The Last Orphan

Gregg Hurwitz is the No. 1 *Sunday Times* bestselling author of the Evan Smoak thrillers *Orphan X*, *The Nowhere Man*, *Hellbent*, *Out of the Dark*, *Into the Fire*, *Prodigal Son* and *Dark Horse*. He is also the author of *You're Next*, *The Survivor*, *Tell No Lies* and *Don't Look Back*. He lives with his family in LA, where he also writes for the screen, TV and comics.

Also by Gregg Hurwitz

The Last Orphan

GREGG HURWITZ

MICHAEL JOSEPH
Est. 1936

PENGUIN MICHAEL JOSEPH

UK | USA | Canada | Ireland | Australia
India | New Zealand | South Africa

Penguin Michael Joseph is part of the Penguin Random House group of companies
whose addresses can be found at global.penguinrandomhouse.com

First published in the United States of America by Minotaur Books,
an imprint of St. Martin's Publishing Group 2023
First published in Great Britain by Penguin Michael Joseph 2023
001

Printed and bound in Great Britain by Clays Ltd, Elcograf S.p.A.

The authorized representative in the EEA is Penguin Random House Ireland,
Morrison Chambers, 32 Nassau Street, Dublin D02 YH68

A CIP catalogue record for this book is available from the British Library

HARDBACK ISBN: 978–0–241–40290–0
TRADE PAPERBACK ISBN: 978–0–241–40291–7

www.greenpenguin.co.uk

MIX
Paper from
responsible sources
FSC® C018179

Penguin Random House is committed to a
sustainable future for our business, our readers
and our planet. This book is made from Forest
Stewardship Council® certified paper.

To Caspian Dennis and Rowland White
My UK copilots
Special Relationship indeed

The mind is its own place, and in itself
Can make a Heav'n of Hell, a Hell of Heaven.

—Milton, *Paradise Lost*

I was in no sense a hypocrite; both sides of me were in dead earnest.
—Robert Louis Stevenson, *The Strange Case of*
Dr Jekyll and Mr Hyde

PROLOGUE

Behind the Scarlet Door

Johnny was twenty-two years old and only wanted to have sex. Other things, too, he was sure of that, but they receded so far into the background haze of his conscious state that they generally went unregistered. That's what had driven him, post–high school, from Massachusetts to Manhattan, where he was ostensibly a stagehand but really just a dude hanging around the theater scene to meet beautiful, smart, talented women drawn to the promise of the Big Apple.

He'd lucked into a square jaw, a decent fastball that gave him athlete cred, an ounce of acting ability from his mom, and if he worked out twenty minutes a day, he could keep a six-pack. It seemed unfair, almost, the advantages the world had given him, and he wanted to make sure he was respectful of those gifts. And grateful.

Lacey was all-American—round face with dimples, long hair with bangs, curves all day. She was young and firm and he was young and firm, and he knew enough to know that he should appreciate every red second of this phase of his life. Johnny Seabrook, a helluva wasp name for a kid whose grampa was a carpet installer. The real family name, Schetter, was changed at Ellis Island for obvious reasons. It had taken his family four generations to get from Needham across Wellesley Avenue. As academic as they were now, they still had blue collar running in their veins. That's what Johnny loved so much about New York. Everyone there was dying to reinvent themselves, and they were all happy to embrace whoever you wanted to be as long as you returned the favor.

He and Lacey had fast and furious sex whenever they could. Over lunch break. On his futon at night, pausing to watch a movie, then twice more before falling asleep. She was great, soft, and her hair smelled like green apples and money. She came from the Hamptons and was hooked into that party scene, too, which he'd only gotten a glimpse of on reality-TV shows. But it seemed like that's where it was at, "it" being the future he'd been aiming at for as long as he could remember.

They'd only been seeing each other a few weeks when she'd rolled over after one of their midday trysts and mentioned a party out there over Labor Day. Some rich finance dude who kept a constant party going, like that Gatsby guy from the novel. Lacey wasn't gonna be around, a family trip to the French Riviera, which to Johnny was as fantastical a place as the fifth moon of Jupiter. But she was fine with his going without her, even booked him an Uber through her account 'cuz she knew he didn't have the dough. She said a few of her girlfriends would be there and it was cool if he wanted to get with them because it's not like she wasn't gonna be hooking up with French guys.

New York women, man! So different from the Boston folks he came from, with their New England rigor, Puritan practicalities, and flinty work ethic.

The place was on Billionaire's Row, Lacey said, and when he asked for the address, she replied with a word: **Tartarus.** *Some of the places there were named, she explained, like on the Cape. He didn't have any paper in reach, but he found a loose marker on the floor next to his futon so he'd written it down on the white midsole of his throwback Vans.*

The next Saturday a bit before ten at night, the Uber dropped him off at the end of a winding road that looked like some kind of royal drive. These weren't oceanfront houses so much as coastal palaces. A wide-open vista overlooking Shinnecock Bay on one side, soft sand beaches on the other. Even at this hour, Johnny could hear the crash of waves and the cries of seagulls pinwheeling in the southwest summer wind. He could taste the sea.

He followed the folks streaming up Meadow Lane to an enormous house with a private dock. Cliques and clusters, the young and gorgeous mixed with the mature and well-preserved. An old-fashioned wooden sign announced it as Tartarus, the wide letters painted with a tartan pattern like from a kilt. Moonlight glinted off the quartz stone of the circular driveway, and valets in red vests were lining up vehicles worth more than his parents' house. He was swept along with a cluster of little-black-dress types through a foyer the size of his apartment building, past a tumbling waterfall feature, and then out into the backyard, where the party was in full swing. A squat man with Warhol glasses—some famous designer?—wheeled and offered him and the women a snort of something from a no-shit silver spoon.

Johnny figured it would be rude to decline.

The party swirled and eddied, and the lights were oh so bright, and he was laughing hard, and anyone whose eye he caught laughed with him.

Chinese paper lanterns tugged at their strings overhead, casting a reddish glow. There were snow crab claws in bathtubs of ice, cheerful bright capsules passed on hors d'oeuvres trays along with fennel puff pastries, the best cover band he'd ever heard throwing down some serious eighties rock. In the churn of the crowd, he thought he spotted that one supermodel and then the journalist who'd had that scandal with the wine bottle. There was that politician—senator? congressman?—he remembered from the news. All those household names in clusters, joking and drinking and snorting and groping.

Someone was getting head on the diving board.

Rich people, man!

Two appetizer poppers down and halfway through his third gin and tonic, he bumped into someone and almost spilled right down her plunging neckline. He had to force his eyes north. She was a goddess, hair picked out in an Afro, bronzed skin, loose backless summer dress. Her cheekbones were accented with fierce strokes of makeup, and she was so attractive it made no human sense.

It felt wrong to even be looking at her.

"Wow," he said.

She gave a regal half turn, her bare shoulder nearly clipping his chin. On the back of her neck was a blue-and-gold awareness ribbon tattoo with small vertical lettering on the left tail: BOSTON STRONG.

Johnny felt his heart lift; it was as good an in as he was gonna get at a party like this. "You're from Boston, huh?" He tapped his chest with his thumb. "Wellesley. You come in for the party?"

She regarded him. "Don't you get it?"

"Get what?"

"You're a toy like me. I'm not looking for another toy. I'm looking for an owner."

A cigarette girl passed between them strapped to a tray sporting cannabis cotton candy and a medley of joints, and then the goddess was gone in a ninja poof, and he wondered if she'd even been real.

He was laughing now. It was so ridiculous that he, Johnny Seabrook, number-two high-school pitcher from the not-too-rich part of Wellesley, was here among the clouds and the stars.

The old guys had money, that was for sure, but he knew he was cuter than he deserved to be, so he had that going for him, at least. Sure enough he caught the eye of a redhead in a red satin dress across the way, and he hoisted his glass for a toast before realizing he'd set it down somewhere. She wiggled a finger at him, and he followed her into the house. They played grown-up hide-and-seek, Johnny pursuing her through the crowd from room to room. God knew the mansion was set up for it, with nooks and crannies, secret passages, hidden rooms behind bookcases. There was crazy shit going on everywhere—metal tubs full of champagne, tables brimming with oysters, a half-clothed orgy on the leather couches of a library. At every turn there was another guy in a tux balancing a tray of cocktails. Johnny drifted through a miasma of pot smoke, the good stuff that tasted like live resin. The contact high compounded his other highs until he felt like he was floating through the halls.

He lost track of the girl in red and then of what room he was in and then of his face, which felt rubbery, like something stretched over his skull.

He came back into himself sprawled on a pool table with a ruddy-cheeked man with wobbly jowls beaming down at him—the anchor on that one morning show—and then he realized the guy's chin was wet and he had his hand shoved down Johnny's 501s.

He tried to say, "No," but it came out babylike—"Nuh"—and then he was stumbling out of the room trying to fasten his belt, the floor refusing to stay steady underfoot. Everything had taken on a horrible cast, like he'd telescoped in beyond where freedom was fun into the place where it became limitless, dizzying, terrifying. He was crying, and he wanted his high-school room with his Red Sox banner on the wall and his mom and dad and his nerdy-cool baby sis who had so many opinions and most of them right, and he felt so far from home.

And he thought about what his parents would say and his teachers, too, and how he'd brought this on himself, thinking that he could be a big man in the world, that he could have this much fun without consequences, and it was all so dirty and awful. And it was his fault for catching a ride to God knew where on the word of some girl he only half knew, and he'd taken all sorts of shit into his body without thinking about it, and now he was getting what he deserved.

Disoriented, he staggered from room to room but didn't seem to get any-where. The mansion was like one big maze where everything led to every-thing else. And he was crying now and thought about how he couldn't tell anyone what had happened and he wouldn't want to drink ever again or see people and he couldn't go home and face his parents and partygoers were looming before him on the stairs, their faces ballooning. A woman in a platinum-blond wig ran a fingertip down his cheek and then sucked his tears off her print, and then he was running up instead of down just to get away from her.

Two security types on the landing of the third floor—one obese and sloppy, the other gym-hardened with pristinely coiffed hair—were dis-tracted with a woman vomiting pyrotechnically into a floor vase. Johnny slipped past, unnoticed. He blacked out a moment and then . . .

. . . the artwork sliding off the walls, but it was quiet at least. He just needed to catch his breath. He realized he was probably near the master suite—wing?—of the house, since no one was up here, and he felt his gorge rising suddenly. There was a big door with no handle that was upholstered with fancy scarlet fabric like a couch, and he figured it might be a rich-person bathroom, so he shouldered into it, but it didn't open and he didn't want to barf on the marble tiles, so he hit it again hard, and it popped open and he spilled inside, landing on a shag carpet and . . .

. . . couldn't believe what he was seeing, a man cocked back in his chair, head thrown back, lips rouged with pleasure, bathed in the light of a hundred sins . . .

. . .

. . . spinning around in the chair, face twisted with fury . . .

. . .

. . . like a punch that went straight through his shoulder blade and out the front . . .

. . .

. . . spewing vomit as he stagger-slid down a tight servant's stair-case . . .

. . .

. . . someone chasing, shouting . . .

. . .

. . . tripping and then falling down step after step . . .

. . .

. . . memory of stumbling into the wrong room, what he had seen there, no one was supposed to see . . .

. . .

. . . fresh air hit him, and he mostly woke up.

Blood trickling from his ear, left knee staved in, crimson blotch spreading at the breast of his cheap button-up shirt, Johnny gasped for oxygen as he tumbled out through French doors to the side of the mansion, his Vans skidding on a stretch of curated Bermuda grass.

The desolate side yard was unlit—no doubt by design.

No signs of life, the mansion so large that the backyard was a good quarter mile away. The cover band was giving the Boss a run for his money.

—liddle gurl is yer daddy home, did he go 'n' leave ya all alone—

He couldn't go there. He couldn't trust any of these crazy rich people.

Help, *he said, or at least he thought he did, but the word was still inside his head.*

His belt remained unbuckled, and the shame of what he'd allowed to be done to him swelled up like a wave, threatening to pull him under. He couldn't get help, couldn't talk about this ever.

Ahead, a rise of trees partially blocked the putting green of the neighboring estate. The house looked a mile away, as distant as a castle on a hill. The wind had shifted from the north, bringing from the bay and marshland the stomach-turning stench of low tide, fresh salt air turned rotten.

Drunk with pain, Johnny swung his head toward the front of the mansion, his vision bright and woozy, the edges of things blending together. A spill of light glowed around the side from the massive circular driveway.

The valets. He could trust the valets.

Footsteps behind him, hammering down the stairs, approaching thunder.

He wobbled a bit, fingers splayed on his torso over the wetness where chest met shoulder. The bullet hole seeped more blood, dark like ink.

Had he . . . had he really been shot?

—and the Boss was singing about a knife, edgy and dull and—

He moved toward the valets, fumbling his iPhone from his pocket, thumbing the three digits, but his fingers were numb, insensate, and the slick case slipped from his hand and tumbled before he could press CALL.

He took a knee to pick it up, but then he couldn't rise and blood was drooling from his bottom lip and he was crying and the news anchor's ruddy face filled his mind and he understood for the first time in his charmed life what it meant to feel violated, demeaned, and he couldn't imagine talking about it ever or about what he'd seen behind the scarlet door, and then the footsteps were coming up behind him, soft on the lush grass, and a shadow stretched slender and sinister beneath the susurrating leaves.

He could see his own face reflected up in the obsidian screen of his phone just beyond his reaching fingers, and then he saw another face appear over his shoulder, the face of the man from the room behind the scarlet door.

Somewhere the backyard band kept ooo-ooo-ooo-ing, and it was floating there, that awful face, inhuman and blank like a ghost's, the rest of the body lost to shadow, and Johnny whimpered and drooled blood and strained for the phone in the grass, his fingertips brushing it, the screen coming to life, that green CALL circle right there millimeters from his fingertips.

But then he heard a thud, and his hand went hot with pain.

He saw that it had been staked to the lawn.

He opened his mouth, but all that came out was a rush of air, and then the man grabbed his hair and a voice whispered in his ear, "Naughty boy."

THE LAST ORPHAN

The knife slid up and clear of Johnny's hand with a tug, and then his head was yanked back further, baring the throat, and sensation blended with song, his heart pounding like the distant music, his ears thrumming to the rush of percussion, his nerves on fiii-ire.

1

Hold My Vodka

It wasn't the first time Evan had drunk vodka atop a glacier.

But it was the first time he'd traveled to a glacier with the express purpose of drinking vodka.

Not just any glacier, but Langjökull, the behemoth nearest Iceland's capital. Fifteen hundred meters above sea level, the air was frigid enough that Evan sensed it leaking between his teeth, even within the fireplace-warmed interior of the pop-up bar.

It had taken some navigating to get here. A connecting flight to Reykjavik followed by a journey across the tundra with sufficient four-wheel-drive turbulence to make his insides feel as though they'd been tumbled by an industrial dryer.

He'd arrived at the precise coordinates—64.565653°N, 20.024822°W—twenty minutes ago, time enough to shake the numbness from his fingertips and take his first sip from the specialty batch of handmade spirit. Its name derived from the word for "smoke," Reyka had a barley base, augmented with water filtered by the rock of a four-thousand-year-old lava stream, making it the purest liquid on earth.

The bar here in the middle of the desolate nowhere was little more than a sparse wooden structure composed of beams and walls. Well-loved chessboards on tables. A foursome of burly Icelanders in football jerseys. Picture windows overlooking miles of blindingly white tundra. Decorative puffins peeked out from the shelves of bottles.

Evan took another sip of the limited-edition batch he'd traveled over four thousand miles to sample. Silky mouthfeel, rose and lavender, a hint of grain on the back half. He set his shot glass, fashioned from glacial ice, down on the bar before him.

It was promptly shattered by the elbow of one of the footballers wheeling drunkenly to grab at the waist of a passing female tourist. Evan exhaled evenly and swept the ice remnants from the bar. Though the young men were rowdy, cocky, and redlining their blood-alcohol, he could sense that they weren't awful guys. But they were on their way to becoming awful if no one provided a course correction.

On Evan's other side, a lantern-jawed retiree was bragging to a gaggle of Australian coeds and anyone else within earshot that he'd been a member of the legendary Viking Squad S.W.A.T. Team known as Sérsveit Ríkislögreglustjórans. A handsome man a few years past his prime, he basked in the glow of the young women's attention.

Buoyant and amused, the Australians fumbled through his pronunciation lessons. Well built, with beautiful smiles and generous laughs, they hung on his words, as pleased by the unlikely company as he was.

"—we have no standing army," the former cop was telling them in near-perfect English. "So we're the last line of defense when it comes to facing deadly threats."

Evan leaned forward and flagged the bartender for another shot. As it was being poured in front of him, another of the footballers snatched it from beneath the bottle and slammed it.

Evan stared at the pool of vodka puddled on the bar between his hands. Then up at the bartender, a pale Nordic towhead. "Would you like to talk to them?" Evan said. "Or should I?"

The bartender shrugged. "There are four of them. And we're way out here. There's nothing to do."

"Well," Evan said. "Not *nothing.*"

The bartender gave him another shot, this time safeguarding it through the handoff. "American?" he asked. "What did you come to Iceland for? Business? Whale watching?"

Evan hoisted the shot glass. "This."

"You flew all the way here?" The bartender's mouth cracked open in disbelief. "For *vodka?*"

Why not? Evan thought.

He'd arrived at a point in his life where he was finally capable of indulging small pleasures. To say the least, his childhood had been rough-and-tumble. Pinballed through a series of foster homes, he'd been ripped out of any semblance of ordinary life at the age of twelve to be trained covertly as an assassin. The fully deniable government program was designed to turn him into an expendable weapon who could execute missions illegal under international law. Orphans were trained alone for solo operations—no peers, no support, no backup. Were it not for Jack Johns, Evan's handler and father figure, the Program would likely have been successful in extinguishing his humanity. The hard part wasn't turning him into a killer, Jack had taught him from the gate. The hard part was keeping him human. Integrating those two opposing drives had been the great challenge of Evan's life.

After a decade and change spent committing unsanctioned hits around the globe, Evan had gone AWOL from the Program and lost Jack all at once. Since then he'd committed himself to staying off the radar while using his skills to help others who were just as powerless as he'd been as a young boy—pro bono missions he conducted as the Nowhere Man.

Right now he was enjoying a break between missions. The closest thing he had to family or an associate, a sixteen-year-old hacker named Joey Morales, had taken an open-ended leave to explore her independence, whatever the hell that meant. Against every last one of his engrained habits, he'd become personally if erratically involved with a district attorney named Mia Hall, enough so that he'd been at her side two months ago as she was wheeled into a life-threatening surgery that had left her in a coma without a clear prognosis. Her ten-year-old son, Peter, another of the select few Evan felt a human attachment to, was now in the capable hands of Mia's brother and sister-in-law. In the collective absence of Joey and Mia, Los Angeles had felt quiet enough for Evan to rediscover the fierce loneliness in freedom.

To his left, the Icelandic cop kept on. "—skydiving and port security, that sort of thing. Drugs and explosives."

"Explosives," one of the Australians cooed. "Cool."

"Think of me as a real-world James Bond," the cop continued. "But tougher."

"Tougher than Bond?"

On Evan's other side, the footballers shouted "*Skál!*" and slammed their shot glasses together, licking puddled ice and vodka from their palms. An older man escorted his wife past the rowdy crew, drawing jeers. The biggest of the foursome, red-faced and sloppy, smacked the husband on the shoulder, sending him tumbling toward the door.

That drew even more of Evan's attention.

The big man wore suspenders, ideal for grappling leverage. Another sported a convenient wrist cast; Evan always liked when a loudmouth came packaged with his own bludgeon. The man who'd stolen Evan's shot had a flat metal lip stud the size of a quarter, with a rune stamped on it; Evan hadn't brushed up on his Icelandic runes in a few decades, but he believed that it was the symbol for protection in battle. And the fourth man sported glasses with solid titanium frames, ideal for denting the delicate flesh around the eye sockets.

Smashed between the two groups, Evan hunkered further into himself and took another sip. He loved drinking.

But not drinkers.

"What was the funniest thing you ever saw on the job?" The Australians gathered closer around the cop now, indulging him.

"When my partner, Rafn, accidentally shot himself in the foot while he was taking a leak. Right through the top of his boot!"

Laughter. The next round of drinks arrived for the ladies—a vomitous concoction sugared up with pink grapefruit, elderflower cordial, soda, and topped with a cherry tomato. It looked like a salad in a glass.

The banter continued. "And what was the *scariest* thing you saw?"

The venerable cop ran a hand through his salt-and-pepper hair. "Well, I could tell you. But then . . ."

As the Australians laughed and pleaded with him, Evan closed his eyes and sampled the specialty Reyka once more. It was unreasonably smooth, the finish short, leaving a lingering hint of spicy cedar.

He admired vodka. Base elements put through a rigorous process, distilled and filtered until the result was transformed into its purest essence.

As a scrawny boy, Evan had undergone a similar process himself. Hand-to-hand, network intrusion, *escrima* knife fighting, psyops, SERE tactics—he'd endured painstaking training to become something more than his humble origins would have suggested he could be.

As Jack used to tell him, *A diamond's just a lump of coal that knows how to deal with pressure.*

In a show of aggressive amusement, one of the footballers pounded his fist into the bar, sending a glass ashtray flipping up past Evan's cheek. It shattered at the ground near his boots.

He ignored them. Instinct drove him to peek at the RoamZone, the high-tech, high-security phone that traveled with him everywhere. After he intervened on someone's behalf as the Nowhere Man, the only payment he requested was that that person pass on his untraceable phone number—1-855-2-NOWHERE—to someone else in need of help. He never knew when the line might ring, what sort of life-or-death predicament the caller might be in, or what he'd be required to do in order to help. The only constant was the first question he asked every time he picked up: *Do you need my help?*

The rugged phone showed no missed calls.

To his left, the cop was warming to the fresh story. ". . . know of the geothermal pools?"

"Of course! The natural springs. We just came from the Blue Lagoon. Omigod, the color! And the mist."

"Well, there's a lesser-known spa an hour east of Akureyri. We pride ourselves on low crime here, but an enterprise was taking advantage of our goodwill, using us as a transport from the EU to North America. Meth. Significant loads out of Dresden."

Evan hunched over the bar, curled the shot glass in tighter, the icy curve tacky against his palm.

"So we get called to a lava field in Mývatn at dusk. Steam thick like curtains. Water churning, heated from below. Heartbreakingly beautiful." The former cop paused a moment. "That glacial blue, a color you can't believe God can make. We get there and . . ."

The young women leaned closer. *"And?"*

"Floating like a stroke of paint in that blue, blue water was a ribbon of crimson thick as my arm. I waded in after it. Sloshing along, following the blood like a shark. And then I saw it. Bobbing against a wall of lava. Waterlogged. Head at an angle that made no anatomical sense." The cop tented his fingertips on the surface of the bar. "The garrote had worked its way through most of the neck. Guy must've put up a helluva struggle."

"Who was he?" one of the Australians asked breathlessly.

"German drug lord. The one who'd set up the operation."

"So who . . . who killed him?"

On Evan's other side, the footballers were stomping their feet now and chanting a drinking song. But his ear was tuned to the tale being spun by the onetime member of Sérsveit Ríkislögreglustjórans.

"Do you believe in fairy tales?" the cop asked.

The women stared at him glassy-eyed.

"There was a government assassin known as Orphan X," he continued. "Think of him as the Big Bad Wolf. Probably American, maybe British. No one knew who he was. No one ever found out. Maybe he didn't even exist. Maybe he was just a name they whispered to bad men to make sure they didn't sleep well at night."

"Do *you* think he was real?"

"I saw his handiwork."

"The dead German drug lord?"

"And five of his colleagues, found in various states of disassembly in a barn at the foot of the Námafjall Mountains. Their stash house. The carnage . . ." The cop shook his head. "Matched our national death rate from the preceding decade. No one saw the assassin come or go. No footprints, no tire tracks, no eyewitnesses. They say that's how he earned his nickname. His *other* nickname."

"What's that?" The Australians were captive now, leaning in, twirling straws in their drinks.

"'The Nowhere Man.' It's said that he left the world of spycraft. But he's still around. In the shadows."

"That's not true," one of the women said. "That can't be true."

"He has a secret phone number. Or so the story goes. The number gets passed around, and when you call it, he answers, 'Can I help you?'"

Evan shook his head. Barely.

The retired cop keyed to him. "What?"

"'Can I help you?'" Evan repeated. "That sounds . . . servile."

"This man is anything but," the cop said.

"I'd imagine he'd say something more muscular," Evan offered. "Like, 'Do you need my help?'"

"Well, whatever he says, he's not someone you want on your tail."

"What's he look like?" another of the young women asked.

"Like not much," the cop said, happily directing his attention back to the clique. "There's scant intel on him. Ordinary size, ordinary build. Just an average guy, not too good-looking."

The women were breathless.

The cop pressed on. "He goes anywhere, they say. Capable of anything. Scared of nothing."

"No one is scared of nothing," Evan said.

The cop fixed him with an irritated glance. "What's a tourist like you know of a man like that? A man who's killed drug deal-ers, terrorists, heads of state? I've seen with my own two eyes the wreckage he's left behind."

Evan shrugged. Flagged the bartender for another pour. It would be his last. He had a long, teeth-rattling drive back to the capital and a longer flight from there.

The cop cupped his hands and blew into them. "They say he's walked straight into the headquarters of some of the most fearsome men alive. Outnumbered twenty to one. And when they sneer at him, he doesn't bat an eye. He just stares at them and says . . ." The theatrical pause overstayed its welcome. "'Do I look like I'm some-one who you can frighten?'"

Evan nearly choked on his sip of Reyka.

The cop wheeled to him on his stool. "What *now*?"

Evan wiped his mouth. "It's just . . . It's not very pithy."

"Okay, Mr. American Loudmouth. What do *you* think he'd say?"

Before Evan could reply, the footballer with the pierced lip bellowed something into his friend's ear, then leaned over and swiped a glass from the hand of the nearest Australian woman. He poured it down his tree-trunk throat and smashed the glass on the floor, roaring until cords stood out in his neck.

Evan swiveled on his barstool to face the foursome. "Now," he said, "you're starting to test my patience."

The man looked down at him. "We wouldn't want to test your patience." His voice was hoarse from alcohol. He placed a hand on Evan's shoulder. Squeezed. "Whatever should I do?"

"Apologize to her," Evan said. "That would be fine."

The man laughed a desiccated laugh.

His friends spread out behind him, kicking the barstools away to clear room.

Evan sighed. Extended his shot glass to the cop. "Hold my vodka."

Surprised, the cop took it, his mouth slightly ajar.

Resting his hands on the bar, Evan leaned to the Australian women. "Will you excuse me a moment?"

In his peripheral vision, he took in the footballers, assessing the props at his disposal.

The red suspenders were heavy-duty elastic with metal clips.

Titanium eyeglasses far enough down on the bridge of the nose to punch right through the cartilage.

Wrist cast hovering in a low guard, one spin kick away from smacking up into the waiting jaw.

Evan felt the grip on his shoulder tighten.

He kept his gaze on the union of his hands set at the edge of the bar. Sensing the space around him.

Half-empty bottle arm's length away by the beer taps.

Stool beneath him, sturdy construction, legs sufficiently thick for jabbing.

A slick of spilled booze on the floor just beyond the heels of the man crowding his space.

"I know you think you're big," Evan said quietly. "And having numbers and being on your home turf makes you confident."

He stood up.

Behind him one of the Australians gave a nervous titter and the cop sucked in a sharp intake of air.

"But I want you to look at me." Evan lifted his gaze to meet the man's stare, sliding his right foot back ever so slightly to set his base. "Look at me closely. And ask yourself . . ."

He assessed the man looming over him, that rune stud floating on his chin like a soul patch. Beckoning.

Evan said, "Do I look scared?"

The flight attendant paused by Evan's aisle seat with the drink cart. Earlier he'd requested a bag of ice to apply to his knuckles.

She mustered a pert if tired smile. "Get you something?"

"What vodkas do you have?"

She listed them.

Evan said, "Water's fine, thank you."

As she poured, an announcement came over the speakers that in forty minutes they'd begin their twilight descent to LAX. She set the drink on his tray, which, to the consternation of his seat-mate, he'd scrubbed vigorously with an antibacterial wipe.

The flight attendant chinned at the pouch of mostly melted ice pressed against his hand. "Take that for you?"

Evan removed the dripping bag, revealing a wicked bruise across the knuckles of the ring and middle fingers of his left hand. Through a surrounding swell of yellow-blue, a spray of broken blood vessels formed an imperfect snowflake pattern. As he passed her the ice bag, her eyes snagged on the painful marks.

"Goodness, that looks awful. What is it?"

"I believe," he said, "it's the Icelandic rune for protection in battle."

2

All That Annoying Zen Shit

A few minutes prior to midnight on the royal-blue padding of a training mat, Evan was on his hands and knees, holding tabletop position. Shoulders directly over wrists, hips over knees, all joints at a clean ninety degrees. But one thing was different. His palms, placed down on the mat, were spun all the way around so his fingers pointed straight back toward his knees.

It looked bizarre, grotesque, as if someone had snapped his hands off and put them back on facing the wrong direction.

The stretch through his forearms, which had absorbed the shock from a number of well-placed punches in Langjökull, took on a biblical level of intensity.

He held the stretch in the quiet of his penthouse, 21A of the Castle Heights Residential Tower. His neck was sore, too. Bar fighters—especially the big ones—tended to go for headlocks, not understanding that that put you inside their guard with easy access to the groin, the stomach, the tender inner arch of the foot. Exhaling, Evan pulled his hips back another few millimeters, the fascia of his arms tugging more intensely around muscle and nerve fibers.

He'd forgotten to breathe again. He centered himself here, in this spot on the planet, a seven-thousand-square-foot modern wonderland of poured concrete and stainless-steel fixtures, as sparse and cold as the Scandinavian terrain he'd traversed just hours before.

There were workout stations and motion-detection hardware. There were floor-to-ceiling bullet-resistant windows and retractable discreet-armor security sunscreens. There was a vodka freezer vault and a Vault of a different nature hidden behind the shower in the master suite. There was a floating bed held three feet off the floor by herculean magnets, and an aloe vera plant named Vera III who thrived on neglect. There was a mounted katana sword and a vertical garden fed by drip irrigation. There was a disco ball and a Velcro wall with compatible body suits for jumping and sticking.

The latter two were a long story.

The ache in his arms gave way to numb tingling, then pins-and-needles lactic-acid release, and then finally surrender. He breathed in the quiet. The air-conditioning here stayed pegged at a cool sixty-six degrees, the freestanding fireplace at rest. As was his habit, he'd already burned the outfit he'd worn on the outing and re-appareled himself in identical clothes. He liked the cold, the silence, the lack of external stimuli. Everything here felt frozen and sterile and safe, like an ice crypt in which he could rest for vampiric rejuvenation.

Since he'd fled the Orphan Program, he'd led a purgatorial existence as the Nowhere Man. With virtually unlimited financial resources and a stellar capacity to enact freelance retribution on behalf of others, he made sure to use his skills in keeping with the Ten Commandments handed down to him by Jack, a set of rules to ensure that he stayed operationally sound.

Given the past missions he'd conducted as Orphan X, he was considered a dangerous asset by those at the highest levels of the United States government. He'd been granted an informal presidential pardon contingent upon his ceasing all extracurricular activities as the Nowhere Man.

He hadn't been very good at ceasing all extracurricular activities.

But he remained in the clear as long as no one found out. Not State, not NSA. Not CIA or FBI. Not Secret Service Special Agent in Charge Naomi Templeton, who'd pursued him relentlessly as her job demanded. Not President Victoria Donahue-Carr, who had herself set the terms of his unofficial clemency.

As long as the RoamZone stayed quiet, he wouldn't have to worry. He could just relax here, take a bit of a break, and make sure—

The RoamZone rang.

Evan released his hands, sat back on his heels, and flapped his hands a few times as the aching subsided.

The caller ID showed nothing.

Curious.

He answered as he always did. "Do you need my help?"

A slight delay as the call routed around the globe through more than a dozen software virtual-telephone-switch destinations.

Then the sound of sobbing.

Answering the phone as the Nowhere Man, he was accustomed to that. He often spoke to people at their worst moment of desperation.

He waited.

And then he recognized who was crying.

Joey Morales.

After she'd washed out of the Orphan Program, he'd been put in a position where, against all his wishes and his protocols as a solitary operator, he'd had to rescue her. In a manner of speaking, she'd rescued him, too. An unlikely familial bond forged between teenage hacker and adult assassin that puzzled him still. Before her he hadn't understood the fierceness of affection. The vulnerability of it, too, how someone else's pain could hurt worse than your own.

He hadn't been trained to consider other people's pain. He'd been taught to barely register his own.

He stopped the rush of questions—*What happened? Did someone hurt you? Who do I need to maim?*—and forced himself to wait.

The Fifth Commandment: *If you don't know what to do, do nothing.*

"Okay," he said. "All right."

THE LAST ORPHAN

Joey kept on weeping, soul-rending cries giving way to what sounded like a panic attack—jerky inhalations, rushed exhalations.

Somehow she forced out a half-formed plea. "Make it su-stop."

"I'm going to breathe," he said quietly. "And you match me. Okay?"

". . . k-kay."

He breathed audibly, slowly. At first they were out of sync, but slowly she started to calm to the rhythm of his respiration.

"Bottom out your exhalations," he told her. "Twice as long."

"I *am*!"

"No. Listen." He modeled it. "Making room for more oxygen."

It took five full minutes for her to mirror his breathing. Then they held the cadence for another two.

Finally he asked, "What happened?"

The RoamZone had a variety of features—a self-repairing screen, nanotech batteries, an antigravity suction case. It could also prop open a broken window. He thumbed on the holographic display and watched Joey's words dance as the RoamZone threw her voice.

"Nothing," she said. "Everything doesn't always have to be a *thing*, X."

He'd set her sound waves to orange so they flickered like a flame. It was all he had of her right now.

"Where are you?" he asked.

"A little motel outside of Phoenix."

It didn't surprise him that her improvised road trip had wound up in Arizona. Or that panic had overtaken her there. Before her beloved maunt—her mom-aunt—had passed, Joey had lived with her there for the first innocent, uncomplicated decade of her childhood. And then had come the foster homes. And her brief stint in Orphan training. Neither of which was innocent. Nor uncomplicated.

"Know what she used to say? My maunt? When I did something funny, she'd say, 'I've created a monster.' And I'd love that, because it meant she was proud I'd taken the best parts of her. She was so, so funny. No matter what kind of shit we were going through. And—" She cut off with a sharp intake of air.

22

Joey hated crying, fought it all the way through.

Evan gave her time. There was nothing else to give her.

Her voice trembled slightly but did not threaten to break. "She was the only person who was there when I came into the world, the last connection to . . . dunno, *me*. Little me. Riding her shoulders, birthday cakes, all that. You know?"

The only responses Evan could think of were trite and dismissive.

He heard a slurping sound—Dog licking Joey's salty face. Evan had rescued the Rhodesian ridgeback as a puppy from a dogfighting ring and given him to Joey. She'd refused to name him properly, not wanting to grow attached, and by the time they'd become inseparable, the name had stuck.

Evan listened carefully, his senses on high alert. One of the goals of the meditation he practiced was to experience everything as if it were happening for the first time. Because everything always was.

"It just . . . came on," Joey said. "All this *stuff*. Gawd, feelings suck. And they're all up in my face. Like, I got sad today at an old man sitting alone at a bus stop. He had a little hat and everything." A pause. "Come on, Dog. Let's get some water." She made a faint groan as she rose.

Evan zeroed in on the noise. "Why are you groaning?"

"I'm not *groaning*, X. Jesus. I made a delicate feminine exhale."

"Why?"

"Nothing. I'm just tight in my hip."

He closed his eyes, focusing. "Ache in the front of the socket?"

A longer pause now. "Yeah. How'd you know?"

"Did you get scared today? Something startle you?"

"*No*," she said, with readily accessible teen irritation. "I didn't get—"

Some epiphany made her cut off. He gave her the silence.

"Well, some dipshit in a Volvo almost hit me earlier," she conceded. "At an intersection. But, you know, I'm a trained tactical driver so it's not like I was *scared*."

He waited.

"But maybe I tensed up. For, like, a femtosecond."

He waited some more.

"Why? Why'd you ask that?"

"The psoas is the first muscle to engage when you go into fight or flight. You know how to release it?"

"Of course I know how to release my psoas. I'm not an *amateur*."

Abrasive noises as the phone got tossed down. He waited while she grunted and shuffled around. Then he heard her breathing turn jagged, move to shuddering releases, and then finally even out.

When she picked up the phone again, her voice was much more subdued. She sounded exhausted, wrung out. "Can't I just, like, not deal with any of this?" she asked. "Emotions or whatever."

She was generally so energized and caffeinated that he relished these softer moments with her, even over the phone. He pictured her big smile that put a dimple in her right cheek. Those translucent emerald eyes, pure as gemstones. The tousle of black-brown hair heaped to one side to show off the shaved strip above her right ear.

He knew she was sleepy now, could hear it in her voice, how the words got slower, her upper eyelids heavying the way they did. She'd be curled up on the bed right now with the hundred-and-ten-pound ridgeback, winding herself into a cocoon. He knew that phase. The chrysalis when everything puddled together, formless and hopeless, a primordial reset before new structure and meaning took hold.

He said, "Sure."

"Then what?"

"You won't feel as much . . ."

"I choose *that* one."

". . . of anything."

A pause.

He said, "'How you do anything is how you do everything.'"

"Don't give me all that annoying Zen shit. The Commandments are only about training."

He said, "Right."

A long silence.

"Part of why I left was to . . . dunno, find myself. I know, sounds stupid. But what if there's nothing new to find?"

"Meaning what?"

"I mean, I was trained as an Orphan even if I never finished. But what if that's all I *can* do? What if I'm really supposed to be a killer li—"

She halted, but he knew where her words had been headed: *like you.*

"I get it," she continued, regrouping. "I'm just sixteen. But I'm also, like, *way* more badass than the majority of so-called adults. Did they make Mozart wait till he was eighteen to let him play the piano?"

"He wasn't killing anyone with his sonatas."

"That's not the point."

"There are places that you can't get back from."

"You've gone there. Why shouldn't I?"

"The cost," he said.

This silence was even longer.

"I'm so screwed up right now, X. Just fucking *damaged*. All the time."

"'The wound is the place where the light enters you.'"

"Snappy. You come up with that on the spot?"

"Nah, a thirteenth-century Muslim poet. It's been kicking around about a thousand years."

"What's it mean?"

"Poetry never *means* something. It evokes."

"Fine. What's it *evoke*?"

"If I could describe it, it wouldn't be poetry."

"Super helpful. So, like, what am I supposed to do?"

"Either let it go," he said, "or you sink with it."

"The pain?"

"No."

"What then?"

"The notion that the pain makes you unique."

Her words were growing slower, drawing out. "'Kay. What happens then?"

"I don't know. I haven't gotten that far yet. But maybe it illuminates—"

"What?"

"What's *actually* unique about you."

"So what's *actually* unique about me?"

"From what I've seen so far? Your ability to eat enormous quantities of Red Vines."

"You're the worst." On the verge of sleep, her drawl intensifying.

"You're the worst, too."

"Night, X."

"Night, Josephine."

3

The Butt-Clappers

The next day Evan did his twice-weekly circuit of the safe houses he maintained around the Greater Los Angeles Area to ensure that they looked lived in and to fine-tune his load-out gear and backup vehicles. As had become routine, he wound up at the home of Mia's brother and sister-in-law for a visit with Peter in the backyard.

Evan's relationship with Mia had been a confusion of starts and stops; though she no doubt sensed the contours of his secret life, as a district attorney she couldn't ever know who he truly was or she'd be forced to arrest him. Despite all that, they had a basic underlying trust, especially when it came to her ten-year-old son. Mia had asked that Evan look out for Peter if anything went wrong on the operating table, to be the kind of old-fashioned influence on him that Evan had never had in his own childhood. When Mia had fallen into a coma, he'd tried to honor that promise as best he could.

It was the first of his standing obligations that involved another human being.

He and Peter ate sandwiches on the patio table while Peter's aunt and uncle banged around inside, shouting at each other from different rooms in a manner that Evan continuously mistook for arguing.

The sandwiches, halved into isosceles triangles, consisted of bologna, yellow mustard, and Wonder Bread. With his tongue Peter shoved a masticated glob through partially clenched teeth, baring his lips to show Evan the result.

"Check it out, Evan Smoak." Peter had a raspy voice that inexplicably made everything he said sound amusing. "Bologna Play-Doh!"

He leaned forward, let the mush dribble onto the paper plate. Then he mashed it with his fingers, building a starchy snowman. He paused, glanced up. "Why aren't you eating?"

Evan looked at the misshapen bologna Play-Doh, streaked red from the traces of Kool-Aid lingering on Peter's tongue, and did his best to calm the OCD swarming his brain stem like wasps. "Not hungry."

The cloying smell of Tropical Fruit tickled Evan's muscle memory. He stared down at the plates set before them, the kind of meal he'd seen on TV growing up in the foster home. Most people didn't understand how broke broke could be. The kind of broke when bologna was too expensive so they'd eat mayonnaise sandwiches for dinner. There was a secret shame to that kind of poverty, carried on the inside like a stain.

"Okay. Didja know"—with a dirty fingernail, Peter dug at some bread lodged between his front teeth—"if your butt cheeks were horizontal, they'd clap when you walked up the stairs?"

"I hadn't considered that."

"Wouldn't that be so funny?"

"No."

"Why not?"

"Because then we'd just consider it normal. Like footsteps."

Peter laughed that big openmouthed laugh, his charcoal eyes lit up. "So, like, at malls and stuff in the stairwells, there'd just be all this butt-clapping. Like a herd of butt-clappers."

"If you start a garage band," Evan said, "that should be your name."

"Herd of Butt-Clappers?"

"Or go classic: the Butt-Clappers."

"Like the Beatles."

"With heavier percussion."

Peter's smile faded. He looked restless. He picked at his remaining half sandwich, tossed a grape and tried to catch it in his mouth.

Evan watched him, gauging the mood shift. Trying to be useful to a child did not come naturally.

"At school—" Peter stopped. Slid his finger into the opposite fist and gave it a squeeze.

"What?"

"Well, like, Mrs. Reimenschnitter says that you have to treat girls and boys the same. But that doesn't make sense. 'Cuz I wouldn't wrestle-tackle a girl, you know? I should be more gentle. And Uncle Wally's different from Aunt Janet. And you're different from Mommy."

"How so?"

"She's smarter."

"Fair," Evan said.

"And she wouldn't like the butt-clapping joke as much."

"She might."

"Yeah, she might. She'd just *pretend* not to." Peter chewed his lip, lowered his eyes, and Evan could sense his thoughts lingering on his mother. "But girls treat *me* different! So how am I supposed to know what to do?"

Evan knew the mnemonic device for the top ten pressure points for inflicting maximum pain in kyusho jitsu. But gender-awareness counseling for elementary students was far from his area of expertise. He prayed for an interruption, a distraction, an incoming rocket-propelled grenade.

But Peter pressed on. "I can't ask Uncle Wally about this, 'cuz he's always wrong about everything. And Aunt Janet just says the opposite of whatever he thinks, which should make her right, but weirdly it doesn't. It just makes her different wrong."

"I usually find," Evan said, "that people will show you how they want to be treated if you pay attention. I'd think that's something that Mrs. Durchdenwald—"

"Reimenschnitter!"

"—would understand. You can rarely go wrong by being gentle. Especially with girls."

Peter pondered this. He took a slurp of Kool-Aid that left his lips glowing mime-red. *"You're* not always gentle."

Evan said, "No."

"But only when you have to not be?"

"That's right."

A slight breeze stirred the golden leaves on the trees. There was a gopher-riddled lawn shaped like a kidney and a play structure that Wally had built with an abbreviated rock-climbing wall installed upside down. There was a rusting skateboard in the weeds, a sun-cracked Frisbee, and a cheap foosball table under the nylon awning of the porch. There was love here. But so much missing from the life Peter had before.

The boy stared down at his forefinger encased in his little fist, squeezing it in pulses that turned his knuckles white. "I read to Mom yesterday like they said to. And . . ."

"And what?"

"Tried to get her to squeeze my finger. But she didn't. What if . . . ?"

The wind riffled the blond cowlick rising to the side of Peter's part. Evan could see him trying to muster the words and thought, *Please don't ask.*

Peter folded his hands at the edge of the table. There was a formality in the pose that Evan found heartbreaking. "What if she doesn't wake up?"

An agonizing question that deserved an honest answer.

"It would be terrible," Evan said. "And then we'd deal with it."

Next stop was Joey's temporarily vacated apartment. She'd texted Evan to swing by because she needed a physical reboot on one of her servers; a memory leak in the video-recording software she'd written had left the system hanging when she tried to access it remotely.

To ensure that she'd be safe living alone here as a sixteen-year-old, he'd bought the building through a tangle of shell corps and had overhauled the security measures. Joey being Joey, she'd figured it out quickly and deemed him overprotective and paranoid. He'd informed her that those were his finest traits.

Approaching the building, he admired the stainless-steel digital call box at the front door. Before he could tap in the code, a college guy with an overburdened backpack hustled in front of him and used his key.

"Man," the guy remarked. "It's hot as balls today."

He swung inside, held the door for Evan.

"Don't let me in," Evan said. "You don't know who I am."

"Dude, come on," the guy said. "You don't look like a problem."

"What if that's the point?" Evan said.

Standing in the foyer, the guy stared back at him, suddenly sweating a bit more profusely. "Um," he said.

Not breaking eye contact, Evan swung the door closed between them. The guy watched him through the glass, frozen. Evan punched in the code, opened the door himself, and brushed past the guy on his way to the stairs.

Joey's place smelled like her, vanilla lotion, Red Vines, and Dr Pepper. Her massive hardware station, a circular desk with mounted monitors stacked three high, was at rest. Dog the dog's fancy pillowtop disk of a bed was in the corner, the skull-and-crossbones water bowl empty. Joey's collection of speedcubes, all tidily solved, rested on the windowsill, and the air was unvented.

He opened a window.

Circling through the pie-slice opening in her desk, he nudged her mouse with his knuckles.

The monitors hummed to life. For a second, standing in the relative silence, he thought he heard the clatter of Joey working a speedcube.

He sat in her gaming chair, which cocked back so severely it nearly dumped him onto the floor. Righting the ship, he clicked the KVM switch like she told him to, performed the reboot, then sat a moment watching the screens repopulate.

His eye snagged on one of them, and his breath caught.

Details of his biological father, the man he'd never known. Jacob Baridon, an honest-to-God rodeo cowboy, as clichéd and ridiculous as that was. Against Evan's wishes Joey had been tracking him down. The open file showed that she'd unearthed a debit card from a checking account that had been closed three months ago. A scattering of gas-station charges grouped around the town of Blessing, Texas, and a few more line items for Mixed Blessing, a local bar.

Before he could dig deeper, the screens wiped, replaced with images of Joey on every monitor. They all looked angry. "Why are you snooping around?"

"I could ask you the same thing."

She was on the bed in a hotel room with a scattering of room-service dishes and Dog the dog stretched inelegantly across the bed beside her. His head hung upside down off the edge of the mattress, mouth stretched in a smile, tongue lolling.

The multitude of Joeys said, "I told you to reboot my server, not look at all my files."

"Why are you searching the man who . . . my biological . . . ?"

"For *you*, X. I mean, he's out there. How can you not want to at least *see* him? Just so you can put it to rest? He's your *father*."

"I didn't have a father," Evan said. "Jack. Jack was my father."

"I mean, if *I* had a chance to talk to my—"

"You're out there looking for answers right now. I'm not."

She exhaled and leaned back from the screen. Dog tried to haul himself all the way up onto the bed, but the sheets avalanched beneath him. He landed with a thump on the carpet, lifted his head sheepishly, then lost himself in an Olympic bout of crotch licking.

"Fine." Joey fiddled with a woven metal-fiber bracelet he'd given her, its magnetic clasp formed by stainless-steel skulls that clinked together. "I only got as far as a town he was in a few months ago."

"Drop it."

"I *said* okay."

He glared at her. All the Joeys glared back. One of her death stares was generally scathing; 270 degrees of them felt nuclear.

"How's your psoas?" he asked.

"Never better. Yours?" She evaporated from the screens, leaving him in her chair. He didn't have long to drink in the silence.

His RoamZone was going, emitting its distinctive chime.

The Butt-Clappers

He extracted it from a cargo pocket, saw the familiar caller ID forwarded around the planet and then from one of his cover numbers. Every time it showed up these past two months, he felt his heart rate tick up.

Steadying himself for the worst, he clicked. Peter's voice rushed through, loud with emotion. "It's Mom!"

Evan's voice stayed as steady as it had ever been. "What happened?"

"She woke up!"

4

More Pressing Objectives

The streets of Beverly Hills don't mind name-dropping. Evan parked a block away from the intersection of George Burns Road and Gracie Allen Drive, a key juncture of the Cedars-Sinai Medical Center, where Mia had slumbered these past two months. It was a glorious Angeleno day, the kind of golden sun that had once provided the magnetic pull for manifest destiny.

An unfamiliar excitement stirred beneath Evan's ribs. In a breathless burst, Peter had filled him in over the phone: Mia was awake and intact. That's all Evan had needed to hear.

A hot breeze carried the scent of gyros from a nearby food truck. A trio of nurses in scrubs walked by slurping frozen Starbucks drinks the size of feed bags. Across the intersection medical workers on break stretched out on the wide concrete steps of Thalians Health Center, checking their phones or tilting their faces to the blue, blue sky. A stooped man rattled over the crosswalk tugging an IV pole, the wind flapping at his hospital gown, threatening a fleshy revelation.

Passing an outdoor lot, Evan scanned the vehicles, noting license plates. A Buick Enclave with tinted windows idled in the front spot. A windowless van with a Red Cross logo pulled past the kiosk. Evan gave it extra notice; driving over, he'd spotted it on the road behind him. A homeless guy sitting on the curb scrutinized an upside-down newspaper. His overcoat was in tatters, his shoes worn but functional. Evan kept his head down, kept moving.

Palm trees lined the center island running between the North and South Towers in case anyone had forgotten that they were in Southern California.

Evan cut beneath the South Tower's overhang into the parking zone, putting his back to a concrete pillar and peering out. The Red Cross van kept rolling right through the outdoor lot and out again. Moving steadily his way. He watched until it drifted past and hooked left onto San Vicente.

The Buick stayed put.

The homeless guy was on his feet now, scratching repetitively at the back of his head. The caffeinated threesome of nurses disappeared into Thalians. The man with the IV pole made sluggish but steady progress in Evan's direction.

Were there patterns in the movements? Or was he attributing patterns to movements?

With their security, choke points, and surveillance cameras, large facilities made him nervous. Mia was one of few people worth the risk.

Evan withdrew from the pillar, entered the hospital through the automated glass sliding doors, and rode up to the plaza level. Mia had spent the duration of her coma in the new critical-care building a block north, but Peter had reported that she'd been moved to the South Tower today for imaging.

The plaza, laid like an epidermis atop the parking structure, was bustling. An ambitiously named healing garden, an elevated squiggle of xeriscaping edged with teak benches, broke up the corrugated concrete of the high-rises. The soporific trickle of water features background-scored people conversing around tables and benches and potted plants. A Henry Moore sculpture broke a reclining figure into three cast-bronze lumps that resembled dog turds. Two middle-schoolers with chemo-bald heads sat on a bench near the bridge to employee parking, peering at an iPhone screen and giggling. Eyes dulled with sleeplessness, a father sipped coffee outside the cafeteria and cradled a newborn with hearing aids. A row of sky-blue umbrellas cast soothing shade, their underbellies adorned with cloud patterns.

There were worse places to be sick.

Patients and workers streamed between the buildings. Evan lost himself in the current, taking a meandering path to flush out potential tails.

Coming around a bend in the garden, he spotted the man with the IV pole emerging from a doorway across the plaza. Moving more swiftly than he had before. Less stooped, too.

Evan felt his pulse quicken ever so slightly.

Backing up, he sidled beneath one of the shade umbrellas, sweeping his gaze across the crowd. Pregnant mother shepherding twin toddlers with pigtails and cornrows. The middle-schoolers stayed lost in their iPhones. An exhausted mom tramped by with an infant rigged to her in a BabyBjörn.

Taking another step back, Evan bumped into a burly guy with a mullet, a sleeveless Nike dri-FIT, and a visitor name tag announcing him as Frank B.

"The fuck?" Frank B. barked.

Evan dropped his eyes to the guy's feet. He was wearing flip-flops, unsuitable footwear for a stakeout or pursuit.

Frank B. bent down, angrily wiping at a smudge on his cargo shorts. "Why don't you watch where you're going?"

But Evan wasn't paying attention to him anymore. He'd already narrowed his focus to the man with the IV pole and the umbra thrown by one of the building's concrete outcroppings. Another man was emerging from the darkness there, his gait familiar.

The homeless guy from the street, moving swiftly on his sneakers.

Evan let his vision blur so he could take in the full sweep of the plaza impressionistically. Through the tumult he discerned figures moving in concert as if connected by invisible strings.

He heard his own breath now, a rush in the ears, sensed his

heartbeat ticking in the side of his neck, felt the brightness of the midday sun, a shard in his eye. The pedestrians around him were talking and bustling along, lost in the daily grind, cell phones pressed to cheeks, mouths moving. They were soundless, their words lost beneath more pressing objectives.

The homeless guy cutting one way, the gowned man with the IV pole another, the swiveling heads of three others at tables around the healing gardens. Coordinating trajectories, lines of sight.

The Third Commandment barked at Evan—*Master your surroundings*—and in a split second he shuffled through the schematics and blueprints he'd stored in his head. Service elevator behind South Tower reception. Utility closet on the top floor with an access hatch to the roof. Cafeteria kitchen rear door that let into a warren of restricted-access corridors. If he could make it to the Medical Offices Tower, there were outlets onto Third Street and Sherbourne Drive. But he didn't know how much manpower they'd brought or how wide a net they'd thrown.

Best bet would be to disappear into the parking structure beneath his feet—dumpsters, stairs, elevators, countless vehicles, a sewer line to get him underground.

Evan stepped back again beneath the shade umbrella, pushing past Frank B. to shoulder against the wooden post.

"Hey, chief, now you're really getting on my last—"

Across the plaza the guy in the hospital gown halted, his eyes sweeping the crowd. They locked on Evan's. The man pushed the IV pole away. It slid a foot or two, tilted.

He skinned the gown off himself. It undulated in the breeze and fell away behind him. He was wearing form-fitting running clothes beneath. Slung around his neck, now in his hands, was a fat-barreled grenade launcher.

Evan felt it then, the conversion of potential threat into kinetic danger, a thrumming of his bones, a firing of the nerves, an imprinting of lesser phenomena like the shard-sharp glint of sunlight, breeze cooling the sweat at his hairline, the man talking at Evan's side, Adam's apple bouncing lethargically.

Without knowing it, Evan had moved to a calming breath

pattern—two-second inhalations, four-second exhalations. His muscle memory had set the tempo, slowing him down, steadying him. This was what his tactical training had taught him: to decelerate real life until it moved in slow motion.

That's what being present was. People think of a superpower as going fast when everyone else moves slow. But that's not as useful as going slow when everyone else is moving fast.

Three-fourths of a second had passed. None of the bystanders in the plaza had keyed to the disruption. The man's IV pole hadn't yet struck the ground. The fat-barreled grenade launcher was still rising to aim at Evan.

The bright orange stripe around the muzzle broadcast it to be a less-lethal weapon. From this distance Evan couldn't be sure, but it looked like a 40-millimeter designed to accommodate less-lethal projectiles. With crushable foam noses packed with irritant powders and hard plastic shells, the projectiles were good up to 130 feet. Despite their reassuring name, they could cause serious damage at close range.

Way to Evan's right, the homeless guy came up with a 40-millimeter launcher of his own. The three men near the healing gardens now rose, bringing matching weapons out from beneath the tables. About a dozen more men spread throughout the plaza announced themselves similarly.

Like a flash mob, but less entertaining.

The only note of comfort was that the bright orange stripes made the operatives highly visible.

There was a moment of perfect stillness.

Then someone screamed.

Evan hoisted the umbrella up out of the weighted base.

And charged toward the stairwell to the parking structure.

Leaping through the healing garden, umbrella held before him like a shield, agave plants whipping at his calves. Shouts and stampeding. A projectile whined in, thumping the awning with nearly enough force to rip the umbrella from his hands. Another flew overhead. A third kicked up a chunk of soil by his boot, spraying his front side with dirt.

More Pressing Objectives

Hurdling a bench, tripping over a stainless-steel footlight, he crashed through the crowd. The tough canvas batted people aside but also obscured his line of sight, the peaceful cloud design discordantly soothing. A full-blown panic had erupted, people shouting and bulling for the exits. Evan pinballed between a few folks, nearly lost his footing, and caught a spray of lukewarm coffee from the side. As he sprinted across an open stretch of concrete, he sensed a few men behind him bucking the throngs of bystanders, circling to close ranks.

Questions flurried: Who was behind this? Why less-lethal? Did they want him alive to torture him? To get intel?

His breathing held, a metronome running of its own accord.

A volley of projectiles hammered the awning, and then one ripped straight through and sliced past Evan's cheek so close that his eyes burned from the chemicals. The next tore away a section of fabric, stopping him in his tracks. He stared through the wreckage of the canvas at the fake homeless guy, standing right in front of him.

The man was fussing with the hinge action on the launcher. He looked up. He and Evan were at the edge of the plaza, no more than six feet apart, the crowd swirling around them.

The guy said, "Shit," an instant before Evan jabbed him in the solar plexus with the umbrella post. He flew back, smashing into a trash can, the launcher clattering away.

A projectile glanced off Evan's side, spinning him in a half turn and sending a flame of nerve pain through his underarm.

Six men closing in from behind.

Evan hauled himself upright, ARES 1911 in hand. His Woolrich tactical shirt rippled open in the front, the discreet magnets beneath the false buttons parted from when he'd drawn straight through the shirt from his appendix holster.

But his pursuers were shooting less-lethal.

And he didn't know who they were. They could be cops, FBI, a sanctioned squad from State.

The First Commandment: *Assume nothing.*

The magnet buttons found their mates, clapping together, the shirt zipping itself back into place over Evan's torso. He swung the sights, aimed at the metal links of a dangling cafeteria sign, pressed the trigger.

And missed.

A fraction of a second's hitch of disbelief.

It was a wide-open shot, twenty or so feet with nothing between him and the target. No brisk wind, no shadows, no distracting reflections. He was moving, sure, but not spinning. He'd been trained to shoot left- and right-handed, off a roll, emerging from water, upside down, in free fall.

Orphan X was not a perfect shooter like Tommy Stojack, his nine-fingered armorer. He missed plenty of shots. But this was not a shot he missed.

Ever.

A significant if minuscule degradation of his shooting reflexes.

An eighth of a second had passed, maybe less.

He could afford no time for reflection. Being rattled was a luxury for later.

Reset the trigger. Sight picture. Smooth, clean press.

He fired again at one of the chains holding the dangling sign, and the round sparked as it severed the link. The sign swung down, scythelike, slamming one of his pursuers in the side of the head. He tumbled into his partner, spilling them both over a table, which toppled accommodatingly.

A trailing pair of operators with matching weapons filled the space the others had just occupied; the effect was uncanny, as if the same men had been set upright again, a couple of bowling pins. They were aiming imperfectly, their jarring steps making their muzzles bounce.

Evan ran toward them but not *at* them. As their projectiles blasted overhead, he veered hard to the side, slanting toward the wall at the last instant. Jumping to stab a boot three feet up into the concrete wall for traction, he kicked off for momentum and wound up for a left cross. His fist struck the lead man across the jaw, snapping his head around and sending him sprawling into his partner.

Four men now on the ground at Evan's feet, blinking up at him and scrabbling toward their weapons. A projectile clipped off his shoulder, ripping a flap of his shirt up like an epaulet. The round punched through the cafeteria window, shattering the sneeze guard at the salad bar.

He ran.

Cutting through the crowd, head low, ducking and weaving to chart an imperfect line toward the stairwell into the parking structure. Now it was easier to spot his pursuers; they were the only ones running *toward* him.

He leapt over an upturned table, rolled into a graceless somersault, and popped up, finding himself face-to-face with the guy who'd sported the hospital gown. The coaster-size bore of the weapon stared straight at Evan. A round fired at this proximity would cave in his skull.

The man jerked the weapon lower to aim at Evan's chest. Evan gave the descending barrel a heel strike, accelerating its trajectory so it whipped down to point at the man's foot.

The trigger clicked, the projectile launching with a *fooomp*. The man gave a high-pitched scream, grabbed for his shredded sneaker, and hopped on one foot. Evan swept past him, catching the 40-millimeter launcher as it tumbled from his grip.

Spinning, he got off thigh shots to the nearest two men before the three behind them readied to launch a volley his way.

Evan do-si-do-ed with the hopping operator, getting behind him just in time for the guy to take three rounds to the spine. He jiggled in Evan's grip, face twisted in anguish.

Evan said, "Sorry," and let him fall away.

Tumbling backward over a two-top, Evan crawled toward the stairwell as a fresh round of projectiles rocked into the tabletop. Teak slats splintered, the overturned table scuttling in Evan's wake as if animated.

He hit the stairwell door off an impromptu roll, finding his feet to stagger through the threshold and shoulder into the midst of four ascending gunmen ensconced in full tac gear.

He'd inadvertently inserted himself in the middle of them on the landing, like a protectee in a diamond formation of bodyguards.

41

Patches stitched onto their black BDUs identified them as members of the Secret Service Counter-Assault Team. From all directions they blinked at him through tactical goggles.

"You're gonna want to let me out of here," Evan said.

Instead two of the CAT members jerked their launchers up, proving that they were in fact just dumb enough to shoot themselves point-blank in the face. Ducking, Evan knocked the barrels askew. The weapons fired, skimming cheeks, the projectiles bouncing off the concrete walls and ricocheting into the backs of their helmets. Their heads snapped forward, and they crumbled.

The remaining men stared at Evan, holding their weapons helplessly in a low-ready position. He grabbed the barrel of the nearest launcher, spun its owner into his partner, and shoved them up against the crash bar on the door. The metal rectangle depressed, the door unlocked, and they spilled out in the fray.

Turning, Evan lunged down the stairs, skipping five, six steps per leap. One side of the stairwell was open at intervals, bringing fresh air from outside and reminding him of how far he was above the ground. Grabbing the railing, he spun himself downward, descending as quickly as he could keep his feet beneath him. The fourth-floor landing flew by, now the third.

Already he heard commotion at ground level, a door creaking open, more boots hammering into the base of the stairwell, rising to meet him.

He risked a peek over the railing, caught sight of gloved hands on the one below. Shouts from above, CAT members piling into the stairwell, squeezing him from top and bottom.

Hammering footsteps converged on him. As he hit the second-floor landing, a wall of operators surged up at him. Skimming past their outstretched gloves, he vaulted through the gap in the wall above the side rail, hip-bumping the concrete ledge to slow his momentum.

He whistled out into thin air.

He was still a story above the street, but it was his only hope. He prayed for an awning, a laundry cart, a magic carpet.

No such luck.

Just a van waiting below.

The Red Cross van.

He smashed belly-down onto the hood, the metal dimpling with a thunderclap.

And stared through the front windshield directly at Special Agent in Charge Naomi Templeton.

5

Something Older Than Fear

Templeton was in the passenger seat, headphones clamped over her bluntly cut blond hair. The driver, a scrawny young man who looked two steps out of RTC, had recoiled in the driver's seat, arms crisscrossed in front of his face like a B-movie actress fending off an encroaching monster. Through a gap in the bulkhead partition, Evan could see into the high-end surveillance setup in the back, four men in a nest of equipment, sweating through button-up shirts.

Evan's ears rang from the impact, and his chin throbbed where it had slammed into the hood of the van.

He and Naomi blinked at each other.

Panicking, the driver grabbed for his sidearm and raised it to the windshield. Evan told his muscles to roll him off the hood, but they lagged, stunned into inertness from the landing. Naomi yelled at the driver, lunging for his arms, but she couldn't reach him before he fired into Evan's face.

The Secret Service service pistol, a P229 in .357 SIG, fired rounds with 506 foot-pounds of force and a muzzle velocity of 1,350 feet per second.

Evan's forehead was barely a yard from the bore, separated only by the pane of the windshield.

He watched in awe as the glass spiderwebbed before his face, cracks spreading from the point of impact.

But there was no collision, no last-instant blaze of light, no gray matter exploding out the back of his skull. The pane had turned opaque, clouded with cracks, and that's when he noticed the small cluster of lead resting in the bull's-eye eighteen inches from his nose.

Bullet-resistant glass.

On a tactical van.

Inside, Naomi was shouting at the driver as she leaned across the console, disarming him.

Evan decided not to stick around.

He slid off the side of the hood, ankles and knees screaming as his boots struck concrete. His flank was knotted up, and his elbows ached.

All around, people were streaming out of the South Tower, a messy evacuation overseen by armed operators. Bizarrely, in the midst of the commotion no one seemed to take note of him.

A familiar *thump-thump-thump* overrode the ringing in Evan's head, and then a blast of wind nearly knocked him over, a Black Hawk setting down in the middle of Gracie Allen Drive. Two more spun into view above. Now the intersection was clogged with dark SUVs screeching in at all angles, sirens screaming, blocking off every avenue of egress. Agents hollered into radios, staticky bursts coming back at hiked volumes.

"—shots fired at street level. Repeat: shots fired—"

"—switching to lethal—"

Evan was in the eye of the storm, and his only hope was to lose himself in the maelstrom.

They'd be expecting him to run away.

So instead he'd run back to where it had started.

As he stumbled beneath the overhang, he could hear Naomi exit the van, charting his movement, yelling into her radio.

A stream of CAT members poured out of the stairwell from which he'd just ejected, and they stopped, heads swiveling to find him amid the turmoil.

But he was gone inside, the glass doors to reception parting politely. He nodded at the receptionist and shuffled past two undercover agents jogging out, their eyes on the crowd outside.

Through their radios, he heard Naomi's voice: *"—no live ammo! He did not fire on us. Repeat: He did not fire on us."*

"—already got orders from the—"

"Keep on less-lethal!"

A wattle-necked worker was leaning out the door to the gift shop, gazing at the bodies washing by.

Ducking into the shop, Evan pulled on a mesh hat, its puffy white front panel sporting bubble letters announcing TACOFORNIA! He grabbed a bouquet of lavender flowers and spun back out, holding them to partially block his face.

A few nurses evacuated patients in wheelchairs. Another agent stood post by reception, ushering them out, chattering into his radio, "—clearing a few more from the rooftop. I'm securing the lobby."

Evan walked briskly toward the heart of the hospital, elbow-knocking a handicap push plate, the sturdy door yawning open to a corridor. He scampered toward a stairwell sign pointing around a corner.

A single pair of footsteps quickened back in the lobby, a radio broadcasting off the hard surfaces: *"—coming down now, flushing the stairs—"*

He picked up the pace, reaching a trot down the long corridor before slicing into the intersecting hall.

And then Naomi's voice came from behind him just around the bend. "Okay, okay. Alpha Team members each take a staircase and start up from ground level to trap him. I got the one off the lobby."

"—lethal if we're gonna—"

"No! Do *not* use—"

"—dealing with Orphan X. I'm not taking any fucking—"

He could hear Naomi sprinting now, her breath coming harder.

It was the closest he'd been to her since that night they'd cat-and-moused around her apartment in D.C.

"Less-lethal only!" An uncharacteristic note of concern animated Naomi's voice. "Those are the ROEs straight from the top! Confirm!"

The rear stairs were up ahead. Evan slipped inside, eased the door shut, flew up and onto the first landing, flowers thrashing against his thigh.

Footsteps way up above, boots hammering. Leaning over, he peered up the stairwell. Gloved hands visible near the top floor, sliding briskly down railings.

He would fight them on the stairs. Close quarters hand-to-hand would cut their numerical advantage. Tight space, metal handrails, concrete walls. He'd claw, fight, and grapple his way to the plaza and then assess other stairwells and fire escapes or lose himself once more in the South Tower.

And then he heard it.

Different footfall, closer to him, two-thirds down. Quiet steps, awkward and rushed.

One or more civilians trapped between him and descending CAT members who were sufficiently alarmed to use lethal ammo.

The Tenth Commandment roared in his head: *Never let an innocent die.*

Evan froze on the landing, his mind flurrying through various civilians he'd seen in the plaza. Pregnant mother with twin toddlers. Chemo-bald middle-schoolers. Father and baby with hearing aids. Exhausted mom toting a newborn in a BabyBjörn.

Evan couldn't risk anyone getting caught in the crossfire. And he didn't have the luxury to move to another plan.

For the first time, fear set in, ice-hot cortisol and epinephrine firing through his bloodstream.

The civilian footsteps neared, the sound becoming distinctive. *Flip-flop. Flip-flop.*

Evan felt his stomach turn with realization an instant before a meaty hand gripped the railing above. A pudgy face, scarlet with fear and framed by a mullet, peered down at Evan.

Frank B.

The guy in the sleeveless dri-FIT who'd collided with Evan beneath the umbrella.

Frank B.'s mouth was agape, square white teeth even whiter against his flushed face.

Evan said, "Goddamn it."

The Tenth Commandment didn't allow wiggle room for assholes.

Cursing, he drew back and leapt down the stairs, hitting the crash bar hard and spilling into the corridor, the stupid Tacofornia! cap tumbling off his head. He'd kept the flowers in the unlikely event he could generate another ruse but had drawn his ARES again, leading the way in his left hand.

Naomi Templeton stood ten meters from him, stark in the bare corridor. She was aiming at his face.

He was aiming at hers.

Her chest was heaving, and he could see a flush at the base of her throat where her white button-up parted beneath her Kevlar vest. She wore her hair in a utilitarian cut—sharp bangs, a small stick of a ponytail, sweat-darkened wisps forming a neat fringe at her neck. With ice-blue eyes and clean features, she was striking but always seemed to underplay her looks, as if she were annoyed at the kind of attention they might bring her.

Just the two of them, alone in the rear hall.

They might as well have been on their own planet.

"Civilian on the stairs," he said. "Call it in."

Keeping her pistol locked on his critical mass, she tilted her shoulder radio's mic toward her lips. "No-shoot on the northwest stairs. There's a no-shoot on the stairs."

Heartbeat fluttering in the side of his neck. The grab of the front frame checkering, eighteen lines per inch, against the inside curl of his fingers. High-profile straight-eight sights zeroed in on the bridge of her nose.

He knew he could get off the shot and roll to safety. She wouldn't stand a chance.

The whites of her eyes were pronounced, but her grip was steady. He'd have expected nothing less.

He could taste his breath, bitter and hot. He felt something older than fear, something deep in his DNA, the terrified surrender of prey skewered in the jaws of an apex predator.

His entire life since the age of twelve had been a narrowing to this moment.

"Okay," he said, more to himself than to her.

And he holstered his pistol.

He held his hands wide, his right fist still ridiculously clutching the bouquet. He took a step back from her, and she lowered her SIG Sauer and fired, the round embedding in the tile a few inches in front of his boot. It sent a spray of chips into his shin, hard flecks like sleet. "Freeze."

"*Freeze* freeze?" Evan asked. "Or can I drop the hydrangeas?"

Naomi looked unsure of herself. "Drop the hydrangeas."

He let them go.

"Hands! Hands!"

He raised them, palms showing.

The sound of men on the staircase was closer now, thundering down at them. He could sense movement through the closed doors behind him and also past Naomi along the corridor.

The noose tightening through the slipknot, cinching in.

"Let me take you, X," she said. "The CAT boys have hot triggers. Best-case they break your ribs with less-lethal. Worst-case someone gets killed."

Her eyes and muzzle steady, she reached for a nylon pouch looped to her belt and withdrew a syringe filled with clear blue liquid. Given the scope of the tactical response, he guessed she was wielding etorphine, a semisynthetic opioid three thousand times more potent than morphine, used by vets to sedate large animals. He would have preferred something more suited to humans but wasn't in a position to get finicky. The corridor was swimmy, the bright lights disorienting.

She bit off the plastic cap, spit it to the side. "I need to put this in your shoulder. You have to give me your word you'll let me."

Shouts and footfall even closer, all around them. A cry from the staircase, no doubt Frank B. being overtaken. Evan and Naomi stared at each other. No one else in the world.

"Please," she said, with the faintest tremor in her voice.

Evan knit his fingers together at the base of his neck and took his knees, one at a time.

Not with a bang, then. But a whimper.

Naomi moved forward, her shadow falling across him, blocking out the harsh glare. She kept her weapon drawn, the needle readied in her right hand.

Now she stood over him.

He looked up at her. She looked down at him.

He felt her breath stir the air, felt it brush his cheeks. There was great respect in her eyes.

"Thank you," she said.

A jab straight through the shirt into the meat of his shoulder.

The buried fire of the injection.

She holstered her SIG, holding his head with her other hand. Weakly, he nuzzled into it.

Somewhere at what felt like a great remove, he heard doors banging open, voices and shouting. Countless shadows flickered along the white, white hospital walls. His muscles started to give, and then he slumped into a fetal position.

The last thing he felt was Naomi's hand cradling his cheek so his head wouldn't strike the floor.

6

Battle-Testing

"The thing you should excel at most is being wrong," Jack says.

The study glows amber from the fire, bronzing Jack's reading glasses, the cut-glass crystal tumbler glass in his hand, the finger of liquor within, the walnut bookcases, even the mallard-green walls.

Evan sits on the worn leather couch, elbow resting on a heap of dusty books. At twelve years old, he's still so small that the tips of his sneakers barely scrape the floor. One of his laces is untied, dangling. He knows that probably drives Jack nuts, but it is a small enough rebellion to be overlooked.

His voice rich with single-barrel gravel, Jack continues. "Pay attention to everything you don't know and everything you're getting wrong while there's still time to learn."

For much of tonight's lesson, Evan has felt antsy, his thoughts desultory. "Time before what?"

"Before you get killed," Jack says, in a tone implying that this is the most naïve question he's ever heard uttered. "That's why the First Commandment comes first."

"'Assume nothing.'"

"Yes. If you have to be hit over the head to learn something about yourself, you'll be someone who thinks that people only learn if you hit them over the head."

"And that's bad?" Evan asks.

"Son, that's what assholes are." Jack takes a swig. Closes his eyes as he swallows. The booze does something to him, warms him, opens him up, too.

Evan feels warm as well. The study is the only place in the rural Virginia farmhouse that could qualify as cozy.

Resting on Jack's wide knee is a vintage cloth-bound book, maroon-brown and tattered, spine letters long faded. "You'll have to work at all this in small ways and build up. That's why the Second Commandment comes next."

"'How you do anything is how you do everything.' That's what I need to know to be an assassin?"

"Being an assassin is easy. I'm raising you to be dangerous."

"Don't you have to be dangerous to be an assassin?"

"There are a lotta ways to be dangerous. You can think dangerously. You can be a dangerous conversationalist or—"

"Conversationalist?" Evan says. "I want to fuck people up and stuff. Shouldn't an Orphan be feared?"

"Feared?" Jack shakes his head, just slightly, but Evan feels the show of disdain in his spinal cord. Though he'd die rather than admit it out loud, he never wants to disappoint Jack. He hasn't felt that way about another person, and the sensation is as terrifying as it is disorienting. "Feared is never the aim. If you're an Orphan, a true Orphan?" Jack leans forward, fixing Evan with a stare. Licks of fire reflect in his dark pupils. "The world will never know your name."

Evan feels it then in his chest, the loneliness that has been his lifelong companion, a black hole of dread. His lower back still hurts from practicing the traditional forty judo throws; his kata guruma needs work, his frame not yet sturdy enough to support the shoulder wheel.

Jack parts the book of military strategy and resumes reading. "'The human heart, and the psychology of the individual fighting man, have always been the ruling factors in warfare, transcending the importance of numbers and equipment.'" He lifts his square baseball catcher's head, the fire tanning the skin of his face. "Who am I quoting?"

"John Boyd."

Jack grimaces. "No. Major General F. W. von Mellenthin."

Evan says, "Wasn't he a Nazi?"

"A brilliant Nazi. You think you get anywhere without learning from your enemies?"

Jack drains the glass, rises to set it down on the mantel next to the framed picture of his deceased wife, Clara. She's on a black-sand beach a few steps into the surf, sundress clinging at her knees. She's laughing big and staring at the camera with an affection Evan can't imagine, can't imagine Jack being the kind of free he must have felt that day having a woman look at him like that. Though Evan never met Clara, she seems to be the animating spirit of the farmhouse, of Jack himself.

"What was she like?" Evan asks, and Jack follows his gaze to the photograph.

For a moment Jack's face loosens. Then snaps back into form. "Study your Musashi now," he says. "Unless your delicate morality is offended by Japanese warriors, too."

Evan doesn't let the disappointment of Jack's redirection show. "I still don't get why I need to read about all these ancient people."

Jack settles back into his seat. Gives Evan's question its due. "You'll be alone. Most of your life." He lifts the venerable book. "These thinkers are your only companions for now. Understand?"

"Yes."

"Don't surround yourself with like-minded people. You'll get limited or radicalized."

"By what?"

Jack looks irritated-amused, one of his go-to settings. "Who the hell knows? The news, the community, the military-industrial complex. The only hope is to stay open to all perspectives as they come in."

Evan shifts on the couch, grimaces.

"What?" Jack says. "You've been unfocused the whole day."

"It's nothing."

"Don't waste time."

Jack hates nonanswers; Evan should have known better.

"My lower back's stiff," he says. "That's all."

Jack gestures with the tumbler, whiskey threatening to swish over the side. "Get up and stretch. Dangling pose, yin style."

Evan obeys, folding over his legs so his chest rests against his thighs and his butt sticks up in the air. He pictures his head as a bowling ball pulling on his spinal column, opening up new spaces.

"Set aside the pain," Jack says. "Let it be. But don't let it run you."

Evan's legs are shaking, but he holds the pose, lets his head grow heavier so his spine elongates, his crown moving millimeter by millimeter closer to the floor.

After a few minutes, Jack snaps his fingers. "Roll up now—"

Evan's voice, muffled against his jeans, joins Jack's: "—one vertebra at a time."

Evan comes vertical and then sits once more.

Jack studies him a moment and then snaps the book shut, releasing a puff of dust. He sets it on the ledge of the armrest: reading time over.

Evan feels it then, that flicker of human connection when Jack opens himself up a crack and lets him in.

Jack waves a hand at the wall of books. "Battle-testing," *he says.* "That's what we're doing here. For what's coming."

Evan tries to eradicate the fear from his voice. "What is coming?"

"You're gonna get beaten and battered and you're gonna look evil in the face. When you do, it won't always look like evil. Sometimes it looks like . . ." *Jack tugs at his mouth, callused fingers rasping over his stubble.* "Power. Someone understanding the infinity of human options more than you and using that to hurt others. It'll be terrifying. It'll mess you up worse than drownproofing or choke holds or enhanced interrogation. Because it'll get inside you, down deep in the marrow. But you can't let it stop you."

Evan's grown to trust Jack enough to risk showing weakness in front of him. "What if it does?"

Jack gives the question some thought, weighing the heft of it. That's what Evan respects in him most; he doesn't serve up ready-made answers like most adults. Finally he says, "When you get stuck, remember that you can deal with physical issues intellectually and intellectual issues emotionally. You can work out emotional issues psychologically and psychological issues spiritually. Those are the spokes of the wheel—one breaks, you can use another to fix it."

"I don't get it. How am I supposed to solve one kind of problem another way?"

"How's your back?"

Evan shifts from side to side. It feels surprisingly loose. "Better."

"How's your brain? Such as it is?"

Evan cracks a smile. "Better."

"There you go."

"Oh," Evan says. And then, "Oh."

Jack takes a weary pause, shadow catching in the texture beneath his eyes. "The emotional spoke will be toughest, because you've had a lotta rough road behind you and I've gotta put a lot more rough road ahead of you. That's just how it has to be."

Evan nods. "Okay."

"We're making you into an actual Renaissance man. Not one of your anti-intellectual street thugs or some dandy Ivy Leaguer. We want all the knowledge with none of the pretention. Mens corpus animus."

The whole thing feels suddenly, crushingly overwhelming. Evan takes a breath. "How the hell am I supposed to do all that? I'm just some throwaway foster kid from East Baltimore."

Jack places his hands on the armrest and leans forward as if to rise. His body is tense, snake-coiled, his face flushed, and his eyes darker than Evan has ever seen them. "Knock it off!"

It's the first time Evan has seen Jack lose his cool. He is the most judgmental man Evan has ever met in all the right ways. And the least judgmental in all the right ways. So if he's angry now, he's angry about something worth being angry about. Evan is scared and secretly thrilled, as if he's burrowed down to something precious.

"You have worth. You do. You." Jack jabs an oft-broken forefinger at him, the joint swollen. "Not whatever shit you learn or what you accomplish or who you think you are to the outside world—and least of all from whatever fucked-up situations I'm gonna put you in. If you don't have worth, no one does."

There it was. The first of Jack's Unofficial Rules.

"Do you understand me?" Jack asks, still mad.

Evan is taken aback, his throat dry.

"Do you understand me?"

"Yes," Evan says. "Yes, sir."

Jack's contained eruption has knocked the book of military strategy onto the floor. He picks it up now, assesses the cover for damage. Then he slides it into its precise slot on the shelf, uses the backs of his knuckles to ease it into line.

Jack sits once more, his features still wearing the aftermath of his anger. "Don't you dare be so arrogant as to forget that."

"I won't, sir."

Evan feels raw and wounded and deeply respected at the same time. He wonders how all these things can be true at once.

For a long time, they breathe the scent of the fire, pine and beech, and listen to the soothing crackle of sap.

There seems nothing else worth saying.

7

High-Value Target

As Evan broke the surface tension of consciousness, the first thing he noticed was the diaper. He was wearing a diaper. The crinkly lining was thankfully dry. It took a moment for him to determine that he was seated. Hard padding beneath him, metal at his back. A bench? An interrogation-room chair?

Wait. Thrumming beneath his legs. Movement. A helo? No—vehicle transport. No bathroom breaks permitted.

His eyes felt crusty and swollen. He opened them, but it made no difference.

Pitch-black.

Okay. A spit hood, then. No, something opaque, like a general-issue sandbag.

Disks clamped over his ears, the world muted. Earmuffs. He brought his attention to his ear canals, sensing the faintest pressure within. Earplugs beneath the earmuffs. It seemed like overkill.

Overkill was a language he spoke fluently.

An acrid chemical taste coated the back of his throat. His tongue was mashed to the floor of his mouth by . . . plastic? A mouth guard. He could feel the strap chafing his neck. His airway was open, but there would be no talking.

Oxygen seemed sparse, but he knew that was only an illusion. They wouldn't go to all this trouble just to let him suffocate.

His first priority was not to hyperventilate.

Steady slow inhalation. Steady slow exhalation.

Again.

Again.

He kept his respiration subtle enough that no observers would notice. There was no advantage in anyone's knowing he was awake just yet.

Next he focused on his skin. Heavy fabric that breathed slightly, a bit of give. Likely a cotton-polyester blend. A standard prison jumpsuit then, probably orange for the highest-security designation. Softness against the tops of his feet. Without moving he altered his feet's pressure against the floor to gauge the give. Soft-soled disposable slippers.

He leaned his calves inconspicuously outward to little yield: an ankle bar with high-security cuffs on each end. The bar was unforgiving, a one-piece rod, probably stainless steel. From what he could tell, the cuffs were also bolted to the floor. No, not the floor. A metal footrest?

Weight tugged at his forearms. He used the same nonmovement to test the range of motion for his arms. Matching bar and cuffs at the wrists with the cuffs secured to the arms of his seat, which meant a restraint chair fastened into a cradle.

He was hunched over slightly, a stitch in his left side. As the vehicle rocked, he bobbed a bit more than necessary, clinking against a hard stop that indicated a security chain linking his wrist bar to his ankle bar.

Crunching down a bit more, he felt metal bite into his Adam's apple paired with rising pressure on his limbs, as if he were clenched in a massive claw. They'd added a choke chain that connected the stainless-steel rods, threaded between his legs, up his back, and noosed around his throat. He noted additional bands of pressure against his torso and legs, restraining straps cinched into place.

He was a lucky recipient of the high-value-target treatment.

That gave him a bit more to work with.

They would have subjected him to a full-body scan while he was unconscious to check for any secret items like a sewing needle burrowed beneath the calluses of his hand or hidden contraband technology like a bazooka masquerading as a suppository.

They'd have run advance-team scouts to check transport routes and identify shelter points along the way—police and fire stations, government buildings with enclosed garages, military bases.

They'd have arranged multiple three-vehicle convoys, each with a driver, a team commander, two gunners, and two handlers armed with less-lethal.

They'd have ensured that no one in the other transport vehicles knew which convoy contained him and that each convoy had a different route and a distinct encoded comms channel.

They'd have put him in neither a lower-security nondescript windowless industrial panel van nor an overly conspicuous Mine-Resistant Ambush Protected light tactical vehicle but in an up-armored SUV that could veer off and blend into traffic once they cleared the area of operation.

They'd have placed air assets over each convoy, probably a fully equipped and armed Black Hawk, a Specter AC-130 gunship on station with a flight of F-16s heated up on the runway of the nearest air force base—the one in El Segundo. Maybe even a quick-reaction force of Boeing Little Bird attack variant AH-6s in case things got sporty.

He was the belle of a multimillion-dollar ball.

It would have been nice to be the recipient of so much attention if he were someone who liked attention.

His body hurt in innumerable places, and his head throbbed from the opioid injection. He took a silent internal inventory. Lots of bruises and aches, perhaps a cracked rib from the fall onto the Red Cross van, but nothing that would require surgery or a fracture reduction. The pain was present and undeniable, but he didn't let it all the way in. He couldn't afford to devote resources to physical suffering right now.

They had total control over his person.

They had total control over his bodily functions.

They had total control over his future.

He realized he had to start unstitching what had happened to him now, because God knew there'd be more to come.

Deep breath. Pushing it all the way out, making room for oxygen as Jack had taught him and as he'd taught Joey. He reached for meditation, found it, lost it, found it again. He lingered there in the relative calm, mustering his courage.

Then he irised himself open ever so slightly to thoughts of the capture. Unfortunately, that was all the opening needed for images to claw their way in. A cold-water hit to his nervous system, a kaleidoscope of horrors like—

her palm against his cheek

flowers thrashing against his thigh

windshield spiderwebbing

IV pole starting to topple

It was like fighting a war with the wind, each sensation stabbing into him anew, blurring past and present, and suddenly he was—

gripping a Makarov pistol, standing behind a round man slumped forward, face in his bowl of soup, the back of his head missing

down on one knee, slender adolescent neck bowed, drooling blood onto the asphalt as the Mystery Man stares down, eyes hidden behind Ray-Bans

asleep on the mattress on the floor between bunk beds, the other boys sliding out with the morning sun, their feet pounding him awake

This is Ethan—er, Evan. His first placement fell through. He doesn't talk much. But I'm sure you'll all make him feel welcome.

baby mobile chiming a nursery rhyme, patterns on the ceiling way up above, a horse, a lion, a zebra, shouts somewhere in the house—A stroke, I think she's had another—red flashing lights through the windowpane eclipsing the animals, the rhyme winding down, his tiny, tiny hand gripping a smooth white rail, and raw sobbing from another room with no more music to disguise it

The transport vehicle bounced over a pothole, throwing him back into the prison of his restraints, encased in darkness, his senses bound.

Sweat trickling down the back of his neck. The smell of French roast, wafting off his skin from the spray he'd caught on the plaza.

And his breath, there for him as it always was. As long as he could breathe, he was okay. He gave himself a brief respite and then re-focused once more.

Rewinding through his takedown, he replayed it inch by inch, forward and backward and forward again, extracting splinters of ancient linked memories, clearing them from his nervous system until each needle punch of sensation lost its sharpness, until they joined the thrumming of his heart and the wheels across the un-even road, until he was no longer locked off from sight and sound and voice, severed from himself, but able to observe his thoughts and emotions, to see clearly what he'd managed to hold at bay.

Panic had been there all along, a constant beckoning, the road not taken. He looked down the barrel of it now to the bottomless dark. Acknowledged it with respect.

Then he closed the door.

It was time to get to work.

8

A Fucking Selfie with Orphan X

Evan straightened up as much as the restraints allowed and feigned choking. Gagging against the mouth guard, knees bouncing, shoulders rattling the metal at his back.

"Shit— He's choking. He's choking."

"Get the fucking hood off, now!"

"Careful—wait—careful—don't—"

Hands seized his shoulders. The GI sandbag was ripped off his head. Drooling around the mouth guard, he kept his eyes fluttering, rolled to white.

Gloved hands grabbed his head roughly, chin and crown. Someone unsnapped the plastic band and yanked the guard free of his mouth, and then the earmuffs were lifted and the earplugs tugged free.

The clamp on his head was released, and then he heard the clank of geared-up bodies flying back to hit the bench across from him, everyone keeping a good safe distance.

He opened his eyes.

He was indeed cuffed and barred and chained and strapped to a restraint chair seated in a metal cradle in the back of an up-armored SUV with blacked-out windows. The vehicle had been reconfigured with facing bench seats.

He was indeed wearing soft-soled disposable slippers and a standard prison jumpsuit, though it was black, not orange.

There were indeed two gunners. They were ensconced in body armor over black BDUs, select fire SR-16s with SureFire suppressors at the ready, SIG P229s in drop-leg holsters, double flashbangs bulging in pouches.

There were indeed two handlers armed with the now-familiar grenade launchers and various caustic sprays and shock devices poking from various cargo pockets.

And seated directly across from him, Naomi Templeton herself playing the role of team commander.

Evan immediately stopped choking and let his face find dead calm. The men's eyes bulged beneath their tactical goggles. Legs bouncing with adrenaline. They couldn't take their eyes off him. Naomi alone looked unflustered.

Evan cleared this throat. Once. "You sure you have enough firepower?"

Naomi's lips tensed, an almost-smile. "Maybe."

The younger of the gunners was breathing hard, his finger curled around the trigger instead of resting alongside the guard. "You're really him?" he asked. A glance at Naomi. "Can I . . ."

"What?" She did not sound pleased.

"If I stay over here, can I take a selfie with Orphan X?"

"No, Chip, you cannot take a fucking selfie with Orphan X," she said.

Chip jerked his head twice in a nod. "Okay."

A car honking. Distant children's laughter. The whine of a lawn mower, someone working a leaf blower. Straining to listen, Evan could barely make out the Black Hawk overhead.

"SR-16s are a bad call in a confined space like this," he said to Naomi. "You should know better."

"Standard operating procedure for CAT," she said. "You know, boys and their toys. So predictable."

THE LAST ORPHAN

Evan watched the baby-faced gunner. Chip's neck muscles had tightened, and the wrinkles of his forehead were centered between the brows. Afraid.

"It's okay," Evan told him. "Breathe deep."

"I'm fine."

"Your safety's off. And the guy next to you would probably feel better if you placed your trigger finger outside the guard."

Chip's throat bobbed with a hard swallow. He made the adjustments.

Evan glanced down as far as the choke chain allowed. "My jumpsuit," he said. "All this and I don't even rate orange?"

"We thought black suited you better."

"Plus, it helps me blend in with you all in case we get hit and we need to switch convoys."

"Perhaps that, too."

"I'd love to see that," the other gunner said. Graying hair showed beneath his helmet, and he had a broad, cynical face. Faded permanent marker on his helmet ID'd him as Paddy. "Even you couldn't come up with an extraction plan for this. Not if you had a year to plan it."

"No?" Evan said.

"No way."

Evan smirked. He sensed amusement in Naomi's face as well.

Chip still looked breathless. "How, then?"

Evan took a breath, considered. "I'd wait for the convoy to reach a relatively populated area, like the suburbs we're passing through right now." A jerk of his chin to the blacked-out windows through which he'd heard landscaping being tended. "I'd have arranged for an associate to hack into every satellite-TV dish in a three-mile radius and reconfigure them to give off sporadic electromagnetic pulses on the same frequency used by ground-to-air targeting systems. The Black Hawks"—he let his eyes pull north through the roof—"and the AC-130 gunship you have standing by at the Los Angeles Air Force Base would be flooded with hundreds of missile-targeting-system alerts a second. That neutralizes your air game."

"No hacker could do that."

Evan thought of Joey's fingers working her keyboards with preternatural proficiency, a half-chewed Red Vine flapping from her mouth as she slurp-devoured it hands-free. "None that *you* know."

"How would he even know which convoy was carrying you?"

"He," Evan said, relishing the assumed pronoun, "would already be inside the visual feeds of the overwatch Black Hawks. From the air it's relatively easy to gauge which convoy is driving the most cautiously. Once that's established, we'd release a massive EMP through every area dish to take targeting and visual tracking offline and kill all your comms. That'd also knock out the engine ignitions. So we're stalled." He gave an emphatic nod. "Right here."

"Fine," one of the handlers said, getting in on the action. "Then what? You'd have to roll in an army regiment to take us."

"Sure," Evan said. "If I thought like you."

Paddy was growing agitated. "So enlighten us," he said, "with your special brand of magical thinking."

"I'd send someone in a tanker truck full of liquid nitrogen to crash into us." Evan felt a ping of amusement at the image of Tommy Stojack commandeering a massive fuel truck, windows down, breeze riffling his biker mustache and dragging smoke from the tip of his Camel Wide. "In the restraint chair, I'd be the most safely secured for the crash. Thank you for that. Then my driver would pop off the valves on the tanker and start hosing down the armored wall right behind your heads."

The men glanced nervously around them. Chip's thumb slipped over to double-check his seat belt.

"Now the vehicle body's at subzero temperatures," Evan continued. "And because it's about to crack like a sheet of ice and the incoming gas is threatening to suffocate those of us unfortunate enough to *not* have a GI sandbag over our heads offering some filtration, you all scramble. Wisely. Once you're clear of the compromised vehicle, the cloud of liquid nitrogen creates a visual barrier and fucks up your helmet- and weapons-mounted thermal vision."

"Okay," Naomi said, finally entering the fray. Leaning toward Evan, she rested her elbows on her knees. "Now what? You and your superhero driver are still surrounded by heavily armed transport specialists from three convoy vehicles."

"In addition to a gas mask, my driver would be wearing a tear-away jumpsuit, which he'd rip off after he liberates me from my restraints."

"What's he wearing beneath it?" Paddy asked. "Wait—lemme guess. Superman Underoos."

"No," Evan said. "Just black BDUs, body armor, helmet, and tactical goggles, and he'd be carrying a select fire SR-16 with a SIG P229 in a drop-leg holster. Boys and their toys. So predictable."

The man's smile grew stale on his face.

Evan continued, "He'd haul me out of the cloud of liquid nitrogen—"

Naomi's eyes were shiny, excited. "And in the commotion, we'd mistake him for one of us."

"Right until he marches me to a decoy Black Hawk with a cloned IFoF beacon stolen during the hacked visual feeds." Evan imagined a chopper and pilot supplied by his friend Aragón Urrea, an unconventional businessman with unlimited extralegal resources. "It would be setting down just about now while your real Black Hawk is off dodging a few hundred fake missile alerts. You all graciously help him load me aboard the helo. He accompanies me, of course. And we're up, up, and away before you realize you've been duped."

A silence asserted itself in the back of the SUV. Naomi stared at Evan thoughtfully, her head cocked. The men looked uneasy.

"Well," the senior gunner said, "it ain't happening today."

"No," Evan said, a note of resignation in his voice. "A different story for a different time."

The only thing clear to him right now was that nothing would go like anything had ever gone before.

Naomi held the sandbag mopped around one hand. "I'll leave the earmuffs and the mouth guard off," she said. "But I'm gonna put this back over your head, okay?"

Evan nodded. "I could use a little rest."

9

So Much Circling for So Many Years

Hooded and embedded in the restraint chair, Evan had been carried from the SUV. Like riding a palanquin but less luxurious.

He'd kept track of his movements as well as he could. After another fifteen minutes in the SUV, he'd been borne through a rattling gate, up three steps, through a door with a hissing hydraulic closer, down a long corridor with air-conditioning vents and significant echoing off hard surfaces, and now into what he gauged—given the reverberation of footfalls—to be a moderate size room.

He was set down with care.

Doors opened and closed, boots scuffling.

Then silence.

Save for the sound of someone breathing in the room with him. He smelled a trace of something fruity and vanilla, a cheap drugstore shampoo.

"Agent Templeton," he said. "Would you mind removing my hood?"

"I'm not supposed to."

A long pause, her shoes ticktocking back and forth as she paced.

Then she said, "Fuck it," the bag lifted, and Evan blinked into the sudden light.

A plain box of a room, walls painted white. No one-way mirror, no furniture, nothing but a recessed light in the ceiling fifteen feet above, well out of reach.

Just him adhered to the restraint chair. Naomi on her feet. And a single folding table, also white, upon which rested a large monitor with heavy-duty cables linking it to an outlet in the wall and no visibly attached computer.

The table was ten feet away from Evan.

Naomi stayed six feet away.

Evan and Naomi had crossed paths enough times for him to have evolved a profile on her.

Her late father had been a legend in the Service, ran the "big show"—the Presidential Protective Detail—for several administrations. Her last name carried an almost hallowed aura within governmental circles. Early on in her career, there'd been whispered claims of nepotism, though her father had in fact lent her scant professional support. She'd made her way up the agency hierarchy on her own undeniable talent, solidifying a lot of good habits in the process of proving herself.

She was indefatigable.

For a time they stared at each other. After so much circling for so many years, it felt surreal to be face-to-face.

Evan broke the silence. "A diaper? Really?"

"Sorry about that," she said.

"You're scanning my clothes?"

"Yes. And your vehicle. Explosive-detection dogs hit on it a few blocks from the hospital. Unless of course someone else was driving a truck with a small arsenal locked in vaults in the bed."

He wasn't worried. They'd find nothing beyond a forged registration, insurance purchased under a false name, and ordnance, including a reusable, unguided, Russian rocket-propelled grenade launcher he'd recently acquired but had yet to try out. His first thought—to ask Tommy to supply him with a replacement—was severed by a pang of dread.

He would likely not breathe free air again.

Naomi crossed her arms. She'd taken off her body armor, her ill-fitting starched white shirt still looked nice on her despite her best efforts. A silver pen clip showed at the corner of the front left pocket of her slate-gray ripstop pants. She had no jewelry, no watch, and wore lightweight tactical shoes with paracord laces of a contrasting color, cinched tight to prevent rattle with her footsteps.

"You could have shot me," she said. "But you didn't."

He stared at her.

"You're an unsanctioned assassin," she said. "You don't believe in the law."

"I don't believe the law is always sufficient," Evan said. "But I believe it's necessary."

"So you're there to fill in the gaps? Like some kind of civil dis-obedience?" she said, her cheeks suddenly flushed. She appeared to notice that she'd drawn closer to him and took a brisk step back, shaking her head. "All these years."

He said, "All these years."

"Never once did you leak an intel dump about the Program, scribble out some manifesto."

"I try not to complain about anything I'm not doing something about. And when I'm actually doing something, I don't have time to complain."

Her mouth popped open. Closed again. She wore no makeup, but her lips looked plenty red against her pale complexion. "You live around here, then?"

"I don't live anywhere."

"Right. The Nowhere Man. Helping the hopeless, one murder at a time."

"Not hopeless. Powerless."

The pressure at his ankles, groin, lap, wrists, shoulders, chest, and neck threatened to tighten him into full-blown claustropho-bia. His chin itched, but he resisted the urge to dip his face to rub it against the strap. He would allow his discomfort no toehold.

Naomi leaned back against the table. "Why do you help people?" she asked. "To atone?"

"Nothing so lofty."

"What then?"

"Because of what you—the government—made me, there's only one thing I am excellent at. And extremely limited circumstances under which I can do it in ways that are . . ."

"What? Moral?"

"No." He contemplated. "Good."

"*Good?*"

"Yes."

"Why do *you* get to choose what's good?"

He thought about it. The choke chain twisted slightly when he swallowed, pinched the skin of his neck. It took him awhile to find words not cloyed with cliché.

"There's no getting around suffering," he said. "But if someone's being terrorized at the hands of another person, that's something different. Not playing victim, not claiming to suffer on behalf of someone else, not being a martyr to themselves. Not suffering over ideas or ideals or some metaphysical bullshit. When it's too painful for any of that. When you see it in their eyes. Bone-deep *suffering*." His voice had intensified, and he took a moment to back down what he felt rising in his chest. "Suffering for no better reason than that someone else wants them to. Then it doesn't matter where they're from or the color of their skin or who they want to fuck or marry or pray to or vote for. They're in pain. And trying to alleviate that? Is the closest thing to good I've found."

That was also why he let his clients choose the next person to pass his covert phone number on to. Because they understood suffering. They could see it, know when it was real.

It was the most he'd ever spoken at once.

Ever.

Naomi hadn't moved. Her attention was locked on him so intently that were it not for the gentle rise and fall of her chest, she could have been a paused image on a screen.

She asked, "Then you kill for them?"

He watched her face closely, no excessive use of the forehead muscles to indicate insincerity. No, he trusted her. Which meant they could honestly disagree on what they disagreed about.

"Then I escalate the situation as far as it needs to go," he said. "That's what my adversaries aren't counting on."

"Someone who will escalate?"

The air was cool, and his throat still felt raw, coated with chemical aftertaste. He wet his lips. "Someone who can escalate higher than they can."

"You've been pretty effective."

"It's amazing what you can accomplish if you go out into the world not feeling like you deserve anything from it."

A muffled sound of amusement escaped her. "That should be *my* motto."

He lowered his eyes to indicate the restraint chair he was captive to. "You've been pretty effective, too."

"We identified you heading into the medical center a few months ago," she said. "A security camera in the parking garage. Your face was blurred, but we got gait recognition."

That would've been when he'd arrived to see Mia into her surgery. Medical confidentiality issues meant scant cameras inside the private areas of the hospital, so they wouldn't have been able to chart his course and connect him to her—a small blessing. He wondered at the scale of NSA surveillance they must've been running across the country in order to find him in one parking garage at the western edge of the nation.

"We've been staking it out since. The manpower alone." Naomi shook her head. "You can't begin to imagine what it's taken to catch you."

"You could've just asked nicely."

"I did." Her smile was melancholy, even doleful. "In the end."

A chime jarred them from the moment. Naomi withdrew a Boeing Black smartphone from her pocket. A quick glance at the incoming message, and then she turned away from Evan, picked up a comically tiny remote control hidden behind the monitor, clicked it, and stood back.

THE LAST ORPHAN

The encryption code scrolled across the screen.
A moment later the monitor went black.
Then blinked to life again.
Evan found himself face-to-face with the president of the United States.

10

A Low-Rent Prometheus

A former constitutional lawyer, President Victoria Donahue-Carr dressed the part of Intrepid World Leader. A midnight-blue pant-suit, the blazer enhancing the lines of her shoulders. Her posture was erect but slightly forward-leaning, hands clasped on the blotter of the Resolute desk. Flags standing sentinel at either side, Old Glory and the presidential coat of arms against a backdrop the same color as her suit. Heavy maroon curtains encroached on the trio of tall windows facing the South Lawn. Nothing else within the scope of the camera recording her.

Bound in his restraint chair like a low-rent Prometheus, Evan returned the gaze she'd launched from the monitor. Now he understood even better the heavy-duty cable, the encryption code.

"Orphan X," she said. "How are you doing?"

"Is that rhetorical?" he asked. Just a little light banter between himself and the leader of the free world.

Donahue-Carr pursed her lips thoughtfully. "Yes."

"In that case," Evan said, "fine, thank you."

Safely out of view of the monitor's camera, Naomi suppressed a grin.

"You've violated the terms of your informal pardon," the president said.

Evan said, "Okay."

Her face made clear she'd been expecting something less succinct. "We've hunted you down as promised. And now we have you in custody."

He felt the bite of the choke chain once more against his throat. "That's apparent."

She blinked twice with discomfort, her second nonverbal tell. "We need to decide what to do with you next."

"Okay."

"Your conduct is not just beyond the purview of American and international law, it's also treasonous beyond any reasonable doubt."

"Okay."

"My predecessor would certainly agree."

"Were he around," Evan added.

This gave Donahue-Carr the briefest pause. "As such, your actions are punishable by death."

"Okay."

"Unless . . ."

The used-car-salesman routine seemed beneath the commander in chief, but who was Evan to judge?

The president looked flustered by his no-response response. "Agent Templeton. You there?"

Naomi stepped into view of the camera. "Yes, Madam President."

"Can we trust him?"

"Yes," Naomi said, with an immediacy and a conviction that did not surprise Evan at all.

The president's focus shifted back to Evan. "Can we trust you?"

"I can't imagine any circumstances under which I'd care less to answer your question."

"Well," she said, "there's that." Another sidebar with Naomi. "You sure about this, Agent Templeton?"

"As sure as I can be about something this insane, Madam President."

Donahue-Carr parted her hands, noticed she'd done so, laced her fingers once more. "You're it," she told Evan. "You're the last Orphan."

"Not quite," Evan said. "There are still bad ones out there."

"You don't think *you're* bad?"

"If I did," Evan said, "imagine what that would do to my self-esteem."

Naomi turned from them both, feigned a cough to cover her mouth.

"Templeton?" the president said briskly. "Why don't we get to it?"

"Yes, Madam President."

Donahue-Carr regarded Evan with her best steely gaze. "Orphan X," she said. "We need your help."

Evan laughed.

She looked puzzled. "I wasn't anticipating that would be amusing."

"Inside joke," Evan said.

"I'll leave you two to it, then," Donahue-Carr announced crisply. She leaned forward to touch an off-screen button or mouse, hesitated just long enough to undermine her curt exit, and then the screen went black once more.

Naomi sighed. "What do you think?" she said.

Evan said, "The presentation needs some work."

"She did go a little boomer with the tech there at the end."

"Now you give me the full sales pitch, right? Time share in the Poconos?"

"Nothing so glam," Naomi said. "Another mission."

"Which, if I complete, restores my informal pardon."

"More or less."

"Let me be clear," Evan said. "I will never operate for the government again."

"Don't you want to meet the target?" Naomi turned the screen back on with a tap of the miniaturized remote.

"Do I have a choice?"

"You could always close your eyes."

A dossier came up, complete with surveillance photos of a puckish man in his forties. Slender of chest and waist, sharply intelligent eyes, thin matte-blond hair that rose to a stylishly mussed tuft at the crown. He had a pronounced widow's peak, the faintest monk's tonsure starting to show through at the back of his head.

"Luke Devine," Naomi said.

"Who is he?"

"Kind of a minigarch, I suppose. Someone who's learned to trade power for more power."

Evan studied the pictures of Devine. Even in the still photos he seemed ethereal, like Ziggy Stardust with that strong dancer's torso and the spectral gaze. "Isn't that how the game's played?"

"Yes," Naomi said. "But he's really good at it."

"And that makes him problematic for you."

"We believe he represents a clear and present danger to national security."

"That's what you say about me."

"Yes. But he's *really* dangerous. He came out of private banking."

"Fetch the smelling salts," Evan said.

"A few dozen wholly owned corporate entities and limited-liability companies, private island near Saint Croix, penthouses in London, Moscow, Beijing, and Zurich, an estate in the Hamptons, a superyacht—you get the drift. But what's he's really good at, what makes him really dangerous? His talent for manipulating people. I don't go in for cult of personality, but it seems he's got a gift to make anyone do pretty much anything he wants them to."

"Which keeps him above the fray."

"With clean hands. He was your typical power player on the rise, but about a year ago he seemed to go into hyperdrive. And now he's gotten so far ahead the laws can't catch up to him."

Evan was familiar with the trajectory of men like Devine. They accrued a certain amount of influence and then began to sense a new frontier beyond the fringes of their endeavors. A place where boundaries dissolved between financial institutions, political leverage, and international law. Uncharted waters where the old precedents and regulations hadn't caught up. Where the stakes were higher. Where a different kind of power was forged and wielded.

"Would you mind loosening my choke chain?"

Naomi turned from the images populating the screen. Removed her holstered pistol and set it on the table. She closed the space warily, circling him. He could smell her shampoo more clearly now. Though she was out of sight, he heard her breaths, slightly rushed with adrenaline. Then he felt the backs of her knuckles brush his neck. Cool, smooth skin.

A bit of pressure, a snap, and the chain fell away.

Her footsteps again as she came back around. She stood closer to him now. She was well built, her clavicles pronounced, a strong swimmer's taper to her lats. "I'm sorry about this."

He said, "I know."

Walking back to the table, she twisted her hair up into that short stick of a ponytail, snapping into place a rubber band that she took from around her wrist. "Devine remains unattached. Single child, parents passed from COVID within days of each other, no living relatives. Known associates and past relationships are compiled here." A gesture at the screen. "These days? He throws parties. Huge, decadent, hedonistic parties. And guess who wants to come? Plenty of fetching young men and women. And? Everyone who's anyone. Political figures, celebs, financiers, foreign ambassadors, scions of industry, academicians, billionaires, royalty, CEOs, prominent scientists—"

"All fine people to bribe for whatever they happen to do at a party with fetching young men and women."

"Bribery carries too much liability. So instead? Why not demand a giant allocation for a hedge fund?"

"I know the drill," Evan said. "Get full power of attorney over the investments, park the fund in a nonreporting country, slam the money into the S&P, take your two and twenty on the management fee, and you've got a legal cash cow for life. So what?"

"What if it's not about the cash at all? What if it's about *leverage*?"

"For the usual? Arms dealing, money laundering, drug trade—"

Naomi said, "Bigger."

Evan rolled his neck, the joints crackling. "Intelligence?"

"Warmer," Naomi said. "Someone with enough leverage on enough powerful people can become . . . Let's say he could become his own nation-state. He would be in a position to shape policy. Financial, legal, political. Have direct dealings with foreign governments. He doesn't just want to play the game. He wants to *run* the game."

"Ah," Evan said. "I'd imagine someone like that would be fairly inconvenient if you were the president of the United States."

"Someone interfering with the democratic process? It's not inconvenient. It's untenable."

"Everyone who can afford a lobbyist interferes with the democratic process," Evan said. "Why's Devine a threat to the president? Specifically."

"What makes you think there's a specific?"

"My few brushes with realpolitik taught me that vague civil concerns don't call for interventions of the type that require my services."

Naomi blinked at him, her lower jaw shifting forward so her teeth met in a tense line. Finally she eased out a breath. "Devine's black book includes two key moderate senators who can put a vote over the top. Or not put it over the top. Whatever he has on them means they take their cues from him on certain votes."

"Such as?"

"Such as the trillion-dollar environmental bill that President Donahue-Carr is trying to push through."

"The one that her reelection hinges on?"

"That is how politics work," Templeton said. "You get shit done if you want to be reelected. The president can play all the usual power games with these senators, trade horses, all that. But she cannot be beholden to Luke Devine to save the planet."

"Sounds pleasingly clear-cut."

"He's a bad guy, Orphan X."

"Like me."

"No," she said. "Not like you at all."

"So our head of state, a onetime constitutional attorney, is willing to act 'outside the purview of American and international law' in order to rid herself of this inconvenience."

Naomi drew in a breath, held it for a moment. "Devine has accrued almost unimaginable influence. He is willing to use it however he pleases. We don't really understand what he wants, what motivates him. And none of his machinations are *technically* illegal."

"That's why you need someone you can deny any knowledge of to neutralize him. Someone you can wash your hands of. Someone expendable."

"Yes." Naomi looked pained. "Look," she said. "This is some DoD secret-handshake shit. I'm not comfortable with it either. I'm not a handler. This isn't my bailiwick."

"Then why are you here?"

"Because the president trusts me. And I'm the only one who knows you. As much as anyone can know you."

"So my job is to infiltrate his superyacht while strapped to this restraint chair and garrote him with my ankle bar?"

Naomi seemed at a loss.

"Yes," she said. She even said it with a straight face, but he could see the skin tighten around her eyes. He showed mercy and grinned first.

"We both know that at some point you have to end the security theater and unlock me, right?" Evan said. "Let's just save time and do it now. Consider me sufficiently cowed into acquiescence. Or do you need me to lie to you first, maybe shed a few tears, tell you I'll do anything you want?"

"After all our effort, that might be rewarding."

He held her gaze. After a moment she crossed to him. Looked down. He was close enough to see the flecks of gold in her eyes. She reached out a hand to the strap at his chest. Her fingers were trembling slightly. Her knee brushed his knuckles.

He kept his stare locked on hers. Pressure released at his chest. He exhaled fully for the first time in hours. He kept his hands motionless in their cuffs, not wanting to startle her.

She exhaled. Her breath smelled clean—like tea and mint. "That'll do for now," she said, easing back a few steps.

"Did you document me in any way while I was unconscious?" he asked. "Photographs, biometrics—anything?"

"No."

"Don't lie to me."

"I'm not. I won't."

He looked at her. Believed her. "Here are my terms," he said.

"You're hardly in a position to—"

"You will not document me in any way. If you do, I will not help you. I want out of this chair. I want out of this building. I'm not staying in a government facility."

She coughed out a note of disbelief. "Where do you think you'll stay?"

"The Beverly Hills Hotel will do for now. If you want to use me as an asset, you'll have to let me go be an asset. And I want my clothes. I want my phone."

"We're processing your phone."

"Don't waste your time. You'll never hack it. It's got three dozen autowipe features. Give it to me."

"Why?"

"You want me to complete a mission for you. It's one of the tools I require for that mission."

"So you'll help us?"

"I won't do anything for you. But I will make a good-faith effort to see if your mission aligns with something I consider worth doing."

The Sixth Commandment, one he'd not had occasion to recall in years: *Question orders.*

"That's not good enough," Naomi said.

"You told me you won't lie to me. I won't lie to you either. So let me be clear: That's the only agreement you're gonna get from me. Ever. Call your boss. Call the director of the Service. Call the president. Tell them to meet my terms. Or throw me in prison. Or kill me."

She leaned against the table once more and studied him. He could hear boots in the corridor outside, the steady hum of the air conditioner overhead. Naomi might have blinked, but he missed it.

"A covert multiagency ops team is being assembled, flying in tomorrow," she finally said. "They will join you for briefing and transport. *If* your conditions are met—and that's a big-ass *if*—they will be with you all the time."

"We'll see about that," Evan said.

"You'll have access to all our databases, weapons, and matériel, fly on private transport. You're not gonna do better than that."

Evan flared his hands, letting the cuffs slough from his wrists, along with the stainless-steel rod connecting them. The pen he'd liberated from Naomi's pocket clattered to the floor next, but he kept the slender silver clip he'd snapped off. It would fit the ankle cuffs just as nicely in case the bozos in the hall took too long with the master key. He rubbed one wrist and then the other, noticed Naomi looking at him.

Her mouth was slightly ajar, but she looked less alarmed than resigned. Her last claim still hung in the air: *You're not gonna do better than that.*

He gave her a cordial nod. "You'd be surprised."

11

The Big Bad Orphan

The Beverly Hills Hotel, perched on a rise above Sunset Boulevard, was a classic Hollywood take on a palatial mansion, its domes and verandas rendered in kitschy peach. From the sprawling gardens to the bungalows nestled behind banana plants and hibiscus to the main building embellished with deco furnishings, Evan knew it well.

That's why he'd chosen it.

The Third Commandment: *Master your surroundings.*

He was dressed in his own clothes, blissfully diaper-free. With extreme caution Naomi released him from the restraint chair at the valet, resecuring his wrists behind him with zip-ties. LAPD had lent a few units who lingered at the periphery of the literal red-carpet entrance, trying to hide their excitement.

To the consternation of leisurewear-appareled guests, Evan was frogwalked in by a cadre of agents, past the perennially burning fireplace in the lobby, up the elevator to the fourth and top floor, and into a suite with a balcony and a Jacuzzi, the interior a haze of apricot, cream, and green.

The agents had changed into tactical-discreet garb so they'd look merely intimidating rather than terrifying. Their conceal-carry pistols and rifles weren't nearly as inconspicuous as they seemed to believe.

Now that they were in the room, Paddy lifted the SR-16 from where he'd tucked it beneath his coat. At a ten-foot standoff, he aimed it at Evan's head. Chip followed suit. The others formed a horseshoe around Evan and the bed, showing him 270 degrees of rifle bores. Naomi was the only one willing to stand within reach of him. She held a Pelican pistol case at her side.

Jumping up and tucking his knees to his chest, Evan swung his zip-tied wrists beneath his boots to bring his bound hands in front of him. He brought them to his mouth, bit hard on the protruding strip of plastic, and yanked the cuffs even tighter. Then he raised his hands and slammed the union of his wrists down against his hip. The zip-ties popped open.

In concert all the men thumbed their safeties to off, a single compounded metallic click immediately followed by fainter clicks as they took slack out of their triggers.

Evan sat on the pristinely made king-size bed, sinking luxuriously into the sea-green comforter. "I see we still have trust issues."

"About that." Naomi set down the Pelican case on a preposterously overscale coffee table and snapped the catches. From the foam interior, she drew a thick, rubber-coated ankle bracelet with a sinister-looking steel locking mechanism. "Tamperproof, GPS, shock- and impact-resistant. This will accompany you until tomorrow's briefing."

At her gesture Paddy stepped forward. Turning the bracelet, Naomi pressed a sensor square on its side to his thumb, and the unit snapped open with a low thrum like a lion's cage door releasing.

"My men'll be in the connecting room," Naomi said, nodding toward an internal door. She removed a metal disk the size of a hockey puck from the Pelican case. "We've arranged for these to be implanted all around the suite's perimeter—in the hallway, next door, in the vents, on the ceiling, outside the windows, beneath the balcony—"

Evan said, "And if I cross them, they play the refrain from Beethoven's Fifth."

"Not just that." She moved to him cautiously, knelt before him. The men looked twitchy, but she'd gained confidence around Evan. Or was it trust?

She held the bracelet wide. He hiked up the leg of his cargo pants and proffered his ankle. She snapped it into place right above the top of his boot.

"A ring of det cord is embedded in the bracelet." She rose, stood within reach of him. "If you move beyond the borders of this suite, your foot will be cleanly severed by pentaerythritol tetranitrate."

"A shock wasn't enough?"

"It has that capability, too." Flicking up a folding knife from her pocket, Naomi leaned over him. She slipped the metal tip beneath the zip tie ringing his left wrist and tugged, the plastic cuff falling free. Her face was close, a wisp of hair arcing past her temple, catching in the side of her mouth. Dried sweat sparkled on her cheek at the soft spot in front of her ear. She severed the right cuff with another confident twist of her blade. "But we figured you'd require a more robust deterrent." With a jerk of her wrist, she snapped the knife shut, and it disappeared into her pocket once more. "You know, as we continue to hone our working relationship."

A young man with narrow features and a shock of black hair entered the front door. He wore overalls and a tool belt and carried the proverbial black bag—a technical security investigator straight out of central casting.

"Agent Templeton, my team—erhm—my team has the units in place." He kept his face lowered, no eye contact, but oriented toward Chip and Paddy. "Surveillance center's set up next door for you. Per your agreement with the—erhm—high-value target, the video won't leave the room, and he can personally oversee the wipe after the team brief tomorrow." His head and narrow shoulders swiveled back in the direction of Naomi. "Boss said to sleep you separate downstairs so you don't have to—erhm—be embarrassed."

"I'm embarrassed?" Naomi asked.

"I'm just saying, bunking in with the—erhm—men, you're probably uncomfortable."

"Uncomfortable," she said. "How else do I feel?"

"C'mon, Templeton," Paddy said. "Give the guy a break. No need to get touchy."

"'Touchy'?" she said. "If we could just work in 'strident,' I'd hit the quadfecta." She glanced over at Evan, lips pursed, and shot him a wink beneath the sway of locks across her eyes. Then back at the men, who looked ill at ease. "Jesus, team, I'm just kidding," she said, and the room seemed to exhale. "I'm happy to have my own suite. You boys should really smile more."

Chip shook his head, bit down on a grin. "Templeton."

Naomi moved toward the door, the bulk of the men following in her wake. Pausing, she turned back to Evan. "Try 'n' behave yourself. For once."

He gave a two-fingered salute.

"And you guys?" A side-eye to Paddy and Chip. "Don't fuck it up."

A turn of her broad shoulders, a fan of straw-blond hair, and she was gone. The others shuffled out after her, heavier on their feet.

Now it was down to Paddy, Chip, and an open adjoining door to their surveillance suite. A spray of white roses on the accent table by the window gave off a waft of perfume and the aroma of fresh-cut stems. Naomi's footsteps and the sounds of her men faded up the hall.

When Evan refocused, Paddy was considering a slender control device that had suddenly appeared in his hands. He was wearing a sideways grin that Evan didn't like one bit.

Chip said, "I'm not sure we should—"

Paddy's wide fist pulsed around the device. An electric shock hit Evan's ankle, locking up his leg and flinging him off the bed. As he writhed on the floor, he could just make out the ding of the elevator out in the hallway closing behind Naomi, carrying her away.

It wasn't just the electroshock, at least fifty thousand volts coursing through Evan's nervous system. It wasn't just the sharp, stabbing pain or the intense muscle spasms, locking up his legs, his hips, the lower abdominal muscles, sheeting his neck with veins, making his eyeballs bulge. It wasn't even the total immobilization, the knowledge that his flesh and fiber no longer obeyed him, that they'd been put at the mercy of a current passing from electrodes on the inside rim of the security bracelet bolted around his ankle. It was the mental haze, the real-time knowledge that his cognitive functioning was being fragmented, turned into snowy static, that he was drooling onto the carpet, shuddering like a stunned fish, and could grasp little beyond—

palm against his cheek

windshield spiderwebbing

not a shot he ever missed

—and then he heard a voice, gauzy and distorted. "Say *aaah.*"

When Evan came back into himself, Paddy was leaning over his face, one kneecap pressed square over his heart, compressing his ribs. Straightening up, Paddy inserted a cotton swab in a transport test tube, a satisfied expression on his face. Evan felt rawness in the side of his mouth and realized that while he'd been rendered useless, Paddy had scraped a DNA sample from his cheek.

Evan still couldn't breathe.

Now an iPhone hovered above his nose, the camera flash spiking through his dilated pupils as his photo was snapped. The pressure lifted from his chest, and Paddy rose and stared down at him.

"For a guy with a big reputation," Paddy said, "you don't look like much."

"Fuck, Paddy." Chip was leaning against the wall, his arms crossed as if to prevent a shiver. "It's not too late to forget it."

"Forget it?" Paddy held the test tube to the light, grinning up at it. "You have any idea what this'll fetch on the black market?" He slid the DNA sample into his breast pocket and patted it for good measure. "We won't interfere with the job. All we have to do is sit on it till the time is right." He headed for the adjoining room. "Now, let's fire up the surveillance cameras and give the big bad Orphan some downtime."

After the adjoining door closed, Evan lay on the carpet for a few minutes, trying to catch his breath. Then he hauled himself up onto the mattress and lay there a few minutes more.

round man slumped into his bowl of soup
Mystery Man staring down at him
a horse, a lion, a zebra

A glint winked from the heating vent overhead, no doubt one of many hidden pinhead surveillance cameras.

When he sat up, he groaned at the ache in his stomach muscles.

Trapped four stories off the ground in a building watched by myriad cops and agents, subject to the finest surveillance at the United States government's disposal, penned in by an invisible fence that if crossed would leave him an amputee.

He needed help.

He took out his RoamZone and gazed down at it. He could see his reflection in the organic polyether thioureas screen. No point in making a call, because anything he said would be overheard. But he had some other ideas.

He nudged the phone to life.

Considered what he was about to do.

Decided for it. Then against it. Then for it again.

Blocking the screen from the view of any potential cameras, he punched in a series of brief texts. Then he did something he'd never done before.

He unmasked his GPS.

12

Fun Fun Fun

Palm Springs suited Candy McClure to a tee. All that retro-campy Americana, retirement communities clustered around fake lakes with water features, vintage boutiques run by retired gay couples who had the best worst taste. Last week she'd bought a porcelain pelican with its head tilted back, beak agape to accommodate umbrellas.

She didn't own any umbrellas, but she liked looking at it in the corner of her Airbnb'd room, as if she were a normal person who collected normal-person things.

She loved Palm Canyon Drive with its shaggy palms, dead fronds ruffled beneath the crowns like the throats of bearded dragons. And the people here, straight out of the 1950s. White couples and elderly folks driving Oldsmobiles and a broad spectrum of Polo-shirt colors and fake-tan skin tones.

Near what constituted downtown, she was attending a culinary class to learn how to bake soufflés, because she was bored fucking senseless and she figured she should at least try something at which she could fail spectacularly.

The industrial kitchen was filled with earnest housewives, well-mannered retirees who called her "hon," and a few ambitious students from the community college. She'd lucked into a station next to a duo of asshats from the casino, blackjack dealers with spiky hair and Philly accents who joked self-consciously about wearing aprons and sprinkled flour onto their shirts to make boob outlines. They were in their late twenties, and yet this still constituted humor for them.

She'd once disposed of a diplomat in a Saint-Germain-des-Prés café using a stainless-steel meat fork with tines spaced precisely for eye sockets and was tempted to do the same here. Especially since said asshats kept glancing at her after each lewd joke, checking if their dude-bro roughhousing had drawn blood in a way that might pique her interest.

She was dressed down, but the problem was that even dressed down she was still sexy as fuck. In order to not draw the attention of males, she'd have to get up an hour earlier than an hour early just to knock some of the shine off her pure animal appeal. It was all so aggravating, the Pavlovian slobbering, the jockeying for position, the pickup approaches she'd heard enough times to X-ray any would-be Lothario in the first instant even were she not trained as a virtuoso of psychological observation.

Candy was the type of woman other women complained about to men, claiming that women like her didn't exist. At least the outside of her. And that was the thing. Maybe if they saw the inside of her—all the broken and dirty bits—they'd realize she wasn't any different from them. And maybe that would help her realize that she wasn't either.

But no one saw her that way.

So she'd resigned herself to roaming this earth as a goddess incarnate, capable of opening any door she wanted with a twist of her hip, a dip of her shoulder, or a demure lowering of her eyes. It was so easy it made her sick with ennui. Ever since the Program had blown apart—along with her role in it as Orphan V—she'd been unable to find challenges sufficiently treacherous to warm her engine, let alone turn it over. So here she was in Palm Springs baking a fucking soufflé next to the Brothers Dimm. A surreal detour for a girl who'd once been snatched out of foster care at the behest of a black government program and schooled in the arts of liquidation, maiming, and the creative disposal of human remains.

She'd spilled her finger bowl of pepper and had yolk spatter on her chef bib from overly exuberant egg cracking.

Another titter from her side. "This one likes it *messy.*"

She did not glance over but felt the heat of the dealers' eyes crawling over her body.

The teacher, a mousy woman with a tremulous voice, proclaimed, "And now we dice the Vidalia onions!"

Candy reached to grab her onion and lobbed it back to herself in the direction of the cutting board. Before it could reperch in her other palm, it was intercepted by one of the neighboring men, his gym-swollen arm trespassing into her space. "Can't help but notice you need a hand. I always cook when I have girls over. Happy to show you some of my tricks." A broad smile displayed perfect orthodontic work. "Kitchen *or* bedroom."

Finally she met his eyes. Clear blue, dull, and empty like a swimming pool that no one used.

Without turning her head, she reached for the chef's knife, flipped it into a triple somersault, caught it by the handle, and jabbed the tip sideways in a single brusque motion at his hand.

His fingers flared wide, matching his eyes. His gaze lowered to check that his palm was still intact.

It was.

But the onion was skewered straight through at the midline.

She flipped the impaled onion free of the blade, pinned it beneath the heel of her hand on the cutting board. Her hands moved in a blur, the knife rat-a-tat-tatting against the butcher block like a tommy gun until there was no onion left, just a small mound of cubed perfection.

It had taken her three seconds, maybe four.

Now she gave him her stare again, the one that could melt

diamonds. "Listen"—her gaze dropped to his name tag—"*Tanner*. You're arrogant. And you think that's charming. But all it really means is that you've never had the balls to attempt something dangerous enough to humble you. Your bro-hole routine might work on meek little club girls with baby purses and selfie duck lips. But I'm not a girl. I'm a woman. And if you were ever blessed enough to reach the altar of my mattress to try to engage me with your 'bedroom tricks,' the ride would tear you to fucking pieces."

Tanner's lips had popped apart, forming a near-perfect O, and he was leaning away from her as if to avoid a good scorching.

Before Candy could continue, her burner phone emitted its notification alert from the wide front pocket of her apron: wild girl Cherie Currie rock-screaming to the world, *I'm your ch-ch-ch-cherry bomb!*

"'Scuse me a moment," she said, reaching for her phone.

Still dazed, Tanner took the opportunity to step back.

When Candy saw who the texts were from, an arrow of adrenaline struck her right in the chest.

The only person alive who could still spike her heart rate. Another human weapon on the lam from the government that created them. They'd been enemies first. An early run-in with him had left her back mottled and ruinous, swirled with scar tissue that still seethed and burned when the weather changed. But that had been her fault as much as his.

They weren't friends, really. They were occasional allies. And something like lovers who hadn't yet bothered with sex.

She read the series of short texts, spelling out the ground truth.

Holy shit.

But also? Fun fun fun.

At last.

Already she was spinning a plan in her head. She was a hundred-twenty-minute drive to Los Angeles, but given the groundwork she'd need to lay once she got there, she might do better to grab a plane and save a precious sixty. On the way in, she'd passed the Bermuda Dunes Airport, spotting a few Cessnas. She wasn't current on her private-pilot cert, but she could figure her way around a single engine and the odds of an FAA ramp check were low.

Besides, it gave her an opportunity to liberate an aircraft, set it down in Santa Monica Airport, and hightail it with a purloined car before anyone figured out she'd faked her call sign.

She peeled the apron off and dropped it on her work counter.

The class had come to a standstill, all eyes on her. But she no longer cared about the class, or soufflés, or continuing Tanner's chiropractic attitude adjustment.

She had a damoiseau in distress to rescue.

13

Tensed-Sphincter Tone

Chip hunched into the makeshift nerve center, staring at various hard-cased laptops, across which danced sound waves and surveillance images, RF, Bluetooth, and wireless packet captures. Behind him Paddy lounged on the jasmine-silver, tufted-velvet sofa with the room-service tray on his not insubstantial belly, dragging steak fry after steak fry through a hillock of ketchup. Three large monitors mapped a mosaic of Evan from every conceivable angle. He reclined on his bed, legs crossed, hands tucked at the nape of his neck—Huck Finn at rest as rendered by Duchamp.

A sheen of sweat turned Chip's forehead reflective. "He sent five texts."

Paddy used another fry as a delivery vehicle for ketchup, plopped it into his mouth, and reached for a bottle of Pellegrino. "So you've mentioned."

Chip had captured the GMI communications from Evan's phone on a DARPA-retrofitted device that iterated on the Stingray

IMSI-catchers used by the three-letter agencies to eavesdrop, record SIM-card activities, and intercept text messages. "They're heavily encrypted, end to end. Can't tell what they say, who they went to."

"Can't you pull the encryption key off with GSM Active Key Extraction?"

"Trying, but there's a substitution cipher in the mix, too. The fifth text looks to be the shortest. Just three words. I've got crypt-analysis hammering at it, like Adnan recommended. I'm calling it a half hour. "

Chip stared impotently at the code churning across the screen, over a trillion cracked hashes aimed at one key.

Paddy grinned. "Maybe the last text says 'I love you.'"

Chip shoved back from the overburdened table, blew out a stale breath. "Doubtful."

"What's he gonna do?" Paddy said. "He can't exit his room, at least not with both feet. We've got men on the lower floors and LAPD units at ground level. Why so nervous?"

Chip shot a glance over at his partner.

Paddy said, "What?"

"I think we should flush the DNA swab. Templeton finds out, it's our ass."

"No way," Paddy said. "That thing is worth more money than we'll make in the rest of our lives a hundred times over." With a groan he pulled himself upright. "Before you even think about getting cold feet, remember three things: You're an accomplice, you're behind on child support, and your new girlfriend's pregnant." He jabbed a finger at Evan resting peacefully on various monitors. "Meanwhile that"—he searched a beat for the word— "*terrorist* has been running around for decades shitting on our laws and norms, living like a prince. You know what my pension's gonna be in three years?"

"Doesn't mean we can overstep—"

"Forty-two thousand seven hundred and sixty-eight dollars. Works out to what? Little more than three grand a month? Mortgage at eighteen hundred, lease and insurance, groceries and everyday shit leaves me what? Enough to take Cathy to Red Lobster and a movie once a week? Twenty-two years I've laid my body on the line to uphold the Constitution. And this fucking criminal gets put up at the Beverly Hills Hotel? Uh-uh. No more."

"Hang on!" Chip swiveled back to his computer screen. "Looks like we've got a byte. Wait—two."

A larger monitor alerted to movement in the hall—an LAPD officer striding in. Chip turned back to the codebreaking software. "PD check-in," he said. "Get the door."

A brisk knock followed.

Paddy lumbered across the room and answered. A female cop in a dark navy uniform a few sizes too tight. Her hair was pulled up beneath a regulation peaked cap with a patent-leather brim. Her name tag read SANCHEZ.

"Don't want to alarm you," the woman said, brushing by him to enter the room, "but we have some action downstairs." She set one black tactical boot up on the bed, hinging her knee wide to expose her crotch, and popped the top two snaps of her shirt. The red lace bra peeked out, restraining a country-star cleavage. "So the boys from the L.A. field office thought you deserved some action up here, too."

Plopping back down on the sofa, Paddy laughed and clapped his hands. "No way. Rodriguez sent you?" A glance at Chip, whose attention was divided between the slowly decrypting text and the undulation of Candy's hips. "At least we get perks."

She peeked up from beneath the cap's brim and twisted her torso so another snap gave way. The men's SIG Sauers were seated in their hip holsters. Given her speed, they might as well have been locked in the minibar.

The laptop chimed, and Chip broke from his hormonal trance, his head snapping back over. "Cracked it!" He read the words, his muscles tensing.

Paddy leaned forward, curious despite himself. "What's it say?"

Chip was now in a seated-elevation in his chair, an indicator of tensed-sphincter tone and testicular retraction—a full-blown fear display.

Paddy said, "Well?"

The words tumbled from Chip's lips, flat and toneless: "'Don't kill anyone.'"

By the time they looked back at Candy, she had her best smile on and four sets of flex-cuffs fanning from one fist.

"You boys ready to party?"

14

Operational Comfort

Reclining on the sea-green comforter, Evan heard a series of thumps from the room next door. A high, clear note of skin striking skin—a slap? A louder thud, perhaps a body hitting carpet. A chair tipping over, not a loud clatter but as if it had been toppled beneath a man's weight. A grunt. Another grunt.

An exclamation reduced to vowel sounds, quickly muffled.

The shrill zippering of flex-cuffs being tightened. Then another set. Two more zippering sounds—ankles, not wrists? A bit more shuffling and commotion.

It really wasn't fair.

The connecting door banged open, struck the wall, and wobbled back, stunned on its hinges.

Then Paddy flew in, his prone body describing a low arc through the air. He struck the carpet at the foot of Evan's bed and emitted a sea-lion bark as his breath left him.

Evan finally unlaced his hands from the base of his neck and sat up, the memory-foam mattress adjusting pleasingly beneath him.

Paddy squirmed on the floor, fighting for oxygen. He'd been hog-tied, wrists behind his back, ankles secured, the two sets of flex-cuffs connected with what seemed to be his belt. His pants had come down several inches, revealing white-and-blue-plaid boxer shorts with a frayed waistband.

After a dramatic pause, Candy entered, buttoning up her LAPD uniform shirt. "Hi, honey," she said. "How was your day?"

"Looking up now," Evan said.

"Given the det cord, I figured I should bring the thumb to you. Though there's still time to remove it if you'd prefer."

The whites of Paddy's eyes were pronounced, and not just from having the wind knocked out of him.

"Tempting," Evan said.

Despite their dissimilarities, Evan had an operational comfort with Candy from their shared background as Orphans; they spoke the same language with different accents.

Paddy struggled for breath. He writhed some more.

Evan walked over to him, dug the toe of his boot into his ribs, and flipped him onto his side. Paddy's fingers stuck out at the base of his back like an abbreviated rooster tail, the digits whitening from lack of circulation.

Crouching, Evan guided Paddy's bloodless thumb to the sensor square on the rubber-coated ankle bracelet. The steel locking mechanism released, and he guided it free of the leg.

"What should we do with this?" he asked.

Candy shrugged. "Find it a new home?"

"What should we use as the security print?"

Candy thought a moment, then tugged off one of Paddy's shoes and the sock, and imprinted his big toe on the bracelet's sensor. She handed the collar back to Evan, and he snapped it around the bare ankle.

Paddy made a low whining noise, his face purpling. Mucus moistened his upper lip.

"You wiped the databases next door?" Evan asked.

"With a military-grade USB eraser," Candy replied. "Nothing left on there. Cameras are shut off, too."

Paddy's lungs finally released, and he sucked in halting breaths.

Evan fished in Paddy's jacket pocket and came up with the swab containing his DNA. Then he found Paddy's iPhone, made use of the bound man's thumbprint once more, deleted the photo of his face, and ensured it hadn't uploaded to the cloud. Heading into the bathroom, he dropped the phone on the floor, shattered it with the heel of his boot, and flushed the pieces.

When he came back out, Candy had drawn aside the curtains and exited onto the balcony, where she was lowering heavy-duty fishing line over the railing. Dusk had started to shade into evening, casting a newspaper gray across the room's cheery furnishings.

Red splotches covered Paddy's face, and his lips were guppying.

Evan detoured to peek through the doorway into the connecting room. Chip was zip-tied to the chair, flat on his stomach atop the bed, his head turned so he could draw wheezing breaths. It looked a bit like the chair was humping him to death.

By the time Evan retreated into his own suite, Candy had hauled up what was on the other end of the fishing line—a black polyester plaited-fiber rope. As she began hauling up the second, thicker rope, Evan checked his pillowcase for stray hairs. None to be found.

When he turned, Candy was in the process of securing the thicker rope to the railing. "I couldn't get any good abseiling equipment on short notice." She removed a pouch hooked onto the rope, dug into it, and tossed something at Evan. It struck him in the chest, and he caught it off the fall. A pair of gloves—no, two pairs. "So we're gonna fastrope."

He layered them both on, tactical gloves followed by a thick leather metalworking pair. Candy was already straddling the railing. Flipping off her LAPD cap, she looked back at him, wind riffling her hair, and winked. Then she dropped out of view.

Evan peered over. Below, the fastrope vanished into a tropical oasis of lipstick-pink impatiens. Aromatic cover.

He came back inside and jotted a note for Naomi Templeton on the lovely hotel stationery.

I'll be in touch.—X

He placed the note in an envelope, rolled it into a tube, and leaned over Paddy. "Say *aaah*."

Paddy's breathing was labored, his lips flecked with sticky white saliva, but he complied. Evan slid the message into his mouth.

"All you have to do to release the collar is get your big toe to your ankle," he said. "If you're not that gymnastic, make sure the bomb tech has steady hands when he cuts it off. Det cord can be temperamental. Might be safer to cut off the toe instead."

He moved onto the balcony, swung one leg over, caught the fast-rope in his double-gloved hands, and flew down fast enough for the leather to smoke at his palms.

His boots struck soil, and he flung the steaming outer gloves off with a quick snap of his wrists. Candy was there in the tropical flowers waiting over an open duffel bag. She'd already shed the LAPD uniform and had changed into a sundress, a wide-brimmed straw hat, and giant Audrey Hepburn sunglasses. Waiting for Evan in the bag was a Havana Joe print shirt and a Ralph Lauren white twill baseball cap.

As he threw them on, she slid behind him to peer out through a spray of auburn-tinged banana fronds. She brushed across his back, the fabric thin enough that he sensed her nakedness against him.

North Crescent Drive was a stone's throw away across a brief strip of manicured grass pinpricked with streetlights. A number of guests strolled along the various paths between the bungalows, well-tanned men in expensive leisure wear, accessorized with children and younger wives sporting spin class–firmed backsides. Candy had appareled herself to fit right in, playing the part of hot suburban housewife. There were so many alluring feminine roles in the social-engineering handbook, and she seemed to embody the most dangerous of each category.

A number of cop cars lined the curb, interspersed with other vehicles. Candy lifted a key fob, and a Mercedes SUV parked across from them chirp-chirped.

She caught Evan admiring her. "What?"

"Every time I see you, you're someone else," he said. "Which one are you?"

"All of them."

He offered his arm. She wove her hand through it. They emerged from the gardens, mingling with the other guests briefly on the path, and climbed into the Mercedes.

As they coasted away from the curb, Candy favored two of the officers leaning against a squad car with an elegant dip of her head. They grinned back wolfishly.

She turned onto Sunset, putting the Beverly Hills Hotel in the rearview.

"We should split up," Evan said. "You can leave me off in Westwood."

"Fine by me," Candy said. "I'm waiting for a soufflé to rise."

He had no idea what to make of that.

They drove a few miles in silence, minding the mirrors and passing cars. She pulled over at the east edge of the UCLA Medical Center to let him out.

When he turned to say good-bye, she met him with a full kiss on the mouth. Her lips were plush, sticky with a glossy lipstick that smelled discordantly and delightfully of sugar cookies. She pulled away, leaving him flushed.

He could feel the lipstick on his mouth. He opened the door, hesitated, and looked back. "I owe you one," he said.

He couldn't see her eyes, only his own reflection in her dark sunglasses. Those lips parted to show a crescent of perfect white teeth. "Next time," she said, "we should at least"—she leaned closer, whispered the verb.

He'd barely cleared the running board when she took off, the passenger door snapping shut from the momentum of her acceleration. He watched the Mercedes blend into traffic, the taste of her still lingering on his lips.

15

A Bad Case of the Crummies

Keeping the Ralph Lauren cap snugged low over his eyes, Evan stalked through nightfall toward Castle Heights. He held focus as best he could, averting his face from store security cams, ATMs, and traffic lights rigged to photograph speeders. The Third Commandment demanded that he master his surroundings but he felt his focus blurring the outside world with the rocky terrain of his internal landscape.

needle punching through his shirt

Crushing his RoamZone underfoot, he kicked it down a sewer drain. Clusters of students were out in front of the movie theaters, laughing and taking selfies. He drifted past a café wafting scents of shisha and barbecued meat, a busker playing a battered guitar down two strings, a green-cross dispensary leaking the earthy reek of pot.

windshield spiderwebbing

He'd held it together while in captivity, but feeling the pavement jarring his heels, breathing the candied smell of vape pens and the waft of grease and potato from the In-N-Out a block over, he sensed the pieces of his capture shifting inside him, sharp bits with jagged edges.

man slumped forward, face in his bowl of soup

He neared the lobby now, images and sensations churning, the barrier between past and present as thin as a film of ice laid atop a well-shaken martini. Screwing his thoughts together, he entered through the glass front doors, Joaquin greeting him from behind the security desk.

"Hello, Mr. Smoak."

other boys' feet pounding him awake

Evan tried to focus on Joaquin's words, lost them, identified what he was saying by tone and cadence: *"Small talk small talk small talk."* Joaquin gave him a grin, reaching to summon the elevator. *"Small talk?"*

Evan nodded, guessed at the meaning, forced an answer up through the constricted channel of his throat. *"Small talk."*

fat-barreled grenade launcher

On numb legs he moved to the elevator door. A flurry of movement from the sofa facing the tall windows looking out at Wilshire Boulevard. And then Lorilee Smithson, 3F, beelining for him.

He turned away as he entered the elevator, but she boarded with him, chirping into his shoulder. *"Small talk small talk small talk small talk."*

He said, "Uh-huh."

"Small talk small talk." She was looking at him now, her Botox-enhanced face shifting into its best approximation of kindly concern. The moment demanded that he meet her gaze. He stared at her, straining to focus.

She rested a manicured hand on his shoulder—

palm against his cheek

—and leaned in, her face spackled with foundation. Her perfume was sickly-sweet, heavy with orchid. A rare crease marked the space between her eyebrows. He forced himself back to the present to take in her words. "Looks like *someone's* got a bad case of the crummies."

He initiated the muscles on his cheeks, pulled his mouth into something resembling a pleasant resting shape. *"Small,"* he said, *"talk."* His eyes stabbed past her luxuriant blowout at the elevator numbers. A ding for the third floor, Lorilee's floor, and then he armed the doors as if to hasten their parting and ushered her out.

She stared back at him, blinking, until the car stitched itself shut once more, wiping her from view.

He blew out a breath, sagged against the wall, buttressing himself with a hip jammed into the thick metal rail.

symphony of paranoia

Now stepping out of the elevator.

gripping a Makarov pistol

Now walking down the hallway.

bright orange stripe around the muzzle

Now opening his door.

his flesh and fiber no longer obeying him

Now stripping off his clothes, boots, socks, boxer briefs, shoving the bundle into the fireplace, stoking up two cedar logs, incinerating all evidence of the outside world that had stained him.

sweat cooling at his hairline

Now into the shower, hot enough to raise welts, scrubbing at his arms, legs, chest with peppermint soap that made his skin burn clean.

drooling blood onto the asphalt

Now leaning over the sink, trimming his fingernails, compulsively running his thumb pad over the sharp spots and edging them with the clippers more and more until he was down to the quick.

shard-sharp glint of sunlight

Now sweeping up the clippings, washing and scrubbing the surfaces they'd touched, washing and scrubbing his hands, forcing himself from the bathroom.

IV pole starting to topple

Now dressing in the closet but there was lint on his shirt and he picked it free and walked it to the trash can in the bedroom but there was a tiny ball of dust on the poured-concrete floor and he crouched to press his thumb to it but saw that there were more specks by the baseboard and they were everywhere and how was he supposed to determine the acceptable size of dust to leave on the floor instead of convey to the trash because how you do anything is how you do everything.

patterns on the ceiling way up above

It was his OCD screaming at him, running him, and he tried to grab hold of the errant operating system, but all he could see was dust and lint, and all he could feel were the minuscule jags on his fingernails, and he closed his eyes and tried to find his breath.

swinging his sights to the metal links of a dangling cafeteria sign, the kind of wide-open shot he never missed

The Second Commandment—*How you do anything is how you do everything*—warred with reality, paring him down to nothing but behavioral loops. He knew he had to put the OCD into a drawer in his mind and close it, but everything was spinning too fast for him to grab hold of.

heartbeat fluttering in the side of his throat

He reached to find his breathing, the floor beneath his bare feet, and pushing out thoughts of lint and dust sticking to his soles, he walked back into the closet and closed the door behind him.

It was dark inside—*white hospital walls*—save for the seam of light at the edges—*Mystery Man's eyes hidden behind Ray-Bans*—so he couldn't see all the clutter and imperfections—*he doesn't talk much*—and he racked aside the Woolrich shirts on their hangers—*tiny hand gripping a smooth white rail*—to clear a space and lowered himself down—*cuffed and barred and chained*—toppling the stack of brand-new Original S.W.A.T. shoe boxes—*a lion, a zebra*—and an image of Joey flickered across the screen of his mind—*fifty thousand volts*—and he realized he'd kept her furthest away from all this in his thoughts, his Achilles' heel, his biggest weakness, and—*no brisk wind, no shadows*—he hadn't let himself entertain for a single instant—*you know what it's like to be powerless*—what it would do to her if he were gone.

He put his back to the wall and tucked his knees into his chest.

He dug in a drawer to his side, and then a replacement Roam-Zone was in his hand, and he'd dialed before he realized who he was calling.

Tommy Stojack picked up after the fourth ring. "Yallo."

The pop of lips around an inhale. Evan could picture the Camel

Wide nested beneath Tommy's biker mustache, could hear the echo of his voice off the hard surfaces of his armorer's lair, a rusty topography of mills and lathes, munitions crates and test-firing tubes.

Evan's voice sounded as though it belonged to someone else. "Tommy."

"What?"

"I'm there."

"Where?"

"In the hurt."

A long pause. Another inhalation, the white noise purr of smoke exhaled. "Need me to come?"

"No."

"All right." More silence. In the background, water dripped and a machine hummed. "Be humble as fuck," Tommy said. "And keep gratitude."

"Okay." Evan pictured the twenty feet between him and the dangling cafeteria sign. No brisk wind, no shadows, no distracting reflections. He opened his mouth. Closed it. Tried again. "I missed the shot, Tommy."

"What'd it cost you?"

"An eighth of a second." Evan's lips felt dry, chapped. "You know how much that is?"

"It is," Tommy said, "a lifetime."

More silence. Evan reminded himself to keep breathing.

"Age comes for us all." A squeak and a faint hiss, no doubt Tommy grinding out his cigarette in that salvaged ship's porthole he used as an ashtray. "So you learn."

"Learn what?" Evan asked.

"To use different muscles."

Evan couldn't wrap his head around that right now.

"The missed shot," Tommy said. "Is that what put you in the hurt?"

"No."

"What did, then?"

"Huh. Three Black Hawks, five Counter Assault Teams, a few

dozen LAPD, a convoy of uparmored SUVs, and a mess of Secret Service agents."

Tommy gave that a few seconds' respect. "And yet here you are."

"That doesn't matter. They got me. They *had* me."

"And now they don't," Tommy said. "So you got two choices. Indulge yourself and lick your wounds. Or. Go all the way down inside yourself. Find the leaks. And plug 'em."

Evan said, "Right."

The snap of a Zippo, the crackle of a new stick. "You got this," Tommy said, and cut the line.

Evan sat with his knees pulled to his chest and for a long time did nothing but breathe in the darkness.

"You're okay," he told himself. His voice was deep, strong, gravelly like Jack's. "You're okay."

16

Four Count

In the dark of the closet, Evan breathed in for four seconds.
   Held his breath for a four count.
   Breathed out for four seconds.
   Held empty for four seconds more.
   Then he did it again.

17

A Very Bad Night

It was a very bad night.

18

Unavailable Men

Evan bellied down beside an industrial A/C unit atop the north-most peak of the upscale Beverly Center mall. His Steiner Tactical binoculars pointed across San Vicente Boulevard, trained on the east-facing bank of windows of the Saperstein Critical Care Center.

The shade of Mia's window was half lowered to cut the morning light, but he could make out the bump of her body beneath the hospital sheets, an IV tube threading into a pale arm, and the shadowed outline of her head nested in her unruly chestnut waves of hair upon the pillow. She appeared to be asleep.

On the web of streets surrounding Cedars-Sinai, LAPD continued a halfhearted stakeout in the event Evan were stupid enough to return. There was no obvious sign of Secret Service, but a pair of dark SUVs running circuits around the nearby streets indicated they'd left some units to sniff out the area. Approaching through the crowded mall, he'd been cautious of surveillance cameras, double-downing with a heel wedge insert inside his left boot to foil any potential gait recognition.

He watched. And he waited.

The sun beat down across his back, the lazy October breeze more summery than autumnal. Against his abdomen he felt the thrum of traffic from the parking decks below.

The RoamZone rested near his face on the blinding white TPO roofing. It rang, throwing up holographic sound waves beside his cheek, the caller ID also projected in 3-D.

Keeping the binocs in place with one hand, he answered.

"You over your bellyaching?" Tommy asked.

Evan said, "Yes."

"Good. Last night sounded like you had piano wire around your nutsack."

"I wish it'd felt that pleasant."

"Well, hell, didn't want to leave you OTF." A favorite Tommy-ism: out there flapping. Tommy groaned as he rose or sat, the war-horse joints talking. "Got any big plans today?"

Evan tracked a familiar dark SUV as it turned onto Beverly below. "Not really. You?"

"Gonna go outside, drink my morning gallon of shut-the-fuck-up, and feed the mosquitoes. Finish up an order for DoD, then hit the rain locker. I got a lady friend coming over."

"Lady friend?"

"Purdy little dental hygienist, wants to save me from myself."

"She has her work cut out for her."

"Yeah, but she's determined."

A rare awkward pause. "All right, then," Tommy said. "If you're done buggin' me."

"I need a new truck."

"Fuck," Tommy said. "Again? What happened this time?"

"Somewhere between the agents, the Black Hawks, Counter Assault Teams, cops, and uparmored SUVs, I misplaced it."

"Ain't that just like you. All right, I'll outfit a new rig for you, have it ready by Saturday."

"Tommy?" Evan pursed his lips. The breeze blew across his face, warm and steady.

"Don't thank me," Tommy said. "Bring cash."

A click as the call ended.

Through the Steiners, Evan watched Mia sleep some more. At daybreak he'd texted Joey to tell her to dig up what she could on Luke Devine. Now that he was free and clear, he wasn't sure why he was bothering. President Donahue-Carr's priorities were not his priorities. Devine was nothing to him. And yet he couldn't help but be curious about a man deemed sufficiently threatening to the leader of the free world to have set into motion the machinations of the preceding days.

Joey's reply displayed her usual tact and candor: where the f were u last nite?

He knew he'd have to read her in at some point. She'd have endless questions and all sorts of big feelings, and he didn't have it in him just yet, not given what he had to handle with Mia.

A movement at Mia's door drew his attention, his grip tightening on the set of glass. An orderly entered bearing a vase of flowers, a lush spray of blue and yellow. Mia did not stir. The orderly set them quietly on the windowsill and withdrew.

Evan waited ten seconds before pressing CALL on his RoamZone.

Mia shifted in the bed. Turned slightly, screwing a fist into one eye. Through a drugged haze, she blinked at the ringing that issued from the begonias. Evan realized he might have underestimated the psychedelic effect of the ruse.

Mia blinked at the bouquet some more.

Evan hung up. Called again.

Mia stared at the flowers suspiciously. Finally she leaned over, slid them onto her lap, and dug around the stems. She came up with a burner phone sealed in a Ziploc. She considered the bizarre sight for another few seconds.

Then she pulled the phone free and answered. "Hello?"

Evan had thought he'd never hear her voice again. Hearing it under these circumstances seemed a particularly nasty trick of fate.

He said, "Mia."

He watched her magnified in the lenses. Her face contorted as if in a sob, but she made no noise. She pressed a knuckle to her mouth. Smoothed out her expression. When she spoke, her voice was steady. "Mr. Danger."

"Sorry for the subterfuge."

He had little choice. If the government discovered the connection between them, anyone else could as well. Every last enemy he'd made in every last country.

"Beats one of those singing get-well cards," she said.

He watched her stroke the petals. Sensed the heaviness passing across the line, him to her, her to him. Outside of an operational setting, he'd rarely felt in sync with someone else like this.

"From what I've come to know of you," she said, "you'd be here if you could."

"Yes."

"Hell or high water."

"Yes."

"For you not to be here . . ." She moved the phone from her face, covered her mouth. Her cheek was glittering. Deep breath. Phone back to face, her voice steady once again. "It would have to be something huge."

"Yes."

"Life or death."

"Yes."

"For you."

"Yes."

A long pause. "And potentially for me and Peter."

"Yes."

She was crying silently, privately, in breaks from their conversation. He gave her the time, tried to unknot the twisting in his chest. "After Roger died, my shrink warned me that I might gravitate toward unavailable men." She was smiling now. "But, Evan? You really take the cake."

A soft noise of amusement escaped him. For a moment they smiled together and apart.

She tilted her head to the ceiling to stop the welling tears. "Peter said you looked after him."

"I tried."

"Thank you," Mia said.

He wasn't sure how to reply.

She nodded a few times. "Okay," she said. "See you around."

She was waiting, but he couldn't generate the right response. No matter how far he'd come, this was still beyond the scope of his training, his expertise, a language he didn't speak fluently.

Lowering the phone to her lap, she severed the call.

Evan lay there for a time with his head bowed, the sun beating down on his shoulders.

19

Charlie Foxtrot

Evan stood inside his dry shower, one hand holding a spherical ice cube, the other hovering over the hot-water lever. A respectful hesitation before he broke the seal and crossed the threshold into his other life.

It struck him that perhaps the delay wasn't motivated by respect but by fear of reentry.

Before the thought could find purchase, he gripped the lever. Embedded digital sensors read his palm print. An electronic hum indicated the green light, and then came a suctioned pop as the hidden door revealed itself, its camouflaged edges coming clear as a rectangular section of patterned tile yawned open.

He stepped through into the Vault.

A hidden room, concrete and dank, one swath of the ceiling an inverse mirror of the public stairs above leading to the roof. Server racks, munitions lockers, a sheet-metal desk crowded with computer hardware. Three of the walls wore a skin of paper-thin OLED screens that glowed to life when Evan sank into his chair and nudged the mouse. He brought his attention to Vera III, his pinecone-shaped aloe vera companion who rested pertly in a bowl filled with rainbow-colored glass pebbles selected by Joey. He was still adjusting to the disorderly palette, a disruption from the usual soothing cobalt blue he preferred. The garishness made his teeth hurt.

He set the ice cube in the clutch of Vera III's fleshy serrated leaves to water her.

She seemed irritable from the lack of attention.

"Got hung up," he told her.

Unimpressed, she shunned him, moodily absorbing carbon dioxide.

He brought up an encrypted videotelephony app, braced himself, and rang Joey.

He was more reliant on her hacking skills than he liked to admit.

Plus, maybe he wanted to see her face.

Joey tapped to answer, and all he saw was a ceiling fan. "X! Hang on, hang on. I have Cheeto fingers."

Some fumbling noises off-camera. He knew the drill, how she scraped the orange fuzz off her prints with her lower incisors. And then didn't wash her hands. And then touched things.

Suddenly her face loomed large, giving him a vantage up her nostrils before the screen rotated vertiginously and found a perch.

She was in a different hotel room, sitting at a circular Formica table amid the wreckage of her lunch order. Her fitted T-shirt read STRONG WOMEN INTIMIDATE BOYS . . . AND EXCITE MEN. She'd ripped the sleeves off to show her toned arms. Her fingers still bore hues of orange, and she had a streak of mustard on her lip. Dog the dog hovered behind her with a scavenger's impatience, snout visible at her elbow, nostrils quivering.

She tossed a Cheeto over her shoulder, and he vanished. The half sandwich in her grip sagged precariously, leaking turkey and lettuce. She nibbled at the overflow, rotated her overladen fist, bit off a chunk of bread, then found some mustard on the heel of her hand. She chewed, cheeks squirrel-pouched.

Wearily, Evan said, "Josephine."

"What?" She spoke through a jumble of half-masticated food.

"I'm having sandwich-ratio problems. Ya know, where the fixings get outta whack and you can't get all the good stuff into the same bite. Don't you *hate* that?"

Evan let out a breath.

She rotated her hand, licked a bit more mustard off her index finger. "What? Doesn't that happen to you?"

"Never," Evan said. "I never have that problem."

Munching, she managed to insert a Cheeto into the mix. "Well, it all goes to the same place."

"True," Evan said. "But some processes are more inelegant than others."

"Well, *excuuuuze-moi*, Miss Manners. Didn't realize that the garrotter of child traffickers whose bladders release as you sever their life thread would be off-put by the inelegant consumption of a club sandwich."

"The bowels."

"Huh?"

"It's the bowels that release."

She paused midchew to stare at him with disgust. Dog the dog threatened another return, so she flung a second Cheeto over her shoulder. "You are the CEO of TMI."

"Three Mile Island?"

"You are *literally* hopeless. As in: without hope." She reached behind her and let the sandwich fall to the floor. It hit out of sight with a wet thud. Evan heard the scrabble of excited canine paws. Joey wiped her hands on a napkin and then dabbed delicately at the corners of her mouth, presumably for his benefit. "Now," she said. "I called you last night and you didn't answer. And you *never* don't answer that phone. Where the hell were you?"

He told her.

It took some time.

When he was done, she said, "WUT?!" flattening the vowel into textspeak. "I know you're not joking, 'cuz you have no sense of humor. Really—you're like a charisma vacuum. So that must've messed you up bad, like, mentally."

"What did you find on Luke Devine?"

"Skillful redirect, X. But seriously. You messed up from all that?"

"Language," Evan said, I'm fine."

"Don't forget you have a negative EQ," Joey said. "Which means you don't know how you are."

"I'll bear that in mind," he said. "Luke Devine."

"Well, I don't have all my hardware with me, but with my spec'd-to-hell EuroCom Sky X9C, I can do pretty much anything. And this guy? He's like a wet dream for conspiracy theorists. All kinds of crazy global business dealings and legal teams and, like, VIPs in his orbit." She leaned in to stage-whisper, "That stands for 'Very Important People.'"

It had been at least fifteen seconds since her last insult. Her consistency was reassuring.

"So I get why President Prissypants is all panty-knotted over him. He's, like, a ruling member of the Urinati. I'm sending you a bunch of other intel I gathered for Your Holy Thanklessness while I was inelegantly nourishing myself."

All around Evan the OLED screens flurried into action, folder after folder depositing themselves on his server. Having long given up on trying to keep her out of his system, he'd resigned himself to letting her joystick it remotely from time to time. He stared at the proliferation of spreadsheets, documents, and reports. It seemed like a lot of work.

"I don't care about all this business stuff," Evan said. "Shady or not. Anything about him seem like . . ."

"What?"

"Like something that might draw my interest?"

"You? As in: the Nowhere Man, savior of the desperate and lost, champion of the downtrodden, paragon of White Knightery?"

"Just answer the—"

"Dead parents, no siblings, never married—Devine's kind of a blank slate. Though his security detail's a bit sus." She leaned forward once more, her breath fogging the lens as she typed. A series of fresh documents tiled the Vault wall to Evan's left. "Private army of seven, led by this guy."

At Joey's remote urging, a dossier came to the fore.

Derek Tenpenny. A cluster of photographs captured him from

various angles. It was rare to see a man that tall and that slender, like a normal guy stretched by a funhouse mirror. He had to be at least six-six. Brown old-fashioned mustache, elongated plain suits, a side-part haircut at least two decades out of style.

"So here's what's weird. The other six? Private military contractors. They're former marines, dishonorably discharged in the wake of a trophy-photo scandal. Pardoned by Andrew Bennett, our favorite dead president."

Evan fiddled with the mouse, clicking through Tenpenny's underlings, memorizing faces and names. "They posed with enemy corpses?"

"Yup," Joey said. "They Abu Ghraib'd their way through a village outside Kandahar. Farmers and civilians, teenage males and a twelve-year-old boy. Of course they documented it on their phones like the dipshits they are."

"Not dipshits." Evan scanned the dossiers, noting each marine's deployments. "They're battle-tested—plenty of life-or-death hours combing through caves and heaps of rubble for high-value targets." He focused on the photos of the leader. "So Tenpenny, he was their staff sergeant?"

"Way more menacing. Media fixer. Worked behind the scenes at a few of the big cable-news stations, even did a stint for Al Jazeera in Qatar. Payouts and settlements, private security, that kind of stuff. What the hell does a world-mover like Devine need with a dirty cadre like these fuckers?"

"Language," Evan said. "And the answer's in the question." A smirk caught him off guard.

"What?" Joey asked.

"'Urinati.'"

"Aren't you quick on the draw," she said. "So? Is any of this of interest to El Hombre de Ninguna Parte?" Her accent was crisp, on point.

"No," Evan said. "It's just more of the same mess and corruption— government, military, private sector. Everything I left in the rearview. I don't see why it should involve me now."

A low-pitched whining issued from behind Joey, and then Dog

the dog's head reared into view. Big doleful eyes, tragic jowls, ears perked in desperate anticipation.

"As you can see, I'm getting hounded by the puparazzi for a walk." Joey pivoted to Dog. "Yes it *is*! Who wants to go for walkies? Who's *the most handsomest boy who wants to . . .*" She seemed to realize that she was still streaming, gave a double take back at the camera, resumed Resting Scowl Face. "Internal DoJ report from a failed insider-trading investigation lists his other business contacts, last-knowns, ex-girlfriend, all that." She leaned over, fastening a skull-and-crossbones collar on Dog the dog, who whinnied with delight. "I'm glad you're not getting involved, X. Seems like a high-grade clusterf—uh, charlie foxtrot, even for you. Especially after everything you went through. If you ever connect with whatever passes for your internal emotional state, feel free to call for expert feminine guidance. Here if you need me."

"I won't."

"Yeah you will. First time I'm gone and you get captured by the government? Sound like a coincidence? I think not."

She blinked off the screen.

Evan sat for a time staring at all the intel arrayed about him. So many reports and investigations, business dealings and spheres of influence. What a relief that Luke Devine and his byzantine affairs were not Evan's concern.

He moved to quit out of the running software when the DoJ report caught his eye, the former girlfriend, Echo Gabriel, named along with a cell number and a Manhattan address. An underlined note jotted in the column read *"psychological abuse?"* They'd split up about twelve months back. He remembered what Naomi Templeton had said about Devine: *He was your typical power player on the rise, but about a year ago he seemed to go into hyperdrive.* He wondered if Echo might shed some light as to what had happened around that time.

His hand hovering above the mouse, Evan stared at the number, waging an internal argument. Vera III lookie-looed from the desktop, a judgmental over-under gaze from beneath the spherical ice cube she held aloft like a vegetative Atlas.

"Fine," he told her. "One exploratory call. Then I'm out."

He tapped the digits into the RoamZone. The line rang more times than made sense. No voice mail. He was about to hang up when he heard the click of someone picking up and a rush of wind.

"Hello?"

"Echo?"

"Yes?"

She sounded younger than her thirty-four years.

"I hoped you might answer some questions about Luke Devine."

A faint laugh, the sound sucked away by a breeze across the receiver. "I'm busy right now," she said dreamily.

"It'll just take a few minutes."

"I'm so sorry. You interrupted me."

Something about her voice. "Doing what?" he asked.

"Killing myself."

20

A Cry for Help

Echo stood beside the tall, narrow pane of her elongated tilt-and-turn bathroom window, bare feet on the wide ledge, gazing down eleven stories at Broadway below. The wind cut straight through her jeans and sweatshirt as if she were wearing nothing at all. She had a good grip on the inside of the window frame, so all in all it was a pretty safe scouting exercise, one she'd undertaken a number of times, venturing to the sheer edge of what her nerve would allow.

She'd forgotten about the phone in her pocket, its ringing nearly startling her off her semisecure perch. She'd debated not answering. If she was going to take the plunge, what would an unanswered phone call matter? And yet not picking up a call that had arrived serendipitously seemed like putting her thumb in the eye of fate. And who could afford to do *that* on the way out?

At first she'd thought it might be her mother, which would have sent her over the edge with haste. Mom derived her pleasure not from luxuries but from the superiority she felt projecting the strictures of her own contorted morality, a perennial litmus test everyone else failed. Not that Echo had stopped trying to pass.

Not all the way through Dartmouth, principal cellist in the orchestra, crew team captain, magna cum laude, four years volunteering in the music-therapy program at the Children's Hospital. She'd been the first in her class to open a business, midway through senior year. It was a music-therapy online start-up—or, in Mom's words, a rent-seeking scheme for Echo to get her snout into the medical-industrial trough.

But the universe had spared her from Mom calling with a few sanctimonious last words and given her a stranger instead.

The man on the other end of the line seemed shockingly calm given what she'd just said.

"Do you have a plan?" he asked.

"Sure," she said. "One more step."

"Oh," he said. "It's like that."

"I come out here from time to time and consider my options." She thought of her Christian Pedersen cello resting unused on its stand inside. When she couldn't play, she felt voiceless. "I can't figure out if I'm serious or if this is just a cry for help. But I don't know who I'm crying to, really."

A gust of wind filled the receiver. A taxi disappeared beneath the awning below, and over on Madison someone honked and held the horn, an aggressive blast. To her side a pigeon set down on the ledge, cocked its head, and regarded her with curiosity, its dumb pigeon eyes frozen wide in that expression of perennial pigeon shock.

"You want to talk about Luke Devine?" she asked.

"Not at the moment," he said. "But I would like to know what you can tell me about him, yes."

What *could* she say about Luke Devine?

That he walked the razor edge between brilliance and insanity? That at times it seemed he could make anyone do anything? It wasn't his money that was intoxicating, it was the fearlessness that had *led* to his having money. No, not just fearlessness. That adventurer's streak so rare among today's entitled and contented.

That's what he exuded, an old-fashioned spark of genius and reck-lessness. That's also what pulled so many luminaries along in his wake, what made so many unmakeable deals snap together at the last minute, what drew everyone to him like a drug they couldn't believe they'd lived without. His conviction that every instant con-tained the whole universe if you were willing to pay close enough attention to it.

In the brief but intense time they'd dated, he had shown her how to see inside herself in a way she never had, all those buttons coded into her genetics and coaxed into prominence by her lived experience. How to let the ebbs and flows of guilt and anxiety roll through her instead of locking them inside where they could drown her.

Luke made her stronger, but he used to say in his playful scher-zando voice that she made him *better*. That she tethered him to the world, brought him into balance. He was an incredibly sensi-tive instrument that she knew how to tune. Without her he was all thundering fortissimo, but she helped remind him to also live in the tender dolce that made the powerful notes so much more powerful.

She'd always thought of the cello as a split personality, swing-ing from warm and low to bright and high, the yellowy heat of bourbon balanced against the cyan coolness of vodka. Its voice spanned three clefs, transforming itself to hold other instruments together, to ground the whine of the violins or lift the growl of the basses. It took a rare soul to allow the instrument to speak with its full vocabulary, and the fact that she belonged to that small com-munity was her biggest secret joy. She liked to think she did that for Luke as well, modulated him to embody his full musicality.

Until she couldn't.

Those last few months, Luke's work and the considerations surrounding it had grown greater and greater. When he spoke, the words crowded together, like there were too many thoughts in his head competing to get out and his mouth was a mile be-hind them, struggling to keep pace. Everything—she included—seemed to bore him. He'd told her that he increasingly felt the same everywhere, like he was in a scene he'd played through enough times that he could have written the dialogue for every role. That he needed new challenges and new frontiers. The energy coming off him in those weeks was brilliant like a diamond and just as hard. He'd even held himself differently, head jutting ahead of his body, his prefrontal cortex out in front leading his chest, heart, guts, overpowering and effective, able to convince itself of anything.

She'd been afraid he was speeding up.

When he was himself, he was the best.

But when he was fast, he was very, very bad.

"I don't know how to describe Luke to you," she told the pigeon and the man on the phone. "Or to anyone else. I just know that since our relationship I feel . . . diminished. It's so humiliating that I was weak enough to let him do this to me."

"It'd be more humiliating if you killed yourself over it."

For the first time in a long time, she felt genuinely amused. "I know," she said. "That's the problem." She kicked at the pigeon, who scuttled back, undeterred, and then shat in the wind with pigeonly entitlement. "Know what's worse?"

"No," he said. "But I'd prefer if you told me once you were inside."

She was surprised to hear herself laugh. "Hang on."

She squirmed back through the window, the heat of the condo enveloping her. Her feet had gone partially numb. She walked through the bathroom and into the studio, burrowing into the plush velvet blanket on the couch. "Okay," she said.

"Tell me what's worse."

"Luke could see everything that was wrong with me." She rubbed an edge of the royal-purple blanket against her cheek, stared at her cello collecting dust next to the side table by the front door. "He saw it in me, in everyone but himself. It wasn't the whole truth. But it was truth. That's how Luke is. And . . . *God.*"

"What?"

"Even talking about him now feels like a betrayal. Of *him*! How insane-making is that? How do you stay angry when parts of him are so . . ."

"So what?"

"So *right.*" Heat in her face, pressure behind her eyes. There was

125

a pause so long that she wondered if the caller had hung up. "Still there?"

"I am." A briefer pause. "Will you tell me more about him?"

"Huh. I suppose so. It's just . . ."

"What?"

"I can't hear an instrument in your voice," she said. "Is that by design?"

"Do most people have an instrument in their voice?"

"Everyone," she said. "Who are you? What's your name?"

"If I flew out to see you, would you promise not to kill yourself until I get there?"

The wind howled against the window, and the building creaked in response. Wrapped in the blanket and the glow of her own body heat, she felt safer than she had in months.

"Why the hell not," she said.

21

Fallen Angel

Seven hours later Evan sat in Echo's upscale studio condo on a chair pulled over from the kitchen set. She was nested in a blanket on the couch where—he assumed—she'd relocated from the ledge when he'd spoken to her this very morning. Shabby-chic furniture and soothing Swiss-coffee-colored walls warmed the place, and yet everything about it seemed to be straining for cheeriness—the Crate & Barrel decor, the area rug beneath his feet, the desperate spray of daisies leaning from the painted soup-can vase on the counter that passed for a kitchen.

Evan's trip to Manhattan had been seamless, thanks to Aragón Urrea's generosity. Urrea had found Evan awhile back and asked for his help to retrieve his missing eighteen-year-old daughter. The mission had been dangerous and grueling, nearly costing Evan his life. The price he'd demanded for his help was that Aragón limit his future dealings to the right side of the law. Or at least the right*ish* side. Overwhelmed with gratitude, Aragón had gone above and beyond that, putting his small fleet of private planes at Evan's disposal whenever he needed to travel discreetly, which was always.

Given the federal government's renewed interest in hunting him down, Evan had been happy to take advantage of a flight that required no TSA checkpoint, no commercial airports, and no documentation, forged or otherwise.

Echo's building was Manhattan-tiny but Tribeca-nice. Aside from the brimming trash barrels in the facing alley and a guy slumbering beneath a shiny thermal blanket on the neighboring steps, the whole block felt scrubbed clean.

The night was sloping toward midnight. Echo gripped a steaming cup of tea with both hands. She'd yet to take a sip; it seemed there for warmth alone.

She'd been talking in desultory stops and starts, painting a mosaic of a relationship that was at turns wonderful and damaging. "Maybe they go hand in hand," she said in that same dreamy tone she'd had on the phone. "I think a part of me still loves him. Do you have any idea how infuriating that is?"

No expert in relationships, Evan kept his mouth shut. Wisps of steam rose from her cup, framing her clean features. She was prettier than she allowed herself to be, limp hair framing the smooth, pale skin of her face. A lean build tilting toward too skinny. Evan wondered at an eating disorder.

"It sounds like there was a change in him, your relationship."

Her eyes darted away.

"What happened?"

"It's hard . . . it's hard to talk about it." Her lips trembled, but her expression remained flat.

"Everything is on your terms," Evan said. "If you don't want to talk anymore, don't."

"But you came all the way here."

"You don't owe me anything."

For a time Echo stared down into her tea. Evan rubbed his fingertips together, each coated with an invisible layer of superglue to obscure his prints. Somewhere in the building, a water pipe banged. The old-fashioned clock in the kitchen had a vigorous second hand that ticked off one minute and then another.

She started to talk, hesitated, pushed through. "He stopped taking his meds." The words came out in a rush, as if she had to force them out before she lost her nerve. "He said . . . he said they were holding him back."

"Meds for what?"

"I don't know exactly. But they slowed him down. Made him kind."

"He wasn't kind when he was sped up?"

"No," she said. "No. If Luke has any gift, it's getting other people to do whatever he wants. He used to say he could see the marionette strings that held people up. He could just tug them this way and that. And if he deemed someone unworthy, he could just . . ." She made a snipping gesture with her fingers. "He's not just a narcissist. No, that would be easier. But Luke, Luke gets in your head. All the way. Makes you do stuff."

"Did he ever hit you?"

"No."

"Threaten you?"

"No."

Evan took a moment to filter the skepticism from his tone. "What then? How does he make you do stuff?"

Her gaze was penetrating. "If you meet him, you'll find out."

He wondered if Echo's feelings revealed more about her than they did about Luke.

She was watching him intently. "*What?*"

An accusation.

Evan trod carefully. "No one can *make* you do anything."

"You don't get it." She shook her head. "All of a sudden you're doing something that you thought was your idea. But it wasn't. It was his."

So much of what she said was slippery and vague and frustrating.

"When he speeds up, there are only two things," she said. "What he wants to have happen. And collateral damage. He starts moving so fast he forgets that other people are . . . well, *people.*

We're so much slower, burdened down with feelings and . . . and consideration."

Luke Devine sounded just as enigmatic as when Naomi Templeton had laid out his profile. And Evan wasn't sure how much more clarity he could get now from a woman who not ten hours ago was out on the brink contemplating the drop.

"What does he use his influence for?" Evan asked.

She gave a mirthless laugh. "Forcing through legislation he deems convenient. Steering billion-dollar defense contracts. Destroying the livelihood of competitors who dare challenge him. Burying inconvenient news stories. Kneecapping foreign leaders whose interests aren't aligned with his." She lifted one shoulder in a halfhearted shrug. "Whatever he desires."

Evan thought of President Donahue-Carr's trillion-dollar environmental bill, hung up pending the approval of two senators Devine controlled.

"Why did you stay with him?" he asked.

"I kept hoping he'd be like he was before. And the thing with people who are . . . "

"Who are what?"

"Crazy. Brilliant. Crazy brilliant. When you're with them, if you're not strong enough, it feels like everything's your fault. You feel like it's you. And . . . "

Evan waited.

"My whole life," Echo finally continued, "I felt like I was waiting. For life to get better, for me to . . . I don't know, *arrive*. To be happier or more secure. Dumb, I realize. With him? It felt like you weren't waiting. It felt like you were *there*. Everything was like"— she closed her eyes, lips pursed—"like the first time you perform the Bach Prelude." Her eyes opened abruptly, as if she'd found the darkness no longer safe. "Until it wasn't like that at all."

The conversation hadn't yet touched on anything Evan had wanted to find out about Luke Devine. But he'd learned from Jack that what he wanted to know wasn't always what he needed to know.

"The best people are the worst people," Echo continued. "All that sensitivity and insight focused on you—the real you. It's like

they know what chords to tap deep down to make you . . . reso-
nate. With yourself, the world. But then once you let them in"—
her expression darkened—"they can hit those same chords with a
mallet. And make you vibrate so hard you think you might come
apart." There were big round tears in her lashes, and she blinked
and blinked, but they wouldn't fall. "It's almost not worth it. Opening up. Do you know what I mean?"

Evan thought of the self-contained ecosystem of his penthouse,
his poured-concrete floors, the speckless countertops, the pristine façade of the Sub-Zero, as cold as the Icelandic landscape. He
thought of the Veras he'd failed, the interior vertical garden that
breathed his opposite, carbon dioxide to his oxygen, and how it
all kept him safe from the chaos of the world. The dollhouse view
through the bank of east-facing windows that looked in on an array of lives in the building across—a female couple singing ka-
raoke, Latin parents teaching a toddler to bang a tambourine, an
elderly man with a bedbound wife who spent hours every night
over his stovetop concocting elaborate French meals for two.
Noise, color, smells. Life in all its richness. Life that Evan could
only watch through aquarium glass while he sipped seven-times-
distilled vodka, purifying his insides, making sure no pollution of
the outside world could take root inside him.

He said, "No."

"Well, Luke was like that. A guy with a mallet. Volatile. Charming. Dangerous. Everything filled with . . . too-much-ness. He went
from the A string to the C string. Nothing in between."

"I don't know what that means."

She pursed her lips thoughtfully. "Dark and powerful, filled
with gravitas. That's the C. And the A string is . . . let's see, domi-
nant. Penetrating. Bright."

He regarded the cello by the door, at rest like a relic, the stand
cradling its hips and supporting its neck with care. The bottom
curve of the waist was powdered with dust. His OCD scratched
at him. He wondered why a cello that fine wasn't in a case. But
Echo was scarcely in a place to care for herself, let alone a stringed
instrument.

He searched for another route in. "You think in music."

131

She nodded faintly, her expression distant, bruised. "Jacqueline du Pré lost feeling in her fingers. Multiple sclerosis. Can you imagine? That left-hand technique—unparalleled. Such a loss. She must have woken up every morning and . . ." She stared over at the cello with enmity.

"You don't play anymore," Evan said.

No answer.

"Why not?"

"Practicing, it's how I work out what's going on inside me. When I'm sad? Bach's Second or Fifth Suite. Angry? Shostakovich's Eighth Quartet sets me right. But I can't anymore. Doesn't feel, I guess, safe. To go all the way inside myself."

"What do you play when you're scared?"

She chewed her lip, breathed in her tea. With her flawless skin and brilliant blue eyes, she looked like a fallen angel. "I don't." She gazed at him through a wobbly rise of Earl Grey steam. "Why are you so interested in Luke?"

"I've been asked to look into him."

"For what?"

"To see if he deserves to be . . . held accountable."

She laughed, but there was no mirth in it. Her mug was set down on the coffee table with a clink. She crossed her slender legs, drew the purple blanket around her like a robe, and leaned forward, confessional.

"There was this girl I really didn't like. In college. Total bitch. Fucked my best friend's boyfriend. We were at . . ." Her voice faltered. "A fraternity party. She was drunk, super flirty. Grabbing guys' crotches through their jeans, all that. Head drooping, barely conscious. And at a certain point, a few of the guys, they just . . ." Her hand waved at the air, a dying motion. "Carried her out. Back to a bedroom. And even though I hated her, I felt sick for her. Worried. I was . . . I don't know, four, five drinks in myself. And I watched them carry her back, and I was scared to speak up—I was just a dumb freshman—and I don't know . . . I don't know if I would've found my voice if I'd liked her more. Do you know how awful that is? I still see it perfectly—them around her, five, six guys like pallbearers. And her arm was the only thing visible between them, just dangling. And I was so drunk and so scared and such a fucking coward. And maybe—" She pressed her knuckles against her mouth, and her chest heaved once, twice, silently. "Maybe this, what happened to me, with Luke, was my punishment. Maybe we all need to be held accountable. What if we're all responsible? For everything?"

"That's what drove you onto the ledge?"

She nodded. "I can't get it out of my brain. How I'm responsible for everything that ever happened to me. And . . . um, to everyone else I've ever met. And I can't remember what it feels like not to feel this way. I think that . . . that I might be going crazy."

Evan looked down. His hands were crossed, body still.

She said, "Can I tell you a secret?" Her thin eyebrows lifted. "I know I'm not going to kill myself. I was just waiting . . ."

"What?"

"For someone to notice. To make me real again."

"You're a music therapist."

"I am."

"Are there therapists for therapists?"

"There are therapists for everyone." She gave a faint nod of acknowledgment. "Right." A smirk. "It's either back in the saddle or out on the ledge. And I think I've exhausted what I have to learn out on the ledge." As he made to rise, she said, "Let me ask you a question, Mr. . . ."

The silence lingered. He let it.

She relented. "You say you're here to see if Luke needs to be held accountable. Do you think he should have to pay for what he did to me? Like he would if he'd assaulted me physically?"

"I can't punish someone based on how they make you feel."

"Why not?"

And here was the mission's end. Evan had dispatched plenty of assholes, but being an asshole wasn't grounds enough for the Nowhere Man. Presidential pardon aside, Naomi Templeton and Victoria Donahue-Carr would have to find someone else to take Luke Devine off the chessboard for them.

"I don't know," Evan said, standing up. "I just can't."

"For what it's worth? I agree with you. I was just curious."

He'd given Naomi his word that he'd make a good-faith effort, and he had. He owed her nothing beyond that. He was eager to get home, burn his clothes, take a long shower, meditate, sip vodka, and then sleep for a week. Until this moment he didn't realize the relief he felt at this mission's not materializing. Whatever mess Luke represented and whatever mess Echo had brought to the party was no longer his concern.

As he turned to leave, Echo fished a phone out of the folds of the blanket. "Do you have a phone number?"

He gave her the digits, not the letters. "1-855-266-9437."

"A toll-free number?"

"A work line."

She screwed her mouth to one side. "Okay, I just texted you a thing."

"What is it?"

"Maybe nothing related. A murder. Double murder, actually. A guy and a woman. Mid-twenties. Their deaths got a bit of attention, and a friend forwarded it along to me. You'll see why. The woman was a wannabe influencer, wrote poetry on driftwood, shot it in sepia filters, that sort of stuff. They stuck in my mind because . . . well, because they were beautiful."

"And you think Luke Devine had something to do with their deaths?"

"You can judge for yourself."

"Do you think he could do something like that?"

Echo regarded him. "You have no instrument in your voice. You flew out here to get information on Luke, not to save my life. You have a kind manner about you, but that's all it is: a *manner*." She sloughed off the blanket and rose to show him out. "I think that you have done terrible, violent things, Mr. No Name. I think I know what you're capable of. But I don't have any idea what Luke's capable of now, and that terrifies me more than you do."

22

Fucking Complicated

A TikTok video in selfie mode. Lens jerking, terrible lighting, sound muffled as the phone camera shifted about.

The first thing that struck Evan about the young woman recording herself was how evident her grief was, resting right there on the surface of her face.

The account handle was @rubyanne, and the bio read: 19, she/her/hers, don't DM me unless u've got mad Mr. Darcy skillz.

Evan sheltered in a porte cochere across the street from Echo's place. The building was grand, sandstone uplit to a golden glow, cobblestone drive, doorman in full regalia who'd sized Evan up, deemed him sufficiently well-heeled, and let him be. The rain had picked up, annoying flecks that pelted him sideways. He had to use a hand to shield the RoamZone's screen.

Aragón's jet waited for him at Teterboro Airport, and he was eager to board, sip on something clean, and arrow back toward Los Angeles.

But first he had to watch this year-old TikTok of a random nineteen-year-old.

"I'm coming on here because there's nowhere else to go. My brother, Johnny Seabrook, was murdered last week, and his"—a hitch in her breath—"body was dumped with someone else's, a woman named Angela Buford, who I don't think he even knew." Ruby was sorrow-stricken, but there was no shortage of anger behind her words. "And he literally wrote a clue on his shoe. *Tartarus*. You know what that is? I mean beyond the fucking Milton look-how-clever shit. It's the name of a mansion in the Hamptons for this big asshole hedge-funder who has crazy Jeffrey Epstein parties and stuff. And guess what happens when you talk to the cops, the FBI—anyone—about looking into it? *Nothing*. It goes up the chain and then just . . . disappears."

She swiped a forearm across her nose, index-fingered the pale pink lower rims of her eyes. "Because if you're super rich, you don't have to answer for anything. I guess I was privileged enough not to ever have to know that. Before now. But when you see it, I mean really get it, it's *terrifying*. To be shown you're not important enough, your brother's not important enough to matter? That there's this other class of people who can do whatever the fuck they want? And to them my brother was nothing. I'm nothing. And no one—" Her features seized, a paroxysm of bone-deep pain—lips tugged in an upside-down U, forehead contorted, chin turned to a walnut. She jerked in a breath, forced out the words. "No one will help us. I hope this never happens to any of you, because the way it hurts . . ." Her face tensed and reddened further, trembling.

The TikTok ended abruptly.

He reviewed it several times more, trying to convince himself that it was not something worth looking into further.

It was the last post that Ruby Anne Seabrook had made, a year ago almost to the day. He scrolled through her preceding videos, struck by how seismic her transformation had been after her brother's murder. He'd seen it time and again, grief snatching someone up in its jaws, shaking them like prey.

Before, Ruby had been pert with an evident excess of intelligence. No makeup, rare for her age, but she'd known how to approach the camera as well as her contemporaries, dishwater-blond hair to one side, dipped chin, lens angled slightly downward.

He watched a clip of her with her brother, a mindless loop of him sitting next to her and then suddenly lunging to snort in her neck. She feigned annoyance, but her smile was bright as she pushed him away and gave a little shriek of delight. In contrast to her flanneled brother, she wore a yellow cable-knit sweater, fitted tightly to her torso, flared sleeves adding a touch of flourish. She looked expensive.

Johnny had been an unreasonably handsome kid with kind, affable features—a rare combination.

The raindrops had grown so tiny they felt aerosoled against Evan's cheeks, his neck, his hands. He thought of the Cirrus Vision Jet awaiting him, how his friend had ensured that the cabin was stocked with the proper caliber of vodka. He thought about the needle going into his shoulder, *the burn of the tranquilizing agent*, the way the choke chain had pinched his windpipe, and how little he wanted to tread back into the web the government had spun to ensnare him.

He thumbed back to Ruby's final plea: *No one will help us.*

He muttered, "Goddamn it."

The doorman cleared his throat pointedly. It was time for Evan to move on. When he glanced up, he noticed the man he'd seen dozing beneath a thermal blanket next door to Echo's place. But he'd moved over to another building with a less sheltered stoop, one with a better sight line to Evan. He stretched languidly and yawned, the shiny blanket shifting to give Evan a clear look at his face.

Bram Folgore, one of Derek Tenpenny's crew of six charged with the private security of Luke Devine.

Joey's dossier had included a photo of Folgore snoozing amid civilian bodies stacked like firewood in the village near Kandahar. While his squadmates had vamped for the camera, Folgore had lain in the dirt, head resting on one corpse, armored helmet tipped over his eyes. His boots, crossed at the shins, were propped up on the chest of a teenage boy. To him they were a pillow, a footrest.

Of all the poses in the trophy photos, Folgore's had been the most grotesque. Devoid of bloodlust or excitement. The situation not significant enough for him to keep his eyes open.

Reclining lazily on the stoop across the way, Folgore laced his hands, flipped them inside out to stretch his shoulders. He looked over at Evan as if to say, *Let's get to it.*

Evan grimaced, dreams of jetliner leisure evanescing in the hard gray air.

With a nod to the doorman, he stepped out from beneath the porte cochere. Folgore shed his space blanket and rose, pawing to cover another yawn.

They made and broke eye contact once more.

Evan walked past the brimming trash cans into the dark alley.

Folgore followed him.

23

This Should Be Easy

Dumpsters and trash cans. The abandoned skeleton of a pram, perforated nylon stretched across the frame like rotted skin. Mist from pipes, a sewer-line reek, the clang and clamor of a back kitchen lurking invisibly behind a pollution-opaque high-set window.

That was good. There was stuff around. To hide behind, to throw, to bounce someone's skull off should the need present itself.

Evan stepped across a caterpillar-bunched sleeping bag. A puddle provided a rain-tapped reflection of the narrow slice above—towering stone walls, fire escape, heaped clouds pellet-shot with moonlight.

He could hear Folgore behind him, the plodding of footsteps, the splash of a puddle. He kept near the trash-lined wall so as not to offer a clearly silhouetted target.

Nearing the depth of the alley, he paused. Way up ahead traffic flashed by, headlights boring through cones of flurried rain. To his left, bloated foam spilled intestinally from an incised futon. A parasol-less umbrella lay scrunched like a dead cellar spider, its once-proud wooden handle thrusting up, a hand from a grave. His wet cargo pants gripped his legs; his socks felt soggy.

The footsteps neither quickened nor paused for Folgore to take aim.

Evan half turned, offering him a slim profile.

Rubbing the nape of his neck, Folgore stopped about five feet away and swept back his jacket like an old-time sheriff showing off a wheel gun beneath a duster. On his hip was a coyote-tan M17 9-millimeter, preferred service pistol of the Corps.

"You here for Echo?" Evan asked.

"Don't give a shit about her." Folgore looked bored. "I'm here for you."

"How'd you know I was coming?"

Folgore shrugged. "Devine knows everything."

"He sent you?"

"I didn't say that. I said he knows everything. Which means *we* know everything." Folgore muffled a yawn, lips closed, one shoulder screwing up toward his ear. He chinned at Evan lazily. "You got a gun?"

"Not at the moment."

"This should be easy, then."

Evan toed up the decrepit umbrella, caught it on the rise by its smooth wooden handle. The naked ribs clattered, a woebegone percussion instrument.

Folgore's lips spread and then curled upright. "Easy there, Mary Poppins."

"If you go for that nine," Evan said, "I'm gonna break your shoulder."

"With a broken umbrella?" Folgore grinned, reached lethargically for the holster. "How you gonna do that?"

Evan hooked the wooden handle around the fire-escape ladder and ripped it downward, Folgore looking up, his draw slowed with surprised curiosity. The ladder unstacked itself rustily, telescoping down past Folgore's ear and slamming onto the meat of his trapezius.

The sound was muffled, like a round hitting a slab of beef.

Folgore's muzzle had just cleared leather, but the downward momentum of his arm slammed it back into the holster.

Folgore stumbled back, his dislocated shoulder floating down near the side of his chest. Certain injuries served as a reminder that skin was primarily a bag for bones.

Folgore didn't look as fazed as he should have been. Marines thought of themselves as the toughest guys in the room, and they were generally right. His head lowered like a bull's, he glowered up at Evan with wild, dangerous eyes.

Evan said, "Reach for it again and I'll break your nose."

This time Folgore moved swiftly, a cross-draw with his left hand. As the pistol swept past his chest, Evan jabbed the slide with the heel of his hand. The side of the frame smacked into Folgore's face, his nose popping theatrically. The pistol tumbled into a puddle.

Twinning streaks of red painted Folgore's upper lip. Trembling with rage, he balled up a fist.

"If you swing at me," Evan said, "I'll break your jaw."

Folgore darted forward in a boxer shuffle and threw a wide left. Evan covered, wrapping his head, biceps to temple, the blow glancing off. Evan threw a left of his own, and he threw it from the ground up—base set, pivoting at the hips, torso snapping around. His knuckles struck a few inches from the point of the chin, solid contact with the mandible. The crunch was horrifying; he felt the vibration through his legs and feet.

Folgore went out, a dead-sack fall onto his back. His pant leg hiked up to reveal the handle of a boot knife, glass-reinforced nylon with three pronounced finger grooves.

Rain pattered across the detritus of the alley. A shift of the wind promoted the sewage reek to noxious, but it reversed just as quickly.

Evan waited patiently.

After a moment Folgore stirred. Rolled sluggishly into the fetal position. He looked almost comfortable. After a few breaths, he pulled himself up to sit without the benefit of one arm, hoisted onto his knees, and stood. He gingerly pressed on his jaw, winced, then drooled a bit into his cupped hand and regarded the blood.

His right arm dangled uselessly at his side, the fingers reaching unhumanly low to his thigh.

"Next is your leg," Evan said. "I'm thinking the left one."

Folgore fanned his good hand wide, showing a bloody palm. "Uncle."

"You want to answer my questions now?" Evan asked. "Because I could do this all day."

"I have something to show you," Folgore said, his words blurred from the injury. "That will answer your questions." Cautiously, still showing his palm, he started to crouch.

"You sure you want to do that?" Evan said.

But already the knife was free of Folgore's boot, held expertly in a reverse grip, blade angled down along the forearm. With the cutting edge out, there was nothing for Evan to grab or deflect. Folgore lunged forward, raking the blade sideways toward Evan's chest. As Evan skipped back, Folgore's heel slipped on a peel of soggy foam, his boot skidding. He overcorrected with his torso, the good shoulder spinning forward. He lost his footing, instinctively went to catch himself with his functional hand, forgetting that it still held the knife.

His chest slammed down, muffling the clank of the nylon handle striking asphalt beneath it. He gasped more in surprise than pain. Facedown humped up over the knife, his body twitched a few times. Then he exhaled once, long and smooth, and lay still.

Evan stared at him. One glassy eye stared up.

Folgore looked like he was slumbering.

Evan rolled him over, marveling at the blade's placement in the solar plexus, buried deep enough to sever the abdominal aorta.

Like any decent operator, Folgore proved to be carrying nothing but cash and weapons. No wallet, no ID, not even a phone.

Evan left him there, sprawled on his back, arms flung wide, like a dozing sunbather.

Before emerging from the alley, Evan checked himself for blood. The doorman eyed him somberly and Evan tipped an imaginary cap to him. He searched the two stoops across the street but found nothing beyond the thermal blanket.

Heading toward Broadway to hail a cab, he texted Joey: I need an

This Should Be Easy

address for Ruby Seabook ASAP. Then get me everything you can find on the Johnny Seabrook—Angela Buford double murder.

The dot-dot-dot appeared instantly. Then: please + thank you?

Evan thumbed in: Please and thank you.

it doesn't mean anything when i have 2 tell u 2 say it.

He raised an arm, and a cab screeched over. Then pretend I thought of it all on my own.

everything go 👍 in ny?

Evan thought of Folgore lying in repose in the trash-strewn alley, raindrops plinking against glazed open eyes.

Swimmingly.

He eased into the cab, breathed in the warmth, the venerable vinyl seats crackling beneath his weight.

"Where to?" the cabbie said in a pleasing lilt. Southern Africa, maybe Botswana.

Already Joey had replied: ruby seabrook is a 2nd-year @ uva but she's living @ home w her rents in wellesley, ma. which u could have figured out w a google + insta search if u werent completely useless.

"Teterboro Airport," Evan said. "Please and thank you."

He typed: But then I wouldn't get to talk with you.

ur the worst, X.

You're the worst, too.

24

Really?

Ring. Ring. Ri—

"Templeton."

"Templeton, it's—"

She knew his voice and didn't wait. "What the *fuck*! We had an agreement. That shit at the Beverly Hills Hotel? Trussing up my agents like rodeo calves?"

"Your man took a DNA swab from my cheek to sell on the black market."

"Wait— *What*? Who?"

"Paddy. You should put pressure on Chip first. He has a pregnant girlfriend."

"You'd better not be lying." Seething silence. Then, "Fuckin' Paddy."

"Go flick him on the nose and tell him he's an asshole. Also? You have a mole. Devine already knows I'm coming for him."

"Wake up to what I already told you." she said. "It's not about a mole. Luke Devine is *everywhere*. That's why we detained you. That's why we were supposed to work together."

"I prefer this."

"Do you have any idea the kind of earth the government is willing to scorch to get to you now? And it goes without saying that your pardon's out the window."

"I don't care about the pardon. But I gave you my word I'd look into Devine."

"So you'll do it?"

"I'll look into it. That's all. Stay out of my way. I'll be in touch if I need you."

"You don't set the rules."

"Templeton. *Really?*"

Click.

At HQ Naomi headed along the catwalk, glass-walled offices scrolling by on her right side. Paddy glanced up from his desk as she entered. His wrists looked raw, and a purple-black bruise had bloomed on his cheek.

She flicked him on the nose.

His eyes widened, and he jerked back in his chair.

"Asshole," she said.

25

A World Apart

The white Colonial clapboard house was accented with a red door and navy shutters so dark they passed for black in the foggy soup of a Massachusetts dusk.

Across the street in the shadow of a NEIGHBORHOOD WATCH sign, Evan sat in a rental car he'd liberated from a Hertz maintenance site in East Boston. The Buick Regal required only light body work on a dinged-up passenger-door panel, but the facility was back-logged, the repair not scheduled until the following week. He'd slipped into the indoor parking lot during lunch break, lifted the key from one of myriad hooks on the service board. The abundance of tools made it easy for him to remove the Lojak, and he'd stashed the NeverLost GPS unit in the trunk of another vehicle before driving off.

He probably could have booked a car safely with one of his fake identities, but he'd been on the receiving end of Naomi Temple-ton's focused competence before he'd given her reason to take her pursuit of him personally. He thought it better to raise his security protocols from highly cautious to paranoid. So as to leave no foot-print at a hotel, he'd returned to the private jet to eat a meal of red wine–braised beef with polenta and take a nap. It was an arrange-ment he could get used to.

Joey had generated a dossier of the double murder. The bod-ies had been dumped in Angela Buford's apartment in a tene-ment building in Mattapan, a Boston neighborhood south of the city center. Before his death Johnny Seabrook had been beaten up badly, bruised face, torn ACL. He'd been shot once from behind, his hand impaled with a blade, and his throat slashed.

Angela Buford's head had been raked around on her swanlike neck, sending C2 vertebra fragments into her brain stem. Even for a woman as delicately boned as Angela, it would have taken an enormous amount of strength and expertise to provide sufficient torque to end her.

Evan had tried and failed at this very move once and had been left to contend with an enraged Serb sporting a sore neck.

According to the medical examiner's report, Johnny and Ange-la's time of death had occurred between eighteen and twenty-four hours before their bodies were discovered, which put the murders on Labor Day. Devine's men had provided investigators with the guest list for the party that evening, establishing that neither vic-tim had been in attendance.

Joey had included Zoom Earth links showing Devine's South-ampton compound. Cushioned on either side with lush green lawns, the mansion perched on the strip of Meadow Lane between the Atlantic and Shinnecock Bay. It was named Tartarus, a wicked bit of wordplay from the original owner, a Scotsman who'd built his fortune producing merino kilts for Royal Mile tailors in Edin-burgh.

If in fact the murders had taken place there as Ruby suspected, it would have required a hell of an operation to move two bodies across state lines to throw investigators off the scent. From every-thing Evan had seen of Luke Devine and his security cadre, they were capable of a hell of an operation.

Evan looked up from the crime-scene photos on his phone to the Seabrook house once more. It was a suburban spectacle. The brick walkway picked up the dulled red of dueling chimneys rising from the steeply pitched roof of the second floor. Colonials could be counted on for pleasing symmetry—a forthright rectangular front with a four-columned porch, geometric shrubs, matching windows below, twinning dormer windows above.

Contrasted with the image on his RoamZone—Johnny Seabrook laid out in a broken-limbed sprawl on a tenement floor—the Wellesley house was a world apart. And yet death had strolled up that brick walkway, rung the doorbell, and brought the horrors of the world across the threshold anyway.

Evan wondered what it said about him that he felt more at ease in dump-site tenements than in a proper home like the one before him.

The Seabrooks had upgraded to a "smart system" a few years back, and Joey had jumped Evan onto the Wi-Fi network with credential stuffing via the ecobee thermostat, giving him control of the security cameras, the video doorbell, and even the dimmers should the need for romantic lighting suddenly present itself as a tactical imperative.

Deborah Seabrook, on the cusp of sixty, was a onetime soap-opera actress. Her husband, Mason, was a psychologist. The amusement of Evan's traveling across the country from Los Angeles to wind up at the house of an actress and a therapist was not lost on him.

He was tempted to avoid both thespian and shrink and talk to Ruby separately, but the thought of someone addressing an issue of this weight with Joey behind his back made him feel murderous. So there it was. A green shoot of familial empathy.

He grimaced, annoyed at himself.

Then he walked up and rang the doorbell, watching his own face appear on the RoamZone as he did.

"So let me get this straight." Deborah Seabrook folded her hands on a stockinged knee peeking from the hem of a conservative tweed A-line dress. "You won't tell us who you are or what you do. You won't tell us your last name. You want to talk with our nineteen-year-old daughter to help solve the murder of her brother in response to an ask for help she made a year ago on FlipFlop—"

At this her husband stirred. "TikTok."

Deborah refused to lose steam. "—and we're supposed to facilitate this?"

Evan had to concentrate in order not to fidget on the upholstered settee. They were in the family room or living room—he'd never figured out how rich people named their spaces of leisure. Deborah leaned forward in her armchair with beautiful straight-backed posture, but Mason was looser-limbed, on a slightly slumped thoughtful recline that—from Evan's limited engagement with popular culture—seemed proprietary to therapists. Bearded, with glasses, he stayed silent and paid attention.

Evan said, "Yes."

A cramped doorway revealed the breakfast seating area of the kitchen, above which CNN murmured from a mounted TV. A fan-shaped graphic of blue and red dots depicted the deadlocked Senate vote on the president's trillion-dollar environmental bill above a split screen of talking heads, their muted mouths flapping. A good half of the kitchen table had been overrun by an abandoned jigsaw puzzle, its thin frame completed and little else. A jumble of loose pieces were mounded in the middle for long-term storage. Beyond several items of abstract art he failed to decipher and a central staircase, Evan couldn't make out much more.

California open-concept floor plans to which he'd grown somewhat accustomed served as a rebuke to the distinct rooms of New England houses like this one. Specified spatial purpose, increased privacy. But formality didn't seem primary in the Seabrook household; they'd invited him right in and listened to his macabre sales pitch. They were serious people who understood the utility of a light touch. And now Deborah was leading the charge right to the heart of the matter.

"Are you . . . what's the word? Official?" Deborah asked.

"Sanctioned," Evan said.

"That one."

Evan took a moment to consider the question. In the kitchen the news had moved on to another dreary commissioning of another combat ship in a Wisconsin shipyard, the military-industrial complex feeding itself.

"In a manner, yes," he said. "At the highest level."

"Why should we believe that?" The left side of Deborah's face bore the faint memory of a stroke, her handsome features slightly reluctant to follow the lead of her expressions, though her speech was barely impeded. She was unnervingly poised. "It's not like you're a door-to-door brush salesman. Given the gravity of the situation and the vagueness of your claims, how should we be expected to trust anything you say?"

Evan took a moment to think about it. There was little sound aside from the susurration of the television. A former vice president droned on at a lectern, Secret Service doing their best to stand at attention among the crisp rows of sailors.

"Would you mind if I made a quick call?" Evan asked.

Mason dipped his head in the affirmative.

Evan dialed the familiar number, reaching the main switchboard. When the featureless voice answered, he said, "Dark Road." A pause while he was transferred to a security command post, and then he said, "Extension thirty-two."

The line rang and rang.

Deborah and Mason watched him, motionless.

The voice, flattened out in annoyance. "What?"

"It's me," he said.

A terse half-second pause and then, "Do you have any idea the kind of response your actions will draw?"

"I'm on the mission as you requested."

"You can't just *call me* as if I'm some—"

"I'm going to put you on speakerphone. Tell the nice people I'm sitting with that I'm sanctioned so they'll trust me."

"You're *not* sanctioned. Not anymore."

"Should I stop?"

A longer silence. And then, slightly muffled, "Tell the Latvian president to hold." Back to Evan. "Go."

He hit speaker, held the phone aloft.

President Donahue-Carr's voice lifted from his RoamZone, rendered in 3-D sound waves. It asked, "Do you recognize my voice?"

Deborah and Mason stared slack-jawed at the phone. "Hello," Mason said dumbly, eliciting a curt glance from Deborah.

"This man can be trusted. He's on"—and here the president's voice sounded slightly strained—"the right side."

Deborah said, "Why should we believe her? I've worked with plenty of voice impersonators."

"Jesus Christ," the commander in chief said. "I don't have time for this shit. I'm having you transferred to Templeton."

A click. A hum of the paused line. Then ringing. Naomi picked up on one ring.

"Excuse me," Evan said, taking the phone off speaker and turning away for privacy. In a muted voice, he told Naomi what he needed.

Then he hung up and said, "Follow me, please."

In a sort of stupor, Deborah and Mason followed him into the kitchen and stood before the TV. Evan pointed to the grandstand behind the dais, indicating the black-suited man nearest the podium.

"Secret Service will scratch his nose," Evan said.

Twenty seconds passed. Perhaps thirty.

Then the agent touched his ear. Caught the eye of the camera. And scratched his nose pointedly.

Deborah said, "Holy hell."

26

Dirtboxes

Derek Tenpenny and his sinful six had a cadre of low-level security schmuckatellis to cover the basics so they could concern themselves with higher-order strategy for Mr. Devine. They also had the run of Tartarus with all its hidden spaces and secret corridors. Lately they'd been commandeering the billiards room as their unofficial HQ. Its plush leather couches and the curved bar in the corner made it ideal for confabulations, and that's where Tenpenny and the extant five met now.

Bram Folgore had been stabbed to death.

As always, word traveled rapidly to Mr. Devine, in this case from patrolman to detective to the commanding officer of the First Precinct to the police commissioner to the mayor of New York City, on whom Tenpenny himself had compiled a substantial file over the course of a lost weekend last autumn.

This glorious job that Mr. Devine had bestowed upon Tenpenny—part security tactician, part interceder, part espionage agent—

seemed uniquely designed to fit his attributes and temperament. Tenpenny's only weakness was women. He got after it every time he found a participant who was willing and properly shaped and, in a pinch, when she was neither. Being a media fixer had provided ample access and plenty of opportunities. After an incident involving cracked hotel drywall (DoubleTree, Times Square) and cheekbone (hooker, Thai), a judge had ordered him to attend Sex Addicts Anonymous, which had proved richer hunting grounds yet. During the six-week stint, he'd nearly worn out the sink basin in that church bathroom.

A Division II hoops player from way back when, Tenpenny was taller than any man had a right to be, his height a useful icebreaker when it came to the dark arts of lechery. He'd had the benefit of pouring the foundation of his career before the #MeToo nonsense had gotten up steam, so he'd had plenty of time to hone his skills at keeping one step ahead of the social-justice mob.

Working for Luke Devine felt like getting called up to the Show after laboring for years in the farm system. Per Mr. Devine's wishes, Tenpenny had dirtboxes installed all over the property, cell-site simulators that threw out powerful pilot signals stronger than those from any cell towers in the area. They made all phones within range switch over to their network. Then—*bam*—you had IMSI numbers, ESNs, and you could snatch encryption-session keys in less than a second. That meant you were logged in. Emails, text histories, all that juicy stuff Mr. Devine used to exploit their owners and, in turn, the world.

Mr. Devine was, if anything, laissez-faire. Tenpenny had plenty of elbow room to work with on the side. He'd grab all the girls' information when they entered Tartarus. If you got into a young woman's phone, you got into her head. There was an art to it. Pulling photos and comments out of Instagram and Snapchat, compiling information on their best-loved attributes. Did they favor their asses? Their long, long legs? Did they post wistful pictures of their deceased daddies? Or were they frosty and immaculate, shelf ornaments like the cable-news ice queens he used to look after who always had to be the prettiest girl in the room? In fact that's what he lusted after most of all—the collection of insecurities those girls put right out there for the world to see, all the poker tells he could use when lubricating his angle of attack.

Tenpenny kept records for himself in a big old-fashioned leather-bound ledger like the ones they used at European bed-and-breakfasts. On the weighty pages, he noted flexibility, mouthfeel, degree of required persuasion, sexual positions. It gave him a kind of power, his big book of exploits. Write her name in the ledger and he owned a piece of her forever.

But now, now they had a problem. And he was at bottom a fixer. So he had to fix it.

The one holy rule of Luke Devine: No one was to see what went on behind the scarlet door.

Ever.

But someone had, and that had opened up the gates of hell, so now Tenpenny was here meeting with his marines.

Years ago they'd been flown into the city for a news segment on their alleged misdeeds in Kandahar, and Tenpenny had been tasked with looking after them. Right away he'd recognized that they were beautiful savages, the purest of what they were, and he'd made clear that he could provide bountiful opportunities to exploit their expertise. Through the course of doing business, he'd learned much about their temperaments.

Like that of Craig Gordon, currently embedded in the couch, thunder thighs parted to allow room for his belly to sag. A great big shiny pink man with a bald head and hot-dog bulges of fat at the base of his skull, Gordo had been an M240 Bravo Gunner with the Corps, lugging the Pig into more firefights than he could keep track of. The front of his shirt carried potato-chip shrapnel and various streaks of lunch condiments, as did his push-broom mustache. A spiral notebook rested, as always, on the slate of his knee, and he doodled now, the pen dwarfed in the catcher's mitt of his hand. He seemed to keep the scribble pad with him as a security blanket; Tenpenny had never seen him take a single actual note.

At Gordo's side Daniel Martinez stood with a ramrod posture that looked reinforced with rebar. On the gym-swollen ball of his biceps, Dapper Dan wore his marines tat with pride, the Eagle, Globe, and Anchor inked in vibrant blue to match his piercing eyes. Waxy black hair, not a strand out of place. Prominent eyebrows manscaped to perfection, waxed chest showing at the open collar of his Polo shirt, waft of Creed Viking cologne giving off smoke and a hint of spice.

Norris Norris, which was actually the dude's fucking name, sat on the pool table with his stick legs dangling. Double N had done a stint as a nonappropriated fund-audit technician within the Force Support Squadron before changing his MOS so he could get his dick dirty out beyond the Green Zone. Lean and dark-skinned, he had a pronounced Adam's apple and a pair of old-school thick-frame eyeglasses that popped his pupils. Of the men he was the easiest to predict and handle; he ran on nothing but money. It was almost shocking what he was willing to do if his price was met.

João Santos perched on the arm of a couch like a gargoyle. He wore an Order of Christ pendant, square and symmetrical with flared tips like an Iron Cross. It was pinched between his lips, white-gold chain drooping on either side of his chin like an eyeglasses strap. He was the smallest and least-liked of the crew, and in some ways the most dangerous. An MMA-ranked fighter in the Gracie tradition, he was underappreciated and undermined, covetous of the camaraderie the others enjoyed. Grapplers rarely got the same respect as snipers and demolition breachers, but if Sandman got someone—anyone—down to the ground, he owned them. During a tavern fight, Tenpenny had seen him hyperextend a guy's elbow in an arm-bar and then rake it so severely to the side it looked as if the limb might twist right off.

Last was Rathsberger. Slouched low and crooked in a leather wing chair studded with bronze nailheads, Rath had one leg flung over the armrest, a wicked prince trying out the throne. He wore his 9-mil on his hip, as Folgore had. The kiss of white phosphorus from an artillery shell burn had turned the right side of his face into a hypertrophic mudslide, but his dark shiny eyes were intact, peering out from the depths of the wreckage.

Rath was the only one the others feared. He'd been the ringleader over in the Sandbox, the guy who'd gone in not quite right and had spent his time inside the war theater giving vent to his worst and darkest instincts. If there was a lighter side to the man, Tenpenny had never glimpsed it.

Rath held up a slender test tube, which he ticktocked like a hypnotist's watch, aggravating its living contents. To satisfy his infinity of perverse habits, he cast his line far and frequently into the dark net and fished out all order of evil delicacies. These latest, bull ants from Tasmania, grew up to an inch and a half. Their nasty scissoring mandibles were so long that, according to Rath, zoologists believed them to be evolutionarily derived from legs. The ants could jump like crickets and were known to hang off their victims once their mandibles were sunk into flesh.

Tenpenny had requested that Rathsberger keep the stopper in the test tube.

Rath had taken the news of Folgore's death the hardest. He'd skipped grief-stricken and headed straight to rageful.

"So he killed him." Rath rattled the test tube before his eyes. The bull ants seethed behind the glass, a tangle of menace. "Left him in an alley like trash. What are we supposed to do about that?"

"Not a damn thing," Norris said. "This is a private job. We all knew that. There's no taps, no flag presentation."

Rath's upper lip curled away from his teeth, and Norris's Adam's apple bobbed once with a swallow. The thick scarring of Rath's chin and throat had led to contractures, the skin tight enough to tug down the right corner of his mouth and expose the gum line.

"But," Tenpenny said, "we gotta cover our tracks."

He lit up another Marlboro Red now, sucked in the inhale, and blew it out through clenched yellow teeth. He was a messy kind of smoker, bits of ash on his tie, stale tobacco wafting from his clothes with every movement. He never understood people who were closet smokers, who could indulge in the vice without having it seep into their pores.

"I thought everything was covered," Sandman said. "What isn't covered?"

"Relax, lil' man," Gordo said. "Let Tenpenny talk."

Tenpenny took a drag, the tobacco hitting the bags of his lungs with a pleasing burn. "We have to lock down the home front hard. And. Those squeaky wheels in Boston surrounding the dear departed? We can no longer afford to have them out there squeaking. Not now that this asshole's showed up prying around, kicking over rocks. Who wants to go to Boston, tie up loose ends?"

Rath jiggled the test tube. Even from here Tenpenny could make out the shapes of individual ants, their red waxy bodies, big compound eyes, and cutting jaws. A leaf trapped inside with them had been turned into jigsaw-puzzle pieces.

Rath slid upward from the chair onto his feet, his olive-drab utility jacket flapping wide to show off a barrel chest and a tapered waist. He tapped the test tube down into an interior pocket and rubbed his hands. "I'd be delighted."

"Pick a battle buddy," Tenpenny said.

Spitting out the Portuguese cross, Santos popped up eagerly, puffed out his own chest, dusted his hands on his jeans. He was a hair below five foot five counting the lifts in his boots.

Rath's gaze swung right past him, and Santos deflated a little.

"I'm out," Dapper Dan said. "I got interval training tonight. Part of a regime."

"Oooh," Rath said, "a *regime.*"

Dan's smile was so white and smooth the teeth looked of a single piece.

Rath flicked a forefinger at Gordo, who shifted onto his left flank, setting off a rippling effect as he prepared to rise. It took considerable effort, and even once he was planted on his feet, his corpus needed some time to settle back into place around him.

"Take the jet," Tenpenny said. "No loose ends."

27

Me Neither

Outside a closed bedroom door on the slightly worn maroon carpet of the second floor, Mason turned to Evan and said in a lowered voice, "You will be honest with us. Completely. Or I will pull the plug on all of this. Understand?"

Evan said, "Yes."

Deborah shouldered past her husband to Evan. For the size of the house, the hallways were surprisingly cramped. "Was Ruby right about Tartarus? Is Luke Devine behind this?"

"I don't know."

Deborah pressed closer. "Can you keep her safe?"

Evan said, "Yes."

"No matter what?"

"Yes."

Through the door issued televised sounds of gunfire and explosions. An action movie?

"Okay," she said. "Then let Ruby tell you."

Evan asked, "Tell me what?"

"That's up to her," Mason said to his wife. "To decide whether she trusts him."

Deborah said, "We should be in there with them."

"We will ask Ruby what she wants," Mason said. "If she's comfortable being alone with him, she'll say so."

Evan picked up the third person: "He will do his best to make her comfortable."

Deborah rapped on the door with a single knuckle.

A voice from beyond: "C'min!"

Deborah opened the door, and the three of them crowded at the threshold like bozos determining how to exit a clown car.

Slumped in a beanbag cast in the sterile blue light of a big-screen TV, Ruby worked an intricate joystick, playing a first-person shooter game. Her face was pallid, slack. It looked like she'd been at it for hours.

It took a moment for Evan to understand the decor. *Sports Illustrated* swimsuit pictures tacked up over a bed with green flannel sheets. A framed Red Sox jersey covered with Sharpie signatures hung on the wall next to a pennant. Photos wedged in the frame of a mirrored closet door showcased Johnny through the years with different friends and girlfriends—and quite a few with his sister.

Ruby nestled deeper into the beanbag, seemingly comfortable in her brother's room.

"Ruby," Deborah said with enviably refined diction, "you have a visitor. Evidently approved by the president of the United States."

Ruby didn't look over. Her hands pulsed around the controller. On the television several shady mercenary types met their end, their heads exploding in tomato bursts. The game was no more demure when it came to their screams of agony. "Really?"

"Yes."

"Cool." Ruby favored them with a single quick glance. "Well, hi."

Deborah said, "Would you like us to stay, dear?"

"I'm fine." Ruby shot a soldier in a gas mask in both knees and then kicked him back into the conveniently located tail propeller of an attack helicopter. Intestinal muck spattered a heretofore invisible lens.

Mason offered Evan a nod of encouragement. "Good luck."

For the first few minutes after Deborah and Mason withdrew, Evan watched Ruby obliterate an entire squad of mercenaries with a .50-cal meat chopper.

She neither spoke nor looked up.

Finally she tossed over a second remote and chinned at the beanbag next to her. "Don't just stand there. Get in."

A challenge.

Evan sat with the remote and tried to figure out the weapon-control system. The movement mechanics were baffling; every time he tried to lead a target, he missed by several inches. The little recoil buzz of the joystick drove him crazy.

He missed all his shots.

He took fire.

He ate a grenade.

He accidentally shot himself in the leg. Twice.

"You really suck at this," Ruby said.

"That seems to be the case," he conceded.

Taking pity on him, she turned off the game. "You're here about my brother."

"Yes."

"Do you actually want to figure out what happened to him? Seriously? Or is this more ass-covering bureaucratic nonsense?"

"The former."

"Why?"

"I saw that video you posted a year ago."

"Right," she said. "And then you just decided to help."

"Yes."

She did a double take, saw that he wasn't joking. "Okay. What do you want to know?"

"Anything you can tell me. What he was like. The kind of

crowd he was running with. You said you don't think he knew the young woman whose body was found with his. Did he date black girls?"

Ruby looked appalled. "That's so *racist!*"

"Why?"

"Why? Because you assume there's, like, a *type* that dates black girls. And a type that *doesn't.*"

"Okay," he said. "Did Johnny just date people who he liked no matter their skin color?"

Her cheeks dimpled ever so slightly with amusement, the effect winning.

"Yeah," she said, "he dated everyone. And everyone dated him. That was him. That was Johnny."

Her eyes lowered and her face softened in that manner he'd seen time and again with Joey when emotion started pressing toward the surface. Evan knew to keep his mouth shut so as not to scare it back down inside her.

The room was warm, and the air bore the faintest tinge of incense. Several worms of ash lay in a cherrywood burner on the nightstand.

Evan marveled at how the room had been preserved, as if Johnny might stroll in at any moment and plop down on the bed. He wondered how much time Ruby spent in here playing video games, burning incense, occupying the space her brother used to fill.

"He was out ahead of everyone else," she said. "Always in a rush to practice, to a party, to fun. The first to drink, the first to have sex, the first to smoke pot. But he was the most naïve, too, somehow." She pursed her lips. "His base setting was . . . faith in the world. He thought the universe was as loving as it presented itself to him. They talk about that as entitlement, but, man, I'd never want to be that kind of ignorant. He was my big brother, right? But also he was so . . . young. And kinda dumb. But sweet all the way through, you know?"

She picked at a fingernail. "And he was . . . beautiful. Like someone Lord Byron would've fallen in love with. He had this dreamy stoner smile like from the seventies. He was insufferable." She was crying. "And if he was just dead because an Acme safe fell on his head or because he drunk-crashed his car, then fine. But if someone *did this* to him? Just *because*? I don't know how to live in a world where that goes unanswered."

Evan said, "Me neither."

She swiped away tears with the pulled-down cuff of her sweater, not breaking eye contact. There wasn't a trace of embarrassment in her for crying.

"Look at that," she said. "We agree on something."

The moment sat there bright and pleasing between them.

"Your parents said you had something to tell me," he said.

She shrugged. "Okay."

The quickness of her response caught him off guard.

"What?" She gave a one-shouldered shrug. "If my parents say I can trust you, I can trust you."

"It's that easy?"

"Have you *met* my parents?"

"Briefly. But I take your point."

"And believe me," Ruby said, "I'm *dying* for more people to trust. It's the only way out of any of this."

"You are terrifyingly astute."

"So I've been told. But there's a thing. Which is. I haven't shown this to anyone else but my parents. And if I show it to you, you have to protect me."

This was proving to be the easiest game of Win Your Trust he'd played in all his years of operating.

He said, "Okay."

Ruby shifted to fish out her iPhone and held it up so it captured facial recognition. Pulling up voice mail, she went to a saved message labeled: UNIDENTIFIED CALLER.

She hesitated. A thin line of sweat sparkled at her brow. She blinked a few times rapidly, bracing herself. Then pressed PLAY.

A voice distorted through horror-movie software, all low growling menace and satanic reverberation: *"Stop talking about your brother. Stop asking questions about your brother. Or I will come for you like I came for him. You'll get your counseling, your medication to try to convince yourself that maybe I forgot, that it's safe to talk to the cops, that the threat is no longer real. But I am. I always will be. You will never be safe from me."*

It clicked off. Her lips were trembling. She quit out of the screen and shoved the phone back into her pocket, then rolled her lips over her teeth and bit down.

He wondered at the kind of strength it would take for a nineteen-year-old girl to be able to carry a message like that around in her pocket. He wondered if the level of anger elicited in him was sustainable or if it would burn a hole straight through the mission.

"There," she said. "I told you. Now you have to keep me safe."

She bounced up and skipped out of her room. Making a mental note to grab a recording of the voice mail later, Evan followed her downstairs to the kitchen.

Mason was slicing heirloom tomatoes at the counter, and Deborah sat on a stool across from him, flipping through a gossip magazine.

"I showed it to him," Ruby announced.

The words had a visible effect on both parents. Mason gave a somber nod and resumed chopping.

Ruby slung an arm across Evan's shoulders, though she had to reach up to do so. "I found him," she said. "So now I get to keep him."

"What do you mean you found him?" Deborah asked.

"I wiled him here. With my damsel-in-distress wiles." Draping the back of her hand across her forehead Lichtenstein-style, Ruby feigned a swoon into Evan. He caught her and propped her neatly back on her feet. "And now? He is my sworn liege forever."

Deborah set down the magazine and strummed the shiny cover once with perfectly manicured nails. "Is that so, Evan No-Last-Name?"

"I meet a lot of characters in my line of work," Evan said. "Your daughter's the first one who's scared me in a while."

THE LAST ORPHAN

Mason migrated the last few perfect circles of burrata from the cutting board onto matching tomato counterparts and drizzled them with a balsamic reduction. "Forever's a long time, Ruby," he said, "so why don't we start with dinner?"

28

Keep Digging

The Caprese salad rested beside a literal silver platter of roast guinea fowl. The unfinished jigsaw puzzle occupied one side of the table, the four of them the other half. A few connected pieces forged down into the puzzle interior—a chunk of a forehead, a fluff of hair. Enough for Evan to discern that it was a photo of some sort. The strays, mounded in the center, had collected a thin sheen of dust. The bow window beyond the table showed off a bucolic backyard, a detached office or guesthouse dwarfed by mature oaks.

Wine was served; Evan declined. Dinner-table patter was a foreign language to him, and it required his full focus. Plus: wine.

Sitting at his side, Ruby kept thumbing through her phone. "Sophia just came out on Instagram."

"Good for her," Mason said.

"Are you kidding me?" Ruby forked a bite into her mouth. "At this rate I'm the only hetero person in my class. I'm trying to get people to *stop* coming out. I barely have any straight friends left."

"I've realized that you don't get more conservative as you get older," Deborah remarked to Evan. "The world gets more liberal."

"And—ug. Colby DM'd me. Again." Ruby flashed the phone. It showed a meme of some actor type captioned with: *HEY GUUURL. YOU'RE SUPER HOT.*

Evan ventured for the first time into the stream of dinner conversation. "Colby?"

"My crazy high-school ex. And look—I get it. Everyone thinks their ex is crazy. You never hear anyone say, 'I broke up with him because I realized I'm borderline and a nightmare to deal with.' But Colby? Supremely limited. It's like, dude, I get it that you think all I really want to hear is how beautiful I am, but the thing is I already know that I have pleasingly symmetrical features and the whole flush-of-youth thing going for me, so it only shows your own failure of imagination when you fall for the evolutionary fitness mask when I'm right here beneath it and I'm so much more and if you weren't busy bragging about my looks, you would've realized I am the best resource you could ever think to have."

Evan's next bite of skewered fowl hovered a few inches from his plate. "Poor Colby."

"Right. Side with him." Ruby gave Evan a little backhanded thwap with her knuckles, her easy affection disarming. "And they're all like that." I even tried one of those wholesome-ish dating apps, but I kept matching with guys named Caden who want to chill and hang but don't have any money to go out. Great. Thanks, dating apps. Something to make males of the species *more* lazy and indecisive." Her thumb flick-flick-flicked. "Arty Caden. Try-Hard Caden. Jock Caden." She held the phone sideways. "At least Jock Caden is kinda cute."

"The big muscly ones always turn into fatsos," Deborah said.

"That's why you date them *now*, Mother."

"That's enough, dear," Deborah said, rising to clear. "Phone away at the table."

"But, Mom," Ruby said with teenage bite, "I'm supposed to be getting back out in the world, remember?"

"Not with *Cadens*."

"Fine." Ruby pocketed the phone. "I took a year off from UVA.

And Dad thinks it's not good for me to 'stay holed up in the house I grew up in.' But am I really supposed to give a shit about studying environmental science anymore when my brother was murdered?"

"I'll let that pass as a rhetorical question," Evan said.

"You are terrifyingly astute." Ruby smirked. "You asked me about Johnny. Why don't you ask *them*? Mom? Dad? Describe Johnny. Habits, personality, quirks."

Evan blinked a few times. Ruby had commandeered the interrogation process, a charming if ruthless coup d'état.

"Describe Johnny?" Deborah sank back into her chair, cupping her hands around a mug of coffee. "He was a free spirit. The . . . hmm . . . the one we could never trust. Except to be kind. He was so gentle-hearted and . . . easy to love. He got all the light in the family."

Ruby said, "Thanks, Mom."

"Don't complain, dear. You got the brains."

"Double thanks, Mom."

"*And* the backbone."

"Keep digging, *mère chérie*."

Mason placed his hand over Ruby's and gave it a little squeeze. "And the work ethic." A cautious glance in Evan's direction. "Johnny lacked discipline. And yet he always managed to get his way. I always said if he'd applied himself, he would have been a brilliant lawyer."

Deborah's smile stiffened. "Yes. You did say that. Always."

Evan pressed through the tension. "Would it be characteristic for him to wind up at a party house in the Hamptons?"

Mason considered for a moment. "I'd say so. He ran with whatever crowd could offer the most adventure. Party people who blow around from this scene to that."

Deborah bristled once more. "My father used to tell me never to shame someone for finding joy. It's so goddamned rare in this world."

Mason's face looked long in the yellow glow of the kitchen. His beard glistened, flecked with gray. A wise, patient face. "He found more than joy, Deborah. He found trouble he couldn't handle."

She looked at him, her gaze unrelenting. He held it. There wasn't enmity between them, only a raw kind of contradiction in their pain. He was like a container for her emotion and she for his.

Ruby said, softly, "Guys."

A discomfort moved through Evan, and he had an abrupt urge to distract himself with something—anything—else: to wipe down the greasy silver platter, to put together the incomplete jigsaw puzzle, to align the edges of Deborah's magazines, which were infuriatingly stacked with no regard for right angles. He'd come here to get information on Luke Devine. Not to witness a family processing their grief. It felt like he'd been shanghaied into participating in an ancient ritual he didn't understand.

Deborah pushed back from the table, rising to fill her mug once more. "You know, Evan, I used to hate coffee, but I needed caffeine to get going in the morning." Her tone was different, performative. "Then I got hooked on the taste. But after Johnny the anxiety was too much. So. I started hating caffeine. Now I drink decaf day and night. Go figure. Would you like a cup?"

"No, thank you."

She flipped through one of the magazines stacked on the counter without looking down at it. "I'd imagine if you're protecting Ruby, we should log you into our security system. It's one of those modern ones with cameras one can view on one's cell phone."

"I'm already in," Evan said.

Ruby shot her father a look across the table, eyebrows raised in delighted astonishment.

"Oh." Deborah took a moment to regain her composure. "Well, don't you dare turn up the thermostat. Women of a certain age require a cool sleeping temperature."

"Yes, ma'am."

Mason said, "I can make up the couch in my office out back for him."

"No." Ruby grabbed for Evan's forearm, caught herself, and, released it. She suppressed her fear beneath a peacock display of sass. "I want him to sleep upstairs next door to me. Like a guard dog." She made a frame with thumbs and forefingers, pretending to take the measure of Evan's neck. One eye closed, teeth pinching her lower lip, a full Kubrickian focus. "If he behaves, I won't even need a collar and leash."

"Guard dogs mistreated by their owners tend to turn on them," Evan said. "And then CSI has to clean the blood spatter off the ceiling."

A moment of stunned silence. And then the Seabrooks all laughed.

29

Family Fill Up

The corporate jet put Rath and Gordo down on a private runway on Hanscom Field, fifteen miles from Boston.

The nearest Home Depot was thirteen minutes away in Waltham.

They arrived comfortably before the nine-o'clock closing.

Gordo waited in the Town Car and dusted off a Family Fill Up meal from KFC.

Rath went in and walked to Aisle 10, Bay 4, his favorite.

He bought a five-roll multipack of industrial-strength duct tape.

30

Looking into the Sun

The guest room looked like a sophisticated boudoir. Floral wallpaper and elaborate drapes. A spray of silver-dollar eucalyptus branches rising from a Murano vase atop a Tiffany-blue nightstand. The mattress, elevated to a pharaonic summit atop a formidable box spring, nearly required a running board to mount and was princessified by a dust ruffle and a puffy duvet weighted for a Siberian winter. A reed diffuser breathed a suffocating blend of holly berry and spruce, the aroma thick enough to glaze a doughnut.

Tassels abounded.

Evan sat on the floor. Fully dressed. Leaning against the rucksack he'd retrieved from the car.

It had been roughly twenty-four hours since he'd dispatched Folgore in a Manhattan alley. Forty-eight since his ankle had been ensconced in an explosive device at the behest of the federal government.

And now? He was asphyxiating on the civet of a Winter Mantel reed diffuser.

Which somehow seemed worse.

He wanted to hurl the diffuser out the window. Lacquer over the rose-vine wallpaper with a pleasing gunmetal gray. Pull the duvet onto the floor to make a nest at a breathable altitude.

From downstairs he heard a creak of warped wood grinding.

He thumbed up the ecobee system. The cameras had been placed with amateurish dipshititude, offering limited vantages of key areas.

But sure enough, one of the kitchen windows had been shoved open.

Evan was on his feet, through the door, padding downstairs.

His ARES 1911 gripped in both hands, pointed down at the floor.

He swung around into the kitchen and spotted Deborah curled up on the cushions of the bow window. A cigarette projected from the knuckles of one slender white hand, and she was leaning to exhale through the gap she'd opened in the sash pane. She wore slippers and a white bathrobe secured high at the throat.

The muted television displayed a youthful Caucasian couple with vigorously bright faces kissing in a haze of soft falling snow before a Christmas-drenched house.

He holstered the pistol before she turned around.

"Caught in the act." She offered him a smirk, her lips pale, bare. "I smoke and my husband pretends not to know about it. I have to be respectful to maintain his suspension of disbelief, you see. No hard evidence." She closed her eyes into another drag and shot the smoke expertly out into the night air. That winning grin, ever so slightly compromised on the left side. "I've come a long way, baby."

The magazines had accompanied her onto the cushions. *Soap Opera Digest, US, Star.* One cover featured her leaving this very house; the wind had drawn back her hair, which looked brittle and thinning, and her face had been captured in an unflattering light, the stroke damage evident. The headline read BEAUTY TURNED TO BEAST!

She followed his gaze down. "Ah," she said. "They're awful, sure. But it's not them. It's everyone who . . . gobbles this up. There's been renewed interest in yours truly since they're doing a reboot

172

of my show. *Winds of Time*." She took in his blank reaction. "You're not exactly the demographic."

"No, ma'am."

On the TV a Hallmark Channel logo popped up briefly. Now the couple were at some sort of festival outside a barn among townsfolk sporting an array of holiday sweaters. Everything soft and warm and soothing like a not-too-hot bath. Evan could understand why Deborah might want to slip into this well-lit world devoid of shadows and sharp edges.

"Another paparazzo caught me at the Whole Foods perusing artisanal mustards. I told him, 'Darling, make us look younger. It'll sell more rags.' And see?" She tugged another magazine from the stack, already open to an internal spread of her grinning coyly: LOOKING GREAT AND LIVING LIFE AT 60! "To be clear, I am fifty-nine. They're shocked to report that I'm still 'living life' rather than just slowly decomposing after the midcentury mark as women are wont to do." Her eyes held a kind of soulful depth. "That's the cost of being an icon. Even a low-rent one. You see the disappointment on their faces, everywhere you go. They're angry with you."

"For aging?"

Another draw set the cigarette crackling. "For not staying a fantasy."

Something on the television drew Evan's focus. There she was, Deborah Seabrook, among the other actors at the snowy festival, wearing a whimsical scarf and pristine winter gloves. She gave the young man from the previous scene a maternal embrace and leaned close to offer him what seemed to be a few words of wisdom. Watching her perform the bland if tender role, Evan felt something twist inside him.

"Sounds claustrophobic," he said.

"That's a good word for it," Deborah said. "One needs to have a face to the public that seems personal but really isn't. You don't want it to be truly personal, and turns out they don't either."

She caught the direction of his focus, her own eyes ticking to the television. A cruel hall of mirrors: Deborah watching Deborah twine her sweatered arm in that of her fictional son as they traipsed through fake falling snow.

She gestured at the kitchen chair nearest, and Evan sat. "And then something happens that . . . rips a hole in the universe, and you realize that you've only been playacting all along."

She stubbed out the cigarette on the outside of the windowsill and then balled it up in a tiny preserves jar she produced Houdini-like, from a bathrobe pocket. "When those two police officers knocked on our door, I was holding a cup of coffee. I had to tell myself to set it down. My hand was trembling, so I knocked it over. Then I had to tell myself not to worry about the spill. It was dripping onto the carpet there"—a gesture through the wall—"and I had to tell myself not to worry about cleaning it up. Or the stain. That nothing I had ever worried about before mattered anymore or ever would again. How foolish and petty all my thoughts and concerns were. Pain just . . . skinning me alive, unwrapping me. I felt *bare*. And I could see the world with all its terribleness everywhere around me." She studied him. "I'd imagine you see that now and again. With your work."

"Yes."

"People at their most naked? Their most real?"

"I don't see people any other way."

"What a blessing."

He did not respond.

"And how lonely."

He said nothing.

"That is unless you have someone to look into you that way, too," Deborah said. "That's the most powerful thing."

"Being understood?"

She shook her head. "Men want to find someone who understands them. Women know they'll never be understood." She took out another cigarette, sniffed it, stuffed it back in the pack. "No. They want to be *known*. It's different. It's . . . hmm, intimacy. And when you have a child, the fierceness of feeling . . ." She shook her head, at a loss before the infinite. "I'm sure you had that from your parents."

Evan thought of the mother he'd known a few short weeks. Then of Joey's search for his biological father, a rodeo cowboy who ran up bar tabs in Blessing, Texas. The man had never once laid eyes on Evan.

He resisted the urge to shake his head.

"To love like that, it's a kind of ache," she continued. "Because you hate every bad thing the world could ever hold for them. And you hurt for them all the way through even when nothing's happened yet." A single tear clung to the tip of her nose, a perfect jewel. "And how many times does it not happen? The fall from the tree house. Choking on undercooked bacon. The not-too-bad car crash. And then? One day it does. And it's like you've been braced for it your whole life." Her voice lowered with a kind of awe. "But it's so much worse than anything you could have imagined. It makes you rethink hell. And heaven. You know what heaven would be for me now?"

Evan looked down at the table. In the mound of loose puzzle pieces, he made out a bright blue eye—Johnny's.

"To see him for one minute more doing something mundane," Deborah said. "Something I never bothered to pay attention to. Eating an apple. Picking at his dirty fingernails. To watch him watching TV. That's all heaven is. It was right there, every instant of my life before. And I couldn't see it."

Now in the mess of jigsaw strays, Evan spotted the outer edge of one of Ruby's almond-shaped eyes.

"Mason had that made," Deborah said of the puzzle. "One of those custom ones. He wanted Ruby to be able to put the family back together again. Thought it would be . . . hmm, therapeutic. But it just sits there. And sits there."

She looked back out at the darkness, and it was clear that she was done talking. On the television the holiday tale came to a soft-focus close, the end credits rolling in fast-forward.

As Evan rose silently to leave, Deborah's name flashed by, there and gone.

He left her with her thoughts.

31

Steve the White Pimp

The hard part was getting the glass straw to stay lodged in the nostril. You'd think it would've been the other considerations—immobilizing the subject, duct-taping the head in place, getting the accoutrements there intact and hungry.

But no.

It was embedding the straw in the nostril firmly enough that it wouldn't blow out with each frenzied exhalation but not so hard that it would clot up with blood.

Rathsberger didn't mind pimps, but he fucking hated *white* pimps.

This dickhole was named Steve, the worst pimp name ever. He drove a 1988 Cadillac with a hula dancer suctioned on the dashboard and wore a shiny pleather jacket with pronounced lapels. A scuzzy loudmouth, he pressed pretty, broke neighborhood girls into service in the Back Bay, Cambridge, and Newton, and shipped the ugly ones off to Atlanta and Vegas.

His thick, curly blond hair had made steering easier. They'd caught him just past the box hedges at the door of his row house,

Gordo grabbing him by the mane and propelling him inside. Steve lived in an end unit, the place next door vacant, which provided beneficial privacy.

Mattapan was shady as fuck, which made the whole thing easy-peasy. No need for recon, lookouts, discretion. The next stop would be different, would require finesse.

Once they'd crossed the threshold, they'd learned that Steve the White Pimp had a ratty medium-size dog with wiry gray-black hair. But she didn't bark or get protective. Her ribs were showing, and she cowered and sniffed at their cuffs even as they tussled with Steve. Rath got the sense that she wasn't too fond of her owner, and he couldn't blame her. What self-respecting dog wants to answer to a white pimp named Steve? Rath related to her buttugliness—the bitch was like a living bottle brush—and he admired her absence of loyalty.

To ensure that Steve didn't move around too much, Gordo had sat on him while Rath severed both of his ACLs, an easy Ka-Bar punch through the U at the base of each thighbone.

That eighties rocker hair provided superb adhesion for the duct tape, which Rath had wrapped around Steve's head and the chipped wooden table of the kitchen more times than he could count. Steve's arms were trapped on the underside of the table, his shoes stuck to the floor, his right cheek smashed flat to the nicked surface. Loops of tape covered the top of his head and his chin, but his mouth and nose were exposed, as well as the band of his eyes. It was important that he take in what was about to happen.

He was crying, snot threatening to clog the straw.

The place was a shithole, splintered floorboards and drafty windows, mousetraps and Chinese take-out cartons on the kitchen counter. It smelled of mold and dog piss. There was no furniture in the main area except for the rickety table and a sticky couch that would fluoresce under a black light. There were only two chairs, one of which they'd considerately adhered to Steve to support his inoperable legs. Rath sat backward in the other, his arms crossed along the top rail, facing him.

Not wanting to risk an encounter with the couch, Gordo had settled on the floor, tumbling the final inches and landing hard

enough to creak the foundation. He'd torn a sheet out of his doo-
dle notebook and was busy folding it into something with his sau-
sage fingers. The ratty dog had taken up at Gordo's side, sitting
and watching the proceedings with sad, wet eyes.

With effort Rath could ratchet shut the scarred right side of his
mouth, but he felt the lower lip tugging down now, wet with saliva.
He fingered the point of his Ka-Bar; he'd already cleaned it in the
sink, which held two dead cockroaches and a puddle of olive pits.
"There's a way to take someone's eye out and turn it clear around
so they can see their own ear," he said. "But I've never done that.
Need proper medical training, I think, to keep the optic nerves
intact."

Steve the White Pimp snuffled. "I don't know what you want,
man. But I got people. People who'll come looking for you."

"They say a decapitated head can still see for ten seconds, but
that's a crock," Rath said. "They always pass out from the shock.
Not so much as a blink of recognition. So." He pulled the test tube
out of his pocket and waggled it, sending the contents into a frenzy.
"We set up something more fun."

"What the fuck is *that*? Wait—just wait, okay? Just hang on.
What did I do? I can make it right. Look, you've made your point,
okay? I won't fuck with you. If I overlapped with . . . with a friend
of yours, a daughter, whatever, I can make it right."

"Oh," Rath said, "We don't care about any of that. We care about
your big mouth."

With the scrap paper, Gordo had made a fortune-teller like the
ones schoolgirls played with, four origami pinchers with hidden
flaps and messages. Grinning with childish pleasure, he snapped
the beaks open and closed in different patterns with his enormous
thumbs and index fingers. The dog observed, cocking her head
with interest. Rath could see that he'd drawn doodles on some of
the flaps.

Gordo could be a hoot.

Steve the White Pimp wheezed a little, drawing Rath's focus
once more.

"You see, Steve, you talk too much," Rath told him. "Whining
to anyone who'll listen. And we were happy to let you do that in

your own little cesspool here, but recent events have made that . . . inconvenient. So." He fixed him with an ugly glare. "You know how this ends, don't you?"

"What . . ." A tendril of drool leaked from the corner of Steve's mouth, thin as a spider thread. Rivulets of blood darkened his jeans, striping the denim from knee to ankle. He tried to jerk his legs, but his duct-taped shoes didn't budge and the internal work of the tendons in his knees made him go stock-still with pain. A guttering breath until he could talk again. "What have I been talking too much about?"

Rath removed the stopper. "That doesn't matter anymore."

"But you don't have to do this. Why do you have to do *this*?"

"Maybe he's right," Rath mused. One of the captives had made it up out of the test tube and circled the lip. Its cutting mandibles trembled. An inch and a half was a lot of ant. "What do you think, Gordo? Should we give him a fighting chance?"

"Yes." Spit bubbled at Steve's lips. "Yes please yes please yes please."

Rath asked, "What's his fortune say?"

Gordo grinned wide. A game. He worked the paper fortune-teller open and closed, open and closed. The dog leaned forward and gave it a sniff. Gordo paused, angled the spread paper cup at Steve. "Choose a number."

"What?"

"Choose. A. Number."

Steve's visible eye bulged and strained. It was funny how an eyeball looked moving around when the head couldn't. "Th-three."

Gordo peeled up the matching flap. Stared at it. "Uh-oh."

"What, man? *What?*" The glass straw protruding from Steve's nostril bobbed with agitation.

Gordo turned the fortune-teller to face the other men. Beneath the numeral was a drawing of a big red ant with jagged jaws.

A row of wiggly creases appeared on Gordo's shiny forehead. "Thass too bad." Frowning down at the paper, he lifted the other flaps. "Whoops," he said. "Looks like I messed up. They're *all* ants."

Leaning in at Steve, Rath gripped the glass straw to steady it and brought the tip of the test tube to meet the tiny opening. There

was some spillage, the diameter only wide enough to accommodate one ant at a time. Finally the living jumble worked itself out
into a flow. Urged by gravity, the bull ants began to stream up the
throat of the straw.

Steve kept one bloodshot eye pegged hard to the side, watching
as the parade approached his face. His grunts yielded to a hoarse
scream that sent flecks of saliva across the wood. But he couldn't
look away.

Though it was an elaborate technique, Rath hoped it wouldn't
stretch too far into the night.

After all, they still had to drive out to Wellesley.

32

Mr. Hard Boundaries

"Sue Ann's Organic Enemas. How can I provide excellent service for you today?"

Staring at the panoply of guest-room tassels, Evan hesitated before replying into the RoamZone, "Tommy?"

Stojack's voice came crisply over the line. "You already spelunking up my sphincter about your replacement truck? You just ordered it."

"No," Evan said. "I need you to arrange a safe house for me."

"I thought you had 'em scattered everywhere like rat turds."

"Not in Boston."

"You want me to set up a safe house in *Boston*? I am an icon of masculinity and a marksman par excellence. Not a fucking travel agent."

A feminine voice cut in. "I can do it."

"Joey?" Evan was on his feet, pacing beside the regal bed, the scent of Winter Mantel diffuser threatening to choke him. "What are you doing? This is an encrypted line."

"Duh," she said. "I'm the one who updated the encryption protocols for you."

"Get off the goddamned call."

Tommy laughed a low, raspy laugh that threatened to deteriorate into a coughing fit. "Hiya, Joey."

"Tommy! Hi!"

"Ain't it cute how his voice gets all tense when he's mad?" Tommy asked.

"Seriously," Joey said. "And he's probably doing that tight-jaw thing, you know, when the corners flex out?"

Evan made an effort to unclench his teeth. "I can't have you popping onto this line, Joey. That's a hard boundary."

"Well," Tommy said, "I'm gonna let you two dog-sniff each other's butts and get this domestic matter resolved. Time for me to rack out."

He hung up.

"So," Joey said. "Does this mean you *don't* need me to set up a safe house in Boston for you?"

"You can't do this again," Evan said. "Ever."

"Got it, Mr. Hard Boundaries. Maybe that should be your new code name. Especially since you're having trouble keeping your comms secure, which seems kinda important if you're running around calling yourself the N—"

"*Josephine.*"

"'Kay. What do you need? Where are you?"

"I'm staying at the Seabrooks' house—"

"You're *what*?"

A long, cold silence Evan was at a loss for how to interpret.

"Mr. Hard Boundaries?" Joey's tone was suddenly, intensely angry. "Staying with a fucking client? Two seconds ago you were, like, in *federal custody.*"

"Ruby had been threatened, so she asked me to—"

"Oh, well, she *asked*. That all makes sense now. There's this thing called the Fourth Commandment you used to care about. 'Never make it—'"

"She's a nineteen-year-old kid who—"

"'—personal.' You can't just blow up your operational protocols.

What is she, like, your surrogate daughter now? Sure you don't want to move in for good, pick out curtains together?"

"She's been through a lot."

"Yeah? Did she survive growing up in the foster-care system?"

"No."

"Has she been hunted and shot by government assassins?"

"No."

"Can she tunnel data over DNS and ICMP packets so she can exfiltrate it without detection?"

"Not that I'm awa—"

"Then I'm not impressed. I mean, look at her life. Look at her *gear*. MacBook Pro, iPhone—she's running a fucking Brother scanner-printer from Staples. She's so *basic*. And her social media, making all these, like, literary allusions, like, 'Look how educated I am.'"

"What are you talking about, Joey? What's going on?"

"I'm just sick of it. How much everyone cares so much about some people when they're not even worth it and not at all about others."

"You don't know what anyone's worth." The door was closed, but Evan made sure to keep his voice down. "You're a sixteen-year-old girl. Not a moral authority."

"No? Who is, then? The assholes running everything? Politicians? Luke Devine? The president? Tell me, X. Who's doing such an excellent job with the moral stewardship of the world that I don't have to worry my pretty little head about it?"

"Joey. Her brother's throat was slit. That's all I care about. The rest is just words."

"No," Joey said. "Fuck that. You know how many of *my* friends died? Foster siblings? Drug use, domestic abuse, shot by cops. And I didn't get to boo-hoo all over social media and have the fucking president of the United States get involved three minutes later."

"That's not how it—"

"Up there in Richville, when something happens to *them*, it's an outrage. All of a sudden it's, like, what? Life might not be fair for *us*? *We* might be powerless? *Our* kids might not be safe? And then the whole world comes crashing to a halt and pays attention to *them* and forgets about everyone else. It's been three days since you got captured, and I almost could've never seen you again, and now you're only paying attention to—"

She caught herself. She was breathing hard, emotion brimming, threatening to break, and he knew she was mortified for what she'd revealed.

"No," Evan said. "I'm not. I won't."

"You will," Joey said. "Everyone always does."

Her anger had burned off. There was nothing left but a lifetime of heartbreak, of being reacquainted time and again with her own insignificance. He knew that pain himself, knew it deep down where he could pretend to forget it most of the time.

He sensed that what he said to her next could matter more than anything he'd ever told her.

A piercing screech sounded from downstairs.

The alarm.

The house had been breached.

ARES drawn, he hurtled toward the door. "Damn it," he said. "Joey. I have to go. I'll call you back."

"Sure," she said, and hung up.

33

Inefficient Idiocy

Bundled in her bathrobe, Deborah stood in the hallway of the ground floor, staring up at the hockey puck of the smoke detector in the ceiling and looking shockingly unalarmed.

She lifted an eyebrow archly. "Evan No-Last-Name," she said, "we have to stop meeting like this."

The detector screeched again like a ravenous pterodactyl.

"What the hell," Evan said, holstering his gun, "is that noise?"

"The battery needs to be changed," she said.

"*That's* the low-battery alert?" It was the worst sound he had ever heard in his life. "It sounds like an incoming-missile siren."

"Yes." She dragged a chair over from the defunct telephone nook. "And, miraculously, they only go off in the middle of the night to create maximum psychological distress. Don't you have one?"

Evan had electronic noses with quartz-crystal microbalance sensor arrays and AI pattern-recognition systems embedded in the door and window frames that could detect and analyze the slightest trace of smoke, airborne pathogens, or dangerous gases. When triggered, they sent a three-toned distress signal to his RoamZone and threw a colored sunrise simulation into the room during sleeping hours.

He said, "No."

Deborah stepped up onto the chair, wobbled a bit as she reached for the ceiling. Another life-ending screech vibrated Evan's brain and nearly sent her toppling.

He said, "Why don't you let me—"

With a wrench she twisted the circular unit free, ripped out the battery, and let both pieces tumble to the carpet.

They breathed the blissful silence.

Evan offered his hand, and she took it daintily and stepped down. She gave him a smile. "As long as we're up," she said, "we might as well eat something."

"You need to send Norris," Rath said into the phone.

The Town Car bobbed smoothly along 1-95 toward the airport. Sitting beside him, Gordo crushed the second of two Nacho Party Packs from Taco Bell. He'd balanced each tray on the wide ledge of a thigh. Sucking liquid cheese from his thumb, he was content to leave Rath to deal with Tenpenny.

"Why can't you just finish out the job?" Tenpenny's voice held its trademark irritation.

"Because the Seabrook girl lives in a fancy-ass college town." Rath scratched the burned morass of his right cheek, which the car heater had set tickling. "They got neighborhood watch, private security patrols, all that shit."

"So you want me to send the black guy?"

"Hell yeah. Everyone'll be too politically correct to call the cops on Double N. You know how rich white people are."

"You're there right now. I need this done."

"Sure. Send Gordo waddling in. He looks like Jabba the Hutt. And I look like Jabba the Hutt's ballsack."

Gordo snorted. "That's us, *semper malus*."

"Fine," Tenpenny said. "Get back to the jet. I'll pay Norris's ass to go tomorrow morning. By nightfall I want the girl to be past tense."

Deborah left her cigarette in the ashtray on the window ledge, the tendril of smoke sucked out through the crack into the cool night air. She opened the freezer and refrigerator doors, took a moment to lean in and breathe the coolness, and when she turned around, her arms held a shelf of items—brown soda bottles, ice-cream carton, two freezer-chilled parlor glasses.

She set them down carefully on the kitchen table, took another drag of her cigarette, stooped to blow, then got to work fixing root-beer floats. "I did all that discipline stuff," she said. "My whole life. But now? When I most should? I don't want to. I want to drink root-beer floats and get fat. *Fatter.*"

She was perfectly slender, but Evan decided that hearing that from him right now was not what she wanted.

She slid a float across to him.

"No, thank you," he said.

"Oh, shut up."

Leaning back on the cushions of the bow window, she took a loud slurp through a straw and followed with another drag from the contraband cigarette. Stubbing it out, she tucked it away in another miniature preserves jar that once again appeared in her palm like a close-up magic trick.

The east-facing bow windows were heavily tinted, but even so Evan made sure to choose a chair out of the sight line from the street. "Doesn't the smoke alarm wake up the others?" he asked.

"Yes, but they pretend it doesn't," she said. "It's a domestic game, you see. Whoever finally can't stand it has to tend to it."

The lights in the side yard clicked on, as well as a second set on the front porch. Deborah clocked the sudden illumination with raised eyebrows.

"I reprogrammed the timers," Evan said. "Through your network."

"Ah," she said. "Home security."

A creaking of the stairs drew his focus, and a moment later Ruby entered, rubbing her eyes. "Hey, Mom."

Deborah said, "Sweetheart."

"Hi, guard dog."

Evan said, "Sweetheart."

"Which kind?" Ruby asked, chinning at the table.

"Sorry?" Evan said.

"There is a generational Seabrookian root-beer-float debate. A&W. Or Mug."

"I don't drink root-beer floats," Evan said.

"Oh, shut up." Ruby retrieved a bottle of Mug and made herself a float. She held the ice-cream carton at arm's length, reading the nutritional facts. "A serving is a *third* of a cup? Who the hell eats a *third* of a cup of ice cream? Smurfs? Screw you, calorie content. At least announce yourself honestly." She vigorously spooned several peels of vanilla into her glass. "I'm gonna hate-eat half the carton now."

"That's my girl," Deborah said. "You show that prevaricating ice cream."

Evan couldn't get his mind off Joey. Was she right that people like the Seabrooks got undue attention? Or was she just mad at his priorities?

What inefficient idiocy, he thought, to be preoccupied with someone else's feelings.

There was more movement in the house, and then Mason padded into the kitchen, wrapped in a royal-blue bathrobe. He sniffed the air. "Wow," he said. "This kitchen. It's so . . . well ventilated."

Deborah said, *"Mason."*

His eyes pulled to the float sitting untouched before Evan. "A&W?" he asked. "Or Mug?"

"I don't drink root-beer floats," Evan said.

"Of course not." Mason trudged to the refrigerator and lifted out the bottle of A&W.

Ruby sneered at her father. "Root-beer barbarian."

He scooped a ball of ice cream into his glass and then poured healthily. "Uncouth soda jerk."

"Johnny liked Mug better," Ruby said.

The abrupt silence was so complete that Evan could hear the bubbles popping in the froth of his untouched float. The Seabrooks stirred their drinks, stared down into them.

Evan wished he could think of one goddamned thing to say.

"You told me," Mason finally said to Deborah, "that we should never shame someone for finding joy."

"Mason," Deborah said. "I don't think we need to revisit—"

"For Johnny? Everything came so easily to him." Mason was looking at Evan now, but it seemed he wasn't talking to him. "Girls, sports. And if it didn't, he didn't care about it. I wanted him to find something to excel at. But he never wanted to bust his ass for anything. Never had to." In the dim light of the kitchen, his beard looked multicolored, gray and brown and black and blond. "I was so hard on him. It wasn't until he was gone that I realized . . . what he excelled at? Was being happy."

It was rare to see a grown man cry so readily.

Deborah rose and embraced him, cradling his head from behind.

He clutched her wrist. Ruby pulled her legs beneath her on the padded chair and leaned her head against Mason's arm. She was crying, too. Deborah slung her other arm around her, and they hugged as a family of three.

Feeling intensely out of place, Evan stood. "Better get ready for tomorrow."

"What's tomorrow?" Deborah asked.

"If Ruby was threatened," Evan said, "it's likely that the people around Angela Buford were threatened as well. Someone's scared about what might come out."

"Buford's from Mattapan," Deborah said. "There's a reason they call it 'Murderpan.'"

Evan said, "I'm not gonna get the answers I need in Wellesley."

"I want to go with you," Ruby said.

"No," Evan said.

"You said you'd stay with me."

"That's true," Evan said. "But it . . ."

"What?" Deborah asked.

"It doesn't work this way. That neighborhood's not safe for her."

"You said you could protect her." Mason had produced a handkerchief and cleaned up his face. "No matter what."

"That's true. But—"

"She's a capable young woman," Mason said. "And this is what she wants. Are you here to help her? Or not?"

34

An Overwhelming Sense of Déjà Vu

Ruby beamed in the passenger seat of Evan's purloined rental car. "I've never been to Mattapan."

After leafy Wellesley the blocks here looked even more dilapidated. Dense streets crammed with triple-deckers, a few mid-century split-levels, and homes with peeling vinyl siding, barred windows, and sagging porches on the verge of decomposing into overgrown weeds. A few burned-out houses, a number more boarded up with mortgage-foreclosure signs nailed to the doors like MARTIN LUTHER'S NINETY-FIVE THESES minus the reformist optimism.

Turning onto Blue Hill Avenue, Evan was hit with a familiar sense of vibrancy and agitation. A number of beautiful former synagogues had been repurposed as Haitian Baptist and Black Pentecostal churches. Mom-and-pop shops advertised rent-to-own furniture, hair braiding, and pay-per-minute cell phones. Caribbean women with headwraps ushered their children along uneven sidewalks. Middle-aged men with dreads sucked off-brand cigarettes. Teens congregated in clusters, their baggy pants low-slung. Gang signs and love letters encoded as graffiti-embellished walls, sidewalks, billboards, and even one unfortunate street dog.

It was a hood not unlike the one Evan had grown up in. Different cultures and currents but the same muddy-rich water he'd pulled himself out of. He felt more comfortable here than in the arid atmosphere of Wellesley.

For the past few blocks, Ruby had gone speechless, a not-unwelcome development, staying focused on the fearsome new world revealing itself beyond her window. A homeless man emerged from an alley without pants, his teeth rotted to tiny nubs. A girl who couldn't have been older than seven watched her younger siblings play in a cracked wading pool devoid of water. She held a baby on her hip with maternal dexterity, his diaper sliding down. An ancient boxy Jaguar glided by, the hood rusted, bass booming from woofers. Painted on the driver's door in black: *Is there a problem, officer?* The dude slumped in the passenger seat smiled at Evan menacingly, gold grill gleaming. When the Jag accelerated away, the modified engine sounded like it might rip a hole in the fabric of the universe.

As the noise faded, Ruby said, "I can't believe this is a half hour from my house."

Joey's words swirled around in Evan's head, and he felt his hackles go up. He'd had dozens of foster brothers representing an assortment of shades and stations. Remembering the First Commandment, he sought to clarify. "It's dangerous," he asked, "having people like this close to your neighborhood?"

"No," she said. "It makes me so upset. No one's taking care of anything."

"A lot of people here," Evan said, "take care of a lot."

"I'm not saying that. I mean . . ." She struggled to grab the tail of a thought. "Did you see that little girl back there?" Her eyes misted. "Taking care of all her siblings? And all those moms alone with their kids . . ." Her anger felt thin, a veneer to hold in more complex emotions. "Why aren't they getting real help? It's just . . . as an empowered woman? It pisses me off."

"It should piss you off no matter what you are."

She held her hand to her mouth and stared out the window some more. The sights were no more uplifting.

Turning onto a dead-end street lined with drab buildings, Evan was hit with an overwhelming sense of déjà vu. Patches of dead grass, faded red stone, bathtub-size balconies crowded with burst armchairs and rusting bikes. Another dismal government project aimed at producing cheap housing. He'd lived in these apartments before. He knew the shortcuts the city builders had taken, how the toilets didn't flush unless you pulled the chain in the tank, the way the breeze blew right through the prison-small window frames, that in the winter you had to wear a jacket to sleep and that the rooms turned into broilers during peak summer hours. He knew what wasn't in the refrigerators. The water stains on the ceilings. The tattered clothes always a size too small. When all you could do is hold on for something, anything to get better.

Two low-riders were parked nose to nose, blocking the road. Young men sat on the hoods and trunks, drinking from brown paper bags. They wore flat-bill hats and pristine sneakers. Their eyes were pinked up, and they looked restless, directionless, dangerous.

They looked like Evan and the other boys from the Pride House Home.

As Evan coasted up to the roadblock, they set down their bottles and slid off their positions. They surrounded the Buick Regal. Ruby made a little noise in the back of her throat.

Evan said, "Stay here," and got out, leaving the car running.

The locks clicked behind him, Ruby taking precautions.

The leader approached Evan, standing uncomfortably close. The kid couldn't have been twenty years old. He wasn't the biggest of the bunch, but he had the requisite gleam in his eyes. Handsome, too. In another life he could've been a movie star. His shirt was unbuttoned, showing off a white sleeveless undershirt and the handle of a crappy 9-mil Ruger with a turquoise frame. One of the boys standing behind him looked like he could be a starting lineman in the NFL.

The leader ducked down to peer in the passenger window. "Who's the pretty white girl?"

"A friend."

"Yeah? A lotta out-of-town motherfuckers like you bring 'friends' 'round here, know what I'm sayin'? Maybe we do something about it this time."

Evan said, "Mind clarifying?"

"These aren't fucking whorehouses. These aren't pedo crash pads. We live here, know what I'm sayin'? Our *moms* live here. I don't care who the fuck you paid off on this block for an hour of time where your wife can't find you. You come in here and do your dirty shit with some white bitch and guess who deals with the fallout when her long-lost daddy calls the PD?"

"I'm not here for that," Evan said. "I want to ask a few questions at ninety two eff three."

Door 90 on the street, second floor, third door. According to Joey's report, that's where the super who managed Angela Buford's building lived.

"Questions 'bout what?" the leader asked.

"About Angela Buford."

"Never heard of her."

"Fuck that, Mack," the big kid said. "I say you chin-check this motherfucker."

Evan stared at Mack evenly. "What respect do you want me to show you to get past?"

Mack hiked up the leg of his loose baggy jeans, showing off old-school Wheat Nubuck Timberland 6"s with the laces undone. He flashed a matinee-idol smile. "Why don't you kiss my boots?"

The others laughed and fanned around Evan in a semicircle, thrumming with low energy like idling cars. Ruby had cracked the window to hear, her flushed face all but pressed to the glass.

Evan said, "Ask for something real."

He held eye contact with Mack even as the others jeered and murmured.

He knew Mack would understand from his stare alone. That he didn't have to do the usual, *Look at me and ask yourself: Do I look scared?* routine. That he was unafraid to escalate the confrontation as far as it needed to escalate. That his request for safe passage had been in good faith.

Mack tilted his head back, sucked his teeth. "Okay. We grew up here. This is *our* hood. It's just us who take care of it, know what I'm sayin'? So don't come and start shit that we have to clean up or act like whyever you're better out there entitles you to a damn thing in here."

"I understand. I'm asking questions. That's it."

Mack nodded. "A few questions."

"If someone starts shit," Evan said, "I might have to rough them up some. Is that okay?"

"If *they* start it?" Mack nodded again. "Yeah."

Evan held out his hand.

Mack stared at it for a moment before shaking. He flicked his chin at his compatriots, and they hopped into the vehicles and backed them up, allowing just enough room for a car to pass through.

Evan went around to the driver's door of the Buick Regal and knuckle-tapped. Ruby unlocked it. She was still wearing her seat belt.

Evan drove slowly through the gap toward the end of the cul-de-sac, faces watching them from either side.

Ruby blew out a breath. "That was incredible." Her voice was ratcheted high, the excited afterglow of fear. "You backed that guy down. All of them. That was badass."

"I didn't back anyone down. I asked for permission." Evan pulled to the curb in front of Angela's building. "And, besides, I'm surprised that impressed you. I mean, as an 'empowered woman.'"

"We want our men to be modern," Ruby said. "We don't want them to be *pussies*."

35

The Kill Site

The super was a fastidious little old man, his apartment crammed with supplies stacked in small labeled boxes. Door latches, drain cleaner, toilet flappers, caulking guns, paint. The place smelled intensely of dust, or perhaps he did. He stood blocking the doorway with his body, which Evan assumed was just habit since he couldn't imagine that he and Ruby looked like a problematic duo.

"Angela Buford," the super said. "The double murder upstairs. Right. Right." He had a pair of wire-frame glasses that he took off and polished on his shirt. On top of the dust, he smelled of shaving cream and aftershave. "It was a mess. Can't rent her room out no more. It was awful. That poor young woman, like so many here."

"Can we see the apartment?"

The man had no eyebrows, but the shiny patches above his eyes knitted together. "You're not PD," he said. "So why would I let you do that?"

Evan started to answer, but Ruby clasped his arm gently and

leaned forward. "The boy whose body was dumped there. He was my brother."

"Right." The man's eyes peered out earnestly through the round lenses. "I'm . . . I'm very sorry. Hold, please." He stepped away, running the tips of his fingers along a row of keys hanging on tiny brass hooks on the wall. Plucking one off, he shouldered past them. "Let's go."

On the way up the stairs, Evan asked, "What can you tell me about Angela?"

"Well, aaaaah. She wasn't really known as Angela around here."

"What was she known as?"

"Desiree."

"Desiree?"

"What I said."

Evan remembered what Echo had told him about Angela—*wrote poetry on driftwood, shot it in sepia filters, that sort of shit.* "Was that her influencer name?" he asked.

The super came to the next landing and leaned on the rail a moment, winded. "Influencer? I wouldn't say that."

"What would you say?"

The man straightened up, all five foot four of him, his glasses fogged from exertion. He pressed through onto the next floor and paused by the first door on the left. "She was a working girl," he said.

Ruby looked at Evan, puzzled, and then she got it.

"She wanted to be more," the super said. "But this is what she had."

He unlocked the door and armed it open. They eased inside.

It wasn't really an apartment, more of a room, as he'd said. Sparse decorations still in place. A faded pink bedspread over a twin bed. Moth-eaten silk pillowcase. Plastic set of drawers. The door to the tiny bathroom was open, a blow dryer resting on the floor, still plugged in. A poster of a Jamaican beach thumbtacked to the wall showed teal waters and white sand. Evan wondered if she'd ever been.

There was an amoeba-shaped splotch on the floor near the window.

Evan had the crime-scene photos in his RoamZone. Angela had been thrown onto the bed, facedown, left arm twisted beneath her. The shoulder had been pulled from the socket posthumously, no doubt when her body was hauled from the kill site. Johnny had been discovered right there at their feet, his head over the stain in the floorboards. There hadn't been a lot of bleeding since his body was moved, but there'd been drainage from his slit neck and orifices as his body had decomposed.

Ruby was frozen, staring at the splotch, her shoulders up around her ears.

Evan said, "Can you give us a moment?"

"I can't leave you in here."

"Just a moment," Evan said.

The super looked at Ruby, then down at his shoes. "I'll wait in the hall."

He crossed to the bathroom, unplugged the blow dryer, then withdrew quietly.

Evan moved toward Ruby. When he brushed her shoulder, she started. Her eyes were wide and a bit wild.

She looked back at the floor. Crouched. Reached for the stain, her fingers trembling.

"Johnny," she said. "This was Johnny."

Evan said, "Yes."

She sank more, her knees striking the floor. "Was he . . . ?" Her throat seemed to have dried up, so she paused to swallow. "Was he left faceup? Or facedown?"

"Facedown."

She lowered to all fours, the discolored patch right under her. Then she eased herself flat to mirror the stain below.

Lying right where Johnny had, perfectly still, her head turned.

A bead of water swelled at the corner of her left eye. It forded the bridge of her nose, ran beneath her other eye, joined the darkness on the floor.

Mack and his crew were right where Evan had left them, the road once again closed by the gate of their vehicles. Evan stopped and got out.

"Desiree," he said to Mack. "Her name was Desiree."

"Oh, man," Mack said. "Desi? Why didn't you just say so?"

"I didn't know to."

"She's Tawnda's cousin," Mack said. "Took a jaunt to NYC, was gonna meet her a real sugar daddy."

"She went to New York?"

"That's right."

"About a year ago?"

"That's right. 'Member her pimp rolled out here, hollering at everyone, lost himself a good piece of business, know what I'm sayin'? We told her she'd be back like everyone comes back. But next time she showed up here, she was dead. With that boy."

Mack looked through the window at Ruby. The rims of her eyes and edges of her nostrils were red. She was staring straight ahead at the dashboard, at nothing.

Mack's eyes stabbed back at Evan, angry. "You hurt that girl?"

"No," Evan said. "She's the sister. Of that boy."

Mack pawed at his mouth.

Evan said, "Got an address for the pimp?"

"Ain't you learned, motherfucker?" Mack flashed that million-dollar smile, and Evan thought he was maybe the most handsome kid he'd seen in his life. "I got everything 'round here."

Evan rang the doorbell twice, but no one answered. Ruby was back in the car, still within eyeshot. She hadn't spoken a word since they'd left Angela Buford's place.

He stood on the ledge of a concrete planter to peer through the barred transom above the front door. Then he knocked a few times.

He heard tiny footsteps inside. Then panting.

A dog wobbled into view from around the corner. Pink tongue dangling, coat like a porcupine, dark around the muzzle.

Something seemed off.

Evan knocked once more, drawing the dog forward another few steps.

Her muzzle looked slick, matted. A drop fell from it, hitting the floor in a patch of thrown sun.

Bloodred.

The dog ambled forward some more, leaving crimson paw prints in her wake.

Evan hopped down, checked on Ruby sitting quietly in the car.

The lock was robust enough to suit the neighborhood. It took Evan a good two minutes with a snake rake and a tension wrench before it yielded.

The smell. He knew the smell.

The dog approached him and yipped a few times, droplets spraying from her bloody muzzle. Then she darted off.

Evan followed the bloody paw prints in reverse, the main room drawing into view.

Duct tape adhered the pimp to a wooden table, his arms secured beneath, his feet bonded to the floor. A strip of saturated denim on his leg looked to have been lapped at roughly by the dog. The visible band of the man's face was twisted at an unnatural angle, contorted in pain and swollen nearly beyond human recognition. Nose and lips enflamed, puffed-up flesh bulging the eyes outward, skin afire with a shiny rash that looked moist. A glass tube stuck up from the top nostril like a golf flagstick.

Not wanting to step in the tacky patch near the man's feet, Evan kept his distance. He had seen plenty of crime scenes, but none like this. He wondered what the hell had gone down here.

A faint movement by the rouged lips drew Evan's attention, the skin seeming to bubble outward. Then something broke the seal of the mouth, pushing through.

A red ant.

Nearly two inches long.

Even from halfway across the room, Evan could make out its jagged mandibles.

He backed out of the room, through the front door, and closed it in his wake.

As he turned, a piece of trash fluttering in the box hedges caught his attention, an ant drawn on one crumpled edge. He picked it up, smoothed it out. A scribble of numbers and images.

He turned the sheet of paper over.

A rough sketch on the back showed a cooked turkey, plump and ridiculous, a wing squiggling at the side, femur bones protruding. But that wasn't what froze Evan's breath in his throat.

In place of a turkey head, a human's was drawn instead, cartoon features looking shocked and scared on the serving platter.

The face of Ruby Seabrook.

36

Monsters

"We say there's no such thing as monsters." Ruby's voice was flat, without intonation.

Racing back to Wellesley, Evan had the speedometer pegged well above the limit. The grotesque drawing was folded up in his back pocket. He hadn't given her details of what he'd seen in the row house, only that the pimp had been killed. It was clear that her mind was still back on the floor of Angela Buford's room, that stain like a chalk outline.

"But then what the hell is a bear?" she said. "If it was, say, a giant reptile with scales that lived in the jungle, we'd think it was a monster. Then some scientist would name it. *Bearius reptilius*. Then we'd all be, like, 'Cool, we named it. Now it's not a monster.' But it's *still* a monster. It doesn't become something less just because we name it."

She swung her gaze to him, and he could see in her expression the full measure of her shock. The earth had cracked open beneath her feet, and she was in free fall. He knew it, the dizzying aftermath of trauma, where the world and your place in it zoom in and out, when notions of dimensions and scale no longer hold, when you're reminded that you're a speck floating through an experiential infinity you cannot possibly comprehend.

"And, well . . ." She scratched at the side of her nose too hard, raising a welt. "People can be like that, too, even if we give them a name. Monsters."

Evan leaned on the gas pedal some more. "Yes," he said.

When Evan entered Mason's office, the middle-aged woman on the couch started as if zapped with a cattle prod, her profusion of wooden jewelry rattling like a rustic wind chime. A Kleenex box rested near her elbow on a side table, and there was an Arrowhead water cooler and a lonely daisy tilting from a crystal vase on the desk.

Mason stiffened in his Le Corbusier lounge chair. "I'm in session," he said in a tight voice. "You can't just come barging in here. This is a safe space."

"Not anymore," Evan said.

Evan had two things Devine's men wouldn't be expecting.

The element of surprise.

And the ecobee network that gave him surveillance angles around the home's perimeter.

Joey had arranged a safe house for the Seabrooks in the form of a long-term Airbnb under a false account she'd created; the owner was even a Superhost. She'd done the job as well as she did every job, the instructions texted to Evan with passive-aggressive curtness. He'd tried calling her, but she hadn't picked up.

After he'd conveyed the Seabrooks to their new location, he had rearranged the camera angles in the Wellesley house to make sure he had maximum visibility before the attack he anticipated to come at nightfall.

He'd pulled the living-room armchair around on the carpet to face the front door. Dusk drained color from the sky, turning the drawn curtains pale yellow and then a ghostly gray. As night came on, he switched off the interior lights. He kept the RoamZone on one knee showing various vantages, his ARES 1911 on the other.

He waited and he breathed, bringing attention first to the bottoms of his feet, his calves, his hip flexors. Then rising up his body, inhaling into each space, directing oxygen, smoothing out knots and discomfort. The fascia of his right cheek remained tense, and he brought a few full breath cycles to it. On the third exhalation, it released, sending a twinge down his neck, through his shoulder, and all the way to the tip of his pinkie. The world slowed down, turning him from matter into focus, connecting him to himself.

Spirit. Derived from Latin and ancient Greek words for *breath*.

Without respiration, there was nothing. And with it he *became* nothing. That's what it all was for—the meditation, the yin yoga he used to pry his body open most nights. Using breath like a bellows to stretch past pain, to yield into new spaces, intercostals bowing outward, the small of his back unstitching itself, his chest cracking open, ribs splayed forward.

He thought about Joey's and Ruby's outrage at the world. Unfairness writ large on the streets of Mattapan, across the face of Mack and his crew of lost boys. How there was nothing left of Johnny Seabrook but a stain on a tenement floor and how Angela Buford changed names and aspirations trying to find a better version of herself. Evan didn't care about the Secret Service or President Donahue-Carr or Luke Devine. They had their own levers to pull, their own untraceable numbers to call.

A figure appeared on the RoamZone on Evan's knee, snapping him from his trance. It hadn't been there before, and he hadn't seen it enter the camera's purview; it had just appeared at the fringe of the Seabrooks' front lawn like an apparition.

A slender masculine form standing at the far reach of the streetlight, illuminated sharply from one side, the outer edge of him glowing like a crescent moon.

The Neighborhood Watch sign hovered above him, depicting a menacing form in essential parts—hat, trench coat, eyes.

The figure beneath—hat, trench coat, eyes.

It was as if he'd stepped out of the sign, a living embodiment of ill will.

His hands seemed to glow white. Latex gloves.

Breathless, Evan watched the immobile figure. Whoever it was emanated calmness. What he was about to do did not frighten him in the least. A moth fluttered near the lens, a frenzy in infrared, and then vanished.

The figure withdrew a phone from a deep pocket and stared at it, the screen uplighting his face for an instant.

Norris Norris. Double N.

An invisible bank of cloud ate the moon, blanketing the neighborhood in dark. Not a sound, not a car, not a movement.

Just a predator outside staring at the house he was about to invade.

And a predator inside awaiting him.

An anticipatory chill moved across Evan's nape, horripilation presaging the arrival of death once again to the Seabrooks' front door.

At least Evan had the cameras, the element of surprise.

Norris's glowing hand pulsed around his phone, and the surveillance feeds on Evan's RoamZone went dark.

37

Butcher's Thigh

Evan peered through the row of tiny square windows inset at the top of the front door.

No one on the lawn.

It was as if Evan had dreamed it.

He moved silently through the kitchen to check the side yard, keeping clear of the bow window. The empty strip of lawn stared back, glistening with dew. The clouds blinked open, straw-colored moonlight falling on the mound of puzzle pieces on the table, the knife block on the counter, the obsidian pane of the mounted television.

Looping through the ground floor, he checked the other windows.

A crunching of rocks announced itself somewhere in the darkness outside, but it was hard to source.

He ducked low. Scooted into a powder room with a view of the east-facing yard. A disused shed sat unevenly on a bank of river stones.

The rasp of wood scraping in a frame, more a vibration than a sound.

Deborah's smoking window?

The house was pitch dark. Evan had lost surveillance visibility but still had the upper hand. Norris believed he was coming to kill a nineteen-year-old girl and two parents.

Flipping off his boots, Evan eased from the powder room, setting down toes first, then the ball of each foot, then the heel. Silent exploratory steps, lifting the feet straight up, sliding the toes down as if digging them beneath a rug—the rare ninjutsu technique he was capable of employing. Long steady breaths through his nostrils, knees slightly bent, hips level.

The rooms of the ground floor formed a loop around the core of the stairs. Moving silently back toward the kitchen with his ARES at the ready, Evan discerned the faintest scuff of tread from one of the adjacent rooms.

Norris likely wasn't aware he was being stalked.

Moving through the room where he'd first sat with Deborah and Mason, Evan cut toward the back of the house, staying attuned to the sound of Norris's shoes quietly touching the floor. They were circling each other in the ring of rooms around the stairs. It seemed Norris was safing the first floor before moving up.

The closed floor plan rendered the house almost pitch black at night, the profusion of walls blocking ambient light. In keeping with the Third Commandment, Evan had mastered the layout.

Avoiding the Chinese porcelain vase with its tentacles of pussy-willow branches, he reached the mudroom by the rear door. Its sash pane was lifted two feet in the frame, the gap just enough for a slender man to slip into.

Speeding his steps, Evan moved through the formal dining room and sliced the pie into the kitchen.

It looked to be empty, but he couldn't see behind the counter or the table beyond. Scanning the room over the sights of his 1911, he pressed forward.

Inch by inch, shifting his weight, ears straining.

Norris's footfall had gone silent.

Evan's concern redlined. Norris wasn't just some thug. He was a United States Marine with extensive operational experience.

Leading with his pistol, Evan leaned around the counter—no one there.

Crouched to check beneath the kitchen table.

He rose silently, willing his right knee not to crack as it was wont to do.

As his head drew level with the counter, he saw the missing slot in the knife block.

The boning knife.

He stilled. The thud of his heart reached his consciousness, barely audible over the rush of blood in his ears.

In a neighborhood like this, Norris would prefer a knife to a gun to keep everything quiet. Using a weapon from the house left a forensic dead end and would paint the picture of a home invasion gone wrong.

Still in his half crouch, Evan cocked his head and stared across the foyer.

There were two brick-size bumps at the base of the stairs. He blinked rapidly, stimulating his night vision. As the bumps resolved, a chill tightened his skin.

A pair of shoes.

In his peripheral vision, he caught a flash of movement reflected in the black screen of the TV. He spun to aim behind him, but a blow struck him at the wrist, knocking the ARES from his grip, a shot firing wildly. He leapt back, his shirt billowing forward as the blade came low and mean, swiping at his gut.

Evan's hip struck the kitchen table, sending up a spray of puzzle pieces. His shirt gaped wide across his solar plexus, split horizontally by the boning knife.

Norris's head drew back slightly—a spark of recognition at Evan's face?—and he lunged again, leading with the tip of the blade. An underhand prison-shiv stab, leaving Evan nothing to grab but the cutting edge.

Evan threw the bar of his forearm down, catching Norris's arm just above the wrist. With his left hand, Norris hooked Evan's neck, pulling him in toward the blade even as he kept jabbing against the pressure of Evan's arm. Muscles screaming, Evan strained to hold the knife at bay, but each stab brought the tip closer until he felt it tapping his stomach, popping through the surface tension of his skin.

When Norris drew his arm back again, Evan swept his hand up Norris's forearm to the wrist, locking it in place. The majority of knife fighters froze up here.

But not a United State Marine.

Norris dropped his grasp of Evan's neck, whipping his hand down to meet his trapped knife hand and plucking the knife from his own clenched fingers.

Now he had it free and clear.

He jabbed it toward Evan's side, but Evan crashed forward inside Norris's guard, chest to chest, the blade whisking just behind his kidney. A double slam into the wall ovens, Norris's shoulder blades striking metal, Evan dipping his chin for a headbutt, his forehead clipping Norris's chin.

Norris grunted out a clod of air, his hat flying free, the boning knife clattering to the tile. As Evan drew back, he dug for the Strider in his cargo pants, snagging the shark fin atop the blade on the edge of his pocket so the knife snapped open.

Evan spun the Strider across the back of his hand, changing to an edge-out reverse grip, and slammed the blade through Norris's thigh at the femoral artery.

Like many of Evan's favorites, this fatal injury had a nickname: butcher's thigh.

Norris wrenched away, the embedded knife coming with him.

Evan staggered back a few steps, and Norris groaned and wobbled against the stacked ovens. They took a beat, panting from the burst of adrenalized exertion. Evan's stomach, peppered with incisions, burned. His sliced shirt flapped idiotically across his gut like sputtering lips.

They stared at each other, Norris's dark skin even darker in the night, his eyes bright and his latex-gloved hands even brighter.

Norris looked down. The Strider stuck straight out from the upper thigh of his jeans, the tip sunk a solid two inches.

But something was wrong. He was still holding his feet.

Norris looked back up at Evan.

In the darkness his grin appeared, a Cheshire Cat float.

Reaching down, Norris gripped the handle of the Strider and tugged it upward.

The black-oxide blade sliced through the denim like butter.

The knife cut a vertical zipper through the pocket and emerged. It had impaled a fat wad of hundred-dollar bills folded once and rubber-banded.

Laughing, Norris held the knife up and wagged the cash on its end like a giant lollipop. "Now, ain't that a—"

Evan stuttered-stepped into a *yeop chagi* side kick, lower body pivoting sideways around his left hip, leg chambered, ankle high, toes pulled back out of the way and angled slightly down. Since he wore only a sock, he led not with the edge of his foot but with the heel.

His foot struck the butt of the Strider on the rise, the knife plowing into Norris's chest. There was a crackle of yielding bone, the wadded cash now rammed all the way down to the guard where blade met handle.

Four inches of S35VN steel buried in Norris's solar plexus.

The awful stench of raw innards meeting air.

Covered in dampness, Norris's face shimmered in the faint light.

He gripped the knife handle, his fingers not able to close.

The bottom of Evan's foot ached from the impact. At least he'd been on the right side of the knife. They were down to minutes now.

"Why were Johnny Seabrook and Angela Buford killed?" Evan asked.

Norris stared at his wet hands, white latex doused in crimson. His Adam's apple bobbed as he made a gurgling sound of disbelief.

"Were you all in on it?"

Norris's eyes rolled up to white, then rolled down once more as if coming back online, the effect supernatural, ghastly.

"Did Luke Devine order their deaths?"

Norris tilted forward, arms spread as if in a hug. Evan caught him under the armpits, felt the cold butt of the sunken knife against his own bare stomach. Norris's legs went out, but he grabbed behind Evan's neck, tugging him down, his face lifted to look into Evan's eyes.

Their noses were inches apart. Evan could taste Norris's breath, bitter and dry, puffing up from parted lips.

Evan eased him sloppily to the floor. One of Norris's stockinged feet pawed loose circles on the kitchen tile. His cheek came to rest against Evan's leg, his arm slung over the knee, clinging with what little strength his fingers had left. It was a meager sort of embrace. Sweat and blood turned his skin tacky.

Death came on like a galloping horse. His whole body shook. His breaths shuddered. His lips wavered, the hollow of his throat sucked in, a pitch-black hollow. He blinked long, blinked longer, his eyes screwed up toward Evan. He didn't want absolution or forgiveness.

He just wanted someone there.

Sprawled in the darkness of the kitchen, Evan held him until he slipped away.

38

The Fine Art of Disappearing Corpses

Ring-ring.

"What *now*?"

"I need to dispose of a body."

Evan had pried the stray round from the kitchen soffit, patched and painted the bullet hole with supplies he'd found in the garage. He'd gathered the jigsaw-puzzle pieces from the floor, placed them back on the kitchen table, and repaired the jostled frame. He'd rolled Norris onto a bed of trash liners, cleaned the blood off the floor, and aired out the kitchen. He'd retrieved his Strider knife and washed it extensively with hot water and bleach. He'd stripped off his boning-knife-incised shirt, bagged his bloody clothes, and showered. He'd left a single drop of blood on the white carpet of the guest room, which he'd scrubbed with water and then cleaning solvent to no avail. He'd dabbed rubbing alcohol on the tiny puncture wounds on his stomach, which hurt more than a minor injury had any right to hurt.

Then he'd called Orphan V, a virtuoso at the fine art of disappearing corpses.

"Start with a hacksaw," Candy said, "preferably lightweight extruded aluminum with a rubberized handle to avoid blisters. You're gonna want a ten pack of replacement blades, at least twelve inches with twenty-four teeth per inch. For the legs I prefer a hand ax to speed things along. Safety goggles, two industrial blenders, a super-heavy poly tarp, call it twenty-three mils to avoid nicks and drips. I've been off hydrofluoric acid lately, playing with concentrated sulfuric acids. The hydrogen peroxide's gotta be added drop by drop—that's the trick. It's called piranha solution. Leaves behind nothing but black organic sludge and gallstones."

"Tasty."

"Don't be a baby. Gallstones are actually quite pretty."

"I'll have earrings made up for you."

"I only need green to complete my collection."

"Seriously?"

"No," Candy said. "You gotta leave the body parts to boil in a hazardous-waste drum. Fifty-five gallons should do you fine."

"Where am I supposed to get that?"

"Any decent-size auto shop. Once it's done, you pour the sludge into a river and it's as though the body never even existed."

"I don't have time for all this. Any way you could get out here to Boston and handle it for me?"

"Can you do *anything* on your own?"

Evan stared down at Norris's body. He lay on his back, the trench coat beneath him flapped open like the wings of a moth. The circular bloodstain at his midsection looked like a cannonball entry wound.

"Apparently not," he said.

"I see how it is. I'm here for cleaning and housekeeping while you're out running around at all hours having fun and killing people."

"I did ask you to rescue me from the clutches of the federal government."

"Fine," she said. "Text me the address."

"One more thing."

"What?"

"How do I get a bloodstain out of white carpet? I tried dishwashing detergent."

"You're a liberated man," she said. "Figure it out."

39

Long Island MacArthur Airport, a regional facility in the comedically named town of Islip, was near the base of the tail of Long Island, forty-five minutes east of Luke Devine's estate.

Evan sunned himself, leaning against the borrowed Hertz rental he'd slotted in the middle of outdoor long-term parking. But he wasn't merely sunning himself.

He was shopping for a new residence. Between Luke Devine's reach and the Secret Service's intensified interest in him, he could risk neither a hotel nor a bed-and-breakfast.

A promising minivan pulled into the lot, coasting along and parking two rows over. Empty bike rack, a custom decal sticker showing a stick family of five. The 3-D version unpacked themselves from the car, the wife blond and fair, the husband dark-skinned, likely Indian, the children an unreasonably beautiful blend of both.

Preparing for his fourth exploratory approach of the afternoon,

Evan ambled past them as they unpacked a fleet of suitcases from the rear. As the parents dealt with the larger luggage, the middle child, who looked to be around six years old, fumbled with two hard-shelled suitcases, decorated with action heroes, and a diminutive set of golf clubs.

She unsheathed a driver and waved it around like a swashbuckler, her toddler brother laughing and clapping his hands. The other clubs tumbled out onto the asphalt, and as she crouched to gather them, the suitcase slid away toward Evan. "Runaway droid!" she cried.

The family alerted all at once, a herd of startled deer.

Evan caught the runaway suitcase by its handle, his thumb snared in the luggage tag. Glancing down, he checked the city on the address before rolling it back.

"Sorry!" the mom called.

"Thank you!" the father said.

The girl laughed a joyful laugh and slung her second suitcase toward Evan.

"Asha!" the mother shouted.

Evan blocked it with his shin.

As mother and father reprimanded Asha, the oldest sibling, a string-bean around Peter's age, hoisted the youngest atop his midsize suitcase behind their backs. He launched passenger and conveyance at Evan, crying, "Runaway Padawan!"

Straddling the rolling suitcase bearing down on Evan, the toddler giggled, air rippling his dark hair.

The parents were screaming.

Evan caught the toddler around the waist, lifting him off his rolling perch, setting him down on his feet, and arresting the suitcase with his heel. The boy jumped up and down, clapping his hands.

As the siblings celebrated uproariously, the parents alternated scolding them to no avail and thanking Evan profusely. Then they gathered up their luggage, the father chirp-chirping the minivan with a key fob. Laden with bags, they trundled off toward the terminal in a simulated jog no faster than a swift walk.

As soon as they passed from view, Evan circled back, removing a relay theft device and a specialized transponder key that had captured the electronic signal.

He unlocked the minivan, climbed in, and punched the keyless ignition. The vehicle was impeccably neat, no trash in the cup holders, and the interior still held that magical new-car smell. Bringing up the GPS, he punched the entry for HOME.

A professional voice with a slight British accent instructed him to pull out of the parking lot and turn onto 27 East. She was firm and a bit pushy. He decided to name her Pleasant Boss.

Pleasant Boss directed him to a quiet street in the town of Hampton Bays, ten miles from Devine's stately pleasure-dome of Tartarus. The residence itself was a high-set Queenslander with bright white wall cladding and an expansive covered veranda. The first button in the minivan's visor lifted the garage door. Evan pulled in.

The main access panel to the house alarm waited behind an unlocked panel in the garage beside the washer and dryer. He unplugged the AC power, used a rake from his pick set to pop the plastic backing, and disconnected the wires attached to the blocky battery.

He entered his temporary residence.

Light spilled through timber archways and across Shaker-style cabinetry, sand-colored stone benchtops, and duck-egg-blue walls. Various school and sports portraits adorned the refrigerator, mostly featuring wide-mouthed grins, delight pouring out of the kids. It seemed impossible to get a photo of the children with their mouths closed. Magnetized above them, a large monthly-format calendar provided an accounting of domestic life. Evan studied it with fascination. Birthdays, *"call HVAC guy,"* holidays, *"family movie night,"* soccer practices, *"refill prescription,"* farmers'-market times, *"lemon chicken pasta,"* carpool schedules.

He liked this family.

The computer on the kitchen desk had no password. One of the open tabs was logged into Instacart, the liquor store up the street carried Kauffman Vintage, and they offered contactless porch drop-offs. Heaven in a single thought. But he demurred.

Dumping his rucksack on an Amish knot rug in the family room, he plopped down on the giant shabby-chic couch. While not his taste, it would make for superb sleeping. The house smelled faintly of lavender.

He was pleased with his selection.

Now he had to attend to Joey. He needed her for operational backup. That's why it made sense to reach out to her. Not because he was worried about her.

He wasn't worried about her.

Not at all.

He was unsure how to approach her. She'd been angry with him before, but not like this.

After a few minutes of pondering, he downloaded an emoji app onto his RoamZone. He sent her an olive branch in the mouth of a dove. A bit saccharine, but it was the only relevant option.

Her response came immediately: i believe u meant to send this: 🏳️

He thumbed: Am I to understand that your only terms are unconditional surrender?

my only terms r u apologizing 4 hanging up on me after being all like 'ur so important 2 me'

She fired off two more texts in rapid succession: im mad @ u, X.
Then: irl.

A quick Google search translated what IRL meant.

Can we talk? he texted. The rationalized orthography is exhausting me.

im not a birdwatcher

Evan searched for an aggravated emoji but found none to his liking.

Before he could reply, Joey's next text popped up: kidding! oops. i mean kdng. but if u want 2 apologize, being a snotty grammarian isnt the best look

Ok, **Evan texted.** im like tots sorry + i wud luv 2 talk 4 reelz

X!
wut?
aaargh! fine!

He dialed.

"You're, like, the most annoying uncle-person ever!" The hint of amusement in her voice undercut the sharp tone. "What do you *want*?"

"I'm in the Hamptons. Ten miles from Luke Devine."

"And?"

"I'm gonna need backup. Start figuring out his network at Tartarus. The encryption will be intense."

"Intense encryption? I'm shuddering in my Adidas slides. Is that all? I mean, I don't want to keep you. I need to make sure I honor your hard boundaries."

"Joey."

Silence. Then, "Did Ruby Seabrook travel with you to the Hamptons? I mean, since your famous hard boundaries don't seem to apply to her?"

"She stayed with her folks in the safe house. She was pretty rattled after I took her to the dump site where they found her brother's body."

A long pause. He could hear her breathing. "Damn it, X. I'm not mad at her. *Obviously.*"

"Who are you mad at?"

A much longer pause.

"Josephine," he said softly.

"I'm mad at my mom and dad for being useless children who should never've had a baby. I'm mad at my maunt for dying. I'm mad at the foster parents who treated me like shit, and I'm mad at the other *asaltantes culeros* who abused me just because I was there and small and had the right anatomy. I'm mad at the Program and the fucking world that doesn't give a shit about people like me, and I'm mad at how unfair it is and how hard it is at the bottom and how no one up top bothers to notice until *their* perfect lives feel threatened. If you have *any kind* of money in this country? Life is so easy. I mean, easy compared to *the entire historical record of the species*. It's safe. There's food. You can say what you want, do what you want, buy stupid shit for cheap. You don't get raped by Huns or die of a bladder infection 'cuz there're no antibiotics or get eaten by pterodactyls—"

"I'm pretty sure there weren't pterodactyls—"

"—so s-t-f-u and enjoy it. Don't act like you're beset with inequities and the suffering of the world pains you endlessly. Just *don't*. 'Cuz if you're at the bottom? Shit *is* really hard. And we don't care what everyone up there *feels*. We don't. We just want them to do something to help or quit taking up all the oxygen."

She was breathing hard from the rant, and Evan wasn't sure if she was done. She was out there alone with the pain cracked from its hiding places, and it was everywhere, all around her. She was in the belly of it, and there was no getting out. It would digest her until it was through with her or she with it.

"Big words," Evan finally said, "from a trust-funder."

"Yeah, X," she said, a smile in her voice. "But we *earned* that shit."

He laughed.

She giggled along with him. He didn't laugh often, and she delighted when she was the cause of it.

"Remember what your maunt used to tell you?" he said. "'*Tiene dos trabajos. Enojarse y contentarse.*'"

"Don't use the language of my people against me. And your accent. *Gawd*. Ear rape."

"Apologies."

"Maybe . . ."

Evan said, "What?"

"Maybe you start your life thinking it's all some big thing that's just for you and no one else gets how special you are and if only the world could just see through how fucked up you are, everything would be great, right? Then: It never happens. You never get to be perfect, like Katy Perry."

"Who?"

"People get older and they're, like, fuck, this is *it*? So they talk about appreciating every moment and living in the present and how today is all you have because what else are they gonna say?"

"I think I read that once in a greeting card."

"I'm just saying. There's no big secret to life. It's just what we decide it is. We can get pissed off about it and make everything suck 'cuz we think we deserve it, or we can . . ." The words came a bit harder now. "Learn how to be with it. And—if we're lucky—even, dunno, try 'n' celebrate it sometimes. People we care about." Her voice dropped to just above a whisper. "Ourselves, maybe."

Evan thought about what Deborah had said about never shaming someone for finding joy. Johnny Seabrook had been that kind of kid, openhearted, generous of spirit. The loss of him was more than just the absence of a person; it was an affront to hard-won goodness in the universe.

He listened to Joey breathe some more.

Her tone was softer now. "Did Ruby and her folks get to the safe house okay?"

"Yes. And Candy's in Boston now if they need anything."

Her voice shot up an octave. "What? Really?! *Ruby Seabrook* gets Orphan V? I had to wait, like, *forever* before—"

"Good-bye, Joey."

"X! You're *tha worst*."

"You're the worst, too."

Hanging up, he tossed the phone beside him.

Twilight dampened the sky, shifting the shadows of the house, pulling them long across the wide-plank flooring. With an exhale, he sought a moment of relaxation, but instead a flood of anger caught him off guard. Joey's outrage had loosed his own.

Since the moment he'd listened to the voice mail intended to terrorize Ruby, he hadn't registered just how furious he was. That Johnny Seabrook's throat had been slit deep enough to expose vertebrae. That Angela Buford's head had been twisted 180 degrees. That a pack of men were at work doing Devine's bidding. That the Seabrooks had been shattered into pieces because of it. That one of Devine's men had come into the home of those good people to kill them.

THE LAST ORPHAN

Evan had tucked it all neatly away.
Until now.
Degree by degree, night blackened the windows.
It was time to visit Tartarus.

40

Torches and Pitchforks

Billionaire's Row on Meadow Lane was a parade of mansions built right up out of the sand atop aprons of hardscaping. No doubt to the consternation of the landowners, the beach itself remained public, stragglers making their way up from the bonfires farther west in rusty pickups to fish or get it on atop silky dunes within breathing distance of the shimmer of affluence. In fact, your average riffraffer could walk undisturbed along the shore all the way to Montauk's lighthouse.

Perhaps not *entirely* undisturbed.

Private security patrols rotated like electrons around the dunes of each estate, delineating bailiwicks. A guard station in every driveway and dark SUVs in every yard. The other houses Evan had passed had private-security types with not-so-concealed weapons hanging in their guard stations. Each tycoon seemed to have his own war force.

Except Luke Devine.

Tartarus kept its muscle tucked in, seeming to prefer electronic surveillance. Myriad-headed black cameras rose in stacks aiming every which way like cartoon trail signs.

Just out of peeping range of Devine's surveillance, Evan idled in the unthreatening minivan, drinking in ocean air through the rolled-down window. On the way over, he'd replaced the license plates with those from a similar-looking minivan he'd spotted parked behind an antiques shop in Art Village.

It took less than a minute for a 4x4 to buzz up to him.

Evan made a show of fumbling with an old-fashioned road map.

A security man wearing tan cargo pants and a decaled jacket hopped off. "Heya pal, help you with something?"

Comfortable demeanor, ample belly, local accent. Forgotten Oakley Blades dangled around his throat on a neoprene switch-back retainer. Evan pegged him for a retired cop.

"Yeah, I'm scouting out a good place to throw a line," Evan said. "I'm in from San Diego. Retired PD."

"Oh, yeah? Me, too. Suffolk County, Seventh Precinct. What brings you?"

"My wife's mom is circling the drain with Alzheimer's, so we take shifts. You know how it goes."

"I do indeed."

"I can't make mother-in-law jokes anymore without feeling guilty," Evan said.

The security guard laughed. "You'll have the best luck all the way at the end of the road where it hits Shinnecock Inlet. I'd say early morning. You can throw from the rocks. Soak a few clams or put on a strip of squid and you might pull out some bluefish or striped bass."

"Local knowledge is the only knowledge worth having." Evan chinned at the nearest mansion, Devine's neighbor to the west. The mist had thickened up around the grounds, bloating into na-scent banks of fog. "Nice little pied-à-terre."

"Well, hedge-funders need a place to summer, too. Where else they gonna count their ducats?"

"That your guy's house?"

"Yeah. He's only half bad."

"Why so much security? Keeping an eye on the beach bums?"

"They worry about corporate kidnappings, ransom, all that. Ever since the Hurricane of '38 took out the bridge over the inlet, this road's the only way in or out. Natural choke point at the intersection of Halsey Neck and Meadow Lane. So they take precautions, keep us in the mix. Ya know, in case Antifa reaches them with torches and pitchforks before they can get their private helicopters in the air. But mostly we're glorified staff."

"Employers like that, at least they make it worth your while."

"I got two kids in college, a third starting in a year. So it's all 'Yes, sir,' 'How high, sir?' from me. My employer had a toilet overflow last week in the middle of the night, spreading out across his reclaimed wooden floors from Amish barns or some shit. I get the call at two A.M., he's freaking out. So I throw on some clothes and drive out there. Go in like a hero to twist a basic turnoff valve." He shook his head. "What good's a hundred-twenty-seven-million-dollar house if you can't stop a leak that'll wreck it?"

"That's increasingly the way of the world."

"Ain't that the truth."

Evan folded up the map, gave a nod at the road ahead. "And that behemoth next door looks even bigger."

"Ah. Belongs to Luke Devine."

"Haven't heard of him."

"He's the swinging dick who makes all the other swinging dicks look like Pee-wee Herman. Has these crazy decadent parties. In fact, we're gonna get some action tomorrow night."

"Why's that?"

"Every year he hosts this big-ass Halloween costume gala. This year's theme? Heaven and Hell. Come tomorrow we'll have all sorts rolling through here. Entitled rich dickwads who think the rules don't apply to them. And entitled party kids who think the rules don't apply to them either. We just keep 'em off our lawn, make sure no one OD's on the beach, that sort of stuff."

"I don't miss that," Evan said.

"No, sir."

"Thanks for the tips on the bluefish. Stay safe out there."

"All right, brother. Be well."

Evan rolled up the window and drove a ways forward before

banking into a three-point turn in front of Tartarus. He cast a glance at the façade of the mansion. The upstairs windows gleamed darkly. Somewhere behind them Luke Devine rested in the heart of his forbidden empire.

The time for a face-to-face had arrived at last.

Tomorrow night.

A Halloween costume gala.

Evan would be there with bells on.

41

Blue-Collar Poet

Ring. Ring. Ri—

"Aunt Hilda's Secondhand Bird Cages."

"Tommy. It's Joey."

"Hiya, kid."

"Do we have to worry about X?"

"No."

"I think we have to."

"Well, then. You're, what, twelve years old now?"

"*Tommy.* I'm just sayin'. He seems off. I mean, after they caught him."

"'Off'? That a medical term or your girlish intuition?"

"Don't be so male. It limits you."

"Sorry. *Womanly* intuition."

"Clever."

"How are *you* right now? In your head?"

"All fucked up."

"Okay, then. Get yourself squared first."

"What if he's not okay? He seems . . . *different*."

"We're all different. Every day. That's the point."

"But not X."

"Everyone. Look. Evan's between one place and another. Understand?"

. . .

"Kid? Still there?"

"Yeah. I was just thinking."

"What?"

"Me, too, I guess. Between places. It feels like . . . feels like being nowhere."

"The fall into the abyss."

"That means he's gonna hit bottom. In the middle of a mission!"

"Or pop through to something else."

"We can't risk that."

"*We* ain't risking shit."

"We have to get him to see—"

"Kiddo. You're smart as fuck. But you're a know-it-all. And you're not as smart as smart-as-fuck people who've been at it longer than you."

"What's that mean?"

"You got two ears and one mouth. Learn to use them proportionally."

"That is excellent advice. I'm definitely not ready to take it yet."

"Course you ain't."

"That's *it*?"

"Whaddaya want? I'm halfway through a handle of Beam and my cable's out. You want pontification I need lead time and an inflated sense of my own importance."

"Tommy, you're a blue-collar poet. I never would've thought it."

"Well. Like the wise man says, you never know who's who in the zoo."

"Who's the wise man?"

"Me, topped off with the proper level of bourbon."

Click.

42

Destroying Angel

Drifting up the quartz circular driveway to Tartarus amid a current of partygoers, Evan caught sight of himself in the polished window of a valeted Rolls-Royce SUV with suicide doors.

A floating skull with exposed teeth painted on his lips, frozen in a macabre grimace-grin. He wore a black shirt and black jeans, his body fading into the dark of night.

He'd applied water-based face paint with the same precision and rigor that Jack had taught him to create camo patterns. Sponge, flat-edged brush, white pencil to delineate the shape of the skull, even a few asymmetrical cracks squiggling through the cheekbones.

He felt downright fearsome.

A destroying angel.

The mansion gave the appearance of expanding as he approached, a mélange of tiers replete with decks, terraces, and patios. The white-stained shingle siding, illuminated with bold sabers of light, gave Tartarus the appearance of a ghostly wedding cake.

Security men were in abundant evidence, distinguished from

the costumed revelers by somber suits and faces. They were checking names at the entry, so Evan detoured through the manicured
gardens and slipped through a servant's door, aided in invisibility
by his dark attire.

A brief hall peeked in on a kitchen sufficient to feed a brigade.
The corridor led out into the main foyer that yawed three floors
upward like the dome of a cathedral. A waterfall feature domi-
nated the inner curve of a *Sunset Boulevard* staircase. Backlit with
glowing crimson, it poured a sheet of water so controlled that it
looked like a frozen wave. In its undulating illumination, guests
milled and sipped and snorted, dressed in all manner of attire.
There were sexy nuns and devils in red tutus, zombie bishops and
lingerie angels with fluffy halos, horned lords of darkness and
vampy vampires. Silver trays circulated, bubbling wines of various tinctures, pills and snuffboxes, Japanese white strawberries
each nestled in its own satin pillow. A string quartet on a dais
performed a playful classical version of "Monster Mash." Someone screamed "Happy Halloween!" and then witch-cackled loud
enough to make Evan wince.

He spotted Tenpenny, a head above the revelers, scanning the
swirls and eddies with a trained eye. He was tall enough to give
the illusion of slimness. Those long bones looked easy to break,
but Evan had clashed with enough towering men to know that the
extra inches added poundage and fighting leverage and the extra
weight strengthened the bones. Even so, Tenpenny stood with the
faintest stoop, his head slightly ducked. A perennial right-hand
man who'd never learned how to stand up straight.

Moving away, Evan bumped into a man painted statue-white
like a cemetery angel, tears of blood staining both cheeks. His pupils were blown wide from MDMA or coke. Fluttering his frosted
fingernails before long snow-white lashes, he poked out a pale
pink tongue and spoke with a baby-girl crackle in the back of his
throat. "Are we even really here?"

Evan said "No" and breezed on.

He circled the ground floor, hoping to make sense of the house,
but it spun this way and that, a muddle of corridors and gathering

rooms with pumping music and strobing lights. Even the weather was made to acquiesce to the theme, various contraptions conveying blasts of heat and frost, fog machines issuing dragon-breaths of mist, rain bars felling water from the ceilings into neat trenches along the walls.

Tartarus felt like a state of mind, an enchantment, a reverie.

It was enough to confound the Third Commandment: *Master your surroundings.*

Lodged in a corner of a loggia overlooking the backyard, Craig "Gordo" Gordon was impossible to miss, his girth substantial enough to crowd his cheeks and pooch his lips so that the bottom fringe of his push-broom mustache aimed directly outward.

Hoping to note the location of Devine's surviving heavy hitters, Evan searched out Dapper Dan Martinez, Sandman Santos, and Rathsberger, to no avail. As Evan headed back for the central stairs, a girl who looked no older than eighteen peeled herself off a wall and danced before him. She wore a quicksilver slip, angel wings composed of real feathers, and jean shorts cut so high that the white bottoms of the pockets stuck out atop her thighs. Without so much as a glance at his face, she writhed and shimmied against him, high to low, and then bounced off to grind against the next passerby.

Tenpenny was where Evan had left him, holding an overwatch position by the stairs, gauging the flow of traffic to the second floor. But now he was distracted, stooping to wrap an arm around the waist of an attenuated young woman dressed as a slutty Catholic-school girl—plaid skirt, thigh-high stockings, unbuttoned blouse. Tall and coltish, she had slender, uniformly tanned legs and long black hair shiny enough to see your reflection in. She giggled, delicate head bobbing on a long stem of a neck. She looked like she'd shatter if someone sneezed near her.

When she wobbled atop high-heeled black patent shoes, Tenpenny used the opportunity to shore up his grip on her, bending further to sniff her hair. And Evan in turn used the opportunity to slide past him onto the stairs.

He came face-to-face with a state governor leading an entourage

of she-devils down the stairs and munching sushi from an actual scallop shell serving as an appetizer plate. She drew back
from Evan's painted face in mock horror and exclaimed "Spooky!"
showing off a half-masticated hand roll gummed in her molars.

Evan eased to the side and let the satin costumes prance by. Protruding from a ledge of what he guessed to be Japanese zelkova
wood perched a carving of the three wise monkeys in the Inami
Chokoku tradition, Mizaru, Iwazaru, Kikazaru hewn in kanji on
the wide base.

Clusters of guests clogged the upper landing, enjoying the
rarefied-air vantage down onto the lobby. Slicing through, Evan
veered left down what appeared to be the master wing of the
house. The crowd was thinner here, only the occasional staff
scurrying about or guest stumbling from the restrooms retucking
flaps of costumery.

A curious door upholstered in a vibrant shade of crimson had
no handle or visible hinges. Standing sentry before it, Dapper Dan
Martinez chewed gum vigorously, his shiny, clean-shaven cheeks
rippling with muscle. He wore fluorescent lime sneakers that
would have looked ridiculous on a high-schooler.

He alerted to Evan at once, so rather than avoid him, Evan approached.

"No one comes in here," Dan said. *"Ever."*

Evan waved him off. "You know the tall guy downstairs? Another security dude?" His disguise was sufficient; he felt the face
paint crack on his lips.

"Yeah." Dan shifted with annoyance, his suit fitted to show off
gym-swollen pecs. "What about him?"

He gripped hand to wrist at his groin, his head tilted back
haughtily. With guys like Dapper Dan, you were never worth their
focus. Everything important was happening one foot over your
left shoulder.

"He got roughed up," Evan said. "Someone got in a jab, knocked
him out cold."

A slender door a few strides up the hall opened, a worker emerging from what looked to be a servants' staircase. Holding a silver tray on which a green smoothie balanced, she proffered it to

Dan, who took it without so much as a glance in her direction. She faded away down the stairs.

Evan's remark had drawn Dan's partial attention. "No shit?"

"I'd get down there, man. He's hurting pretty good."

Dan and his smoothie jogged off.

Evan tested the scarlet door, fingertips dimpling the fabric. It didn't budge.

It practically hummed with relevance, guarding something of importance.

He pressed on.

Double architectural doors at the end of the hall were pinned open, letting into a vast master suite. Dimly lit, it had its own foyer, coat closet, and an ensuite office the size of a small restaurant. Evan caught sight of himself in a brass-framed mirror, a decapitated skull drifting through the air. As he advanced, the room kept drawing into view, telescoping in scale.

Behind a massive wrought-iron screen, a fireplace roared ocher and true orange.

A man stood facing it, hands clasped at the small of his back. The dappled light shone off a thinning patch at the rear of his head.

He didn't turn so much as rotate with a ballet dancer's fluidity. Shoulders pinned back, erect spine, a dignified diminutive bearing like that of the Little Prince. The vast hearth rose at least ten feet, backdropping him so he seemed to wear the flames like a living robe.

"'Hell is empty and all the devils are here.'" Luke Devine's smile seemed as warm as the blaze surrounding him. "Welcome, Mr. Nowhere Man. I've been waiting for you."

43

A Dark Kind of Lovely

Evan stood maybe twenty feet from Luke Devine at the edge of an expensive-looking silk splash rug that stretched to the fireplace. On the rug by the hearth were two facing love seats. Between them sat a rectangular cuboid of a glass table with a naked male mannequin trapped within, a piece that Devine must have fancied to be art. A series of radius windows looked out on what felt like perpetual darkness with no glimmer of the backyard party. Evan's internal compass was exceptional, but he had no sense which way he or the room was oriented; it was as though they were floating in the gloom.

For a moment the men regarded each other, neither blinking. The inferno raged behind Devine, flames leaping from his shoulders.

"How did you know I was coming?" Evan asked.

"We'll get to that."

"How do you know who I am?"

"We'll get to that, too," Luke said.

Evan had the unnerving sense of being outplayed and out of

his depth. He was reminded of the shot he'd missed from twenty feet at the hospital plaza. Wide open, no wind factor, no glints or shadows.

needle punching through his shirt
windshield spiderwebbing
missed shot at twenty feet

He felt vulnerable.
He hated feeling vulnerable.
"Please," Luke said with an artful flare of his hand. "Sit."
They took positions on the love seats, squaring off across the glass table.

Luke's eye contact was direct, unremitting. There was no sign of the mania that Echo had warned Evan about, and he wondered what it would take to get Luke there. Or had Echo made it up, exaggerated his flaws through the prism of her own inadequacies?

"I'm fascinated by people who are exceptional at something," Luke said, his tone as calm as ever. "Because excellence is the way we burrow through to meaning and—if we're lucky—wisdom. Dancing, thinking, sculpting . . ." He cast an eye at Evan, translucent blue like Icelandic water. *"Killing."*

The mannequin peered up, its smooth, featureless face conveying terror, plastic palms pressed to the glass, mouth agape in a silent scream.

"I want to know what they know," Luke said. "I want to feel what they feel. I admire people like you. The mercilessness required to get done what you get done—I'd imagine you pay a terrible price for it. I'd imagine you have to turn off many parts of yourself. You have to be so much less to be so much more. It's a sacrifice, really. But you were made for it. If the rumors are true, you're like . . . like a demigod."

"No," Evan said. "Just a guy with no patience for theatricality."

"Amusing coming from someone dressed up like an avenging angel," Luke said. "You put on the garb, but you won't own what's beneath. I understand. There's nothing more terrifying than embracing that which is great in you."

"I'm not certain about much," Evan said, "but I'm sure that there's no greatness in what I do."

Luke cocked his head. Being at the receiving end of his focus was like staring into a klieg light. "Your humility seems unfeigned."

"I was taught to remain aware of how many ways I can be better," Evan said. "But I'm not interested in myself. I'm interested in you."

"I'm the recipient of a great deal of interest from a great number of powerful people. They think I'm dangerous. No one can rise this high without dealing outside the boundaries of accepted law. The rules change as you ascend. That's why you're here." The fire made cat's-eyes of Devine's pupils. "Because of the power I hold."

Evan wondered why Devine wanted to block a trillion-dollar environmental bill. Money was the obvious answer, but he seemed governed by other impulses. Evan, too, had different concerns beyond a bill and a Senate vote, neither of which had motivated him to arrive at Devine's door dressed in the black garb of death.

The heat of the fireplace warmed the right side of Evan's face. "You had a kid killed. And a young woman."

He looked at the cat's-eyes, and the cat's-eyes looked back. Or they did not.

Luke's light blond brows vanished when the flames licked a particular way, but the skin of his forehead rose a quarter inch. Evan read his posture, his expression, looking for a forward lip purse or some other alpha display that indicated a clandestine plan. There was none. Luke seemed genuinely surprised.

"I did no such thing."

"Then why did your man come after me in New York?"

"Because you went after Echo. We thought we'd catch you there."

"To do what?"

"Invite you here."

"Mr. Folgore didn't seem interested in *inviting* me anywhere."

Again Luke looked surprised.

"Your other man came after me in Massachusetts," Evan said. "And after the family of the kid who was killed."

"What kid? What are you talking about?"

"Johnny Seabrook."

Luke concentrated, his non-eyebrows bunching, his face shiny and smooth in the firelight. "I remember a report about this. There was a girl, too."

"When young women are killed, no one seems to remember their names."

"Her name was Angela Buford," Luke said.

There was a ruckus behind Evan, and then a quintet of men tumbled into the room breathing hard, faces red. The full roll call: Tenpenny, Rath, Dapper Dan, Santos, and Gordo.

They spotted Evan and charged him, veering off only when Luke held up a palm. Evan remained sitting.

"Goddamn it," Tenpenny said. "He slipped by us. Are you okay?"

"As you see," Devine said.

Tenpenny came around to face Evan. He reeked of cigarette smoke, bits of ash dotting his tie. "You piece of shit," he said. "I've coordinated protection for Al Jazeera in Qatar against terrorists, for Tucker Carlson against Antifa wackjobs, for Rachel Maddow against crazed right-wingers. Compared to what I'm used to, to what these men are used to, you're a speck of spinach caught in my teeth."

Evan said, "And you haven't learned that dropping names means you're still someone who has to drop names."

"Get the fuck up. And march the fuck out."

"Derek." Luke Devine's voice, no more than a whisper. "Let me offer you something. People are never feared for being threatening or making demands. But by their silence. Their unimpeachable politeness. Because they're above it."

Tenpenny lost an inch or two in his posture, that long spine retracting at Devine's rebuke. The others lurked behind Evan or in his periphery.

"He's right," Evan said. "I've killed quite a few of them."

"Get up," Tenpenny said. "Move. *Now*."

Evan said, "I'm not done with your boss."

Devine stiffened in his chair, his first show of displeasure. "I don't care if you want to kill me," he said to Evan, "but at least be polite." He dusted his small hands, though there was nothing to dust. "I'll see you when you're ready to discuss our . . . antagonism with some measure of civility. Security will show you out."

Barely moving, Evan gauged the men's placement around him, tapped into a sixth sense to read body heat and disturbed air. "That might not go well for security."

The widest shadow shifted on the silk rug. A creak of floorboard behind him.

"I'll make sure they're respectful," Luke said.

"Kind of you."

Gordo's meaty hand reached across the back of the love seat to clamp down on Evan's shoulder. Reaching across his chest, Evan grabbed the hand at the ledge of the pinkie and pried it up, locking the elbow and torquing the arm. A grunt that stank of salami wafted over his shoulder as Gordo pressed his substantial weight in for a better grab. Rather than resist, Evan kept the arm and tucked forward onto his feet in a crouch, tugging the big man with him. He felt about 350 pounds roll up across his back and shoulders. There was a hitch at the apex as Gordo's mass slowed the momentum, and then he rotated across Evan's shoulder blades and smashed through the glass table, crushing the mannequin.

Behind Evan the love seat toppled, providing a charming little coda to Gordo's downfall.

Tenpenny skipped back to let the real fighters have their space.

Rathsberger was already lunging, but Evan dropped low and swept the leg. Rath hit the rug hard on his shoulders, ruinous face contorted, his lungs ejecting a noise sounding like a displeased seal.

Dapper Dan snatched Evan up from behind in a sleeper hold, arching his back to pull Evan's feet off the floor and choke him out. His massive biceps crowded Evan's cheek. Evan could sense the crinkle of Dan's smile, the fresh scent of wintergreen gum.

In front of him, Gordo had labored up to a knee, one hand pressed to the shattered glass to support his substantial weight. Blood veined the silk beneath his palm. Evan kicked out his elbow, and the big man crashed once more, cheek finding shards. Dapper Dan tightened his hold, static crowding in, and Evan shuddered once, made a gurgling sound, and went limp.

A Dark Kind of Lovely

The losing-consciousness act worked, Dan relaxing just enough for Evan's boots to lower a few inches. Evan heel-stomped the inner arch of Dan's foot through the trendy sneaker, crushing bone, and Dan grunted and released him. Evan threw an elbow hard back into Dan's solar plexus, knocking the wind out of him but missing the floating rib he'd intended to break. Dan staggered back into the upended love seat, which struck him at the backs of the legs. He tumbled over it, deposited in rocket-launch position staring up at the ceiling with his back and legs parallel to the floor.

Evan whirled to face Santos, the least threatening, but Sandman's bearing showed him to be anything but. The small man had taken a medium-wide stance, heels elevated, springy on his feet. Arms partially extended, elbows bent, hands open and searching. Spine flexed and curved forward, center of gravity eased slightly over his lead leg, readying for a lunge.

A grappler.

Grapplers were always the most dangerous.

It had all gone down so fast—less than ten seconds.

The others were on the floor or picking glass out of themselves. They were gasping and panting, breaths echoing like crosscurrents in the vast hard room. The acrid stink of body odor made itself known above the burning cedar.

As Santos moved, an Order of Christ pendant, square with flared tips, swayed at his chest. He was short and compact, low center of gravity. Evan shuffle-stepped with him and tried to track his eye movements to see if he'd give up a target glance telegraphing where he'd strike first.

That's when he heard the click of a hammer drawing back on a pistol.

Tenpenny peered over a 9-mil, gripping it like a mall warrior with the thumb of his support hand behind the slide. Evan could see that the sights were aimed under his left elbow, and the deltoid of Tenpenny's shooting arm was tensed, which meant he'd likely anticipate recoil and place the shot even lower and wider. If Evan could shake Santos for a moment, he could get inside Tenpenny's reach and introduce his Adam's apple to his neck vertebrae.

But Santos drew in toward the other marines, and Tenpenny

239

shuffled behind them as well. On the floor Rath rolled onto his side and coughed out more air, his sleeve smeared with white paint from Evan's face. A test tube had slid from his pocket, and it took Evan a moment to distinguish the insectoid scrambling within. He thought of the pimp's face adhered to the table in that pigsty in Mattapan. Skin swollen tight like cellophane, glass cylinder protruding from the nostril, a grotesque feeding tube. The way the swollen lips had bulged at the corner before the red ant had wriggled through and popped free.

Rath tracked Evan's gaze to the test tube, then grabbed for it and lunged up, his twisted features a blur of scar tissue. His hand found the coyote-tan pistol in his hip holster, but he didn't draw; his angle would put his own men in the danger-close area and his principal within ricochet distance. Gordo had risen as well, as slow as a mounting ocean swell. Glass studded his left cheek, blood dribbling from both palms. Dapper Dan was next up. Tenpenny edged farther behind his men, still aiming the pistol imprecisely at Evan over their shoulders.

Devine was also on his feet, though Evan hadn't seen him move; it was as though he'd teleported from the love seat.

It occurred to Evan that for the past few seconds there'd been no memories, no doubts, no uncertainty. He had occupied himself without distraction. And it had been a dark kind of lovely.

He stared at the crew of men. They stared back. They were more bruised and bloody than he was, and that pleased him.

He offered Devine the faintest tip of his head. "Please inform security that I'll show myself out."

44

Letting Go

Rathsberger and Tenpenny bookended Evan down the stairs, through the partygoers, past the tumbling waterfall and string quartet, and to the massive pivot door in the front, where a rugby scrum's worth of no-necks continued to check faces and names. The two marines were sure not to touch Evan. Contact would be reserved for a future date.

They walked him out into a soft spitting rain, across the quartz driveway to the edge of the property where the front gardens met Meadow Lane. They halted once Evan's boots hit asphalt, facing him from the rim of the lawn.

Line in the sand.

A half step behind Rath, Tenpenny glowered at him. Dew had caught in his dated mustache. His eyes were brown and forgettable.

Evan flat-out fucking hated him.

Hated his cowardice in how he'd hidden behind his men upstairs. Hated how he'd clutched the younger woman inside and nuzzled her neck while pretending to steady her. Hated how he wielded his height as if it were something earned rather than a throw of the genetic die.

Evan stared up at Tenpenny, his best ask-yourself-do-I-look-scared glare. Rath withdrew the test tube once more, tapped it against his knuckles.

"You enjoy yourself," Evan asked, "feeding ants through the face of Angela Buford's pimp?"

When Rath smiled, it looked like a wound reopening.

Tenpenny answered, "Angela Buford? Never heard of her." Forehead elevating, eyelids dimming, a partially suppressed grin twitching the edges of his mouth—microexpressions correlated with deception. "There's so many girls around here." He kept Rath's bulk between himself and Evan. "I know your type. I learned folks like you inside and out from a lifetime as a fixer. You're one of those guys who thinks well of yourself, who thinks he rises above it all. When we both know that if you had the access I do, you'd get your dick dirty every chance you got." A gleam of a smile. "Just like me."

The rain was lighter now, little more than a summer mist stirred into the fog. Evan's skin felt cold and raw, and he could feel paint melting down his cheeks. The mansion loomed at Tenpenny's back, seeming to grow right out of him, an edifice of power, of faceless dominance. An echo of Joey's words returned to Evan, cutting through the soupy air: *I'm mad at the other* asaltantes culeros *who abused me just because I was there and small and had the right anatomy.* He thought about how much bigger the other foster boys had been than him—the Mystery Man, too. How he'd once been a twelve-year-old knocked down on his hands and knees, drooling blood onto the cracked asphalt of a handball court.

For a moment it felt like there was no bottom. That it would never end. Just an everlasting cycle of might against those with nothing more than a prayer and whatever grit they could summon out of thin air.

Tenpenny seemed to sense his thoughts. "You know the *most* fun part?" His leer hung crooked on his face. His sideburns were coarse, unclipped. "Knowing how to undress someone who needs

convincing. It's hard business. Getting the jeans off. They bunch at the shoes. You want to fuck them when they're lively, you see. If you have to force it outright, then they get disoriented. That's less fun. So you make them do the calculation. Will it hurt more if they get knocked around a little? Choked a bit in the heat of the action? If they get their face banged against the headboard? You want them to understand it's most enjoyable for everyone if they. Just. Give. Up."

Evan blinked against the rain. His thoughts pooled, dark and rageful.

"We're locking down the estate," Tenpenny said. "No more sneaking inside with your Halloween getup, cute as it is."

The right side of Rath's chin was shiny with rain or drool that had leaked past the seal of his malformed lips.

"I'll leave the chitchat to you two." Rath set the heel of his hand on the butt of his holstered pistol. "And I'll leave the airy-fairy bullshit to Mr. Devine. But I want you to know. I'm a knife-and-bullets man. Just like you. But better." He shuffled forward a half step, close enough for Evan to smell his sweat. His eyes were pretty blue, one clear as day, the other stabbing out through a morass of necrotic flesh. His voice came as a grumble bleared through his misshapen mouth. "You know how this ends, don't you?"

The line sounded rehearsed, like something said by a sheriff in a two-bit western.

The rain picked up, fuzzing everything at a hard slant. The men didn't retreat so much as fade back toward the house, and then Evan was alone on the desolate extravagant edge of Billionaire's Row.

He stood with his face uptilted, feeling the mask melt off it.

The dynamics inside Luke Devine's domain felt surreal and disorienting. Was he a nation-state as Naomi feared? His own center of gravity around which other power players rotated captively? The crazed genius whom Echo had described? He did emanate a kind of influence that was hard to put to words. It was as though he had a distortion field around him that warped perspective. Evan couldn't get a handle on him.

Evan had approached Tartarus and Devine as he had targets in the past. But this mission was unlike any other. And Devine—in his unerring coolness, in his inscrutable manner, in the intel at his command—was different from anyone Evan had encountered.

Which meant that to face him Evan had to be different, too.

baby mobile chiming a nursery rhyme

The water ran chalky and opaque down his black shirt. He peeled it off, used it to wipe his face. Beneath he wore a lab-engineered undershirt designed with an adversarial pattern to confuse machine-vision algorithms and thwart facial-recognition software.

raw sobbing from another room

The air smelled of salt and perfume and champagne. The front of the house was surprisingly free of guests, a peaceful break in the storm after the late arrivals had trickled in. Twinning rows of exotic foreign cars funneled to the porch. The massive front door was closed, guards and valets sheltering from the rain inside.

his tiny, tiny hand gripping a smooth white rail

And then

letting

go.

The rain tapped Evan's bare face as he looked up at the broken sky. He dropped the black shirt, smudged white with makeup, in the mud, strode back onto the property, and rang the doorbell. Even over the din of the party, he heard throaty chimes, deep like organ pipes.

The towering pivot door yawned open, a break in the sheer face of the mansion.

A half dozen guards formed a semicircle in the foyer. In their suits they looked like a receiving line at a wedding. Behind them the party pulsed and roared. Tenpenny and the surviving marines were nowhere in evidence.

"The Nowhere Man here to see Mr. Devine," Evan said. "Please ask if he'll receive me."

The guards instinctively stepped away from him, widening their gaps but holding the line. One patted Evan down over his clothes, his hand freezing when it reached the outline of the ARES pistol snugged in the Kydex appendix holster. When Evan re-

moved the 1911, the men tensed as if braced for an intercontinental ballistic missile to come through the roof. When Evan handed his weapon over, the guard breathed out a gust of relief.

One of the others pressed forefinger to earpiece, turning away and murmuring something in a Slavic accent. A bead of sweat trailed from his sideburn to his collar. He kept his eyes on Evan the entire time.

The guard nodded at the voice on the other end and then nodded again. "Please," he said to Evan. "Come in."

As Evan moved a few steps into the enormous foyer, the lights pulsed—the gargantuan chandelier, the sconces, the accent lights—all of them all at once. The string quartet stopped midnote. The rain-bars ceased, their final downpour vanishing into the floor. The staff stopped moving—the guards, the busboys, the caterer's assistants with their silver trays—and a moment later the guests did as well. A silence asserted itself through Tartarus, everyone paralyzed in a kind of awe.

And then the staff members clapped their white gloves briskly and the partygoers streamed out, some still holding glasses and appetizer plates. The string quartet folded up their act as neatly as street musicians. Staff left platters and stations. The throng surged toward the entrance, funneling past Evan and out the colossal door at his back.

He stood in place, holding firm against the current.

As the last guests flowed out, Evan sensed movement way up above on the second-floor landing.

Luke Devine stood near the top of the staircase, his palms resting on the railing. He wore a beautifully fitted suit—a costume change?—and it struck Evan that he hadn't taken note of Devine's clothing before, an uncharacteristic lapse.

Devine beamed down; he looked positively delighted.

"Didn't mean to interrupt the whole evening," Evan said.

"This is what the party was for," Devine said. "*You.*" His voice found resonance off the walls and ceiling and came back legion.

"Are we gonna keep shouting like Romeo and Juliet?" Bizarrely, Evan's voice did not echo as Devine's did. "I'm rusty on my iambic pentameter."

"Of course not." Devine nodded at the stairs. "If you'll join me."

He made a magnanimous gesture eastward toward the master wing of the building. The place was so massive that cardinal points seemed necessary; it was like orienting on a mountain range or an open prairie.

Evan moved up the stairs past the three monkeys. His boots made the only sound, rapping against the wooden steps hollowly, as if requesting entry.

Devine stood on the landing above, backlit severely so he was nothing more than an outline of a man. Somehow, magically, he was holding the ARES 1911, though Evan had not seen his pistol conveyed upstairs during the mass exodus.

The interminable staircase seemed to grow longer even as Evan mounted it. Devine held the pistol out to his side. Tenpenny appeared to claim it, glared at Evan, and then retreated from view, leaving a suspended trail of smoke from his cigarette.

At last Evan reached the top, Devine waiting patiently with a posture suited to a military portrait. Over the small man's shoulder, Evan cast an eye at the alluring scarlet door. He wondered just what it would take for him to see behind the curtain.

"Welcome back," Devine said.

He coasted smoothly across the Calacatta marble. His head and torso glided evenly at Evan's side; his footfall made no sound.

They reached the door. The upholstery was tufted silk with big glossy buttons.

"Why don't you come in." Devine palmed the previously locked door, which swung inward on lubricated hinges without so much as a creak. "I'd like to show you exactly what I'm up to."

45

Eye of God

The inside of the door was padded as well, and it sucked closed behind Evan and Devine with a soundproofed thunk. Devine slid home a barrel bolt as thick as a .50 BMG round. After the expansiveness of the mansion, the windowless room felt cramped.

Plush scarlet carpet. Two baroque gilded chaise longues with scarlet upholstery against opposing walls. Flocked scarlet wallpaper with fleurs-de-lis.

In the center was a Faraday cage the size of a railroad car, its slatted door ajar.

Inside: A desk with a wireless keyboard and mouse. A chair. Wall-mounted racks holding hard drives.

The far side of the cage was an unbroken screen the size of five large TVs stacked top to bottom.

"I've been waiting to talk to you for so long," Devine said. "I have so much to share with you."

Evan looked at him.

"Please." Devine indicated the chair. "Sit."

Evan sat.

In the dark monitors, Evan could see his own reflection in front of Devine's. Even standing, Devine was only a bit taller than Evan, backdropping him like a shadow's shadow.

And then Devine was gone, having receded silently to one of the chaise longues outside the Faraday cage next to a side table that served as a charging station.

"When you're ready." Devine's words reverberated in the private scarlet room.

The sleek ergonomic mouse fit smoothly in Evan's palm. He nudged the screens to life as he did in his own Vault in his own fortress.

A tiling of surveillance vantages filled his view, showing every conceivable nook and cranny of Tartarus. A time stamp rendered the current date and time. Empty corridors. Staff cleaning up detritus from the party. Tenpenny and his men were clustered in what looked like a billiard room. Countless guest bedrooms. Bathrooms the size of studios. Pool. Gardens. Crawl space. Attic. A ten-car garage. One square was even devoted to the scarlet room itself, Evan sitting watching himself watch himself. Or, more precisely, watching the spot where his head—fuzzed into a cubist confusion of overlapping invisibilities by his engineered shirt—watched another cubist confusion of overlapping invisibilities. And so on.

"Witness." Devine now held an elaborate controller device, part joystick, part keyboard. Its thick cable threaded through the bars of the cage.

The tiled mosaic rotated, and now the time stamp showed an hour prior. Guests drinking, eating, snorting. Fucking on beds. Drunkenly fussing with bidets in the bathroom. An obese man was getting a hand job behind the garden shed.

Facial-, biometric-, and gait-recognition software identified the people despite their costumes, keying to separate text boxes linked to Wikipedia pages, social-media platforms, criminal records, dating website profiles, bank accounts, iPhone videos pulled straight off their devices. Evan caught sight of the governor he'd passed on the stairs snorting coke off the bare back of one of her underlings in the pantry.

Devine clicked and zoomed, the images deep-diving into profiles, collating public records. The flickering images played across
Evan's face, his body, dozens of scandals occurring in real time.
The sheer amount of intel was dizzying, the eye of God, making
the room itself seem to spin.

Evan stayed seated and held his balance.

"This?" Devine spread his arms as if to encompass Tartarus. "Is
Pleasure Island. My guests are presented with options. They run
to those that call to them. All I do is capture who they already are."

Evan pivoted in the chair. "And use that against them."

"Isn't that the purest thing to use against people? Themselves?"

Evan had no ready answer.

"So you're going to assassinate me for stealing personal data?
Mostly compiled from posts and images that people fall all over
themselves to publicize to the world?" The pace of his words
had quickened, the first trace of the mental velocity Echo had described. "If *that* ticks the box of your knight-errant code, you'd
better kill *everyone*." A gleam of teeth. "The masterminds behind
the social-media platforms, e-commerce, NSA, FBI, your friendly
neighborhood PD."

The Fifth Commandment: *If you don't know what to do, do nothing.*

Evan did nothing.

Devine had no problem filling the negative space. "Or perhaps it's
the sex that concerns you? The recreational drugs? I don't let anyone
through my doors who isn't at least twenty-one because, let's face
it, the age of consent isn't the age of maturity. They choose to come
here as adults, or at least their best version of it. I have medics on
standby. Not a single overdose. I don't do drugs myself. I don't even
take any"—the faintest hitch—"medications."

"It's not the sex," Evan said. "Or the drugs."

"Then it must be the power I've amassed from others who are
willing to be corrupted. Want to execute me for that? Why not
kill the president as well for sending you here to kill me? The Secret Service, too, while you're at it. Even that nice special agent in
charge, the one who caught you. There are so many power players
out there with their hands on the levers."

"Not all of them can swing a Senate vote."

"Ah." Devine's eyes gleamed with a dark kind of delight. "The environmental bill."

"How much do you stand to gain if it goes down?"

"Not a dime."

Devine's stare was unwavering, and Evan was surprised to find that he believed him. "Why, then?"

"Because," Devine said. "The bill is nonsense. It's not about the climate. It's to assure Victoria's reelection while funneling a trillion dollars to government contractors with noncompete clauses."

The first-name drop did not go unnoticed.

"Same military-industrial hogs with their snouts in a different trough," Devine said. "Have you read the bill?"

"Of course not."

"The corn lobby's pushing through a hundred billion dollars in subsidies to pursue corn ethanol even though sugarcane is cheaper and seven times more efficient. The primary contractor for wind pivoted from aeronautics last quarter in anticipation of the bill. Zero institutional expertise. The hexagonal head bolts for the turbines cost thirty-two dollars to manufacture—they're planning on charging fourteen hundred and forty-three dollars per bolt. Each wind park has a profit margin of four thousand four hundred thirty-six percent. And that's the *fairest* bit of price gouging. There's massive resource misallocation, zero transparency, pork-barrel earmarks, collusion among subsidiaries. It's not a free market fed by innovation and competition. It's a captive market. And I am attempting to free it."

"Why do you get to decide?" Evan asked.

"Because no one else is willing to," Devine said. "Sound familiar?"

Evan didn't rise to the bait.

"There's always a bigger bully. Until me." Devine hesitated. "And you."

"Why are you telling me all this?" Evan asked. "Why do you want to be understood by me?"

"Because . . ." Devine froze on an image of Evan from earlier in the evening, crossing behind Tenpenny's back to the stairs. A disembodied skull drifting above black clothes. The biometrics were at him hard, but all the connecting slots and windows were blank. No identifying features, no social media, no websites or images online. "You are the Nowhere Man. If you want to kill me, you will succeed. One way or another, you will accomplish it. I have not a prayer against you. My only hope is to convince you."

"How do you know who I am? How did you—"

"*I* don't do anything." Devine raised an eyebrow to the screen. "I get others to do my bidding for me. Why keep an ear to the ground when I can have well-placed people doing it instead? Why go to the trouble of running a major fake-news network when I can own the man who does? Why waste time politicking when I can motivate cabinet members and Supreme Court justices by alternative means?"

He leaned forward on the chaise, fingertips pressed together between his parted knees, the digits forming a globe. His face was flushed, and his speech had picked up to a canter. "They fear the kind of power I hold. Just like they fear yours. So they want me gone. But they can't touch me lawfully. They need you. That's why we are having this discussion. I believe that if you understand, you will leave me to my kingdom."

Evan started to answer, but Devine held up a hand. "Let's continue this somewhere more comfortable. I've always thought that there are few things in life that can't be better discussed over two ounces of chilled vodka."

"Finally," Evan said, "we agree on something."

Devine's mouth reshaped itself into a smile that said that somehow he knew that already.

46

I Was Told There'd Be Vodka

"Ever since we pretended to outgrow religion, we've ceased to value humility, forgiveness, surrender. So what do we have? An arrogant generation that doesn't know how to forgive or surrender. And who are we letting point our way?" Devine faced Evan from behind a curved mahogany bar immense enough to seat a Broadway chorus line.

The space, a drawing room of sorts, featured bookshelves, wainscoting, and a spectacular array of bottles. On the wall to Evan's side, an enormous pencil-and-watercolor wash showed the face of the great Lebanese poet, his famous words writ large in melodic calligraphy:

> *Your pain is the breaking of The Shell*
> *that encloses your understanding.*

"Bureaucracies disemboweled by meekness? Media-seeking crybullies? Leaders who armor themselves in the ideology of left or right and mouth calculated sentiments to lord over their respective dung heaps?"

The voluble host had spoken unbroken for the past ten minutes, his words coming so fast they'd started to run together. No sign remained of the measured speech or inscrutable façade he'd presented earlier. It was as though once he loosed his thoughts, he could no longer control them; he just had to hold on and let them bull their way through the china shop. Evan sensed that the acceleration had something to do with the understanding Luke craved from those he deemed worthy—this tonnage of words shoved before him like the blade of a bulldozer, scarring his signature into the topography. It wasn't enough for him to be the holder of the strings; he had to be revered for what he was, what he saw, what he could do.

"I was told there'd be vodka," Evan said.

Half turning to run a finger solicitously across the spirits, Devine kept on. "They want to take the bloodsport out of business." His finger ticked across a bottle of Beaufort, custom-made for the lower bar at the Savoy in London. "The iron-testing from education." Next a squat Black Cow container that mimicked a milk bottle; a West Dorset dairy farmer had derived a pure milk vodka from whey. "The teeth out of art."

Devine's digit slid past Wyborowa with its twisted glass bottle designed by Frank Gehry. When it reached the next bottle, fat and round with a running wild boar on it, Evan gave a nod.

He'd not yet been able to get his hands on Atomik vodka, created with water pumped from a local aquifer in Chernobyl and grain grown on a plot inside the Exclusion Zone. The distillation process cut the radiation to almost zero. Almost.

Devine said, "They're trying to rearrange the world to avoid any possible suffering. But we can never eliminate suffering. There's no wisdom without it. It's a tale as old as the Greeks."

"And you're good enough to provide the service?" Evan asked.

"No. I'm just not afraid to do it."

"You think you're pretty grand," Evan said.

"Only in comparison to everyone else." Devine didn't grin; he was in dead earnest. He poured two fingers into a crystal tumbler.

"One rock," Evan said. "Cube or sphere."

Devine plopped a spherical ice cube into Evan's glass and then poured himself a good five ounces of Macallan No. 6. "Shouldn't we cultivate men and women who know how to withstand pressure, to persevere, to think outrageously? Did we forget that menace has to be met with will? That we're competing against other nations? That we're collectively responsible for the future of a planet?" He leaned forward on the mahogany plain like an old-fashioned barman. "We're so far out of touch with our animal instincts we've made ourselves vulnerable to being ruled by the worst of them."

Evan sipped. Atomik was rounded off but still hair-on-your-chest strong, more a grain spirit than true vodka. The water base had qualities of similar limestone aquifers from the south of England or France's Champagne region.

He'd been fascinated by Atomik since he'd heard of it. A pure spirit summoned from the most contaminated place on earth. That's where items of greatest value lay: *In sterquiliniis invenitur.* Treasure guarded by the dragon. The alchemist's jewel in the toad's head. Pearl in an oyster's mouth. Every last freedom he'd found within himself, buried in caves hewn from his worst self.

"I haven't," Evan said, when he came up for air.

"What?" Devine seemed surprised to be interrupted, as if just remembering that he wasn't alone.

"Forgotten I'm an animal."

"That's why I'm talking to you." Devine took down half the whiskey, a single five-hundred-dollar gulp. He leaned on the bar unfazed and unslowed. "You and I, we don't hide from the heat of reality beneath the parasol of the latest ideology. When you don't have a tribe or a party or a doctrine to clad yourself in? When you're not captured by belief? When you're *free*? It's goddamned lonely."

His penetrating gaze felt like a violation. Instinctively, Evan lowered his eyes to his drink, a tell he instantly regretted.

Devine kept on. "Most people need their guardrails. They build their own prison cells thought by thought. Milton spent the 1650s reading by light of candle. Latin, Greek, Hebrew, French, Spanish, Dutch, Italian, Old English—every known book in existence. He went blind. From reading too much? No. From *knowing* too much. He wrote *Paradise Lost* from the depths of his sightless mind. Can you imagine? Shouldering the crushing weight of centuries of tradition to spin his own heaven and hell into being?"

His eyes were glazed but present, an unsettling effect as if he were looking straight through Evan, across the room, and through the opposing wall at something imperceptible to the human eye.

"But today? We decide what we believe minute by minute, sound bite by sound bite, tweet by tweet. And we assume it's the most moral, the most just. Why? Because it's the *latest*. Our beliefs have no time to age. To consider the broad sweep that delivered us here, to this instant in history. And everyone's running so fast to keep up that they can't grasp just how treacherous this is. When our culture gets this ill, this unbalanced, it requires *daring* to heal it."

Now the second half of Devine's glass went down.

"Maybe that's all the devil is," he continued. "Maybe he just embraces the worst of what's inside"—a wicked pause—"*everybody*. So we don't forget. Everywhere we look, people are scrambling to tell us how infallibly *moral* they are. Politicians. Preachers. Pop stars. Journalists. Corporations, for God's sake. That's why someone like me is needed—a vice merchant, a collector of sins. Someone who refuses to let them get away with it." Devine hummed with energy. "Label me bad if you like, but people willing to be bad are *necessary*. They're the only ones who can wake us up so we'll have the strength to avoid worse people later."

Evan tasted the vodka once more, felt the burn forge down his throat, coat his stomach. "Maybe that's what worse people tell themselves when they're still only bad."

"You were dispatched to kill me," Devine said. "So. As one should do in any situation no matter how hard, I asked myself, what is the opportunity this presents to me? How might we fit together?"

"We don't."

"Someone has to do up here what you do down there." Devine searched the shelves behind him for his next pour. "You only neutralize people for good reason. I only control them for such. What makes me a greater abuser of human law and custom than you?" He found a Glenfiddich Reserve to his liking and dashed a sloppy pour into his glass without bothering to rinse it out first. "I extort senators. You knife someone in an alley. The question isn't *what* I do. But *why*. What if it's to torpedo a law written by lobbyists to let corporations dump radioactive waste on Native American reservations because they're exempt from federal environmental regulations? Or to sink a pork-laden bill that's about the environment in name only?" A robust gulp. "You could use an ally like me."

"The last thing I need," Evan said, "is an ally like you."

Devine blinked at him. He looked not so much offended as surprised by Evan's lack of imagination. "I'm the *only* kind of ally you need."

"Why's that?"

"Because. We are nothing alike." Holding his eyes on Evan, Luke drained the scotch in a few swift swallows. The alcohol seemed not to affect him at all. "You and I have different gifts. We're familiar with yours. Mine?" He set the empty glass down hard. "When my brain speeds up, it feels like the rest of the world is moving in slow motion. And the less I sleep, the less sleep I need, until I'm nothing more than a body hooked to the network of my thoughts." As he spoke faster, his body canted forward, weight shifted onto the balls of his feet, head cocked slightly out ahead of his neck. "Do you know what it feels like? Moving that fast when everyone else is wading through sludge?"

Evan wondered if Devine's superpower was just wearing people the hell out.

"I understand your reticence," Luke said. "At a certain point, the world doesn't make sense anymore. It's not supposed to. It's because you've outgrown it. You need my expansiveness. I need someone who can ensure I hold . . . perspective. Imagine what you could do if I threw all my power, my reach, my resources behind you. Imagine who you could be if we joined forces. I'm offering you an alliance that will open up the universe to us both."

He reached beneath the bar and came up with a pistol. Evan's ARES 1911.

"What's it gonna be?" Devine asked. "The rules you've always lived by?" He set the pistol on the mahogany between them. "Or what lies beyond?"

Without breaking eye contact with Luke, Evan picked up his pistol, wrapped his left hand over the top of the slide with his middle finger touching the rear of the ejection port, and pulled back until he felt the cartridge case at the breech face. Chamber loaded. Letting the slide go, he thumbed the safety up, ejected the magazine into his palm, and pushed the top cartridge down hard with his index finger. No budge. He reseated the full mag with a click and set the loaded pistol back down on the bar, aimed half-way between him and Luke, an indicator arrow deciding which way to point.

Weapon-status check by touch, less than three seconds.

Devine's stare was unblinking, hawklike. Evan felt the heat of it as surely as he'd felt the fireplace glow on the side of his face.

"Johnny Seabrook," Evan said. "Angela Buford."

Devine's sigh smelled of charred oak casks and warm spices. "You are," he said, "so fucking disappointing."

They stared at each other. Ten seconds passed. Then thirty. One full minute was a long time to hold hostile eye contact.

"Ethics," Luke said tartly, "are a good boy's version of morality. It's coloring inside the lines. Don't worry. You'll outgrow it one day."

Evan allowed himself another sip.

Luke's focus hadn't wavered. His intensity like a spotlight directed into Evan's face. A dark sort of anger seethed beneath his features. Evan watched the frustration work its way up from the pit of Devine's stomach until it reached his mouth; it was as though he could not prevent himself from speaking. "You're not supposed to be here because of a dead boy I've never met."

"And girl," Evan said. "Why am I supposed to be here?"

"Because as the unofficial fourth co-equal branch of government, I'm a threat to President Donahue-Carr and the entire rotten system she represents."

"I don't care about any of that."

"What then?" Luke's tone, as sharp as a blade. "What do you care about?"

Evan thought of the unfinished jigsaw puzzle on the Seabrooks' kitchen table. Ruby slouched in her brother's beanbag. Deborah smoking her taboo cigarettes. Mason's multicolored beard glistening with tears. He thought about a young woman who wrote poetry on driftwood, who'd changed her name to Desiree, whose head had been twisted around on her skull farther than bone and tendon allowed.

"Nothing you'd understand," Evan said.

"Perhaps you're right," Luke said. "You concern yourself with trifles. I'm trying to wake up the world."

"The world is already perfect, Devine. It's people that are broken. And all your talking won't fix that. It's too abstract, too many ways to get lost. We only learn anything in the doing."

"I know you believe that," Devine said. "But I am offering you a rare gift. The opportunity to be wrong."

Evan took another sip and set down his glass, half full. "Labor Day," he said. "A year and a month ago."

Devine blinked three times in rapid succession. "What?"

"That's the date Johnny Seabrook and Angela Buford were murdered. I think it happened here at Tartarus. At one of your parties. You've displayed your extensive time-stamped surveillance footage. So. Show me."

"Gladly."

"I'll make you a deal," Evan said. "If their deaths had nothing to do with you or this place, then we'll continue the discussion."

Luke said, "And if they did?"

Evan reached for the ARES and gave it a spin. It rotated lazily around and came to rest aiming at Luke.

He picked up the pistol and slid it into his holster.

He stood.

Luke followed him out.

47

This Kind of Mind-Fuckery

Tenpenny halted in the doorway, his head nearly brushing the top of the frame. "You let him in here? No one's allowed in here. Ever."

He'd been summoned to the scarlet room, brought up short by the sight of Evan inside the Faraday cage with Luke.

Luke pointed at the computer. "Labor Day last year," he said.

Tenpenny shuffled over reluctantly and began working the database with practiced dexterity. He looked like an organist, long fingers flurrying over the controls, calling up various programs on the massive screen.

Evan and Luke stood shoulder to shoulder, watching Tenpenny zero in on the proper date. Though the tall man didn't have a cigarette, his clothes respired stale smoke, tingeing the windowless room with a bleary gray smell.

At last he found the file for Labor Day and clicked on it.

A proliferation of camera angles filled the screens, showing Tartarus in the quiet of early morning. They watched the estate stir to life, gardeners and house staff readying for the day. Tenpenny zipped along on fast-forward, the time stamp spinning through the morning. The sped-up afternoon saw more jerky progress—tables rolled into place, bar stations set up, outdoor lights strung.

"You'll see with your own two eyes that your concerns are unjustified," Luke said to Evan. "That young man and woman were never here. Then we can get back to what really—"

The footage turned to fuzz.

Tenpenny stiffened. His movements grew frustrated. He clicked more vigorously on the mouse and tapped the wireless keyboard hard enough that the keys gave off little snapping noises.

"What," Devine said, "is wrong?"

Evan had never heard so much cold rage compressed into three words.

"Looks like some kind of file corruption." Tenpenny's voice sounded muffled, though there was no reason it should be. "I don't get it."

The slightest coloring had crept in at the wings of Luke's nostrils, his eyes enlarged by what looked like true surprise.

Evan reached for his pocket.

Luke and Tenpenny froze.

Evan's hand emerged with the RoamZone. He thumbed up the recording he'd made. Pressed PLAY.

The altered voice came low and growling: *"Stop talking about your brother. Stop asking questions about your brother. Or I will come for you like I came for him. You'll get your counseling, your medication to try to convince yourself that maybe I forgot, that it's safe to talk to the cops, that the threat is no longer real. But I am. I always will be. You will never be safe from me."*

Tenpenny kept his back turned, his focus on the noncompliant computer. Luke's face had tightened, his lips a bloodless stroke. He looked livid.

Evan said, "Sounds like you."

"No. That sounds like a *coward*. I've never been afraid to speak in my own voice." Devine pivoted to Tenpenny, who looked diminished by fear, stooped, his shoulders melting forward off his spine. "I'll deal with you later."

Tenpenny rubbed his palms together. They made a dry, scratching sound. He eased awkwardly around Devine, who did not budge, and exited meekly.

Devine walked over to the chaise longue and sat with his hands on his knees, nostrils flaring as he breathed.

Evan moved to the one opposite.

They stared at each other through the scarlet glow of the room.

"My house will be set in order," Devine said. "This is a mistake. And it will be rectified. You'll see. I'll get to the bottom of this."

"Me, too," Evan said.

"It's an unforeseen hurdle. Nothing more."

"That's the thing when you move too fast. You miss stuff."

"No," Luke said.

"Then you're not looking hard enough."

"At what?"

"Everything. Anything. Pick one thing you've done. Stare at it. And follow it down. All the way down."

"I've done that," Luke said. "I've examined every last self-deception, every blind spot, every confirmation bias—"

"Not for *you*," Evan said. "For those people you shove around like pawn pieces. If you really looked at what you've done and who you had to be to do it, you'd feel like you were free-falling through darkness. With no bottom."

"Why do you think that?"

Evan just looked at him.

"You don't know a goddamned thing about where I've been or where I need to go." Devine's expression stayed calm, but there was menace lurking behind his words. He jabbed a finger at the Faraday cage. "You think I can't read you as surely as that software does when people pop up on the screen? It's written all over your face. That you lost your internal life before you had one. That you were too sensitive to handle the pain of existing in reality, so you receded into something else, an archetype. That you can't tolerate ordinary life, so you go to greater and greater extremes just to feel *something*. That you've spent a lifetime building that tolerance, trying to convince yourself that you're not really subject to human emotions and frailties like everyone else. When the truth is you're too weak to contain them. Without your missions, the hapless victims you compulsively rescue, who are you? Nothing. The No-where Man. A scared little boy wearing a lifetime of armor, living in a state of arrested development with your guns and your kung fu. You haven't even learned to age yet. How to let yourself grow older. How can anyone respect a man-child like that?"

The words came sharp and hard like pellets. The room seemed filled with them.

Evan breathed and then breathed some more. "Did you say 'kung fu'?"

But Devine didn't bite.

"The thing is," Evan said, "I'm immune to this kind of mind-fuckery. Know why?" He rose. "Because I don't fear being misunderstood."

"But it's obvious what you *do* fear," Devine said. "Losing control."

Evan pondered a moment. "No," he said. "If I lose control? *I'm* not the one who should be scared."

Devine found his feet. He was unintimidating physically, but that ramrod posture—as if he were hammered from steel—and the words packed inside him waiting to be ignited imbued him with an energy of restrained viciousness. "Do your worst."

Evan tipped his head in a respectful nod and left him in the room.

Tenpenny was nowhere to be seen, but Rathsberger was waiting for Evan at the base of the sweeping stairs. In the grim, stark light of the foyer, his face was hard to look at. A few workers tidied up at the periphery of the enormous room, sweeping and mopping and gathering glassware. The cavernous space smelled of cleaning solutions and spilled champagne.

Rath stepped back as Evan neared and walked him out, holding five feet off Evan's shoulder like a fighter-jet escort.

There were no guards in evidence anymore. Tugging the enormous door open, Evan was hit with a waft of cool, wet air smelling of salt and the stench of low tide.

Rath halted, keeping well away from Evan. "Guess we'll be seeing you again."

Evan looked back. "That's a promise."

"We'll be ready. You'll never get through this door. You'll never make it inside Tartarus again. Not on our watch."

"We'll see."

Two-thirds of Rath's face grinned. "You know how this ends, don't you?"

Evan said, "You don't want a catchphrase."

The grin intensified, the sworl of hard red scar tissue at Rath's chin tugging his right lip down until the line of his lower gums showed, gleaming wetly. "Why not?"

"Because of what happens to guys with catchphrases."

Evan stepped out into the night. The minivan waited on the quartz rocks with the key fob placed on the front right tire. At his back the door shut with bank-vault heft. Standing in the soft rain, he heard nothing through the thick wood but silence. No scuff of feet, no clang of trays or plates, no sounds of life at all.

He listened for a time longer, but there was only the pitter-patter of rain working its way through his clothes. It was as though he'd passed out of one world into another and the portal had sealed behind him. But he knew now what he had to do out here before he returned.

He would honor the First Commandment.

Find the answers he required.

And see the mission through no matter the cost.

48

A Glimpse of Freedom

Evan cleaned everywhere he'd touched in the Hampton Bays house, readying himself to take leave of his temporary residence. He removed twenty thousand dollars in bundled hundreds from his rucksack and left the cash on the kitchen counter. The minivan he'd take care of later, restoring the original plates and returning it to the airport parking lot, the tank refilled halfway as he'd found it.

Devine's words were still at him, wriggling beneath his skin, winding around the base of his brain and squeezing, making his thoughts bulge this way and that. He thought about the people Devine held himself above, the ones striving for something better within themselves, searching for a hidden path that might pull them one more rung up out of chaos toward order.

He didn't have disdain for them.

Where Devine found their striving pitiful, Evan found it valiant, worth protecting.

As there was something worth sheltering inside him, that first pure impression of self, alone in a room serenaded by a nursery rhyme and distant sobs, a baby mobile throwing patterns on the ceiling and then red flashing lights.

That was it, life in a microcosm.

Grip the guardrails.

And then let go.

The spice rack on the counter wasn't arranged properly, the bottles shoved into their wooden slots haphazardly. Cinnamon below cumin, thyme next to dill. It was a fucking mess.

Evan stared at it for a time, suppressing his abecedarian instincts. Keeping his hands still, he reorganized them mentally by size and then cap color and then degrees of sweetness and spice. The Hungarian paprika was on the worst tilt, and he allowed himself to nudge it so the lettering was horizontal.

On the large-format calendar stuck to the refrigerator, the blue-highlighted *"Vacay!"* note showed the family to be gone for the following week, useful to know in the likely event of his return. He let his eyes scan across the other entries. Birthdays and social engagements, logistics and coordinated family time, celebrations and responsibilities.

He wondered what it would be like to keep a schedule like this, weaving his hours into the flow of various lives. Then he considered the brief list of human duties he had to consider.

Feed Vera III.
Check living-wall irrigation.
Joey.

Aragón Urrea's pilot was at home base in Eden, Texas, but he and Evan had arranged to meet at Teterboro Airport in the morning. Tommy had texted Evan that his new truck was ready and he'd better hurry the fuck up and get it and bring ducats, too. Evan had also coordinated with Candy and the Seabrooks, planning next steps. It felt good to have people to check in with, boxes to tick.

Rucksack over one shoulder, he hesitated on his way to the garage, glancing back at the neat stack of cash on the counter. It might freak them out, this nice family, to come home to it.

He found a manila envelope in a drawer, shoved the bundled hundreds in, and then let it fall just inside the front door's mail slot on the tile of the foyer.

He hoped that would make his thank-you less creepy.

Echo felt guilty.

That was her default setting. She knew and hated that she was one of those women who said "sorry" too much. When she asked a person to turn down the air-conditioning. When she asserted her rightful place in line at a shop. When someone else bumped into *her*.

She felt guilty about how long she ran the shower given how far some African women had to walk with a forty-pound jug for water collection. Guilty when takeout arrived in Styrofoam boxes that she knew took five hundred years to decompose. Guilty about buying a seven-dollar cappuccino when that was half the average hourly wage for workers in America. Guilty that she'd bought too much Halloween candy that would go to waste since there weren't many kids in the building. Guilty about owning a nine-thousand-dollar cello that languished on its stand, a varnished rebuke. Guilty for letting Luke Devine into her heart and her head. And guilty for feeling guilty about that, which a liberated woman should not.

She was sorry.

Sorry for everything.

A big bleeding heart that ached all the day long except when she was working with kids, helping them access feelings through music, to express themselves with melodies. Kids like her, who felt everything too much. That was the solution, she'd found. Doing something about it where she could and trying to forgive herself as much as possible for everything else. That was her insurance policy to keep herself from ossifying into someone like her mother, someone who aimed all that guilt outward at everyone else and deemed them lacking.

A Glimpse of Freedom

It was terrifying.

Waiting for Mr. No Name, she needed a break from it all now. Noise and movement and color. The TV was on, and her finger had been clicking for longer than she realized, spinning through the endless wheel of channels. Home-remodeling show. Eighties sitcom. Somber newscaster. *Friends* spinning umbrellas in the water fountain. Oprah Oprah-ing. Buffed-bald Keanu stuck with a thousand futuristic acupuncture needles asking, "Why do my eyes hurt?"

Her doorbell rang. When she checked the peephole, he was standing back in full view, a nice consideration for a woman living alone.

She let him in and made herself a cup of tea. He declined as before.

They took up their seats, she wrapped in her plush velvet blanket on the couch, he sitting on the chair from her kitchen set. As he recounted details of his interactions with Luke, she felt surreal, as if she were listening to a fantastical story, a myth, a parable: *The Tale of the Unhinged Ex.*

She wondered how much of the story Mr. No Name left out.

When he finished, she shook her head and said, "That sounds like Luke left to his own brain chemistry." She held the warm mug, and it held her right back. "Thank you for telling me. That's why you came by?"

Mr. No Name shook his head. "I need your help."

"How so?"

"Do you think Devine knew about Johnny Seabrook and Angela Buford?"

She stared down, watched the mist curl off her mug. "The thing about Luke? He can be all kinds of wonderful. And all kinds of awful. But I've never known him to lie."

Mr. No Name nodded.

"He surrounds himself with these excesses and extreme people," she said. "But he's oddly . . . pure that way. I don't know if that's still the case. But that's how I always experienced him. I'm sorry"—*ugh*—"if that's not super helpful."

"It is."

"Okay. I don't really get it. Why what I think about all this is useful to you."

"Because you see things other people don't."

"Why do you think that?"

"I don't think it. I know it. Just like you do."

He held her stare, but it wasn't threatening, not at all. It was more like he was willing to look into her if she was willing to let herself be looked into. Breathing a haze of chamomile, she decided that maybe it might be okay.

His face wasn't particularly interesting. He was so plain-looking. Not much to see, really. And yet he had such presence, as if he was right where he was and nowhere else.

"I'm scared," she said. "All the time."

"You're either that," he said, "or you're that while working on *not* being that."

She thought for a very long time. And then she nodded.

He moved to rise.

"I said there wasn't any music in your voice." She'd begun speaking the thought without realizing it. "But I think there is. It's just ancient, really deep. Maybe it's a pitch most people can't hear anymore. Like a dog whistle."

Mr. No Name gave a partial grin. "If that's true," he said, "I'm glad you hear it."

She lost herself in the mist rising from her tea, in her blanket, in a wave of emotion she didn't understand. When she came back to herself, he was gone.

He'd replaced the chair over by the table in the kitchen.

It was as though he was never even there.

She stared at the empty chair. And then at her cello reclining on its stand by the front door.

She was up on her feet, gliding across the studio, and then she was gazing down at the narrow-grained-spruce face of her cello, the steel-core strings stretching from the neck across the beautiful wide hips, each a fifth apart. There and waiting, ready to give voice to sensation, to speak in tongues, to span the universe.

Music flooded her mind. Her hands twitched with muscle

memory. For the first time in a long time, she felt a pull back to brightness, an opening of the heart she recognized as a glimpse of freedom.

She reached for her instrument.

49

All the Way Down

Luke Devine had a dream that he was all his worst parts.

And nothing else.

Pick one thing you've done.

He came to with the sheets whipped into a frenzy around him, a whirlpool dragging him down. He struggled against them, but they clung to his bare flesh, damp with sweat. He lay there and watched his thoughts gather like storm clouds until they stopped drifting. Until they layered one on top of the other, blotting out the blue sky of his mind.

Fighting free of the sheets, he tumbled out of bed, feet slapping the cold marble tile. It felt as though something were coming for him, an inkling from the other side of himself.

It had been an arduous day. He'd intervened meaningfully in a lieutenant-governor race in Virginia, in the hostile takeover of a global telecoms corp out of Taiwan specializing in highly intrusive AI technology, and in a hacker group's auction for access to compromised Iranian security networks on a dark web forum. But none of that compared to his face-off with the Nowhere Man.

He was shivering, his teeth clattering.

Stare at it.

Pulling on a robe, he moved to the bar cart and drank down one scotch and then another. The warmth pulled the veil back on the dividing line between the two hims, and he caught a peek of the other half and it scorched his mind's eye.

And follow it down.

He padded across his master bedroom, throwing open the French doors, his churning thoughts seeking escape, and his palms hit the wrought-iron railing, and he was assaulted by the roar of the waves and the mist in his nostrils and eyes and the smudged dot of the moon peering down like an eye and the clean reek of the seaside, decay and seaweed, salt and life, and he thought about the transgression that had been allowed here under his own roof, he anticipated the necessary horrors it would bring, and he felt the veins pulsing with blood in his neck, the words boiling up from his chest, sandpapering the inside of his throat, his roiling inner state reflected in the crashing waves beyond and the smudged eye of God above.

The dark firmament was too much, the endless night peering into him, blank and all-knowing, so he filled another glass and hurried to the elevator, riding it lower and lower.

The dry wine cellar smelled of redwood and the faintest hint of mildew. It calmed him being down here, twirling the aged bottles, the dusty labels of years gone by. Gave him a sense of scope, of patience, of the long game that was the only game worth playing. But tonight his hands shook too much for him to take joy in the bottles' rustling turns. He felt weak and unmoored, swaying on sea legs, and then—

All the way down.

The floor was ice against his cheek, blocky dungeon stones. He was curled on his side embryonically, contorting. For so long his head had been moving fast, so fast, poked up above the clouds into heaven, but now he sensed the roots, too, that had anchored his rise. They were thin and spidery, but they stretched all the way down.

He could chase them down to his former self, but his brain wouldn't allow the necessary stillness. A thousand thoughts running like hamsters on wheels inside his skull, a thousand things to desire and dread.

Not least of all the blood that would now have to be spilled.

50

Don't Even Try

Evan drove to the Seabrooks' house in the long-suffering Hertz Buick Regal he'd left in the free parking lot at Hanscom Field.

At the top of the walkway, he took a moment to admire the stolid Colonial. It looked like a house was supposed to look, a good safe place to grow a family.

Candy answered the door before he could ring. Her long blond hair was straightened and worn up in a twist skewered by a single black-lacquered chopstick. A bustier showed off her chest and a slice of bare stomach. The back dipped low at the hem, covering her scars. Glazed lipstick coated her plush lips, a shimmer of berry and bronze.

"OxiClean," she said.

"What?"

"To get blood out of carpet."

She breezed past him, smelling of sweetness and sunlight, and Evan wondered just how in hell she'd managed to put herself together like that within hours of disposing of a corpse. She was halfway to his car when he caught up.

"Still need me to keep an eye on the safe house?" She threw back the line over her shoulder.

"Just for a bit."

"Where will you be?"

"Figuring out my next move."

Evan unlocked the car and held the passenger door for her. She paused before getting in, their faces close. "Will it involve me?"

"Depends how violent it gets."

She poured herself into the car, her lashes dipping slyly. She was a hard woman to read—the hardest—but Evan could have sworn she seemed flattered.

The Seabrooks' safe house that Joey had arranged was a historic brownstone in Jamaica Plain. Evan stood in full view of the call-box camera, Candy behind him. They were buzzed in from a room to the interior, the three Seabrooks staying out of the foyer as instructed. Candy held back, assessing the locks on the front windows.

Evan came around the corner to find Ruby, Mason, and Deborah perched nervously on stools around a breakfast-bar extension of the ugly tiled kitchen counter. Mason was dressed for the day, but Deborah still wore her bathrobe and slippers and Ruby had on a too-big Wellesley High Baseball sweatshirt. Since Evan had instructed them to leave their phones at their house, he'd provided them a burner, which rested on the counter before them. The shelves were bare, the place spartan, utilitarian, ready for quick turnovers. A fine enough space, but certainly not a home. The Seabrooks looked as temporary as the decorative glass flour and sugar canisters sitting empty beneath a built-in microwave.

"Is everything all right?" Deborah asked.

"Yes," Evan said. "I'm still looking into things. I'm going to have someone watch over you until it's done."

Candy stepped into view, hips on tilt, left leg knee-locked and kicked to the side. At the sight of her, all three Seabrooks rose, their faces frozen in something like astonishment.

Candy surveyed the windows and rear door, barely taking note of the family.

Striding past them, she tapped at Deborah's bathrobe pocket, withdrew the hidden pack of Glamour Super Slim Amber 100s, and snicked up a single stick with a flick of her wrist. She tweaked a knob on the stovetop, bent to the flame, and lit up. As she straightened back up, she checked the cam lock on the window over the sink, her expression making clear it was not to her liking. She swiped an index finger across her front teeth to check for smeared lipstick, then turned to face the Seabrooks, one arm crossed at her hourglass waist, the opposing elbow resting upon it, cigarette hand flared to the side of her cheek.

The Seabrooks still had not moved. Or spoken.

"You'll be fine," Evan said. "Feed her red meat and stay out of her way."

"I love her," Ruby said breathlessly. "I want to *be* her."

"Oh, honey . . ." Candy blew a smoke ring, shot another smaller one through it. With a slender cardinal-red fingernail, she dimpled the top of the second ring as it floated forward, turning it into a heart an instant before it dissipated gracefully on the space between Ruby's eyes.

Ruby looked like she might die in a stroke of ecstatic rapture.

Candy smiled. "Don't even try."

51

Can't Take the Mythology Outta Man

When Evan pulled up to Tommy Stojack's armorer shop, a new Ford F-150 was waiting in the dirt strip that passed for a driveway. A rusting auto-repair sign, freshly peppered with buckshot, swung creakily on its chains above the metal front door. One of the neon tubes was blown out. In the apron of land fronting the shop, car hoods, doors, and engine blocks had rusted into the desert sand, adding fresh orange to the reds and burnt siennas of the Las Vegas landscape. The auto parts had become one with the brush and cacti much as Tommy had become one with the secret lair they disguised.

Unlisted in any directory, this was where Tommy did his work for various government-sanctioned groups, everything from weapons procurement to prototyping to proof-of-concept.

Evan circled his replacement truck. The long-standing top-selling vehicle in the country, the F-150 was—like Tommy's shop and Evan himself—hardly deserving of a second glance. And yet it housed countless hidden tactical features—laminated armor glass, Kevlar inside the door panels, self-sealing run-flat tires. A custom push bumper in the front protected the radiator from explosions or incoming rounds. Rectangular vaults in the bed could store plentiful ordnance. Tommy would have beefed up the suspension, removed the air bags, and disabled the inertia-sensing switches in the bumpers that shut off power to the fuel pump in the event of a crash.

The machine was designed to keep functioning no matter the beating it took.

Evan admired it for that.

He heard a *shuck-shuck* behind him and boots crunching gravel.

"In Buddha we trust," Tommy growled. "Everyone else, show me empty hands."

Evan held his arms wide and turned around. Tommy kept the Benelli M1 combat shotgun angled to the side, but his base was set and ready, knees bent to absorb recoil, boots shoulder-width apart with one slightly forward, weight on the balls of his feet.

Seeing Evan, he lowered the shotgun, smiled wide, and shot a stream of tobacco juice through the gap in his front teeth. A few drops lingered on his biker's mustache, so he swiped at them with the back of his sleeve and spit once more into the dirt. "Like the warrior-monk says, 'Be polite, be professional, but have a plan to kill everybody you meet.'"

"Good to see you, Tommy."

Tommy shuffled a few steps forward gingerly on his warhorse joints. His boots dragged slightly, kicking up dust. He squinted at Evan. "You dig yerself outta that S3?"

"S3?"

"Shit show supreme."

"Mostly."

Tommy nodded pensively, those hound-dog eyes taking Evan's measure. Then he chinned at the truck. "She's ready." Another flash of teeth beneath that horseshoe mustache. "I take cash, Bitcoin, or squirrel pelts."

Evan handed him a manila envelope stuffed with bundles of hundreds, and Tommy shoved it in the front of his camo pants without counting for once and dangled the truck keys off the stub of the finger he'd lost at the first knuckle. He smelled like chewing tobacco and Old Spice.

"Stash this in the garage a few days?" Evan nodded at his backup car, a battered Civic from the Diamond Bar safe house. "I'll pick it up when it's over."

"On your way, then," Tommy said, turning to go. "Don't let the door hit ya where the good Lord split ya."

"One more thing."

From a cargo pocket, Evan withdrew a small black velvet pouch containing what was perhaps his only truly personal possession. He'd pit-stopped at home to grab it from his bureau, where he kept it hidden beneath a stack of precision-folded boxer briefs and the false drawer bottom. He let the item within tumble out to glimmer in Tommy's callused palm.

"Pump the brakes," Tommy said. "I don't do this kind of delicate shit."

"You're plenty delicate," Evan said. "And I don't trust it to anyone else."

"What do you need?"

Evan told him.

Tommy gritted his teeth audibly. His shrug was higher on the left side, no doubt due to a pinched nerve. "When you need it by?"

"I'll wait."

Tommy rolled his eyes to the heavens. "Lord, give me patience. Because if you give me strength, I'm gonna need bail money to go with it."

He turned crisply on his heel and lumbered inside.

Evan followed him. The interior was dungeon-dim and smelled of gun oil. Weapon crates and machinery loomed: test-firing tubes and old-fashioned bank safes, cutting torches and gunsmithing lathes. Through the clutter of equipment, narrow pathways had been cleared, scored with greasy wheel marks from Tommy's rolling chair.

Tommy collapsed into an Aeron with a groan and kicked his way through the labyrinth to a workbench. He shoved a clip-mounted magnifier light in front of his face, his eye enlarged to the size of a Frisbee, and examined what Evan had given him.

"Got any vodka here better than SKYY watermelon?" Evan asked.

"No."

Evan high-stepped over a pallet of Chinese stick grenades and reached beneath a witch's cauldron of a coffeepot gurgling atop a dilapidated cabinet. "That's why I stashed something."

He retrieved Kauffman Vintage from the cabinet where he'd hidden it behind a plastic tub of saturated gun-oil wipes. The bottle was peak elegance, silver and glass curves that brought to mind the silhouette of a penguin. In here it stuck out like a Royal Delft vase in a junkyard.

"You don't happen to have glassware?"

"I got a Solo cup." Tommy picked up a red plastic cup, sniffed it, then squinted into it. He'd slung a pair of welding goggles around his neck, and they dangled from their elastic band. "Nope. This one's fulla Skoal juice. Should be a coffee mug somewhere over by the rifle-cleaning rods. You can wash it out in the bathroom."

Evan grimaced.

"Sorry the service ain't up to your standards." Tommy reached below his workbench, came up with a bottle of Beam, and took a sip of bourbon. He closed his eyes.

"Tommy?"

"Huh."

"Do you think guys like you and me, that we're archetypes?"

"Where'd you hear a thing like that?"

"Guy I'm up against. Brainy."

"I don't trust intellectuals," Tommy said. "They think too much." The magnifying glass cast a contained glow, bringing out the sags of skin beneath his eyes. "And besides, deep down everyone's an archetype of one sort or another. Most folks just prefer to cover themselves up in modern bullshit and pretend otherwise."

"How do you mean?"

"There are no new stories. We're all in thrall to the old ways. Take this . . ." Tommy held the bottle aloft and tilted it so the light caught the rich amber glow. "If I told you we take a grain mixture that's gotta be fifty-one-percent corn, put it in charred oak barrels— but they gotta be *first-time-use* barrels—for a buncha years, that we'd rotate these barrels through different spots in a warehouse, and that when it was done and we sipped it, we'd screw up our faces and say we tasted undercurrents of vanilla and caramel, you'd say I was as batshit as a witch doctor spouting 'bout rhino-horn powder and eye of newt." He shook his head. "You can take the man outta mythology, but you can't take the mythology outta man."

Evan took a light pull from his bottle, the Kauffman going down with more grace and silkiness than seemed possible given the rules of the physical universe. "Tommy, if you'd decided to become an academic," Evan said, "you'd have been a whole different force to be reckoned with."

Tommy knocked back another slug of bourbon, snapped his welding goggles into place, and settled into his workbench for the duration. "Son," he said, "All Souls College wouldn't contain me."

52

One of a Kind

For his first act of homecoming, Evan brought Vera III an ice cube, nesting it in her fleshy serrated leaves. Rather than express appreciation, she glared with reprobation from her bowl of rainbow pebbles. She was even more emotionally demanding than Veras past, though all of the aloe plants had been mouthy.

Exiting the Vault, he walked past his floating bed, pausing to pick a fleck of lint from the sheets. Moving through the great room into the kitchen, he set up at the island.

Then sat at one of the stools to wait.

Returning here now was the first time he'd made a move based on emotional logic alone. It occurred to him that it was not unlikely that he'd guessed wrong.

An hour passed and then another, the shadows attenuating on the poured-concrete floor. He'd lifted the discreet armored blinds, the windows of the building opposite throwing back magenta and orange interpretations of the sunset. It was calm and quiet in his penthouse and he could smell mint from the living wall.

He contemplated Luke Devine's twisty manner of thinking, powerful judgment undergirded by sneaky logic. He wondered if Devine was lying outright or if he'd found a way to outthink his culpability in the deaths of Johnny Seabrook and Angela Buford. He considered willful blindness, shades of responsibility, plausible deniability, degrees of moral separation.

And out of respect for the First Commandment, Evan pried at his own assumptions, searching out weak spots. The facts formed different patterns depending on how he twisted the kaleidoscope.

When it came to Devine, he didn't yet know enough in order to do what it was he did. And Devine knew that somehow. Which meant he'd have to dig deeper to get at the marrow of the truth.

It grew darker.

Evan felt foolish sitting there doing nothing.

He was about to abandon his plan for the evening when he heard a faint scratch at his front door.

He'd left it unlocked.

It swung open.

And there Joey was.

It was the longest he'd gone without seeing her since her stint at Swiss boarding school. She looked tired but undaunted. Her undercut was more severe, buzzed higher on the right side than usual, thick wavy black-brown hair cascading down to frame her face. A tiny green stone pierced her nostril, picking up the vivid emerald of her wide-set eyes. She wore jeans torn at one knee, scuffed Doc Martens, and a tank top that showed off her toned arms. The red-and-black flannel tied around her waist resembled a woebegone kilt.

She halted in the doorway, pick set in hand, backpack slung over one shoulder, Dog the dog tucked in tight at her side. They stared at Evan. One of them wagged their tail.

"What are you doing here?" Joey said.

Evan said, "Shouldn't I ask you that?"

That dimple showed up in her right cheek. "Well, you saved me having to pick your shitty lock."

His front door, with its extensive internal security bars, water core to defeat battering rams, and drill-resistant, pick-resistant, bump-proof dead bolt were hardly shitty. But resistance of most types tended to crumble before the will of Josephine Morales, so Evan figured it unworthwhile to argue the point.

"Go," she said, releasing Dog. He scrambled forward, paws failing to find sufficient purchase on the slick floor. Evan stood as the hundred-ten-pound lion hunter slammed into him, muzzle buried in his crotch.

Evan absorbed the intimate greeting, scratching the ridgeback behind the ears. Dog kept his head smashed between Evan's legs, tail thwapping to and fro, ringing against the barstool and nearly toppling it.

Joey had taken a step inside, the door swinging shut behind her. "I only came back 'cuz Devine's system is tricky and I needed better hardware."

"Uh-huh."

Joey hadn't budged. She fussed with her skull bracelet. "And I just came here 'cuz I set up that sick new water-cooled hashing rig for you in the Vault. It's got more horsepower than I have at my place."

Evan kept petting Dog.

Joey said, "*What?*"

"I didn't say anything."

Dog circled the concrete, padding down imaginary leaves of grass. Then he harrumphed onto the floor and went full tipped-cow on his side, tongue lolling.

"Why'd *you* come home?" She'd mastered the teenage art of turning every question into an accusation.

"I wanted to see you."

She blinked at him. "How'd you know I'd be here?"

"Just a guess."

"Whatever, X. I'm *not* homesick, okay?"

"Okay."

"I was fine on my own."

"I know that."

She scratched at her nose, ambled a few more steps inside, and donned her too-big flannel. She was staring around the great room, taking in the leather couches, the workout stations, the living wall, the view. "So maybe I thought it was time to be back here." Her face had softened the way it did, making her look younger. "Do you . . . ?"

"What?"

She wet her lips. "Know what today is?"

Evan stood and walked around the kitchen island to where he'd set up two military MREs. Of the meals ready-to-eat, chili mac was the least shitty, the entrée augmented with crackers and jalapeño cheese spread, instant fruit punch, and vanilla pound cake. He'd smoothed the crumpled napkins and set the brown plastic cutlery on them to make proper place settings. The accessory packet contained matches, and he'd bent one from the comb and placed the book atop the pound cake so the solitary match stuck straight up.

He flicked the head against the striker. The match bobbed back up.

A makeshift candle.

"Happy birthday, Josephine."

She stood there across the cold, hard concrete floor staring at him, and her lips were trembling and her cheeks were trembling and her beautiful big eyes glimmered. Her hands were at her sides, and all of a sudden she didn't look so tough; she looked like a girl on her seventeenth birthday.

She walked over slowly, dazed, as if in a dream. Then she bent forward, her hair curtaining her cheeks, arcing to nearly meet just beneath her chin. She closed her eyes for several seconds, wish-making, and then blew out the match.

He started up both flameless heater pouches, mixing water into magnesium and sodium to warm up the chow. She sat and watched him.

She wiped at her nose, looked down, looked at the meal, looked up at the ceiling. It was as though it was too much for her to take in at once.

"What about the mission?" she finally asked.

"It can wait a day."

She wiped at her cheeks with one flannel cuff she'd pulled over her hand like a mitten. He made sure not to look at her.

"What's . . ." Her voice cracked. "What's this?"

She chinned at the black velvet pouch resting at her place setting. Evan kept warming the entrées. "Why don't you find out?"

She opened the drawstring, peeked inside. A sharp intake of air. Evan swore he could see the refracted light in her eyes.

She reached inside. And pulled out a classic round-cut diamond solitaire necklace held in a near-invisible prong setting and suspended by a platinum filigree chain as delicate as a spider thread.

The gemstone seemed to catch the light of the entire penthouse and hold it in its living heart.

"The thing about natural diamonds is, they're one of a kind," Evan said. "Like a thumbprint. An iris."

Joey turned away so he couldn't see her face, but her elbow poked out as her hand rose to her cheeks once more.

"Remember what Jack used to say?" Evan asked.

Still facing away, she nodded. "'A diamond's just a lump of coal that knows how to deal with pressure.'"

"Down deep, just above the molten core. Temperatures around two thousand degrees Fahrenheit, pressure something like seven hundred thousand pounds per square inch. Enough to modify crystalline carbon at the atomic level. Enough to transform it into something pure."

"Like your vodka." She looked at him now, finally. She was more composed, but her cheeks were flushed and her expression showed that wide-open vulnerability it got when she was fully within herself. She spoke breathlessly. "Where'd it come from?"

"It belonged to a Persian monarch. It was given to me by an Iranian admiral I did a favor for once."

"Really?"

"I'll tell you the story one day."

"No you won't."

She held it up, and it sparkled transcendentally, finding communion with her eyes. Her mouth was slightly ajar, showing that hair-thin gap in her front teeth.

Evan remembered Deborah's talking about all the times she'd forgotten to pay attention to her son. *Picking at his dirty fingernails. To watch him watching TV. That's all heaven is. It was right there, every instant of my life before. And I couldn't see it.*

The diamond spun and spun before Joey's face. Her mouth tugged to the side. "This better not be bugged, X!"

She gave her openmouthed laugh, graceful in its gracelessness, pure Joey and nothing else. Then she handed him the necklace and turned, lifting the hair from her nape so he could fasten the slender catch.

She turned back, cupping it in her palm beneath her chin. Then she opened her chili mac, dug in her plastic fork, and shoved in a bite. She spoke through a full mouth. "Better eat up so I can get out of your hair."

"It's pretty late," Evan said. "Maybe you should crash here."

"Me? And Dog?"

At his name Dog lifted his head from the cool concrete, furrowed his brow with momentary interest, then laid it back down with a jangle of his collar.

Evan said, "Why not."

"Because if he starts howling, it'll be the Castle Heights *Not Happy Hour*." Her eyes were smiling. "And because of, like, all those hard boundaries you're always bragging about."

She smiled privately and kept her eyes on the MRE. They finished eating together, basking in the most pleasant silence Evan could remember.

When they were done, he cleaned up and she went upstairs into the reading loft to settle in. There was a sofa up there and a small bathroom, with sheets and spare toiletries tucked into a cabinet. The lights clicked on above, casting a glow down through the twisting steps, shadowing the spiral pattern against the floor so it looked like the staircase was a beanpole climbing up from a whirlpool.

Dog raised his head to look wearily at Evan, weighing if it was worth getting up to be closer to his Human. Evan said, "Up to you, pal," and Dog lowered his head once more with a clink of his tags.

A few moments later, they heard Doc Martens clanging down the stairs. Joey ran across the great room, a pillowcase flapping in her hand. "X! OMG! You bought *skull-and-crossbone sheets*? That's *so cute*."

"It was the only pattern they had left."

"Don't *even*. There's not a pattern in this whole condo. You're, like, allergic to patterns—a patternless human." She shook the incriminating pillowcase. "You hoped I'd come. You were hoping I'd come."

"I like having backup gear," he said. "That's all."

She was close to him, bouncing on the balls of her feet, the necklace glittering against her white-ribbed muscle shirt. She jokingly palm-slapped at him. He countered with an inside block to a *pencak silat* strike, but she caught him in a wrist lock and he let her force the elbow and spin him around.

"Mercy," he said, tapping out against her arm for good measure, and she laughed and let go.

When he came around, she dove into him, her cheek smashed to his chest, arms tight around his waist. He could smell her vanilla lotion, the citrus shampoo in her hair, and her breath carried the tang of Dr Pepper. Her shoulders were rising and falling, rising and falling. The wall-to-ceiling windows offered an unparalleled view of Wilshire Boulevard beelining downtown, cars and lights and commerce, a vibrant, dangerous, wondrous city and them here in their tiny piece of it.

She pulled away, heading across the great room without so much as a glance back. Winding up the stairs, she paused halfway. Her eyes glinted and that diamond, too, just above her heart. "You're the worst, X."

His voice had more gravel in it than he'd anticipated. "You're the worst, too."

But she'd already ascended.

53

Chastenment and Humblement

Evan awoke to a clattering in the Vault. He sat up on his floating bed, momentarily disoriented.

He was home. There was human noise inside his penthouse. And yet some half-remembered impulse stopped him from grabbing his ARES 1911 and rushing to neutralize the intruder.

Then he heard, "Dog! Get off! X'll freak if you put your paws up on there."

And he lay back down with a sigh.

Out of bed, into his cargo pants, pulling on a T-shirt, through the shower into the Vault.

Joey sat at his L-shaped desk with her bare feet up, keyboard in her lap, diamond around her neck, hacking away at Devine's system. The OLED screens horseshoeing the walls flurried with code and various progress-update bars. Dog the dog was beside her, both paws up on the desk, drinking water out of a Dorset crystal highball glass that she held loosely around the base.

Evan raced over and seized the glass. "What are you doing?"

Joey and Dog aimed matching expressions of disappointment at him. "I couldn't find a water bowl."

"So you served him in hand-cut lead crystal from southwest England?"

"What was I supposed to use?"

"I don't know. A bucket?"

"Well, ex-*cuuuze* me, I didn't know I should let my dog dehydrate to death rather than drink from some barware you never use."

He breathed into himself, trying to loosen the grip of the Second Commandment. Dog the dog heaped on the guilt, sad yellow eyes beneath a tragic furrowing of brow. He brushed past Evan and plopped down in the corner near the weapon lockers.

Evan leaked an exhalation through his teeth and reoriented toward the screens. The right wall of the horseshoe showed an array of surveillance-cam angles from around the building; Evan had infiltrated the Castle Heights system so he could keep facial-recognition software continuously monitoring incoming traffic. The sight of the software overlay looked eerily similar to Luke Devine's setup in the scarlet room, a parallel Evan chose not to dwell on.

Right now the lobby was empty aside from Joaquin behind the security desk, tossing Corn Nuts into the air and trying to catch them in his mouth. His performance was subpar.

A movement at the door to the underground parking garage caught Evan's attention.

He stiffened at the sight of them, emotion arrowing through his gut.

Mia walking in slowly, Peter at her side. With one arm slung across his shoulders, she moved gingerly toward the elevator, her muscles stiff from the hospital stay. She wore a tired smile, taking in the familiar sights of the lobby. Aunt Janet bustled along behind them, followed by Wally, loaded down with various bags and groceries like a pack mule. Peter scurried ahead excitedly, gesturing at Joaquin, who found his feet to welcome Mia home.

As the family waited for the elevator, Evan reached across Joey to kill the surveillance feeds from the building. It felt impolite to watch them.

His finger hesitated over the mouse as he gave Mia a final look—that lovely bearing, the wild heap of chestnut curls, the birthmark kiss on her temple. And Peter, clutching her hand as if he'd never let it go.

Evan felt their safe return as a warmth in his chest. But there was no place for him there. He said good-bye to them silently.

And clicked.

The feed blinked out horizontally, darkness extinguishing them.

He felt Joey's gaze on the side of his face. "It sucks," she said. "In some other universe, you and Mia would've been great together."

Evan said, "I'm gonna have a shower."

"Fine." She looked peeved. Or perhaps that was just her face.

She resumed riding the keyboard as if it were a wild mustang in need of breaking. Evan felt a pang of empathy for it.

He hesitated halfway through the concealed door, one foot in the Vault and the other in the shower. "Please keep this door closed."

"Of course. Gross. No one needs that. Like, the worst thing *ever* would be seeing you naked."

"Thank you."

"I'd gouge my eyes out with sporks like Oedipus."

"I believe he used gold hair pins—"

"It'd be like birth control for *life*."

"Understood."

"Literally, I'd probably never want to—"

"Got it, Joey."

He closed the door, muffling her next reply.

Freshly showered, Evan returned to the Vault.

Joey didn't look up from her keyboard. "Did the shower cool your raging OCD?"

Evan stared at her dirty toes curled around the edge of the desk, one near the mouse pad, the other close to Vera III, who seemed to be relishing Evan's discomfort. He stood behind Joey and stared at the screens, understanding very little of what she was doing. "Devine's system is pretty robust," he said. "The Faraday cage, plus—"

"Can I, like, save us some time?"

"Sure."

"Cool-cool." Joey snapped her gum and kept clacking at her MX Cherry Blues. It seemed impossible that she was typing with any accuracy, and yet the system continued to obey her every command. "Pretend I explain a bunch of tech stuff to you. Then you get all confuzzled and say 'Huh' and pretend you have any clue what I'm talking about. Then I make fun of you in, like, a super-funny way you don't fully get because: limitations. Then you tell me I can't break into this network, that it's impossible. And I go, 'Yeah. You're right.' But! Then I come up with something awesome. I show you how I'll save the day. Then you're chastened and humbled by my superior being."

He was reluctant to acknowledge that that was in fact how most of their conversations went.

"So, X?" Another gum snap. "Just stay outta my way and I'll tell you when it's time to go get the bad guys."

Vera III seemed to find this all exceedingly amusing.

"Look," Evan said, "I have to get some idea what you're doing."

Joey's hands stopped, the abrupt silence intimidating. "Why? You don't trust me?"

"No."

"What then?"

"So I, you know . . . keep up to date with it."

Joey bounced forward, popping to her feet. "Awww, X. That's totes adorbs. Are you having a tough time keepin' up with the kray-kray kidz these days?"

"Josephine."

He took her by her shoulders, spun her around, and deposited her back in the chair.

She resumed typing as though no interruption had occurred. "When rich-ass people like Devine hire fancypants digital-security folks, they sometimes forget random shit that's internet connected. Like, say, bidets."

"Bidets?"

"'Member what I said about you getting confuzzled? Try'n be a smidge less on-brand, X. Yes, bidets. Of the Japanese variety. The

ID of the automation device that manages the spout, cleaner, lights, dryer—all that—it doesn't have some long string. It's only, like, five hex digits, easy to brute-force, and it just happens to be the default password for the API that they so helpfully documented in leaked internal docs I got from a friend on IRC. And it grabs firmware updates over the internet. So guess who built her own firmware with a backdoor and shipped it over the air to said device?" She jerked dueling thumbs toward her chest, the dangling diamond providing a sparkly bull's-eye. "This guy. Then I used it as a beachhead into everything else, popped into Devine's private network. *Uh*-maze-ballz, right? Oh, and also, as a kind gesture to bidet users the world over, I patched the firmware at the bidet company called—I shit you not—Pee-Pee Fresh, to make it more secure than it was before, 'cuz I'm Robina Hood."

"I'm told *Robin* is also the feminine of *Robin*."

"Whatevs. Either way it's a hacker's wet dream. Own something and leave it better than you found it. Except for the one belonging to the asshole hedge-funder with a God complex."

"Impressive," Evan said. "But you still can't get past the Faraday cage. The system is air-gapped—"

"Unless AHFWAGC charged the wireless keyboard *outside* the cage on the side table beside the chaise longue he likes to sprawl on when he's messing with the minds of impressionable aging Orphans. And unless that keyboard *also* required the occasional over-the-air software update. Which I may have just pushed before he took it back inside the Faraday cage. So while you were busy drooling into your pillow on your floating bed all morning, I've been perusing his files."

"And you learned what?"

"The Labor Day files are full-wiped. Secure deletions, written over, not retrievable."

"Shit."

"But."

"But?"

"Of course *but*. Weren't you listening? This is the part where I come up with something awesome, show you how I'll save the day, and you're chastened and humbled by my superior being. So. Are you prepared for chastenment and humblement?"

"I am."

"Nothing can leave there not on a flash or physical drive. But the zsh shell log happens to show when a physical copy last got made. And one was made. A year and change ago."

"Just after Labor Day."

"Someone saved footage of what went down that night. Someone made a copy."

"Tenpenny," Evan said.

Joey flung her arms wide, let her hands flop out to the sides. "Wa-la." She took in his expression. "What?"

"I thought you'd be able to retrieve the footage here. So I could just watch it."

Her lips set in a firm line of disappointment, mirroring Vera III's expression. "You know what, X? You're getting lazy in your dotage. Flyin' on private jets, making me do all the legwork digitally, forgetting the analog world you came up in. You're X! Go break into a motherfucker's house already and see what's up."

She looked so goddamned put out that, despite his best efforts, he was charmed.

She scowled at him. "What?"

He shook his head. "I've created a monster."

54

Uncharted Territories

When Evan ducked through the clamshell door into the Cirrus Vision Jet in the northside hangar of the Santa Monica Municipal Airport, a heavyset gentleman waited for him in the second row.

Aragón Urrea pulled himself to his feet. He was striking and homely at once, a grin lighting his broad, bold features. His wild shock of thick, wavy hair now tilted more salt than pepper and his bearlike build had grown a bit more stocky around the midsection since Evan had seen him last. Even so, he looked hearty, robust. A few days' worth of stubble textured his face. It struck Evan that he'd never seen the man clean-shaven.

Aragón wrapped Evan in a hug, pinning his arms to his sides, picking him up, and planting a smooch on his cheek. He set Evan back on his feet, and they took up executive leather seats side by side.

"Thanks for coming," Evan said.

"The hell else am I gonna do? You won't let me be an international criminal mastermind anymore. And besides"—a gesture to the full-stocked bar—"I can't let you drink alone."

It was just past 7:00 A.M.

Evan found a cocktail napkin and wiped his cheek, which seemed to delight Aragón further. "How are you?" Evan asked.

Aragón gave a world-weary toggle of the head. "I've reached the age where what I see in the mirror is unrecognizable as a body that would ever belong to me."

"You look fine."

"I am clothed."

"And I thank you for that."

Aragón smiled. "If the Nowhere Man develops a sense of humor, it will no longer be fair to those of us who compete with him for our feelings of self-worth."

"Withdrawn," Evan said.

"I've been working at letting go of parts of myself bit by bit." Aragón's broad shoulders lifted and fell. "You have to move on before you're ready. It's a great pain and a great sadness. To kill pieces of yourself so the rest of you can grow. Like pruning a tree."

Evan thought about that open shot he'd missed at twenty feet. The noose of Secret Service agents closing around him. The pinch of the needle through his shirt and Naomi Templeton's hand on his cheek as she helped ease him to the floor. There were pieces of himself that would let go of him whether he pretended to reciprocate or not. The thought poked at him.

He diverted. "How's Belicia?"

"My wife, she is still infuriatingly sharper than me."

"And Anjelina?"

"She gave us a beautiful granddaughter. And that . . . It changed everything." Aragón paused, musing. He was an unparalleled muser. "I never knew my father. So I spent my life searching for some image of what it meant to be a man. I wish I could've looked him in the face just once and seen what it was I was striving for. Or running from."

Evan's mind pulled to the file Joey had opened up on the man who he had reason to believe was *his* father. That grouping of gas-station and bar charges around the town of Blessing, Texas. Was there something to be learned if he looked Jacob Baridon in the eye? Something he had to embrace or let go of?

No.

Jack was the only father he'd ever known or cared to know. There was nothing he needed from a man he'd never met. This mission had already done plenty enough to strip him of his armor, piece by piece. He wasn't eager to risk losing more.

"Having a granddaughter, it's the opposite of that," Aragón was saying. "The first time I held her, I knew *exactly* who I was supposed to be. I endured a lot of hard decades to get to an understanding like that."

"What's her name?"

Aragón glowered at him but there was humor in it. "Xochitl. Anjelina calls her X. Can you imagine? I finally have a granddaughter, and my child names her after some white asshole?"

Evan laughed. "Despite the insult I appreciate your help."

Aragón scowled, unimpressed with himself. "I'm so rich it annoys me. You know the whole point of having money? Making sure that no one you love *ever* has to suffer from hardships that money can prevent. And then? Trying to do the same for others. That's why I help. Like all . . . *philanthropists*"—he gave the word an amused spin—"I have to make up for all the awful shit I did to get to a place where I could *be* a *pinche* philanthropist." His crooked smile was wide, infectious. "So. Why did you want to see me?"

"I'm trying to decide whether or not to kill a guy."

"That happen often?"

"Only once before."

"Who was that?"

"You."

After a two-second tape delay, Aragón's laugh came on, building up from his belly, a great joyful rumble. "Okay," he said when he'd settled down. "Tell me about him."

Evan did. Aragón listened with powerful focus.

"Is he a psychopath?" Aragón asked when Evan was done.

"That'd be much simpler."

"He likes spouting all this heaven-and-hell *meshugas*."

Evan half grinned. *"Meshugas?"*

Aragón coaxed one shoulder forward in a sheepish shrug. "My lawyer." He ran his fingers through his dense silver-and-black hair. "He makes everything complicated, your guy. But it's simple. Heaven is when you have a romance with your wife, your job, and your house—and your children make you laugh."

"And hell?"

"Hell, well, hell *is* complicated. It looks different for everyone. This mission, it's a mess. Many tentacles."

Evan said, "I know where it starts and ends for me."

"With one young man," Aragón said. "And one young woman."

"If they'd died at his hands or at his command, I'd know what to do."

"Yes," Aragón said. "That is an easy story. We know how that story ends." He gave Evan a few moments of silence. "But you don't think that's the case?"

"I'm not sure what to think. There's so much to be reckoned with. There's . . . a lot to him."

"This man, he sounds like a force to be reckoned with. And it seems . . . it seems he got his first taste of wisdom. It can be intoxicating. There's so much to see that you were blind to before. The problem? He thinks he *has* it. Wisdom. But no one *has* it. We just wear it from time to time when we're lucky."

"He knows things I don't," Evan said. "He sees things I don't."

"And that rattles you?"

Evan considered. "I'm smart enough to be scared of him. And smart enough not to let that influence what I need to do."

"What do you need to do?"

Evan bit his lip, noticed he was doing it and stopped. He shook his head and then shook it again.

Aragón said, "Maybe that's okay."

"What?"

"Not knowing how this story will end. Until you get there."

A faint vibration in the cabin drew Evan's attention. The pilot finished mounting the steps, stooping on his way through the door and saluting casually with a flare of his fingers. "Are we ready to go, *Patrón*?"

"I'll be staying in Los Angeles, attending to some business. I'm having Arturo pick me up tonight in the Embraer Lineage 1000." A wink to Evan. "My new toy." Aragón gave Evan's knee a solid pat with his hand and rose, pausing by the cockpit to face the pilot. "But please take good care of *mi hermano*." His face was at once rugged and patrician, weathered beechnut skin and regal jowls. His rich brown eyes held great affection and perhaps even admiration. "He is heading into uncharted territories."

55

A Cityscape of Unguency

The top nightstand drawer held a medley of sex toys.

The middle one was devoted to crops, paddles, floggers, and other S&M accoutrements.

Flavored condoms filled the bottom drawer to the brim.

Flavored condoms seemed to Evan about as subtle as flavored vodka, but he hadn't broken into Derek Tenpenny's condo to pass judgment on prophylactics.

Rising from his crouch, he nearly knocked his head on the sex swing attached to the ceiling with steel anchor bolts. Bottles of various lubricants covered the top of the nightstand, forming a cityscape of unguency.

He'd searched the two-bedroom place meticulously, finding nothing. Being here elicited an intense disgust reaction in him, not because of the paraphernalia per se but because it felt not like a home but a venue. The habitat was operationalized, bringing to mind human-trafficking operations he'd torn apart.

The single-mindedness, too, added to his aversion—there was

precious little decor aside from the mirrored ceiling. White porcelain dinnerware set and a pack of stainless-steel flatware in
the kitchen. Soap, shampoo, conditioner, bathroom spray. Big-
and-tall suits hanging in the closet above a set of black Tumi
luggage. He'd used a padded stool to hoist himself through the
hatch into the crawl space, which was crowded with HVAC duct-
ing and little else.

The second bedroom, a makeshift study, was sparse: desk,
computer, no paperwork to speak of. Empty drawers, empty
closet, and the ensuite bathroom looked to be unused. There was
no password on the computer and no documents whatsoever. The
search history on the browser had been set to autowipe every
day; the log of the past twenty-four hours showed porn sites and
nothing else.

Everything was bare-bones functional; all the extravagance
had gone into the pursuit of erotic exploits. It was odd to inhabit
the space of a man given over to one part of himself, a solitary
primal drive.

No useful evidence, no damning documents, no flash drive
with purloined Labor Day footage.

Frustrated, Evan scanned the master bedroom once more. It
smelled of fabric softener and lemon-scented Lysol, but the stench
of cigarette smoke lingered. Afternoon light filtered through the
fabric Roman shades. The air conditioner blew air down his collar.
He closed his eyes, imagined being in this space as Derek Tenpenny.

For starters he'd be nearly a foot taller, giving him a different view.

And different opportunities.

Evan opened his eyes. The honeycomb brass vent above, inset
horizontally in the side of the ceiling soffit, dried his eyes. He
studied the knurled screws, one on each side.

Then he moved into the kitchen, searching the bulkhead. Similar brass wall registers blew steady currents of air.

Keeping his eyes on the soffits, he drifted into the study. A
matching honeycomb brass vent above the desk. One of its screws
was loose.

Going on his tiptoes, Evan reached up his palm. The airflow was meager.

Interesting.

Back to the master closet to grab the padded stool. He required it; Tenpenny would not. The knurled screws were easy to twist free by hand. Balancing on the stool, Evan removed the vent. He peered inside.

Nothing. Just a black maw.

He was about to replace the vent when a glistening thread at the side caught his eye. Fishing line, tied in a loop at the end.

A handle.

He pulled at it. Whatever was on the other end was heavy. It came grudgingly.

A large item the size of a board game but heavier, wrapped in a gun cloth.

Evan pulled it down and unwrapped it.

An old-fashioned ledger with page edges that threw a golden glow up into his face when he cracked it open.

Sitting on the floor, he paged through.

Women's names. Dates. Descriptions. It was like reading a catalog of wine or spirit reviews, everything rendered dispassionately, aesthetically, the subjects reduced to physical matter and little more. Scrawled marginalia documented encounters: *held her down, both wrists with one hand; cried a bit but made no noise; quite loud, lots of dirty talk.*

Evan flipped the substantial pages, running a finger along the date column.

There it was. Labor Day, one year ago.

Angela Buford.

Beyond the listing of her approximate height, weight, dimensions, and sensory characteristics, there was a list of several sexual positions, ending with: *"coitus interruptus."*

Evan recalled Tenpenny looking down at him in the spitting rain outside Tartarus: *Angela Buford? Never heard of her.*

He leafed through the other pages. All those encounters, many of them violations of differing degrees. Something dropped from the back cover, literally falling into Evan's lap.

A flash drive.

Brick red, capless aside from a swivel cover.

Score another point for Joey Morales.

Evan walked over to the desk, plugged the flash drive into the computer, and sat in the chair. Hundreds of entries organized by date.

Evan clicked through a few. A few was sufficient.

Tenpenny in full congress with various women, the camera angles suggesting surreptitious recording. Many were inside this condo, but a few were from clubs and private orgies. Evan scrolled down, found the date he was looking for.

Tenpenny had already curated the clip as he had the others.

There he was at Tartarus, outside by the pool dancing with Angela Buford. Her hair was natural, a medium Afro with side bantu knots. She wore a sundress the color of ocher with a deep neckline, and she was turned around, grinding her rear end into him to the beat. Tenpenny's face was flushed; he looked in a near frenzy.

Then they were inside, making out in various hallways, the party booming with wall-to-wall revelers. Tenpenny tried different doors and found most of the places occupied with other couples who'd beaten them to the punch.

Holding Angela's hand, he led her upstairs. The crowd parted for him, but she turned her slender body sideways to cut through the current. Tenpenny went for a bathroom—occupied; the drawing room—packed; a guest room, engaged by a threesome. He was moving more quickly now, driven by what seemed like desperation, all but dragging Angela in his wake.

Back along the second-floor corridor, head swiveling this way and that, searching for a private space. He bumped into Rathsberger exiting the scarlet room. They had a brief exchange, Tenpenny gesturing.

Both men gave furtive glances up the hall toward Luke Devine's master suite.

And then Tenpenny pulled Angela into the room, the camera selection switching perspective to follow them.

No one's allowed in here, Tenpenny had said. *Ever.*

A Cityscape of Unguency

In his haste Tenpenny threw the barrel bolt early, not noticing that it wound up outside the steel catch.

Angela looked surprised at the setup, but he gripped her face forcefully, turned it away from the screens, and crushed his mouth to hers. They stumbled into the Faraday cage. Then they were fucking on the desk, against the bars, on the floor.

He wound up in the chair with Angela on her knees, servicing him.

After a time the door swung inward.

Johnny Seabrook stood stooped in the doorway, glassy-eyed and drunk. He was staring in disbelief at the wall of monitors and everything they held.

Tenpenny swung around in the chair, Angela clinging to his knees. He looked irate. But Evan saw panic working beneath the surface of his face.

In a single motion, Tenpenny rose, gripping Angela's chin from above and snapping her head around. Johnny turned, reached for the doorframe, missed, and wobbled on his feet. Tenpenny rooted in his heap of clothes, came up with the 9-mil, and shot him through the back.

Johnny stumbled into the hall.

Hurriedly yanking on clothes, Tenpenny followed Johnny outside.

Another perspective switch showed the corridor outside with no sign of Johnny. The few partygoers straggling by looked smashed beyond coherence.

Rathsberger ran into the frame, conferred briefly with Tenpenny, trying to calm him down, then dashed toward the stairs to the foyer. Tenpenny put his hands on his knees, his chest heaving, panic-stricken. His gaze caught on the door just to the right, the one leading to the servant staircase. When Evan leaned close, he could discern a dark smudge on the wood.

Blood.

Tenpenny shouldered through the door, wiping the smudge off with a sleeve as he passed.

The door eased shut behind him. The corridor was empty.

303

The perspective blinked back to the scarlet room. Angela Buford lying naked on her back inside the Faraday cage, her head turned to one side. She almost looked peaceful.

No one was allowed in the scarlet room.

Ever.

But Tenpenny had needed what he'd needed.

He'd tripped on a single sin.

And that had undone a little part of the universe.

56

Ground Truth

Evan trudged along the sand just above the shoreline, a night
wind blowing grit into his eyes and teeth. The air felt wet and
heavy, matting his hair. He wore an oilskin coat and a full-zip
hooded sweatshirt over a flannel, and he lugged a fishing pole and
tackle box. The lights of the mansions above were bright, radiating
an otherworldly glow. He'd made his way along the coast from that
choke point at Halsey Neck, getting a read on the ground truth
and timing the fog shrouding the dunes for maximum thickness.

The private patrols were out in force again, but now there was a
significant uniform presence as well. Tenpenny had clearly wanted
proper law enforcement in place, everyone on high alert. Cruisers
were parked at intervals along Meadow Lane, cops bullshitting
with the private security guys.

As Evan cut toward Tartarus, a spotlight stabbed his eyes from
the road about fifteen yards away. An officer, backlit with his
peaked cap, called down at him. "Sir, we're gonna need you to
clear out."

"The hell, man," Evan said, shaking the tackle box. "It's public property."

"We have a credible threat. And we've initiated a lockdown of this area.

Evan squinted up into the glare. "Threat? What threat?"

"I'm not at liberty to disclose that information."

Evan shook his head like a world-weary local. "You don't even know, do you?"

"One of the residents has reason to believe there's a clear and present danger. And? He pays more taxes than you."

Evan scowled and turned to head off. "These billionaires?" he said. "Probably not."

Back at the Hampton Bays house, Evan sat on the shabby-chic couch. He stared at his RoamZone for a long time before dialing.

She picked up on the first ring. "Templeton."

Evan said, "It's me."

A long silence. He pictured her frantically scrambling to record the call or gesticulating at a coworker. He didn't care. They'd never backtrace through the dozen software virtual-telephone switch destinations, and besides, he'd recently transferred the phone service to a pop-up telecoms joint that kept no logs, located in a corner of Skopje.

"Is the mission complete?" Templeton asked.

"No."

"Have you made contact with the principal?"

"I've been looking into everything."

"Does your curiosity align with the president's . . . goals?"

Evan chewed his lip. "Her goal of pushing through a trillion-dollar corporate giveaway to win reelection?"

A brief, heated pause. Then, "Grow the hell up, X. There's corruption in the system? No shit. Things could be more effective? No shit. Whether we go to war or build infrastructure, this is how it works. It's ugly and dirty, and no one gets a hundred percent of what they want. But it's the only way to get anything done. You've got a better plan to run a twenty-three-trillion-dollar economy?"

"No," Evan said. "But Devine thinks he does."

"Sounds like he's winning you over."

"No," Evan said. "I think he's just as full of shit as the president."

"Spare me the moral relativism. At least she's democratically elected."

"Was she?" Evan said. "I seem to recall she assumed the office after her predecessor prematurely expired."

"Are you going to complete the mission?"

Evan pictured Ruby lying on the floor of that Mattapan apartment, the shape of her brother outlined in blood on the wood beneath her. "If I do," he said, "it won't be because of legislation."

The silence stretched out and out. "I've been instructed to remind you that if the mission isn't completed on the specified terms, there will be no reinstatement of unofficial immunity for you."

Evan smiled gently, gazed down at his bare toes on the knot rug. The soft texture felt soothing. "You're better than this, Naomi."

"Your move, X. What are you going to do?"

Evan cut the line.

It was time to meditate.

Tomorrow was going to be a big day.

57

Sticky and Immovable Tonnage

It is harder than one might think to produce a dump truck full of old tires.

But not impossible.

Less difficult to douse said tires with gasoline.

Tipping the truck over takes some doing, sure, but if one is trained in tactical driving and knows how to hit a curb sideways off a skid, it's not as hard as it might seem.

Seat belt recommended.

Ignition is of course a breeze. A flicked match as you fade away into the thickening night, and everything goes boom.

The conflagration of sticky and immovable tonnage provides an excellent clog to a choke point like, say, the one at Halsey Neck and Meadow Lane.

It will likely demand a response not readily mustered by beefed-up private security teams and local PD.

You should try it sometime.

Sticky and Immovable Tonnage

* * *

Shouting and commotion erupted on Meadow Lane. Agitated officers bellowed into their radios, getting back equally adrenalized squawking. Cruisers lighting up, peeling out from the curb, sirens squealing. Security teams tightening around perimeters. Shouted exchanges from guard stations to patrolmen, everyone in a tizzy.

You'd think it was the first time they'd ever dealt with a flaming overturned dump truck heaped with tires.

A low fog had crept in from the sea, puffy wisps and streamers that cut visibility, adding to the commotion. As the cops washed up the beachfront strip toward its intersection at Halsey Neck, a female cop in a formfitting police uniform sliced through the front gardens of Tartarus.

Candy kept the brim of her peaked cap low over her eyes and the generic long-sleeve uniform shirt unbuttoned slightly but not yet seductively.

She rang the doorbell, which echoed sonorously throughout the house.

Rathsberger ripped the massive door open, coyote-tan M17 9-millimeter aimed through the gap at her boots.

"What are you doing?" Candy said. "I'm police."

Rath's face trembled with alertness, his right eye lost to a smear of scar tissue. "Lemme see badge and creds. Badge and creds or no one comes in."

Candy swallowed, took an uncharacteristically nervous half step back. "Sir, I'm gonna have to ask you to holster your—"

A Southampton Village police officer appeared out of nowhere, approaching her from the side, screaming. "Hands! Hands!" He wore a proper uniform with a regulation cap and a tactical neck gaiter covering half his face. "Show me your fucking hands *now*!"

"Shit," Candy said, quietly through clenched teeth, seemingly to no one. "We have a problem."

"Step back," the cop said to Rath. "Close the door."

As Rath narrowed the gap, the cop frisked Candy roughly and then slapped cuffs on her. He noticed she was wearing an earpiece and yanked it out. It was a match for his own comms setup, which he initiated now. "We've got an impostor. Repeat: We have an intrusion attempt at Tartarus. Get backup here. Four units. *Now*. I have her in custody, and I'm sending her to my partner."

A tough feminine voice came back over the radio. *"Copy that. Units en route."*

The cop took a few steps off the wide porch and then propelled her into the fog. Candy nearly tumbled on the quartz stone. "What the fuck?" she said. "I'm a stripper, okay? It was just a joke."

"Got her?" the cop shouted to his partner through the mist. He spun back around, hustling to the front door. "Have you safed the property?"

Rath said, "We have cameras everywhere—"

The cop pushed past him into the foyer. "Secure this door. We're gonna lock down the perimeter."

Rath threw the weighty dead bolt, sealing Tartarus. He scurried back around the cop into the lobby. "Tenpenny, get on surveillance. Let's safe the floors from the bottom up. *Move*."

Tenpenny stumbled to the second-floor landing, hands spread, staring down. Santos was halfway down the stairs already, Gordo wheezing behind him. Dapper Dan stood in front of the waterfall feature, which had resumed its tireless downpour; with his 9-mil drawn, he peered up the corridor toward the back of the house.

Rath caught himself partway to the stairs, seemingly halted by an epiphany. He swung back around to face the cop.

Evan pulled down the regulation neck gaiter.

And smiled.

58

Old-Fashioned Duel

Five Adam's apples clicked up and down in unison.

Rathsberger gaped at Evan.

They were about ten yards apart.

Evan skewered him with a glare. Rath's hand hovered over his holster.

Evan's hands were loose at his sides, the ARES 1911 snugged in an appendix holster beneath the uniform shirt. He'd replaced the original buttons with magnetic ones so when the time came, he could draw straight through the shirt.

The time had come.

As far as an old-fashioned duel went, Rath had the advantaged hand position by at least six inches. Evan preferred it that way.

No one could say it was unfair.

And he had something to prove after that missed shot at twenty feet. That losing a scrap of himself to age was nothing compared to what he still had to gain.

The other men stayed motionless in the background, turned to statues.

Rath's fingers twitched.

"Forgive me," Evan said. "But I don't have time for the whole fire-ants thing."

He watched Rath's eyes. Kept his peripheral vision loose to note any movement of those hovering fingers.

Rath's hand dove for the pistol.

Evan drew, the magnetic buttons parting so the shirt flapped wide, his barrel coming level. He shot Rath through the gut.

Rath's muzzle hadn't even cleared leather.

Evan felt the fabric ripple inward around him, and then the buttons found their mates with a metallic clink, his shirt zipping up around him as if nothing had ever happened. A curl of powdered smoke twisted up before him, and Evan thought that even if he didn't want to *be* an archetype, he sure as hell didn't mind acting like one from time to time.

Rath was gripping the glittering mess beneath his ribs. He managed to clench the gun weakly and lift it just enough for it to tumble out of the holster onto the floor, and then Evan kicked it.

It skittered across the marble, spinning.

Rath dropped to his knees, stopped there a moment, then fell onto his face with a pained grunt.

Evan said quietly, "Now, please."

That tough feminine voice came over his radio. "Your wish is my command."

Joey cut the Lutron light switches, and Tartarus fell to darkness.

59

An Infinity of X's

Rath started dragging himself elbow over elbow across the foyer in the direction of his gun, emitting pained slaughterhouse grunts.

The others fired in the darkness, a stupidity that Evan had assumed would have been trained out of them.

But panic was running high.

Boots stomping this way and that, Gordo's labored breathing, the stink of Dapper Dan's cologne in the air. From the second floor, Tenpenny was shouting instructions that made little tactical sense, his voice ratcheted squeaky-high with excitement. "Gordo, Sandman—deploy! Dan, get to Devine. I'll run command in the surveillance room."

A cacophony of voices answered: "—power's cut, you pussy, there *is* no surveillance—"

"—the hell is he?"

"Rath? Jesus, Rath, you okay?"

"No cross fire! Hang on, no cross fire!"

Another two pops telegraphed Dan's location over by the waterfall.

Night vision was coming on, shadows within shadows, the men sprinting around. A woman screamed somewhere deep in the house, a side door swinging open as the staff fled. Outdoor light filtering through several doorways managed to spill into the foyer, enough to cast elongated shadows across the marble.

There was no sign of Evan.

Gordo had circled through the kitchen, Santos was nowhere to be seen, and Tenpenny seemed to be hiding somewhere above, perhaps in the scarlet room. Rath grunted and groaned, hauling himself inch by inch with his forearms, leaving a snail trail of crimson.

Dan moved slowly across the face of the waterfall, setting down his feet with care though the soporific rush covered the sound of his boots. He had a firm two-handed grip on his pistol, arms directly in line with the barrel of the firearm, elbows slightly bent, a perfect balance of tension and flexibility.

It was tactically sound and looked good. Both were of equal consequence to Dan.

In fact, he paused a moment in the dimness to admire his shadowy mirror image in the wall of water to his side.

And then something bizarre happened.

The cheek of his reflection disappeared, a neat streak of darkness opening up beneath it.

He blinked twice as a floating eye appeared in the blackness behind the waterfall, right where his own reflected eye should have been. The gears of his mind turned and turned and finally clicked: A blade had been jabbed through the water and turned on its side to open up the strip beneath.

A strip through which the muzzle of a 1911 appeared, as indistinct as the haunted eye itself.

He saw the muzzle flash but never heard the bang.

Evan emerged from the side of the towering water feature. There was nothing to see except for Rath rasping his way across the floor. And given the tumbling sheet of liquid, there was nothing to hear.

Keeping his back to the wall, Evan moved away from the waterfall to see what noises he might pick up. Joey would have moved on to phase two by now, flooding local PD with false alarms, impelling them this way and that across Southampton, but even so, time was of the essence. Easing down a back corridor, keeping a low silhouette, he heard the clacking of pool balls.

Leading with his ARES, he vectored into the billiard room. A boudoir lampshade had been knocked askew. The three ball was still rolling on the felt.

The billiard room branched off to two different halls.

He picked the one indicated by the lampshade and kept on. Wide corridor, lots of doors. He checked the rooms as he went—study, guest room, library, gym. The sprawling house was disorienting, a confusion of passages and doors, the spaces bleeding into one another.

Squeezing through a slender doorway, he went down three stone steps into a slimmer corridor, the walls cluttered with Mirós and Rothkos and a creepy Chagall of a goat playing a violin. Despite the minimal descent, the temperature seemed to have risen by ten degrees. He felt sweat beading at his hairline.

Footfall came audible, but given the hard surfaces Evan couldn't source its direction. Aside from the art, the hall was bare. He slipped through the next doorway, finding himself inside a powder room.

A candle guttered on a gold-plated dish, casting a wobbly glow. Beigey-pink marble surfaces veined with quartz. The faucets were two shiny brass Cupids, one playing a harp, the other armed with a tambourine. Angel wings formed the backplate of the toilet-paper holder. Three of the walls had mirrors, reflections of Evan compounding into an infinity of X's.

He pressed his ear to the closed door, heard the vibration of approaching steps. Readying his gun, he backed to the mirrored wall by the toilet, and it suddenly gave way, swinging around.

He stumbled back onto a metal landing, struggling to keep his balance. His heel slipped into nothingness, and then he was tumbling painfully down a steep, narrow flight of stairs. Slamming onto oil-stained concrete, he felt a throbbing in his hip and wondered for a moment if his left shoulder had popped out of the socket. He started to raise his arm, felt a bone-on-bone grind, and buried a shout in his closed mouth.

He preferred his left hand for shooting and could not have it out of commission. Hesitating, he took a series of fast deep breaths and then forced his arm higher yet. The ball rolled screamingly through tendon and muscle and popped back into the socket.

If he had more time, he might've cried.

The rusty steps towering up before him were serrated with perforated raised buttons and debossed holes designed to make them annoyingly antislip. He turned his head to look around, a nerve sending fire through his jaw and down his left side.

A defunct boiler room. Rusted valve bonnets and pipes, metal hand wheels snapped jaggedly in two. In the rear behind a crumbled masonry wall rose the twenty-foot behemoth itself, soot memorializing where it had once belched fire. A rusted FITZGIBBONS brand plate lay on the floor at Evan's side. His ARES must have landed nearby, but he didn't know where.

He told himself to sit up, but his body wasn't having it.

It seemed impossible that the ringing inside his skull didn't exist outside his body as well.

He rolled onto his side, groping in the darkness, forcing his way through the pain in his shoulder. Metal bits and old screws poked at his fingertips, drawing blood. His held breath burned beneath the intercostals of his left side. When he rolled onto his back and told himself to exhale, the effort left him shuddering.

As if in a nightmare, he heard a creak above, the secret mirrored wall opening once more.

Through the mesh of the landing, two large spots of greater darkness telegraphed someone's approach. The metal bowed.

And then Gordo's round, shiny head peeked into view.

Sweat dripped from his forehead. In his fat boxing-glove hands, the service pistol aimed down at Evan looked like a toy gun. Evan felt like he was staring up from the bottom of a well.

Weakly, he reached some more, his shoulder protesting, his

hand grazing shattered bricks and old nails. His 1911 couldn't have tumbled far.

Gordo cocked his head, that broomlike mustache curling with a smile. "I've fallen," he said, "and I can't get up."

Santos appeared now at his back, barely visible behind Gordo's mass. "I got him," he said. "Let me get him."

"Back off, lil' man," Gordo said. "He gutshot Rath. I want him for me."

He set a sturdy leg down to test the rusted top step, which complained but held. That smile grew wider. He kept the gun pointed down at Evan. Peering helplessly up the dozen steep steps had a dizzying effect on Evan, the distance stretching like taffy.

Tilting his expansive hips, Gordo sidled down another step. And then another. His elbows splayed out to the sides with each step to help him hold balance, the effect ridiculously avian. Santos was all but hopping behind him, but there was no way to get around the big man to the waiting prize; in fact, he was barely visible behind Gordo's girth. Moving cautiously, Gordo neared the halfway point.

Evan strained to reach behind him, fire spreading through his injured shoulder.

A nail pricked him. A splinter dug at his wrist. And then—his thumb brushed the familiar aluminum frame.

"Uh-uh," Gordo said, bringing the 9-mil up. His elephantine leg took the next plunge, and then he gulped, his hips wedged between the narrow handrails. Grimacing, he lowered his hands to pry himself free, but that only settled his weight further. He gave a cry of pain, one metal rail pinching above his hip to bite a solid two feet into his gelatinous side.

He was stuck.

Evan lunged for the ARES, gripped it in both hands, and aimed up at the looming target.

Gordo lifted his head, his glistening brow grooved with horizontal wrinkles.

Evan shot him between the eyes.

Gordo jerked violently, his bowels releasing audibly. He slumped forward, arms drooping into thin air, blood spooling from the neat hole in his skull.

For a terrible moment, Evan thought Gordo was going to pop free and plummet on top of him, but the giant hung there, his massive torso canted out above the remaining stairs.

Before Evan could regroup, Santos had vaulted over Gordo, swinging from a handrail and jumping down to bypass the lower steps. Evan fired once, but Santos was small and swift, and he half dove, half fell atop Evan, knocking the ARES away once more.

Santos's features were contorted, his neck straining. *"I'm* the one," he grimaced through bared teeth. *"I'm* the one who can do you."

He flurried at Evan, elbows to the jaw, twining his limbs in Evan's, locking down his legs. Punching him was like hitting tar. He suctioned, controlled, locked joints, that crazy square cross pendant dancing around on its chain. Evan squirmed and battered at him but lost ground quickly.

Tight in, the stink of Sandman's sweat was overpowering. The grime of the boiler room coated Evan's skin until they were a squirming mass of slippery limbs flailing and beating at each other. They rolled and rolled once more, banging off the crumbling masonry wall and winding up with Evan on his back in the full guard position, kicking for his life.

Santos slithered through the guard, ramming his knees beneath Evan's legs, head lowered to avoid eye gouges, chin dug into Evan's solar plexus. Wheezing, Evan countered by going for a guillotine choke hold, curling up around Santos to embrace him tighter, clasping the small man with his legs, locking his ankles around his back. Wrapping his arm around Santos's throat, Evan cinched the blade of his wrist and forearm across the carotid, applying pressure. He grabbed his own wrist with his opposite hand to tighten the choke and pulled up on Santos's neck for a hanging effect.

But Evan was weak from the fall, his skin slimy with their combined sweat, and he couldn't hold the grip against Santos's counter. Evan was losing strength, but Santos seemed invigorated. Once the grappler got free, he would beat Evan senseless.

Sure enough, Santos burst through Evan's hold, bucking out

of the clasp. He reared up, fingers tangled in Evan's, snatching, wrenching, clamping.

Evan spit in his eyes.

It bought a quarter of a second, Santos's hand jerking toward his face before he halted the instinct.

But in that quarter second, Evan reached up, grabbed the dangling Order of Christ pendant, and jabbed one of the flared ends into the side of Santos's neck.

Santos coughed out a spray of saliva.

An arterial spurt shot two feet to the side, blood tapping the concrete audibly.

Santos turned to look at the spray, swung his head back to Evan in disbelief. He dove onto Evan once more, snapping up his injured arm in a top shoulder lock, torquing his shoulder and elbow to the point of breaking.

The pain was incredible. Evan slapped at him weakly; he'd spent his strength.

Another spurt exited Santos's neck. Releasing Evan, he rolled back up, confused, clamping his hand over the puncture. His fingers forked the spray into three spouts.

He couldn't fight Evan and hold the blood in his body at the same time.

Releasing his neck, Santos reached for Evan's throat, sagged a bit, reached back to cover the wound once more.

Evan's shoulder blades ground against the floor. His head felt filled with cotton. He could barely muster the strength to lift his arm, but he gave a feeble punch to Santos's clamped hand, knocking it off the gash. More blood spurted out, painting the left side of Evan's face and matting his shirt at the shoulder.

Santos wobbled, his weight uneven. His eyelids drooped; his head lolled. He reached again for the side of his throat, and again Evan knocked his hand away.

Santos's arm quivered. Hunching forward, he shoved his hand impotently against the flowing blood. With great effort Evan lifted his head and used the crown to nudge Santos's fingers away before collapsing flat once more. For a moment they stayed like that, Santos sitting on Evan, Evan flat on his back, gasping for air.

And then Santos toppled stiffly to the side.

He lay curled in a fetal position, his legs cycling on the oil-slick concrete, the blood coming steady now, a perfectly dark, perfectly round expanding circle.

Evan rolled onto all fours and coughed until he dry-heaved. He spit out a cord of crimson-laced mucus and wiped Santos's blood from his eye. He got up onto one foot and then the other, staggered a bit before he held his weight.

Santos was still.

Evan picked up his pistol and headed for the stairs. Scrabbling over Gordo's wedged body promised to be painful and grotesque beyond compare.

But he didn't have much of a choice.

There was only one way out of hell.

60

The Devil's Work

Evan leaned against the walls of the ground floor, making hand-prints of blood not unlike the one Johnny had left on the fatal night. He was light-headed, but he would not pass out. And despite the throbbing in his shoulder, his grip on the ARES was intact.

A door slammed to the rear of the house, punctuated by the sound of breaking glass. Evan staggered in that direction. Stale cigarette smoke laced the air, the scent of Derek Tenpenny.

A French door swung free in the wet night air, one pane shattered from the force with which it had been flung open. Leaning out into the chill, Evan heard a big truck turn over in the blackness beyond and peel out.

Brake lights flared to life as the 4x4 shot up the side of the house and across Meadow Lane and then bounced over a sand dune and disappeared.

Tenpenny had fled, leaving his soldiers to die.

Evan pulled away from the French doors and moved back toward the foyer, his legs growing stronger beneath him with each step.

Rath squirmed against the marble floor, still trying to get at his gun, a windup toy that wouldn't quit. He was whimpering wetly now. He'd managed to drag himself only about ten feet. The 9-mil was gleaming there on the floor just a few more away.

Evan gauged the distance.

It would be awhile.

He moved upstairs and pretended that nothing hurt.

The architectural doors of Devine's suite were closed. Evan trudged through, his hand sticky against the doorknob. The brass-framed mirror threw back a macabre reflection, half of Evan's face darkened with Santos's blood.

Not surprisingly, the fireplace was roaring.

Luke Devine sat on one of the love seats, waiting patiently, it seemed, for Evan.

It took Evan longer than he anticipated to cross the vast room. His boots felt tacky against the silk splash rug. He sat on the facing love seat, rested the ARES on his thigh aimed at Devine.

The bizarre cuboid glass table with the trapped male mannequin had returned or, more likely given its obliteration, been replaced. Evan wondered how many spares of freaky art Devine kept around.

Luke had set a 9-mil pistol on the table between them, the magazine extracted and laid by its side, the slide locked back to show an empty chamber.

"No point trying to fight you," he said. "I'd just hurt myself."

Evan stared at him.

"You got to the bottom of it. You did the devil's work."

"No," Evan said.

"Sure you did. My employees went off the reservation. They broke my code. It was unacceptable, and they had to answer for it. I promised you: My house will be set in order."

Evan noted now that the passive construction had been intentional.

"But I don't kill people," Devine continued. "As I told you"—that white sickle of a grin—"I get others to do my bidding for me."

The radius windows showed no flashing lights, no distant dump-truck fire, nothing but blackness and more blackness. From the beginning Evan had been warned about Luke's gift of manipulation, his ability to get others to do what he wanted them to. In Echo's apartment Evan had put the question to her: *How does he make you do stuff?* Her reply came to him now, a reverberation worthy of her name: *If you meet him, you'll find out.*

He'd met him.

He'd found out.

The orange glow guttered across Devine's smooth, boyish features. "I heard Tenpenny get away."

"Oh," Evan said, "I wouldn't worry about him."

Devine nodded once slowly, a downward tip of the chin. "Have you decided"—for the first time his voice trembled, but it was so slight that it might have been a figment of Evan's imagination—"what you're going to do about me?"

Evan stared at him.

The ARES felt snug in his hand, a part of himself. A 4.5-millimeter press of his trigger finger would restore his presidential pardon.

"You have a code, too," Luke said. "Before God."

Evan broke eye contact just for an instant, but Luke keyed to it.

"Of course there's a God," Devine said. "Because there's *me*."

On Evan's knee the ARES stayed pointed at Devine. The fire roared and roared, and it was as if they were at the edge of the world on some godforsaken frontier and the flames were all that were left to fend off the darkness.

It took concentration for Evan to pull himself to his feet. Pistol at his side, he stood facing Devine over the trapped soul in the glass table.

Devine was his own center of gravity, everything around him enigmatic and complex, obscured by shades of gray. One thing was certain: He was willing to extort and manipulate to further his own ends. He was willing to employ soldiers who were known murderers. He kept eyes on everything that happened in his orbit and inside his citadel. He'd built the game board, set up the pieces, stoked his sphere of influence to the point of mortal ignition. It seemed clear he hadn't known about the murders committed right under his nose. He'd insulated himself behind a wall of his own making. And yet insulated he was. It was rage-inducing, corrupt, and unjust in more ways than could be tallied.

But he had neither pulled the trigger nor given the order.

Evan's hand tightened around the grip of the ARES, the checkering of the Simonich gunner grips biting his palm. An urge overwhelmed him to raise the pistol and put three rounds through the man before him—two in the chest, one in the head. He let it rage through him and finally abate.

"One day you'll cross the line," Evan said. "And I'll be there."

Luke made no show of relief, but Evan saw his chest deflate as he eased out a breath. "I'd expect nothing else."

Evan turned his back on Luke Devine and the 9-mil.

He figured Luke was not the kind of man to shoot him in the back.

His supposition was correct.

Rath had made it another few feet, his fingertips nudging the edge of his gun. He couldn't move beyond that. He was sobbing dryly, pitiful broken cries.

The swath of blood from his gutshot detailed the painstaking progress he'd made in the past half hour.

Evan's Original S.W.A.T.s tapped across the marble of the dark foyer. The lights were still off, but he could see more clearly now, ambient light coaxing texture from the darkness. At his back the waterfall rushed and rushed.

Evan reached Rath and paused, staring ahead at the door. Rath's head was turned, and he breathed moistly, fogging the marble near Evan's boots. Evan stood, his shadow long, the reflection of the fluttering water washing over him and the polished Calacatta marble. He held the ARES aimed down at his side parallel to his thigh, the muzzle hovering three feet above Rath's temple.

"*This* is how it ends," Evan said.

He shot Rath through the head and walked out the lofty front door into the swirling mist.

61

Strong Woman

Candy was waiting for him on an easement running alongside the neighboring estate in a Yulong white Range Rover she'd borrowed for precisely this occasion. She'd already changed from her cop-stripper getup into a wardrobe befitting a mogul's steely wife, a tennis leisurewear outfit that also somehow passed for evening wear.

He hauled himself into the passenger seat, and she just looked at him. "Baby wipes in the console," she said. "Your face."

He wiped the caked blood off his cheek and neck.

"How much of that is yours?"

"Not most of it."

"The marines?"

He nodded.

"Devine?"

Slowly, Evan shook his head.

She slotted the transmission into drive, signaled like a law-abiding citizen, and pulled out into the murky soup.

They drove in silence.

"Thanks," Evan said.

"It was fun."

"I meant for watching the Seabrooks."

Candy shrugged. "That girl is something else. Spunky."

"Yeah," Evan said.

"Gets it from her mother. Strong woman."

"Yeah."

"A strong man, too, in Mason, to help them be."

The stink of burned rubber hit them first, and then they reached the puddled mess at Halsey Neck. Emergency services had extinguished the blaze and cleared a narrow lane through the wreckage. Candy slowed at the checkpoint, letting the automatic window purr down.

A tired cop with a coffee-stained mustache said, "Ma'am, where are you coming f—"

"This mess better be cleaned up by tomorrow." Candy waved her hands around. Her nails had somehow in the preceding hour picked up a French manicure. "This *entire* mess. My husband comes in from Zurich at daybreak, he's been gone for two weeks, and he will absolutely lose his shit that you allowed this to happen on your watch. We have maxed contributions to the Southampton Village Police Benevolent Association *every single year* since we moved here, and I must tell you—"

The cop tilted onto his heels, reverse-waddled back a few steps with as much passive-aggressiveness as he could get away with, and waved them through.

Candy snapped her head forward, the tinted window coasted up, and she drove on. They snaked north toward Route 27, tires humming across asphalt. Candy checked her rearview mirror and then checked it again.

They looked at each other and cracked up.

He wasn't even sure why he was laughing, and he would've bet she didn't know either. But she was, a big laugh he'd never seen on her. For the first time, he saw straight through Orphan V to the vulnerable girl and the brash young lady and the full-spectrum woman that she was.

THE LAST ORPHAN

She was all of them.
She was herself.
She was beautiful.

62

Root-Beer Truce

Evan lay on his back on the Seabrooks' guest-room bed, staring at tassels.

Perhaps it would've been more accurate to say tassels were staring at him—from the valances, the corners of the comforter and throw pillows, the fringe of the bed skirt. They were making him nauseated.

He'd gotten Ruby, Deborah, and Mason back into their house earlier, and all three had requested, with hospitality bordering on insistence, that he stay the night before catching the jet out at the first crack of morning.

Rather than hurt their feelings, he'd been lying here staring at the ceiling.

It did not seem like a reasonable choice, and yet that was the choice he'd made.

A screech emanated through the floor from downstairs.

Evan sighed.

Another teeth-wobbling screech. And then another.

When he came down, Ruby, Mason, and Deborah were clustered around the smoke alarm in the kitchen. The off-white puck was up high where the ceiling slanted to a peak. Mason stood on a barstool waving a wooden pasta spoon at it, Deborah and Ruby holding the seat to keep it from spinning. They were all talking over one another, shouting instructions, and they didn't hear Evan come up behind them.

"I could just shoot it," he said.

The barstool rotated a few degrees, and Mason almost went down. He crouched awkwardly and stepped off, defeated.

The detector screeched again for good measure.

Ruby stomped off to the mudroom and came back wielding a field-hockey stick. She hopped up onto the kitchen table, careful to straddle the jigsaw puzzle, and swung, knocking the detector to the floor, where it issued a woeful, static-fuzzed bleep and died.

Ruby slid off the table, set down her hockey stick, and dusted her hands.

"Bravo," Deborah said. "Bravo."

"Sorry it woke you," Mason said.

"I was up," Evan said.

"We were, too," Deborah said. "I was . . . not smoking."

"And I was about to make root-beer floats." Mason nodded to the counter where the fixings had been laid out. Two liters of A&W and Mug waited, ready to pour. The parlor glasses were still frosted from the freezer, a vanilla scoop dropped into each.

There were four of them.

"Might you join us?" Mason asked.

Evan looked at the four glasses. Then at the family of three.

"What the hell," he said.

Mason reached for the A&W, but Ruby said, "Uh-uh-*uh*!"

His hand reversed course to the other bottle. He filled all four glasses with Mug and handed them around. He caught his daughter's eye, hoisted his drink for a toast. "Root-beer truce."

"Root-beer truce," she said, and they all clinked.

Evan took a sip.

It was one of the finest things he had ever tasted.

Almost as good as vodka.

But also: sugary.

He indulged himself in another sip. When he set his glass down on the kitchen table, something caught his eye.

The puzzle had been completed in the past few hours. The Seabrooks four sitting in the bleachers at a baseball game. Johnny was in his uniform, snorting into Ruby's neck. She was shoving him away, recoiling with delighted disgust. Deborah had struck an arch actressy pose, arms unfurled overhead as if she'd just taken a hot-tub plunge into a giant martini glass. Mason's grin was faint but pronounced, the contented if bemused patriarch.

So much character frozen into a single image, broken into a thousand pieces.

And then put back together.

Ruby followed Evan's stare, her chin dipping demurely. "I finished it when everyone went to bed," she said. "I wanted to do it before you left."

Her vulnerable gaze was almost more than Evan could take. It moved past him to the foot of the stairs, and then her eyes misted and she swallowed once, hard.

He'd placed his rucksack there in the foyer.

Deborah and Mason took note as well, and a heaviness descended on them that Evan didn't fully grasp until he realized that it was inside him as well.

His intercostals still burned each time he inhaled, and he could barely lift his left arm over his head. The kitchen felt homey and warm. No one could find the spot in the soffit where he'd dug out the slug and patched the bullet hole. And no one would guess that a few nights prior a man had bled out on the very tiles beneath their feet. Evan was glad they'd never know anything about that. That he had preserved this home for this family, a family of survivors.

"It was a pleasure meeting you." Evan offered his hand.

Deborah took it, her grip cool and firm, and gave a stately tilt of her head. "Evan No-Last-Name."

Mason shook next, nodding a few times at Evan as if they both knew what more he wanted to say.

Evan turned to Ruby next, and she stepped forward and hugged him. "I thought I got to keep you."

He hugged her back.

Let go.

She didn't.

Her voice was muffled against his chest. "What do I do if the monsters come back?"

He bent his face to the top of her head and said, "You call me."

63

A New Man

The elderly man with tousled white hair walked with some dif-
ficulty across Concourse C of the Dubai International Airport. His
nose was wide and puttylike, his spine curled arthritically, and he
relied heavily on a cane to move his right leg. Behind him he pulled
a rolling carry-on composed of Tumi's trademark black ballistic nylon. Attached to the handle was a canary-yellow circular luggage
tag emblazoned with a tour-group name: GOLDEN YEARS CRUISES.

It was slow going.

The beautiful modern facility exuded a timeless weariness and
excitement, the forever-day and forever-night of airport terminals.
Between gates C21 and C23 waited the cheery leprechaun-green
façade of McGettigan's Irish Pub, its neon sign sprouting the inevi-
table clover.

DXB served as a gateway to most of America's endless wars, operators and mercenaries rolling through on their way to Baghdad,
Sana'a, and countless other hotspots. For them McGettigan's was
the pub of choice.

The elderly man entered and scanned the cheery interior. A long, curved bar underlit with a purple glow, TVs piping in US football and European *fútbol*, a library wall of antique books and another composed of a neat stack of stripped firewood on which customers had written initials or love equations with permanent markers. One set of windows overlooked a runway, the other offering a glimpse of distant green hills. The elaborate fabric lamps dangling from the ceiling looked like roses or crumpled tissues depending on one's Rorschachian tendencies. Along with illuminated glass shelves housing spirits, they suffused the bar with a welcoming light.

Trudging forward on that bum leg, the man took a seat at the bar next to a tall, slender man nervously sipping a pint and slotted his carry-on between their stools where the other man had left his.

"Hallo," the elderly man said, offering a hand. "Matthew Ross, but you can call me Matty."

The slender man gave an irritated shake and turned back to his drink. "Derek Tenpenny."

The sole TV devoted to news scrolled headlines on the crawl—a fresh outbreak of violence in the Gaza Strip, another celebrity divorce, the American environmental bill stalled out.

"Where you headed to, friend?" the old man asked.

"Look, I'd prefer not to chitchat, okay?"

"I suppose you don't want to see pictures of my grandkids, then?"

"That would be correct."

"Suit yourself, friend."

The old man leaned his cane against his stool, but it clattered to the floor by the carry-ons. With a groan he bent down and picked it up. Given his age, it took awhile, but he found his way back up. The music was a bit louder than he would have liked.

He hailed the bartender with a tremulous hand, and the handsome Arab man bounced over. "What'll it be, sir?" he asked in pristine English. "We have cold beers on tap."

"No, thanks," the old guy said, peering around the barkeep at the beautifully displayed vodka bottles. "Is that Kauffman Vintage?"

* * *

A New Man

The elderly man shuffled his way through the private-jet terminal, his pace starting to quicken. His gait evened out as he straightened up by degrees, trashing his cane into a metal waste receptacle. He rolled a Tumi international carry-on just like the one he'd entered McGettigan's with, the same circular tag bobbing atop the handle.

But it wasn't the same piece of luggage.

The matching piece he'd brought into the pub, the one that Derek Tenpenny had left with, contained several ounces of gunpowder for the explosives-sniffing canines and numerous documents accusing members of the House of Al Falasi, the royal ruling family of Dubai, of pedophilia and treason.

Boarding the Embraer Lineage 1000 he'd reserved for the long haul, Evan peeled off his putty nose and cracked his back.

Tenpenny had name-dropped Qatar-based Al Jazeera enough times that Evan had asked Joey to monitor travel into the Middle East. Sure enough, Tenpenny's name had popped up on the databases, a flight from JFK to Dubai on Emirates, after which he'd switch planes for the shorter hop to Doha.

That is, if he cleared security.

Aragón Urrea needed the luxury jet back in Texas, but Evan would certainly enjoy it while he had it. A queen-size bed, a full-length couch, silk cut pile carpet—everything at peak design.

He collapsed into a leather seat and let out an exhale.

Mission complete.

It was bizarre how it had started and where it had wound up. The more distance he got from Tartarus, the more vague his recollections of Luke Devine had grown, as if he were something from a dream.

Evan's blinks grew longer. He needed a short rest. And afterward he could relax and clean up.

The bar was stocked to his liking. The plane even had a shower in which he could rinse the dye out of his hair and the old-age makeup from his face.

He'd be a new man.

64

Toe-to-Toe

Evan was over the Greenland Sea when his RoamZone rang. He'd set up the phone to route calls through low-earth-orbit satellites when he was airborne; they placed less demand on antennae.

The caller ID was blank, and yet he knew precisely who it would be.

In the privacy of the luxury cabin, swathed in the golden light of the midnight sun, he answered.

President Victoria Donahue-Carr said, "To say I'm dissatisfied would be an understatement."

Evan said, "That makes two of us."

"May I ask why you refused? After all the missions you've completed?"

He thought for a moment, then told her what he'd told Luke Devine. "Nothing you'd understand."

"You'd be amazed at what I understand," she said. "The complexities I have to contain for myself, for the country, the world.

The presidential race is the greatest nonlethal competition in the history of humankind."

"Nonlethal," Evan repeated.

"You can be snide. But you've never done it."

"Neither have you," Evan said. "You didn't win it. You were put there."

The implication of at whose hands hung as heavily between them as a black cloud.

"I thought you were smarter than this. We got you before. We will get you again." There was a steel in her voice that reminded him that this was a woman who'd gone toe-to-toe with Putin. "You don't want us after you."

"True," Evan said. "But you don't want to come after me."

"And why is that?"

"If I can focus on my own missions," he said, "it means I'm not focusing on you."

There was a long pause. Or else she'd hung up already.

Either way he cut the line and settled back to enjoy the view.

65

Whatever Passed for Fate

To call Mixed Blessing a dive bar was to insult dive bars.

Evan still didn't fully register that he'd come here. It hadn't felt like a conscious decision, more like an inevitability driven by some subconscious urge that refused to poke its head above the surface. After flying back to Aragón's home in Eden, Texas, he'd noticed that Blessing was a mere four-hour drive away.

This was the town where the man he thought to be his father had used his credit cards as recently as a few months ago.

Evan stood inside the dim bar. The fan, missing one paddle, spun lazily, providing entertainment for a haze of flies. A few good ole boys were shooting pool, a drunk woman in a wheelchair was throwing darts with surprising precision, and Willie was spinning on the jukebox, apologizing that he'd been blind.

Evan walked over to where an ancient barkeep wearing biker leathers mopped at the varnished wood with a rag the color of urine. He looked up from beneath a red bandanna tied around his head, no doubt in keeping with the Shotgun Willie theme.

"I'm looking for Jacob Baridon," Evan said.

The barkeep bobbed his head. "He in some kinda trouble?"

"No," Evan said. "It's personal."

"You a friend of his?"

"No," Evan said. "But not an enemy either."

The man kept mopping, though at what Evan had no idea. Perhaps he was using the bar to clean the rag instead of vice versa.

"Go right outta the lot. First right, second left, ride 'er to the end."

"Thank you."

On the crackling jukebox, Willie bemoaned all the things he should've said and done.

Evan stood a moment longer and then withdrew.

The long dirt road ended not so much in a cul-de-sac but at an arbitrary spot where the sunbaked terrain reasserted its dominance over civilization. The double-wide manufactured home seemed about six hundred square feet. Foam showed through cracks in the cement boards, the roof was partially caved in at one corner, and the black trash bag covering a broken window snapped angrily in the wind. The house had been pale pink once, though the gritty wind had sandblasted off most of the paint. The mailbox was knocked over.

No one was home.

Evan stood a moment by the Jeep that Aragón had lent him, staring back at the residence.

It made him feel.

It made him feel sad.

He got back into the Wrangler.

What now?

He had no idea.

It occurred to him that he should've asked the barkeep if he'd seen Baridon lately. Evan didn't particularly want to hang around Blessing to try again.

Maybe it was fate.

Or whatever passed for fate.

Whipping the Jeep around turned up the volume on the ache in his left shoulder, but he didn't care. He sped back up the narrow dirt road. No nearby homes, no neighbors. He wondered what kind of man would live like this.

Spotting an approaching truck, he veered to the shoulder and slowed. It got closer.

An ancient Ford F-150, chipped dark blue paint, rust over the wheel wells.

The driver didn't slow and didn't look over.

Through a dust-clouded window, Evan caught a flash of whiskered cheek.

He pulled over and watched in the rearview.

The truck didn't turn on the sole fork in the road behind Evan but continued on straight for the house.

There was nowhere else the man could be headed.

Evan remained staring ahead at the road back to Eden, the Jeep idling roughly.

He wasn't sure how long he sat there.

But then his hands were spinning the wheel for a U-turn, his foot on the gas, everything moving with that same fated inexorability he'd felt before.

He drove back.

Sure enough the empty truck was parked on a slant in front of the double-wide. No signs of life through the functional windows.

Evan parked and climbed out once more. His shadow lay across the hard, flat earth, and as he turned for the house, it pulled back beneath his boots, swallowed up.

He felt numb, not entirely present and yet fully aware.

The splintered planks of the porch creaked under his weight.

He gathered himself.

And he knocked.

Acknowledgments

Once again I went hat in hand to X's longtime partners in crime: Michael "Borski" Borohovski (hacking), Kurata Tadashi (weapons), Dr. Melissa Hurwitz and Dr. Bret Nelson (battle wounds), Stephen F. Breimer (legal maneuvers), and Philip Eisner and Maureen Sugden (masters of the word) remain key players in Evan's world. Thank you for your continued expertise and generosity.

Ross Hangebrauck and Joe Musselman advised on financial trickery.

McKenna Jordan offered musical guidance to a certain tone-deaf author.

Chris Mooney and Jon Cullen lent additional Bostonian insight into one of my adopted cities.

Michael Sendlenski, the original Papa Z, added grace notes to my depiction of the Hamptons and its denizens.

It remains difficult to express my appreciation for Lisa Erbach Vance of the Aaron Priest Agency, my beyond-compare agent,

Acknowledgments

whose perennial competence allows me to focus on what I should be focusing on: the writing.

And my rock-solid manager, Angela Cheng Caplan of Cheng Caplan Company, Inc., who has been an integral addition to my team.

In Minotaur Books I have an exceptional team of publishing experts to whom I am grateful daily for their hard work, strategy, and passion. Many of us have worked together for fourteen novels now, and my appreciation for you remains undiminished. And in Michael Joseph/Penguin Group UK, I have a slightly more gin-centric version of the same. They wield an iron fist of dedication wrapped in a velvet glove of merriment.

Natalie Corinne, my Joey, complete with ridgeback sidekicks.

And of course Delinah Raya, my anchor to everything.